The Pelican Affair

by

R. J. Reilly

First published by Dog Ear Publishing
4011 Vincennes Rd
Indianapolis, IN 46268
www.dogearpublishing.net

ISBN: 978-1-4575-4034-9

This book is printed on acid-free paper.

Printed in the United States of America

Dedication

To my late wife, Lena, the light of our world

Acknowledgements

My thanks to Ed Wolff, Margaret Pigott, Jim McDonald, and Kate Farrell, who read the first drafts. I also want to thank John Schmittroth, David Lavery, and Linda Klem, who were early supporters of my publishing efforts, as well as Mary Rupp Grillo, Mildred Davis Harding, and Wendy Napiantek for their ongoing encouragement. Norman and Alison Beech, our hosts during my Oxford semester, became life-long friends for Lena and me, and I treasure their kindness. Other kind and helpful friends are Marlene and George Heitmanis.

As always, I wish to thank my daughters, Kathleen and Mary, and my granddaughter, Margaret, for their assistance with my book project.

Contents

The Pelican Affair

Prelude

In his later years James Moore, reviewing his life, recognized 1976 not just as the year of his fiftieth birthday and the country's two-hundredth, but as a year of violent rebirth for both. Like most other Americans, he shared the country's mixed feelings about the national birthday. The agony of Vietnam had ended on the ground but not in the national consciousness. The image of the American rescue helicopter hovering over the embassy in Saigon had become an emblem of national shame and loss, a sad reversal of the image of the flag raising on Iwo Jima. The violent emotions of the sixties—in the hippies and the druggies and the war protesters—the emotions that had shaken the government and had stopped a war had cooled but had left a residue even in Middle America; young Americans had frightened older Americans and had revealed the fragility of the social order. Although the Women's Liberation movement could not formally enlist a majority of American women, its insistence on sexual equality undermined for many people the legal and traditional foundations of marriage, and changed forever the way that women and men would look at each other. Politicians pronounced the time one of healing after the scandals of Watergate, but Moore suspected that most Americans felt as he did: that government and politicians in general were never to be trusted again, that what scraps of honor the nation had once possessed had died with the Kennedys and Martin Luther King in the sixties.

While America was being reborn as a more egalitarian society, Moore, a pensive man, was questioning his roles as teacher, husband, and father. He thought the decade of the seventies was for most Americans a time of profound uneasiness about their national identity, of uncertainty about what they and their country had become. The decade was the last before the arrival of the internet and cell phones and e-mail, Moore reflected, but he doubted that even those instruments of instant communication would have answered the questions that Americans were asking, because the questions could not be answered in words, only in the heart and soul. A quietly patriotic American, Moore felt in himself back then something of the nation's unease, but it was a more personal sense of unrest that had grown in the few weeks since he had left America for his summer semester in England. For him, this would be a time of loss and acceptance as he was forced to reimagine himself in ways he had never considered.

CHAPTER 1

Oxford

M oore was in a specific place at a specific time—in the White Horse pub in Oxford in the year he had turned fifty—yet it seemed to him that he was not securely set in either time or place. If someone had said, "A penny for your thoughts," he would have said he was meditating on the fluidity of time and personal identity. But he knew that that wasn't really so, that the answer gave a kind of coherence and logic to what was really an eddy in the river of consciousness, currents of past and present and of Oxford and Detroit drifting and merging. It seemed to him, after his second pint of lager, that if he was here, then he was not wholly here, that he was still partly back in Detroit, talking with Helen about coming to Oxford. If this other self, this Detroit self, had suddenly pushed through the swinging doors and come up to him at the bar, he thought he would be only mildly surprised. This other Moore—the real Moore?—would come over to the bar and lean against it and the person leaning there now would simply disappear. No one else in the bar would notice. There would still be the fifty-year old man in the raincoat sipping lager. But the man would now be the old untroubled Moore who had come over to Oxford to teach a course in the romantic poets, not this present Moore, leaning, sipping lager, his mind muzzy with half thoughts and emotions he was ashamed of.

Like many other literary people, Moore thought largely in images drawn from literature, to the point that he often hardly knew what he thought until it had been verified by someone else's language. Moore knew he thought like this. So if he was thinking of double identities now, or multiple personalities (Jekyll and Hyde, James' Spencer Brydon, Conrad's secret sharer), he knew it was only his way of thinking about, really worrying about, the odd turn his character seemed to have taken here in Oxford. He had always believed he knew himself pretty well, but now he found himself surprised at himself. His mind seemed too full for comfort, and full of contradictory currents. On the one hand there was Oxford itself overwhelming him with a sense of history, of a glorious past, of language soaring like the spires of Oxford itself. Oxford for him was like being on Whitman's Brooklyn Ferry, a place to feel somehow at one with Newman and Shelley and Cranmer. This sense Moore could understand, though he was surprised at its power. But the other conflicting current he could not understand at all. At the age of fifty, three-thousand miles from Detroit, and after twenty-five years of marriage to Helen, he had suddenly become intensely aware of women—more precisely, young women—and even more precisely, young women in tight blue jeans, who were everywhere in Oxford that summer. He was moved to a sense of history by the massive wooden gates of Corpus Christi College, but he was also moved to embarrassing desire by young women's buttocks in jeans that shaped them so lovingly. There were blue-jeaned women at home, of course, and Moore had been aware of them, but he had never felt this resurgence of sensuality at home. If he tried to explain it, he could only image it as a door that for the first time had been opened. He had walked through that doorway into Oxford and into this puzzling world where both past and present were so remarkably alive. That doorway was the doorway from home, from Helen, from his familiar self, the self he was comfortable with—the tenured professor, husband, father, and (recently) grandfather.

"It would be better if you'd come for the whole thing," he had told Helen. They had been sitting at the breakfast nook table in Detroit, early in January, and the heavy snow in the backyard was sparkling in the morning sun. A single black bird, a crow or starling, perched on the back fence and shook its feathers. Summer and the Oxford program at Corpus Christi had seemed far away and not quite real.

"You'll be busy," Helen had said. "I just hope you'll be busy enough so you won't be lonesome. You know you're not a good mixer, dear."

He had nodded absently, as if she had remarked about the weather. He wasn't a good mixer. It was something they both knew and accepted. So he had come over prepared to be a little lonesome for a month, until Helen came for the last two weeks, but he had not been prepared for the chaos he felt now. He had gone for a Sunday sail just off shore and had been blown out to sea by a sudden squall. He had not been prepared for an emergency.

Student voices swirled around Moore, the deep sounds of German and Dutch, the higher, lighter sounds of French and Spanish, the flat sounds of American English. All the world came to Oxford in these summer sessions for six weeks of culture and fun. *Honneur*, the voices around him said, and *freiheit*, and *amour*, and history, and God: the endless arguments that never changed. The words settled on the outskirts of his mind next to his awareness of the

Museum of the History of Science on his left, and Blackwell's bookstore in front of him behind the bar of the White Horse, and Wadham and Keble colleges on his right, and the road to London. All these things on the outskirts of his mind, and in the center his shifting self, whoever that was. The man with a wife and daughter and granddaughter, the man who had come here to teach romanticism? Or the man whose mind surged back and forth between the tranquil oldness of Oxford and the upsetting crotches and buttocks packed into tight blue jeans? He looked at the swinging doors again, wanting deliverance. But the other self didn't come, and he knew that the other self was already here, strange and yet familiar. He was the same man who had come over here and yet he was different. Thirty days he had been at Oxford and thirty nights at the White Horse, and now he admitted to himself that he had been aware of the change all along. But it had been so gradual. He had come as a tourist looking for old things, and he had gradually become a tourist-voyeur, a man of double vision who could almost simultaneously look at the Radcliffe Camera and blue-jeaned bottoms and savor them both. Yes, he thought, I looked at the Shelley memorial in University and at the rump of the Girl Guide, and I remember them equally.

A disco record began to play on the jukebox, and the barmaid began to move in rhythm to it. Moore's eyes went to her moving crotch like the nose of an inquisitive dog while his mental eyes saw the rows of books behind her at Blackwell's.

I should have insisted, he thought for the hundredth time, I should have insisted that Helen come with me. Then I would have stayed good old Dr. Jekyll and never have become Mr. Hyde. But that notion bothered him. Surely he didn't need Helen to prevent his becoming Mr. Hyde? And Jekyll couldn't control the chemicals he drank, but surely Moore could control Oxford?

He hated stale phrases, but one of them surely described his condition: obsessed with sex. Obsessed like a teenager. He had not so much as touched a woman since he had kissed Helen goodbye; but day by day here in Oxford his sexual awareness had become more intense. (And wasn't the only sin not in the act but in the will?) What bothers me most, he said to himself, staring down at his lager, is this almost rapist mentality. I see a crotch and I want it. I don't care whose it is. I'm not interested in the girl, or the woman. I don't want to know anything about her, I don't want to talk to her, I don't want to interest her in me. I don't imagine scenarios in which young girls fall in love with aging men. I'm like a painter who doesn't care about anything except structure. Or like some mad Nazi scientist who wants to examine a vagina just because it's there. He stared again at the bar maid's moving crotch. I don't want to know her name, he thought, or what she wants from life. I don't want her to fall in love with me, I only want that one thing to touch and probe. Like a badly trained dog, he thought again, that would embarrass his owners until they finally had to get rid of him. If I could imagine falling in love with her, he thought, that at least would give it a touch of humaneness, of dignity.

The male menopause. The phrase jumped into his mind as if someone had spoken the words aloud. Someone *had* spoken them, of course, but that had been months before, just before Christmas and the end of the semester. Tom Miller, the department bachelor, had said them to Moore one morning in the coffee room just before their ten o'clock classes. Moore had never really either liked or disliked Tom Miller, though he had known him for fifteen years. But in the last year or so he had gotten a little tired of him, as you sometimes get tired of a professional comic you have heard too often. Miller's field was Restoration, but Moore had never heard him talk much about it. What Miller had always talked about was sex, and specifically the girls in his classes. A few years earlier he had even invented a rating sheet for them that he had called Miller's LAB Test—legs, ass, boobs. For a few months it had been a kind of departmental joke and they had all compared notes at department meetings. But the joke had worn thin and had finally died, or so Moore had thought. But Miller brought it up again that morning, talking about a blond junior. "I'd say a strong B+ on the old LAB scale," he had said. Moore had smiled dutifully, a little embarrassed that Miller didn't seem to know his joke was dead. But then he realized that Miller had made the reference almost absent mindedly, as if from habit. Something else was on his mind.

"You know, Jim," he had said to Moore, "we're victims of the male menopause, you and I." He and Moore were the same age, but Moore had never thought much of that except to wonder that Miller had stayed single for so long.

"You've been reading Ann Landers again," Moore had said, just to be saying something.

"As a matter of fact I have, along with some other things," Miller had said seriously. "She isn't all bad, you know. She passes on the standard info from good sources."

"Well, what did she pass on about the male menopause?"

"It's very simple. Men our age don't see themselves growing older. They see their wives growing older instead. They think they themselves are still the way they were and it seems unfair to them that they should be tied to older women. So they look for younger women."

"*At*, Tom, not for. *At*."

"Same difference. Some of us for, some at."

"Well, that's certainly simple, all right," Moore had said and laughed. "It's a grand universal principle except that it doesn't apply to us. I don't feel that way and you're not married."

"It applies to me in principle," Miller had said. "And of course you don't think you feel that way. That's all part of it."

Sipping his lager, staring for the moment at nothing, Moore wondered why Miller and his comment had come back to him, and then suddenly it seemed obvious enough. If his other, saner self had come through the doors of the White Horse, that self would have come directly to the bar and said, "Hello, you look like Jim Moore, but you're really Tom Miller. When did you change?" Oh, no, Moore thought, I haven't changed like that. The way I feel now is an aberration. It's normal to look at good-looking young women, and if I'm a little intense about it it's because—because they seem to be everywhere, I don't seem to get any rest from them. This seemed incomplete to Moore, so he went on, I would look at older women if they were here and if they were still attractive, like Helen. It stands to reason that young women are more attractive than older women, just as older buildings here are more beautiful than new ones. Some things are just so. An aberration: the word was soothing; it admitted a condition but explained it as temporary, an illness caused by a place, like the cholera in Rome that had killed Daisy Miller. When you left the place you left the condition behind.

These nights at the White Horse he had sometimes thought of writing a kind of comic letter to Helen that began: I'm having a love affair here, and I want you to be the first to know. The other party is quite old, about six-hundred years old in fact. Her name is Oxford. But he had never begun it, and never would begin it. He had written her many letters about Oxford, but not that one, the one that he thought of as the true one. Too many things kept creeping into that letter, just because he thought of it as the true one. He would not be in complete control of that letter—not even if he believed the defense of himself that he had just made—so he only composed it here at the White Horse and left it here each night at closing time.

He dragged his eyes away from the bar maid's crotch still moving to the disco music and made himself look at the clock over the bar that was moving steadily on to half-ten, closing time. He signaled for another lager and could hardly say whether he felt relief or disappointment when she so routinely drew it for him and so routinely took his thirty pence.

It's not just a different place, Helen, he said in his imaginary letter, it's a different way of life. I know that's a dusty old phrase, but what I mean is that there's a kind of pleasantness here. I like the oldness and the inconvenience. I like the old wood paneling in the pubs, even though they close early. I like the spires. Did I tell you they call Oxford the city of spires? But I like the bells the most. I live between Merton and Christ Church, and their bells measure out my days and nights by the quarter hour. Most of the time I don't hear them any more, but they've become old friends because I know they're there. I like the little cars with the steering wheels on the wrong side scooting down the wrong side of these narrow streets. I like the workmen wearing neckties. I like the way they set up scaffolding and replace the stones one by one at Magdalen and here at Corpus Christi. If I could have invented a place for myself I would have invented Oxford. (Here his control lapsed and the other kind of truth slipped in for a moment.) Oh, and the crotches, Helen, I love the crotches because all the girls wear tight blue jeans. No offense, my dear, but, sad to say, your crotch has given us only minimal pleasure these last few years. But I'm only window shopping, I haven't touched the merchandise. (Then he was in charge again.) How can I say it? A different way of life, a fantasy way of life that won't last much longer. I'll be glad when you get here, because part of it I can share with you. You'll like evensong at Christ Church, and eating in the hall, and the deer park at Magdalen (that's *maudlin*, you know). Oh, you'll like it, but you won't like it the way I do, because you haven't been missing what I've been missing these past years, whatever that is, and so you won't find something like that here, as I have. That pleasantness, that rightness—I don't know what else to call it.

"Time!" the proprietor barked, and Moore's imaginary letter ended for the night. All around him conversations stopped or went into their final phases. He liked that, too, the obedience to tradition and order, though he was aware that he disliked that same thing in Germans because he associated it with the Nazis and the wish to be commanded. He was aware of the contradiction: it was part of his love affair with Oxford; Oxford somehow made everything all right. He waited ten minutes for the last bit of the ritual—"Glahsses, please!"—then filed out with the others onto Broad Street and moved along among knots of students past the Science Museum to Catte Street. He could walk home with his eyes closed if he had to, he thought, past Brasenose and the Radcliffe Camera to the High Street, then down little Magpie Lane to Merton, then the last few paces to the great wooden doors of Corpus Christi. As he walked these last steps now he noted again the path between Corpus and Merton—closed now by an iron gate—that ran beneath his bedroom window and down to the river. That was a walk that Helen would like. You followed the winding Cherwell with its swans and quaint houseboats into Christ Church Meadows, and there was surely the different way of life, the different world of his imaginary letter. The first time he had walked there, on a Sunday morning with the mist still lying over the river and the faint sunlight diffused in the heavy damp air, he had thought that Eden must have been something like this garden place. He had sat for a long while on a bench and savored the ultimate quiet of the place, cut off from the rest of Oxford by the massive walls of the college and by the chapel that was so grand that it was the town cathedral. He had been almost afraid to go back the next Sunday morning for fear of being disappointed, afraid that his mood of the first day might have created the special beauty of the place. But he had been back several times since, and the Meadows had never failed him. Their quality was in themselves, not in him.

He unlocked the small door set into the gigantic wooden doors of Corpus and went in, past the porter's lodge, and across the quad where the golden Corpus Christi pelican reared up in the darkness. He turned into the passage that ran past the junior commons room and a minute later was making his way up the old and creaking steps of Staircase Twelve. He unlocked the heavy door that still had the nameplates of last year's students on it—reminding him that he was a visitor—and went into his sitting room.

It was a room that pleased him immensely. It was enormous, and enormously ugly. Its heavy paneled walls were painted a dead white, and so was the ceiling, some fourteen feet high. From the dimness of that ceiling a single shaded light bulb hung like a light over a pool table. The furniture was old and battered, an odd assortment of over-stuffed chairs with the cushions missing, a couple of old writing tables with little lamps that looked like bedside lights, and several homemade bookcases. A worn Persian carpet covered the center of the room, tacked down here and there. A fireplace with an electric heater set into it, the mantel painted the same dead white, stretched between two casement windows at the far end of the room. Overall, the room was a cross between someone's attic and a cottage carelessly furnished, but he had become very fond of it. He opened a can of warm lager and sat down at the writing table he used as a desk and turned on one of the little lamps.

This time was his ritual end of the day. In the morning he would turn himself on again to lecture on Shelley and Coleridge to the ten dutiful students who scattered themselves around the same sitting room, but tonight he didn't have to think of that reality. Tonight, and every night at this time, he could sip his last lager and let himself float pleasantly and aimlessly in the caressing stream of half-thought that was his prime life at Oxford, the half-thought that he felt to be more truly his than the preoccupation with blue-jeaned girls' bottoms. The odd sense of doubleness came to him again, though not as sharply as it had at the White Horse, and he realized that it had been present here in this room in a quiet way every night at this time for quite a while now. Like a silent acquaintance he had gotten used to and hardly noticed now. Not really a fantasy of what might have been, because he knew he didn't belong here, but rather a mild fantasy of what it might have been to be someone else, someone who really did belong here. Not Newman or Keble. Just some anonymous scholarship student who had fought his way through the competitive examinations and now for four years could call this monstrous room his home, and call this blackening and antique pile his college. Someone like one of the real inhabitants of this room, Michael Carey, whose nameplate was on the door, and who by coincidence bore Moore's father's first name and his mother's maiden name. Only a coincidence, yet Moore often had the feeling as he came into the room that he was entering the room of someone who was not quite a stranger.

Moore unfolded the map of Oxfordshire that he kept on his table for this time of night. Every night he drowsed over the names of towns and villages near Oxford and then the next day forgot them, the odd and homely names that would never be familiar to him because he was a tourist. Garsington, Shabbington, Great Milton, Appleford and Didcot and Sotwell, Wallingford. Suddenly the last name jumped up at him as if he'd been reading the name through a magnifying glass. Wallingford. He looked at the white wall in astonishment. Was it really possible that he had looked at this map these dozens of times and never seen that name? Apparently so. There it was, about ten miles due south of Oxford, on the Thames. He had been there in 1944—he was sure of it—though as he looked at the map it seemed absurd that his engineering regiment would have come all the way from Weston-super-Mare to practice building pontoon bridges at Wallingford. But many things had been absurd in 1944, D-Day plus six months, and he was positive about the name.

They had driven endlessly through the blackout night, he remembered, with the pontoon boats stacked high on the trucks. Just before daybreak they had reached the muddy bank of the Thames—very narrow there, only a stream, as it was here at Oxford—and they had unloaded the boats in a riot of cold and mud and confusion. Then his job was over—they were in the headquarters and supply company—and the line companies took over. Presumably the bridge had been built, but he couldn't remember now. All that came back to him was the memory of bedding down somewhere and being very cold for an hour or two, and then getting back into the truck and driving (he and Lane) somewhere, he couldn't remember where. He seemed to recall cobbled streets, so maybe they'd driven into Wallingford, but then they must have driven out again, because they had stopped abreast of a farmer's field and Lane had said, "Look at those haystacks. Did you ever bed down in a haystack?" And Lane had turned the six-by-six off the road and into the field, and they had pulled up to a haystack and parked and crawled into the blessed dry warmth.

He remembered worrying about rats, and then he must have fallen asleep because the next thing he was aware of was the girl's voice saying, "Come look, Nancy, there're two handsome Yanks asleep in the haystack." He remembered the name, Nancy, and he remembered the adjective, handsome. He and Lane had crawled excitedly out of the stack—two nineteen year olds who'd heard a girl's voice call them handsome. Moore could remember their disappointment very well—the feeling but not the details, not even what the girls looked like, really. They were about twelve and had braided hair and wore heavy sweaters, and they sat perched on the rail fence that ran alongside the road, and they chatted with Moore and Lane for perhaps a half hour. And that was all. He and Lane must have left then, gone back to the company, and the company must have gone back to Weston-super-Mare, because not long afterward they had shipped out to France and the next bridge they had built had been over the Saar.

Nothing had happened at Wallingford, or at least many more important things had happened to Moore later on in France and Germany, yet he remembered now that when he had come home from the war and was swapping stories with the other vets he had always sooner or later remembered Wallingford and had told the story of the haystack incident. Partly as just a funny story, he thought now, but partly because he had been nineteen in Wallingford, and something about the experience had caught his imagination. He remembered that in those romantic days—or in those days when *he* had been romantic—in the glamour of Europe and the war, he had tried hard to capture what he thought of as the essence of whatever country he was in—a place or event or person that would convey the true quality of England or France or Germany. He had later seen the same sort of attempt in simplistic novels and travelogues, but back then he had not thought of it as simplistic. So there had probably been something at Wallingford, something with the young girls and the haystack, that had caught in his imagination, some essence of England that he had long ago dismissed as trivial and now forgotten. Now only the meaningless symbols remained: Wallingford, Nancy, November of 1944.

He had been so close to Oxford back then and hadn't known it, and now he was so close to Wallingford and had nearly not known that. The coincidence for some reason seemed important, though it was probably only an effect of his present mood; maybe it was the sudden sense of discovery while looking at the map that just for a moment made him stare vacantly at the white wall and wonder about obscure connections. He had been brought up as a middle-class, middle-west Catholic, but now he found it hard to say what he seriously believed. Or, rather, a few years earlier he had discovered that emptiness, and for a long while after that he had thought mostly in negatives: not what he believed but what he didn't believe. But in the past year or two both the positives and negatives of belief had come to seem too rigorous for him, and without much mental discomfort he had simply left the problem alone. But he knew that if he was no longer a Christian in any very specific sense, he was at least an ex-Christian. If he had no present positive identity, at least he had once had one. He was like a man who has his name legally changed but still responds to the old when someone calls him.

He did not really think there was any occult relationship between Wallingford and his present delight with Oxford, yet he found himself curious to know what at nineteen he had found so compelling at Wallingford.

Two young girls—hardly more than children—sitting on a rail fence next to a haystack in the English countryside, a few forgotten words—a cameo picture with no claim on memory and yet remembered. He wondered if Lane remembered it, wherever he was now. Here at Oxford, Moore was living an almost hypothetical life: what *if* he had been someone else who loved Oxford as he did? But at Wallingford, time had been real time, when he had been as young as the students he now rubbed elbows with every night at the White Horse. Then and now he had found something in England—perhaps not an essence—but something, and he wondered if somehow the two things matched.

He dropped his lager can into the waste basket and went out into the hall to the toilet, being careful to leave his door ajar—a ritual, so that he didn't have to carry his key with him. When he came back he had decided. He would go down to Wallingford over the weekend and see what was to be seen, either there or in himself.

In the little bedroom with the two cots set end to end (till Helen came) he brushed his teeth in the tiny washbowl under the bleared mirror, and the bells of Merton next door thudded out midnight. Drifting into sleep, he saw again the snub hood of the six-by-six and the name they had painted on it— The Jersey Bounce—and the two young girls perched on the fence like two young birds, laughing.

CHAPTER 2

Wallingford — Part I

Wallingford might have been any one of a dozen country towns Moore had been through in the past few weeks. It looked familiar not because he remembered it but because it was generic. The High Street looked like other country High Streets, the pub signs looked like old acquaintances, the church spire could have been one of a hundred he had seen. Even the Royal George, where he booked a cramped little room, seemed a repetition.

He left his bag in the room and went out to explore. Coming into town on the local bus, he had seen no farms that rang a bell in his memory—though, really, how could you identify a farm by a haystack that wouldn't be there any longer?—and so now he walked in the other direction on the High Street, heading out of town toward London. He walked quickly in the warm moist afternoon, past a bakery and an iron monger's and a stationery shop, then past a long series of neat stone houses with rose gardens and on out into the dreaming countryside. It was tiring because he had to walk on the shoulder of the road to stay out of the way of traffic. In an hour he was sweating uncomfortably beneath his sweater and raincoat and stopped at a stone bridge over a stream. He leaned against the stone fence and tried to get an overview of the country, but he was too low, and for all he could tell there were ten farms around the bend, or none. He made his eyes follow the course of the stream as far as they could to the west, since one direction was as good as another. About a mile off he thought he could see a rail fence, though whether the road bent around near it he couldn't tell. He decided to follow the stream to the fence; he was already too tired and too bored to walk much farther along the road. He scrambled down the bank to the stream and began to pick his way along it. It was slow going, and in fifteen minutes he had slung his raincoat over his shoulder and had fallen to his knees twice in the muddy bank and had begun to wish he had never left Oxford. It was a whim that had brought him to Wallingford, he thought angrily, and an even more stupid whim that had made him leave the road. Yet he headed on toward the fence; if he could reach one tangible goal maybe the whole scheme wouldn't seem quite so absurd. Glad that no one but himself knew of his foolishness, he tramped on for another fifteen minutes, and as he came out of a grove of willows he saw the fence ahead of him, a football field away.

As he came up to it he saw that the fence enclosed low green plants that he took to be barley or rye. There were no haystacks, but why would there be haystacks in July? He vaguely associated haystacks with late summer and fall and harvest time. He draped his raincoat over the top rail of the fence and climbed up and sat next to it. Far off to his left he could see a barn, with a thatched roof, whitewashed stone walls, and two black cows grazing nearby. Straight across the field he could see the canvas top of a lorry going south toward London. The far fence could have been the one he recalled, but he was in no mood to cross the field and try to find out. He was sure that the road ran alongside the fence, but he was just as sure that nothing would look familiar once he got there. You had to be pretty stupid, he thought, to look for something that you couldn't recognize. Last night he must have thought that somehow once he found the fence the whole scene, and the meaning of it, would spread outward from it like the opening petals of a flower and what he had thought and felt at nineteen would be retrieved and the two parts of his life would be connected. But now he thought that maybe the fence would be only a generic fence, like the town itself, and any meaning clinging to it would be one that he would have to find only in himself. He sat for a while, cooling off, then slid down from the fence, slung his coat over his shoulder again and headed back the way he had come.

It was after six when he finally got back to Wallingford. Tired, sweaty, and low in spirit, he got his towel and soap from his room and went down the hall to the bathroom. Sitting in rusty, tepid water, he thought seriously of taking the next bus back to Oxford, then decided not to. It was too much of an effort, and he would only get back there when it was too late to do anything but go to bed. He would have a few lagers at the local and go back in the morning. Sooner or later the Wallingford fiasco would fade in importance; maybe in a week or so it would even be comical. It was best to start putting it behind him.

He had never found an English pub he didn't like, because they were all so much alike, so when he went into the Fox and Grape, just down the street from the George, he felt perfectly at home. There was the usual front room, oak paneled, with miscellaneous little oak tables and stools. There were fox hunting prints on the walls, a small oak bar, a passageway that led to the toilets and probably to a walled yard with outside tables. He ordered a lager, a sausage roll, and a hardboiled egg from the elderly lady behind the bar, who discreetly sized him up, he was sure, first as a stranger and then as an American. He ordinarily liked to stand at the bar to drink, but he disliked eating there, and took his food and beer over to a corner table and sat down on the window seat that slanted uncomfortably forward. He looked around him as he chewed the rubbery roll. The pub was not crowded this early in the evening—three or four men at the bar talking seriously about Wimbledon, the usual two or three loners drinking their bitter, staring straight ahead. To Moore's right, hunched over a table next to the electric fireplace, was a six-tyish man huddled up in a shapeless mackintosh, with a brimmed hat covered by a plastic rain protector set squarely on his head, as if he had just come out of a November rain instead of a mild clear night in July. He was looking past Moore and talking in a low conversational voice. Moore could catch a word or two—bloody, London—but no more. He looked around, but the man wasn't talking to anyone there. No one else in the pub paid any attention to him. Another English eccentric, Moore thought. He'd seen several odd people in Oxford pubs—many of them much odder than this man—but the English seemed to have a great tolerance for eccentricity and a remarkable capacity for ignoring it. Like the theatrical old man one afternoon in the White Horse, swinging a velvet cape around his shoulders and reciting *Lear* in a very loud voice. Moore, new to Oxford then, had been embarrassed for him, but it was wasted feeling. No one paid the man any mind at all until he had exited in a kind of rush, like Lear running mad on the heath, and then one of the regulars had said casually, "Brainy old chap, he is." Moore had been delighted, and thirty years before he might have thought of the incident as part of the essence of England.

So now, after another lager, Moore too got used to the huddled-up man talking to nobody, and in spite of his wish to forget his mission to Wallingford, he found himself thinking of it again, but more tolerantly now, as a harmless eccentricity. Certainly it was foolish to set out looking for a fence that had once had a haystack next to it thirty years before, but it had done no one any harm, not even himself. Now that he had entered his fifties he was beginning to understand the enormous charm that one's personal past held. When he was young he had marveled at the endless evenings when miscellaneous aunts and uncles had argued over just where a certain grocery store had stood in their childhood, just how many children a long gone neighbor lady had had, just who had scored the winning touchdown for a high school that hadn't existed for forty years or more. He understood these things better now. To recall old things precisely was to be a kind of historian, to somehow triumph over time: over failures and disappointments and middle-age fat and the quiet horror of growing old. Today he hadn't been able to verify a certain point in his personal history, but the attempt was perhaps not really absurd. It was a small historical failure only because there were not sufficient data. If he had written something down back then, something in a letter or diary, he might have had a clue. But apparently he hadn't. When he'd come home he'd seen the letters he'd written to his parents and one or two girls and had been embarrassed at their mawkishness, but there had been nothing about Wallingford. If there was a meaning there it was a meaning that had come only in retrospect.

The Fox and Grape was beginning to fill up, and he was surprised to find that it was already nine o'clock. He edged up to the bar and ordered another lager, but it was too crowded for him to stay there. As he turned to go back to his table a group of young people came piling in—boys and girls in their twenties in the usual uniform of blue jeans and jackets—and his table was lost. He went over to the fireplace, but found the mantel too high for comfortable leaning. He looked around—he still had the American reluctance to sit down with people he didn't know—and saw that the eccentric man was the only person still sitting alone at a table. Fortified by the lager, and in imitation of the English tolerance, he went over, pulled out a little stool from under the table, said the ritual "Do you mind?" and hovered there for a moment waiting for an answer. The man made a vague gesture that Moore took to be an assent, and so Moore sat down. He had intended to turn halfway away from the man to show that he didn't want conversation, but the man said something that Moore didn't catch amid the other noises around them.

"I'm sorry?" Moore said, leaning over the table.

"American, are you?" the man said, still not distinctly. Moore now saw that the right side of the man's face was lower than the left and that the mouth moved stiffly as he forced his words. A stroke, Moore guessed, and wished he had stayed by the fireplace. Deformity always embarrassed him. "Easy to see," the man said. His jaws moved as if he were chewing the words before they came out, and when they did come out they were in a lisping monotone, with no inflection, like words coming out of a computer. "The clothes," the flat voice said, "the way you look at us. Easy to see."

Moore squirmed inwardly in discomfort. He hadn't thought he was looking at anyone, especially this man, in any special way at all. He felt the twitch of guilt that most tourists feel at some time or other, just because they are tourists. "I'm just passing through," he said, and then was annoyed with himself for being defensive.

The man turned an odd expression on him that might have been a smile but probably wasn't. "You're all just passing through," he lisped, "you've just been passing through for thirty years."

"Well, in point of fact," Moore said, savoring the English phrase, "I'm not really just passing through. I'm up at Oxford for the summer. Teaching there."

"So you've got in there too, have you?" the man said. "You'll leave us nothing of our own in the long run."

Moore's annoyance faded into a kind of pity as he looked at the lopsided face beneath the ridiculous hat. I shouldn't be arguing with him, he thought. It's cruel, it's like challenging him to fight. "We haven't got in there," he said quietly. "I'm teaching American students in a summer program at Corpus Christi. We'll be going back to the States in two weeks."

But the man had turned away from Moore, still talking, though apparently not to Moore any more, and Moore couldn't tell whether his own words had got through or not. He finished his lager at a gulp, feeling as if he had made a perfunctory visit to a mental ward and could leave now. But as he was about to get up a girl appeared from nowhere at the table, and for a moment Moore thought she was a waitress, and then remembered that he wasn't in America and that there are no waitresses in English pubs. She was in jeans and a short jacket like the old Eisenhower jackets. She looked about twenty-five. Her heavy dark hair was parted in the middle and drawn back in two wings over her ears, and her eyes were very dark. Her face wasn't pretty, Moore thought, but if you believed you could read character in a face you would have said it was a strong face—narrow and high cheek boned and almost masculine. She was looking down at the crippled man with an expression that Moore couldn't read.

"Time to go, Dad," she said, and put her hand on the man's shoulder. He went on talking to no one for a moment, then peered up at her as if she were standing on some high place and nodded. He made struggling movements inside the mackintosh and Moore realized that he was trying to stand up.

Moore got up, a little ashamed at his own agility, and put a hand under the man's arm and he and the girl hoisted him erect. A middle-aged man in work clothes and a cloth cap came over from the bar, as if on signal, and took the man by the arm.

"Come along, Ted," he said cheerfully, "a little stop before you leave." The man nodded again, fumbled at his hat brim till he had pulled it down even tighter, and seemed to be trying to square his shoulders under the mackintosh. The man from the bar hooked his arm through the other man's and slowly steered him down the passageway to the toilets. The crippled man didn't quite lean against the other man but didn't quite walk by himself. He bobbed as he moved, dipping far to his right. His right foot splayed out to the side, and he dragged it along as if he were wearing a lead shoe. Again Moore felt a flush of something like guilt at his own good health. He turned his eyes away and looked at the girl.

She was standing with her arms folded across her breast, staring after her father, again with no expression that Moore was able to read. He saw no resemblance to her father, but of course the man had once looked very different. Watching her watch her father, Moore suddenly felt the horror of change, felt it like a flash of pain. Not the mutability that the poets loved, gradual and almost imperceptible, but the sudden rush to destruction that there could be no preparation for and no adapting to, the time so brief you couldn't segment it. That was the real horror, to be transformed like the girl's father in an instant into something new and awful, as if by an evil magician's wand. In the blink of an eye you could be no longer in the game, huddled on the sidelines, watching the lucky ones play. Then the moment passed, and he was simply watching the girl again, wondering why she attracted him so.

She looked after her father and the other man until they went round a corner, then turned to Moore. "It's easy to see you're a stranger," she said, and she seemed about to smile at him. "Most people don't sit and chat with Dad."

"We weren't really chatting," Moore said, recalling his annoyance and now feeling even more guilty about it. "I'm afraid I upset him."

"A lot of things upset Dad," she said. Her eyes went over him lightly. "Especially Americans."

"So you've pegged me too," Moore said. "It reminds me of aircraft identification. Five seconds to identify an enemy aircraft. Does everyone in Wallingford hate Americans?"

"No, only my father. We don't see many Americans here. Most of them are either down in London or up at Oxford." Her eyes went over him again and she smiled a little. "But you really do stand out, you know."

"Really? How?"

"Oh, everything. Your shoes, the cut of your trousers. We see a lot of American films, you know."

Three more young people in jeans came over and sat down at the table and Moore and the girl were pressed back toward the bar. Moore found himself unable to take his eyes off her face for more than a moment. It had looked so very stern when she looked down at her father, but after she had smiled she seemed more accessible. "So it *is* something like aircraft identification," he said, "only I'm not an enemy aircraft?" I'm flirting, he thought with amazement, I could never say anything so silly unless I was flirting. She smiled again. No, it wasn't a pretty face, Moore thought, but there was something there in the face and behind the face, something in the way the dark eyes looked so directly at him. I've looked at a hundred young women in blue jeans in the last month, he thought, a lot of them prettier than she is. Why do I find her so attractive?

"No, you're not an enemy aircraft," she said. "There's only one American I hate."

Moore couldn't tell if she was joking. "President Ford?"

"No one that grand. Just an ordinary person." She looked down the passage to the toilets, and Moore remembered her father.

"What will you do with your father now?"

"Take him home and see him to bed. My car's outside. He'll sleep now. He's had his pub time."

"Can I help you take him home?"

"An American take him home? That *would* make him sick. No, we manage very well. We've had a good bit of practice. It's good of you to offer though."

So now she'll leave, Moore thought, maybe it's just as well.

"Are you staying long in Wallingford?" she said.

"Just tonight, I think. I came down from Oxford looking for something, but I don't think I'll find it."

"Looking for something? For what?"

"Almost a needle in a haystack. It's a long story."

"I like mystery stories," she said. "Is it a person, place, or thing?"

Moore thought seriously. "All three."

"Let me guess," she said. "Wallingford must be the place."

"You're warm."

"So the person and thing must be in Wallingford?"

"More or less. I don't have to answer yes or no, do I?"

She turned and looked down toward the toilets, and Moore saw the light amused expression fade. Her father and the other man were moving slowly back down the passage, her father bobbing and dipping as if he were breasting a heavy current. She turned back to Moore. "I'm afraid our game is over," she said.

Moore nodded, and thought, Yes, it's over, it was just something to kill a few minutes. How could it be more?

"You look so solemn," she said. "Is it really serious, this thing you're looking for? It's not just a joke?"

"It's serious to me," Moore said.

"Not just a game?"

"No."

She looked at him in the direct way she had that he was already coming to know. "I sometimes come back Friday nights when I've got Dad home," she said. "Perhaps you'd tell me about it."

"Yes, I'd tell you about it," Moore said quickly. Her father and his helper were slowly rounding the end of the bar, and people stood back to make room for them. Moore looked at her face again, as many years before he had looked at pictures of favorite actresses. He wanted to touch her face, as if to see if she was real, and his hand even made a little jump upward until his mind stopped it. Then he heard his voice saying abruptly, "I'm too old for you. I don't flirt with girls your age. But you're different. I can't really say why." While the words were still sounding in the smoky air he wondered why he had said them, and for an instant he hoped that maybe he had only thought them. He felt as if in the middle of a pleasant and civilized conversation he had suddenly and without reason said a gutter word.

Her eyes widened in surprise, or maybe only amusement—Moore couldn't say which. "Were you flirting?" she said. "I thought you were just being friendly."

"I *was* being friendly. I *am* being friendly," Moore said, "but I can't just be friendly with you. You're too attractive."

"Now you really *are* flirting," she said.

"No, I'm just trying to be honest."

She looked down the bar toward her father, then back to Moore. "And were you being honest about looking for something here?"

"Oh yes," Moore said, "that's why I'm here, to find out about something. And I really would like to tell you about it." He stopped, looking for words. "I hope you'll come back for that. But I find you very attractive. That's another reason I hope you'll come back."

"You don't flirt with girls my age?" she said. "Well, what do you do with them?"

Caught up in his honesty, Moore said, "Mostly I look at their bottoms."

"Really? And have you looked at mine?"

"No," Moore said, " I haven't had a chance."

"Maybe that's why I'm different."

"No, it's more than that," Moore said, "it's something about you—or maybe something about me. I want to talk to you, but that's not all that's in my mind."

Her dark eyes looked at him, evaluating. "You send out strange warning signals," she said. "Perhaps we should just let it go. Perhaps it would be better if I just didn't come back."

"I don't know," Moore said. "I hope you will. But I can't play games."

"That sounds dreadfully serious," she said.

He couldn't tell if she was being ironic. Probably she was. "I suppose it does," he said. "I'd make it more amusing if I could."

"I'll think about it on the way home," she said. "I don't meet many serious American gentlemen."

Moore was almost sure she was laughing at him now, but nothing in her face showed it.

"He's all yours, Gwen," her father's helper said.

"Thanks, Bill," she said to the man. She put her arm around her father's shoulders and together they turned toward the door. With no one but Moore watching them they began their slow shuffle across the room. Moore found himself looking at her bottom, etched against the tight jeans, and felt a twitch in his genitals. But he had meant what he said: there was something more. As they reached the door the girl turned and half looked back at Moore, and Moore, hoping no one was watching him, raised his hand in a little salute.

CHAPTER 3

Wallingford – Part II

Back up at the bar, sipping another lager, Moore tried to pull his thoughts together. In different ways Gwen and her father had shaken him severely. Her father was obviously not sound of mind, yet Moore was bothered that the man should dislike him so. It damaged his private view of himself as a man whom everyone liked. And as for Gwen: he felt his heart beat heavier, and a pulse throbbed in his forehead. I have to be careful there, he thought, My God, I have to be careful. Except that she probably wouldn't come back, or at least not to him, or only as what the English would call a lark with a solemn old American. Even so, it would be so easy to make a fool of himself. Maybe he had already done that. He wondered why it was so hard for him to think of Helen just now. He had never been unfaithful to her except in his imagination. But he had never been away from her so long since their marriage, and he had a deep feeling that whatever kept him unentangled in Oxford might not operate here in Wallingford. Staring at crotches in the White Horse was one thing, and a safe thing, but having a drink with an attractive young woman in Wallingford was something else. He was on a kind of holiday here, with no censors except those inside him, and now he didn't think they were very strong.

He glanced at the clock. It was nine-thirty, only an hour and a half to closing. It would be better if she didn't come back, he thought, better all the way around. He tried to decide whether he was more afraid of being unfaithful or of making a fool of himself with a girl young enough to be his daughter. It wasn't a hard problem as soon as he had set it out in those terms. He didn't have much faith in his sexual morality, untested as it was, but he had a deep concern, almost physical, not to seem foolish to young people. He supposed it came with the teaching territory. The self-assessment depressed him. Suddenly he felt like Tom Miller again rather than himself. I was so sure of myself before I came over here, he thought, I never thought I could do anything that would surprise me, any more than I could grow three inches.

Groping for his pipe, he happened to look at the doorway just as the girl came through it. He saw her clearly for a moment before he actually recognized her, and he had time to wonder whether she had come back to be with him or whether she would simply nod to him and then sit down with old friends and neighbors, leaving him alone but safe at the bar. She seemed tall coming into the room, tall and almost thin in her jeans and jacket. Her face was decidedly angular, Moore thought, and she had done something with her hair, though it was still parted sharply down the middle. She looked Italian to Moore, though he knew she probably wasn't. Her eyes, strikingly dark even at a distance, went around the room till they came to Moore. He wanted to wave but didn't. He had to be sure she'd come back for him, not someone else. When she came straight over to him at the bar he couldn't have said what he felt. He could only say to himself, Now don't, Now *don't* make a fool of yourself.

He turned sideways to let her slide in next to him.

"I came back in spite of your warning," she said, "but I almost didn't. Then I decided you didn't really mean it."

"I didn't mean to say it. I mean I didn't plan to say it. It just came out."

"It was a curious thing to say. As if you'd been flirting with me for hours and suddenly had an attack of conscience. It seemed to shorten things up, as if we'd known each other for a long time. Hours into minutes, you know, the way they do in films."

"I didn't think of that. It's a good idea."

"No, it isn't. We don't really know each other at all." The lady behind the bar appeared in front of them and her eyes moved briefly back and forth between them. "The usual, Meg," the girl said. Moore watched the woman draw a half pint of bitter and set it down in front of the girl and he hurriedly paid for it. As years ago I would have hurried to pay for a girl's Coke, he thought, to establish a small obligation. Some things don't change.

"You don't think some people can know each other quickly?" he said.

"No," she said seriously, "do you?"

"No, I don't suppose I do. But you can like or dislike quickly."

"But that's not the same thing."

"No."

"I think I know one thing about you though," she said. "Flirting isn't your game. If I were an analyst I'd say you were afraid to flirt."

"Why afraid?"

"Because it might work."

The teacher in Moore was too strong to let that pass. "That can only be a guess, you know, even if it was right."

"Oh? Why?"

"Because it's a judgment that you can't make except on the basis of knowledge of me that you don't have. You just said we don't really know each other."

"Then why did you warn me off if you weren't afraid?"

"There could be a hundred reasons for that."

"Could there? I prefer my own."

Moore lifted his hands in mock despair. "We may not know each other well," he said, "but we're heading for a quarrel if we're not careful."

She smiled for the first time since she had come back. "I know, I can see you getting annoyed."

"I'm not annoyed. It's just a matter of logic." She was still smiling at him, and he found himself smiling back. "All right, I give up," he said. "But tell me, Doctor, as long as you're playing analyst, why did you come back?"

"Analysts don't have to tell their own secrets," she said, and took a long drink of bitter. "But I will. There were a lot of reasons, but the main one is that I'm rather balky. I was sure you wouldn't really expect me back, so I came back."

Moore laughed at her word. "Balky? Yes, I'll buy that."

She put her glass down empty. "Speaking of buying, it's getting on toward closing."

"Right you are," Moore said, "let's have beer, not analysis."

He waved and the lady came and drew their drinks. He touched the girl's glass with his. "Here's to more beer and less thought."

They lifted their glasses and drank together. A wave of warmth and good feeling washed over Moore. She had come back and they were having a good time together. It was more than he had really hoped for. They were standing shoulder to shoulder in this English pub, this most companionable institution in the world. He looked around him with immense satisfaction, taking in the tobacco smoke, the rise and fall of voices, the oak paneling and the upholstered stools, the heat, the smallness. "I'm glad you came back," he said, "never mind about why. Let's drink to your coming back."

"My, you are one for toasts," she said. "I should never have guessed that." They drank, and then she said, "Why do you keep looking around? What do you see?"

"The essence of England, maybe. Or that's what I would have called it a long time ago."

"I think you're getting tight," she said. "I should never have guessed that either."

"If I am, it's not the lager, it's the essence of England," Moore said and waved to the lady for more beer. Moments of expansiveness were rare with Moore, and he knew it. He had to be a little drunk, as he was now, not too drunk, just mellow. The girl was laughing at him and he laughed back.

"What's the essence of England?" she asked him.

He gestured around them, to take everything in. "This place and this time," he said, pushing his glass against hers on the bar with a quiet clink, "you and I and all these people here in this little place called the Fox and Grape in this little town called Wallingford in this jewel England set in the silver sea. Let's drink to the essence of England."

"All right," she said, "to the essence of England," and they drank.

"What was the toast, mate?" said a voice behind him.

"He was toasting England, love," the lady behind the bar said.

"Right you are," the voice said. "Here's a Yank drinking to England. We can't do less, then, can we?"

Moore turned around. A barrel chested man of about fifty in a shapeless brown suit was raising his glass. Here and there along the bar other glasses were raised. Moore, embarrassed that he had been heard, raised his glass again, and the girl did, too, laughing. "Here's to England, God bless her," the man said, and several voices repeated "God bless."

"And God save her from the bloody Yanks," a voice said from farther down the bar.

"Manners," said the man in the brown suit, glaring down the bar. "Mind your bloody manners."

"Screw your bloody manners," said the other voice.

"Gentlemen," the lady behind the bar said, "Gentlemen, *please!*"

"So much for the essence of England," the girl said, still laughing.

Moore hunched down over the bar, his moment of expansiveness gone. "I wish I was in the toilet," he said. "I'm not often so loud."

"You weren't loud, love, just American. Your accent carries. Don't be so embarrassed."

"I don't like to be the center of attention."

"They've forgotten you already. Just mind your toasts."

"I will." She had called him "love," but he knew it didn't mean anything in England. He looked down the bar. The man in the brown suit was staring moodily at the hunting print over the bar. Moore looked beyond him but couldn't identify the man who hated Yanks. "That man down the bar made me think of your father," he said, keeping his voice very low. "Did you get him home all right?"

"No more trouble than usual." Her face and voice had gotten very serious again, and she looked as if she had never smiled. "He has another nip at home and then he's usually good for the night." She took a long drink of her bitter. "He's not a drunkard, you know. I wouldn't want you to think that. He's had a bad time these past few years. He needs something to make him sleep."

Moore nodded sympathetically, and some of the companionable feeling came back. People who liked each other shared their troubles. "Was it a stroke?"

"Several. I think he may still be having them. Small ones, I mean, even with the medication."

Moore's sympathy was genuine. "That happened to my mother. She was a quiet person, but after the stroke, when she got her strength back, she talked like a magpie. They finally found a tranquilizer that slowed her down, but she was never quite the same again." But she hadn't been twisted, either in her mind or her body, like the girl's father.

"Dad's not right in his mind, but he's not really different from the way he was."

"Why does he hate Americans so much? I mean, is there any special reason?"

"Oh yes, there's a very special reason," she said, and took a long swallow that finished her drink. "But that's a long story." She looked at him. "And I came back to hear *your* story."

"I thought you came back because you're balky."

"I *am* balky. I told you there were a lot of reasons."

Moore, looking at the clock, ordered more drinks. He looked at her angular face and dark eyes for what seemed the hundredth time and found them as pleasing as ever. Dimly he wondered again what was so special about her, and whether it was wholly hers or something he gave her. He couldn't decide, and didn't want to. But he thought he could tell her about the haystack and Nancy; somehow he knew she wouldn't laugh—he knew her well enough already to be sure of that. Only it had happened so long ago. He would hate to tell her how long ago. So when the drinks came he said, "My story can wait a little. Tell me something about you."

"Ah," she said, as if she had known something all along, "so you don't really have something to find out about Wallingford. You were really having me on."

"No, I wasn't," Moore said, and then told the truth, or part of it, because he couldn't think of anything else to say. "It's just that you might not find it so silly after another drink."

"After another drink I might find everything silly. I'm getting tight."

"You don't look tight," he said. But there was a brightness in her eyes that he hadn't noticed before. Someone down the bar moved and they were pushed together like lovers. Moore, only a little taller than she was, found his face only an inch from her hair, and barely kept himself from putting his face against it. He thought briefly of a hundred conversations with Helen about a hundred important things, when they had seemed to be always separated by a table, or a room.

When they had pulled themselves back on balance she said, "All right, here's something about myself. I married a man from Edinburgh. He was an engineer in the offshore oil fields. I lived there for a while. It's a fine city, nicer than London, I think. Have you ever been there?" Moore shook his head no. "The weather's cool and changeable there. I always thought of it as a northern place somehow, different from down here. There's an old fortress on a hill overlooking the city, and there are bridges connecting the old town and the new one, and when you stand on those bridges and look over the city it's like nothing I ever saw anywhere else." She stopped for a minute. "But the marriage didn't work out. I was too balky, he said. He was the one who called me that. So we were divorced. I stayed there for a while. I think I was more fond of the city than I was of him. I might be there yet except that my mother died and Dad got sick soon after." She set her glass carefully down on the bar. "And now I take care of Dad. That's it, in miniature. It's not a very special story."

She stared ahead of her across the bar, and in profile her nose was slightly beaked. Feelings churned in Moore, feelings that had as much to do with himself as with her. "That's only because it's in miniature," he said. His own life with Helen wasn't a very special story either, because the general outline told nothing about the people in the story. All stories were basically the same. The people in them lived for a while and then they died. You could say that about anyone. But nobody lived and died in quite the same way. That was the difference. Not the story but the people *in* the story; they were what counted. Like the story here at the Fox and Grape, he and this young woman: not a middle-aged man and a young woman meeting, but *this* middle-aged man and *this* young woman, each of them private and unique. Only the particulars counted, not the generalities. This seemed very important to Moore, important enough for him to try to say it to her. "We're all special if we're known well enough," he said. "Not necessarily likeable, but special, interesting."

She looked at him gravely. "That's how we started, talking about people knowing each other. Are we going to argue again?"

"No, we gave that up for beer, remember?" Again he thought she looked Italian. Italian women had always seemed the loveliest women to Moore. He even liked what little he knew of the language because it had always struck him as deliciously malleable. That was the way the girl looked to him now, soft and sensuous beneath the boyish blue-jean uniform.

"You look like a don," she said, "and you talk like one. But you don't call them dons, do you?"

"No, just teachers."

"Well, are you one?"

"Yes, masquerading as a don up at Oxford."

"You always look as if you're sorting things out. Not just talking or listening, like most people. I knew some dons in Edinburgh."

"What were they like?"

"Like the rest of us, after they'd had enough to drink."

"Well, in that case we should have another drink. Or at least I should." For a while he'd forgotten that he was a don and not like other people, but she'd spotted him, just as she'd spotted him as an American.

Something of what he felt must have come out in his voice, because she put her hand on his wrist, awkwardly, because they were so pushed together. "I'm sorry," she said. "I meant *them*, not you."

It was the first time she had touched him, except by accident, and Moore thought he could feel the touch even down to his loins. "Are you Italian by any chance?" he said. "I mean, by ancestry." He put his hand on hers and their fingers linked on the wet bar.

"You say the oddest things," she said. "No, if I'm anything I'm Welsh, at least on Dad's side. Gwen Morgan. A good Welsh name. I took it back after the divorce."

"You look Italian to me. You seem so—intense."

"I suppose I am intense. Richard Burton is intense. Maybe all Welsh people are intense. I get on with people very quickly or I don't get on with them at all."

Moore looked at her. He had been looking down at their hands as they talked, but now he looked full at her. "Are you getting on with me?"

When she looked back at him for what seemed a long moment Moore thought he had been too direct. But then, quite soberly, she said, "Famously, I'd say. How are you getting on with me?"

"Famously. Intensely. And I'm not even Welsh."

"I don't even know your name," she said. When he told her she said, "Ah, Irish, Welsh, aren't they all half mad?"

Then their eyes dropped as if by agreement and their hands came apart and went back to their glasses. They had seemed for a moment to be alone, Moore thought, but she must have realized as he did that she was an English woman in a public bar with an American. "A last toast," Moore said. "To full portraits, not to miniatures."

"That's a good toast," she said, "I'll drink to that." They drank, and when Moore put his glass down he saw that she was looking at the clock. We've said something to each other, he thought, or have we? Or was it just the lager and the bitter talking? Old scenes slid into his mind: closing time at other bars long ago when other girls had faded away from him like Cinderellas, leaving the rest of the night long and empty. Gwen Morgan had been both right and wrong about him, he thought. He didn't flirt because he was afraid of success, but he didn't flirt because he was afraid of failure too. He didn't now know which he was more afraid of.

A man in a cloth cap and sweater pushed up to the bar next to Gwen Morgan and ordered a bitter in a loud and urgent voice, and once again they were pushed together so that they stood hip to hip. In Moore's agitated state they might as well have been standing naked together. Moore's fear of success and failure dissolved and he was left with only his need not to seem foolish, and even that was now slippery and hard to keep hold of. It was hardly more than a kind of passiveness. He was eager to fall, but she had to push first. That was all that was left.

"Time, please," the lady behind the bar said and rang a little hand bell that reminded Moore of an altar boy's bell.

"I thought I was used to your early closings," Moore said, "but I guess I'm not. Not tonight anyway."

"Haven't you had enough?"

"That depends. Enough to be pretty tight, but not enough to want everything to be over. You know. Some nights you just want to last."

He felt her move against him as she lifted her glass and finished it. "There's always drink to be had, love. No problem, as you Americans say."

"I didn't mean just drink."

"What then?"

But Moore wouldn't push first. "Oh, everything. The whole evening."

"Glasses please," the lady said, "glasses please." All around them people obediently took last drinks from their glasses and set them on the bar, and there was a general movement toward the door. The man behind Gwen finished his pint, set it quietly on the bar and moved away. Able to move again, they turned and faced each other.

"Time to leave," she said, but he couldn't read her face. An instinct surviving from his old single days made him move in spite of his passivity, and he put his left hand on her waist and his right hand on hers on the bar, so that they stood for a moment as if they were about to dance. But he could think of nothing to say. She was looking at him, and he wondered what she saw. She took his hands between hers and held them for a moment as if she were warming them, and then she turned and he found himself walking hand in hand with her out of the pub.

Outside in the High Street the night air hung heavy and damp with a hint of chill that would have meant October in Michigan. Still holding hands, they moved away from the pub door, then stopped.

"Where are you staying?" she asked him.

"The George." Memories rioted through Moore's mind: other dimly lighted streets from the old days, other hands, other nights when simple questions and answers had seemed to carry the meaning of the world and more.

"We drank to full portraits," she said in the darkness. "You do like me, don't you?"

"More than I can say." And in fact Moore couldn't have said more than that just then.

"That's good," she said. She raised his hand and rubbed it along her cheek. "I thought you did. I didn't think you were just out for an easy piece. You aren't, are you?"

Her directness startled him as much as her language. It was like an unexpected question in class when somehow you knew that even the dullest students would know whether your answer was really honest. "I don't want to think I am," he said, "but maybe I'm kidding myself."

He could feel her cheekbone beneath his fingers and her mouth against the palm of his hand and he knew she was smiling. "That's what I meant before," she said. "You never talk without thinking, do you?"

Again Moore couldn't say what he felt, caught in the cross winds of emotion: the urge to kiss her and pull her against him; the bad feeling about Helen, now suddenly present and so strong that he could almost sense her standing next to them in the High Street and crying in that special way she had; the dark forbidden feeling of wanting someone young enough to be his daughter; the old feeling he had always carried with him like a birthmark— the urge to say true things, the urge that had made him a bad conversationalist all his life and whatever kind of teacher he was.

"You don't have to tell me you're married," she said. "I know that. I know the way married people act."

Moore took her by the shoulders and held her at arms' length as if he were going to shake her like a child, but she was nearly as tall as he was. "Why are you with me tonight?" he said. "Why aren't you with someone your own age?"

"Don't talk to me as if you were my father," she said. "I've had someone my own age. In fact I've had several." She took a step forward and his hands dropped to her waist. "I like you, you ass. Why do you find that so hard to believe? Don't you have any ego at all?"

"Okay," Moore said, thinking in some dim part of his mind that she had pushed first. His whirling feelings funneled down to one and he pulled her two steps into a doorway of a bakery shop and kissed her, leaning heavily against her. They kissed for a long time, until Moore's hands began to move down from her shoulders to her back and then to her buttocks beneath the jeans. Once he opened his eyes and saw shadowy rows of ginger cookies and tarts. Then she stepped back and pushed him gently away.

"Let's go back to my place," she said. "I don't want to go to the George."

"Okay," Moore said again, and he thought he had never been happier. The kiss had been like a drug to him and he knew it, knew it would wear off, but like a condemned man he savored the present. He hadn't forgotten his age, but he thought maybe she had, and that was almost as good as being young with her again. They walked hand in hand without speaking down the High Street to her little Morris. Around them other men and women were disappearing into the night, their voices dying in the darkness, and Moore felt at one with them all. In his exalted state he wondered what Gwen was thinking and feeling. Not what he was thinking and feeling, he knew, but he hoped it was something good enough to make her happy for a while. Crowded next to her in the tiny car, he kept his hand familiarly on her left shoulder as she drove, watching her shift the gears with her left hand.

Everything is backward and upside down tonight, he thought. In a moment she turned off the High Street and onto a brick road that wound past a dim church and the broad grayness of a cricket field. She stopped in the middle of a block of semi-detached houses—duplexes they would have been called in the States, Moore thought, neat squarish little houses with rose gardens in the front yards behind low stone fences. He couldn't see the roses in the darkness, but he knew they were there. He had seen a thousand houses just like these and every one of them had had a rose garden. The house was dark. He followed her up the walk and waited while she unlocked the front door, wondering for the hundredth time why door locks were so often shoulder high in England and never that way at home.

She took his hand and led him through darkness down a little hallway and into the parlor. She touched a wall switch and two table lamps went on at either end of a sofa. The room was square and small and neat, with an electric fireplace in the far wall, an old roll top desk and chair in one corner by the front window, and an overstuffed easy chair in the other.

"I want to pop up and check on Dad," she said. "Make yourself comfortable."

"Okay," he said, keeping his voice low. She had spoken in her normal tone, but coming into the dark house where her father was sleeping had stirred old teen age feelings of caution in Moore. Then when she had gone out he realized suddenly that his bladder was bursting from the lager. He went out of the room hurriedly and back down the dark hallway to the front door. He opened it quietly and stepped out into the rose garden. The parlor lights showed dimly through the drawn blinds. He moved quietly over to the far side of the house and urinated heavily against the stone fence, trying to miss the rose bushes almost invisible in the darkness. He got back to the parlor a moment before she did. She was carrying two brown bottles.

"I hope you can go bitter," she said, "it's all we have."

"That's great," Moore said. He hated bitter, but it didn't matter now.

"Are you chilly? I can turn on the fireplace." She handed Moore the bottles and went over to the fireplace. She clicked the switches and in a moment the coils lighted up and Moore could smell the dry heat.

"That's fine," he said. His voice was as dry as the fire and a little raspy. He put the bottles down and went over and turned off the far table lamp. When he came back to the other he looked at her and she nodded. He turned the other lamp off and the room dropped into darkness except for where she stood in the glow of the fireplace. Moore stood staring at her. With light behind her she looked tall and her face was lost in shadow. She might have been an actress waiting quietly on stage for an important scene to begin.

Moore stepped out of the darkness onto the little stage and she gave him her hands. He could think of nothing to say, nothing romantic, nothing true. He simply took her in his arms now because he knew he could and because he wanted to so badly, and again he leaned against her and they kissed for a long time. This time when his hands slid down over her buttocks she didn't pull away but pressed herself harder against him. Slowly they slipped down together until they were kneeling against each other and it seemed to Moore that the warmth of the fireplace was coming from deep inside him. Memories of a hundred blue-jeaned crotches pounded in his mind as he fumbled with the boy's fly on her jeans and he felt her hands on his belt, loosening it. After a moment of twisting and pulling they finally knelt with their naked loins jammed together and Moore, almost disinterestedly, felt their bodies begin to do a little dance of friction against each other. In a minute they pulled apart and hunkered down awkwardly to get their trousers off.

"The couch?" she said.

"No, right here." His hands braced on the warm tiles, he tried to see her face beneath him but could see only the sharp white line of the part in her hair. Then it was over, and he didn't want it to be. Soon it would be time again for the words that came so hard. He put his face down into her heavy hair and held it there until he felt her hands on his cheeks. Then he lifted his head and she kissed him. Down below, their loins were turning to mush and the fireplace was beginning to scorch their bare legs.

"My God but we're wet," she said, and Moore thought her voice sounded happy. He felt his heart turn over with feeling and he bent down and kissed her. Then for what seemed a long time they simply looked at each other. Moore, half hypnotized by the large dark eyes, felt deeply that it was time for great statements, but he could say nothing, and in a few minutes he began to feel the awkwardness of their position and knew she did too. If they had been lying naked in bed they might have lain indefinitely, but lying on the warm tiles of the fireplace, naked only from the waist down, was different. Yet it might have been all right, he thought, might not have been awkward at all, if words had come out of him a moment before. But what words? If I had known what words, he thought, I would have said them. Any words that would have meant she wasn't just an easy piece. But the words hadn't come.

He had just pulled himself loose from her when other words did come. The voice wasn't loud, but the words filled the room like a blast from a pipe organ. He felt her body jerk beneath him and for a second their eyes locked together in terror as if the room had been suddenly rocked by earthquake. The words came again in the flat and lisping monotone that they both identified now and their heads turned away from the fireplace as if they were on a single axis, and there in the half-light they saw him. He stood almost at the edge of the fireplace tiles, stood on a tilt in faded blue flannel pajamas, the right side of his face sagging, and he held a rolled umbrella half aloft like a long clumsy dagger. The words came slowly out again in a drool of saliva. "So the fucking Yanks are still fucking, are they—" The flat voice didn't rise at the end to make a question, only began to say the words again, and the rolled umbrella began to come uncertainly down toward them. Somehow they got loose from one another, and Moore felt his muscles tighten instinctively, whether to lunge for the man or to roll aside he didn't know. But the girl moved quickly and with purpose. She was on her feet before Moore knew it, talking. She took a single long step and threw herself against her father, and for a moment the two of them balanced there, while Moore's eyes moved sluggishly from the raised umbrella to her buttocks so glaringly naked beneath the blue-jean jacket. "It's all right, Dad," she was saying over and over, "It's all right." Her father's face twisted and bulged, but whatever words he wanted to come out wouldn't come. His arm wavered and dropped and the umbrella fell almost at Moore's knees. "It's all right, it's all right, you're not to get excited," her voice went on. She put her arm around him and turned him around as if he were a mannequin. He staggered a little and put his arm around her waist, apparently not feeling her nakedness, and they began to move ever so slowly across the parlor as they had moved in the pub, the girl in short deliberate steps, her father with his right foot dragging.

Moore, still on his knees, petrified, watched them go. When they got through the parlor arch he saw Gwen reach for a light switch and the light went on in the hallway. They moved slowly out of Moore's sight and in a moment he heard the creak of the staircase and Gwen saying quietly, "Up we go now, Dad, up we go."

Then Moore collapsed back onto his heels and drew the deepest breath he'd ever taken. He looked around for his trousers. He had never in his life so badly wanted to have his trousers on. He snatched them up from in front of the fireplace and in seconds was dressed.

Standing now with his clothes on, he found his mind beginning to work again. It had been an absurd episode, but there really had been no danger. He doubted that the man could have hurt him much with the umbrella. But then he looked down at it, and the spike looked wickedly sharp. A little shiver passed over his whole body. He picked up the umbrella and leaned it against the wall, then noticed Gwen's jeans and underpants on the tiles. He picked them up and put them neatly on the sofa. It hadn't been an absurd episode for her. He could walk away from it, but she couldn't.

He turned on one of the table lamps and sat down on the sofa. The urge to run after being caught was very strong, but the urge to stay now that he had had Gwen was even stronger, the need to see her now that they had made love. One was the whorehouse urge, he thought, the other the ego urge. Neither was admirable. Or was there something else as well? He sat inert, an object held immobile by opposing forces, but he didn't know how many forces there were. Images from the past hour poured through his mind, each image drenched with what he had felt, like plants pulled up and showing roots. Some of the images he looked at over and over, like a man showing his favorite home movies. The way Gwen had looked when she had come back to him at the pub, trim and boyish in her snug jeans. The way her face had looked in the dim light of the High Street just before they kissed. Most of all the way she had looked in that moment when they had knelt together before the fireplace. He felt himself excited again at the recalled feeling of her buttocks in his hands. That stayed best in his memory, the anticipation, the just-before.

The marvels that followed were blurred by comparison, and kept sliding into the doomsday voice and the figure in the blue pajamas with the raised umbrella. I have never gone through anything like this, he thought, nothing so—but he couldn't find a word to describe it. I wonder how it will come out, he thought, and then it occurred to him that maybe it had already come out, had already ended. Maybe she would simply come downstairs and say goodbye. Maybe, whatever she was doing upstairs with her father, she was thinking, Well, that's over, we had our little fling. The thought chilled him. He looked down at her clothes next to him on the sofa, then put his hand on the underpants he had folded on top of her jeans. Something—the notion of laundry perhaps—made him think consciously of Helen. I've been untrue to her, he thought, but with no real feeling of either surprise or remorse. At the moment Gwen Morgan filled his mind and there wasn't room for Helen. Thinking again of the past hour, he said to himself that he didn't want to be untrue to Gwen as well, but even as he said it he knew the words had no meaning. He sat with his hands on the underpants, feeling the warmth of the fireplace, feeling Gwen Morgan's presence in his fingertips.

He heard her footsteps on the stairs, light and stable, and in a moment she came in. She was wearing white lounging pajamas that looked vaguely oriental to Moore. The jacket fitted her tightly and went up to a stiff collar like that of a bellboy's tunic, and she was wearing white furry slippers. She stood just inside the arch and Moore felt just as he had when she had come back to the pub. He didn't know what she would do. He wondered whether if he had somehow known her in some other life he would ever have been sure of her. Her face told him nothing, and he thought, Even after what we've done she's still a stranger. She came over to the sofa and stood in front of him, looking down at him. "It's all right now," she said. "I gave him another Seconal. But I locked his door just in case."

Moore's heart lifted. She wasn't saying goodbye. He put his arms around her legs and pulled her to him until his face was against her stomach. He felt her hands touch his hair. She turned and sat down in his lap and he put his face against her jacket, feeling for her breasts. She pulled his head against her and Moore moved his face across her breasts and thought, absurdly, I never knew quiet like this before.

"I wasn't sure you'd be here when I came down," she said.

Moore raised his head. "I wasn't sure you'd want me to be."

"I wouldn't have blamed you for leaving. That was a bit much."

"I'm sorry about it all. That sounds stupid. I mean, how will you handle him now?"

"He may forget it," she said. Her fingers were playing with his hair and she was staring at the fireplace. "Or he may get it mixed up with other things. As a matter of fact I think that's what happened."

"With what other things?"

"I'm too heavy for you," she said, and kissed him on the forehead and stood up. "Other things that happened with my mother."

She went over to the mantel and took a cigarette from an enamel box and lit it. She came back and picked up one of the bottles of bitter and handed it to Moore and took a long drink from the other. "My mother was—" She stopped while she sorted out her words. "My mother had an affair with an American. Dad found out about it."

"I see," Moore said. "So now he hates Americans on principle."

She didn't answer for a moment, smoking, staring at the fireplace. "I think she meant to go off with the American after Dad found out. But she never got the chance. One day the American wasn't here any more. I don't think she ever heard from him again."

"What finally happened?" Moore had a sense of something bad coming even as he asked the question. He saw again the raised umbrella and heard the metallic words.

"She waited for about six months. Living with Dad couldn't have been very pleasant those days. Then one night she took sleeping pills and Dad found her dead the next morning. They were sleeping in different rooms by then, or he might have found her sooner. Dad had his first stroke a week later, two days after the funeral."

Moore got up and paced around the little parlor and back to stand next to her by the fireplace. It was an ugly story and by slow degrees he was realizing that he had become a part of it. "So when he saw us here tonight—"

She nodded. "God knows what he thought. Or felt."

"You mean he may have thought it was happening all over again? Or he may have mixed you up with your mother and me with the other American?"

She nodded again. "God knows. He does mix me up with Mum sometimes. Other times he's clear enough."

"I'm sorry," Moore said. "God, I'm sorry."

"I'm sorry too. For him. Sorry for us. I've never seen him violent before. I'd never have brought you home if I had."

He put his arm around her and they went over to the sofa and sat down. Something was puzzling Moore, not the story so much as the way she had told it, so flatly, as if it had happened to people she didn't really know. "It must have been a bad time for you," he said. "Did you know the American well? What was he like?" He tried to imagine her with her dark hair in pigtails, like the girls at the haystack, sitting here in the parlor and being teased by an American, someone rather like Lane or himself.

"I never saw him," she said. "I wasn't here. I was in Edinburgh. I'd just been divorced. The neighbors wired me the day she died and I came down. That was the first I knew."

Moore was still puzzled. "When did this happen?"

"Three years ago."

"I'm sorry," Moore said, "I had it all wrong. I thought all this happened a long time ago. In the war or right after it."

"Oh no," she said, "we're still living over it. It's quite fresh in Dad's mind. Mum was only a little girl in the war."

Of course, Moore thought, how could I be so stupid? Gwen couldn't be more than twenty-five. Her mother would of course have been a young girl in the war, probably no older than the two girls who had perched on the fence that cold morning and talked to the handsome Americans.

"He came into the pub one night, out of nowhere," Gwen said, "into the Fox and Grape. Bill told me about it. Dad never did. He was very engaging, Bill said. He bought drinks. He'd been here during the war. Everyone liked him, Bill said. He talked to Mum and Dad too. That's how it got started, I suppose." She stopped for a moment, then said, "He's the one American I hate. I shouldn't have said that to you before, but sometimes it slips out. I'm intense, remember?"

She went over to the fireplace and held out her hands to its warmth, but something she had said about the American made the room seem suddenly cold for Moore: everyone had liked the American who had been here in the war. Everyone had liked Lane too. Years later Moore had come across Mark Twain's joke that people had confused him with good weather, and the joke had reminded Moore of the effect that Lane had had on people. He had been a joy to be with. Moore's sense of probability had suffered a good deal in the past twenty-four hours. He had improbably been in Oxford, where he didn't belong, and after looking at a map for several nights had happened to see the name Wallingford on it. And these improbabilities had brought him here to this most improbable night with Gwen Morgan. Now he had a sense that probability might not apply at all here in Wallingford, that this small segment of reality might be free of that constraint. Coincidence might be the bane of bad fiction, but life must be sometimes stranger than fiction, or he wouldn't have been here at all.

Yet he hung on to the law of probability, because it was frightening to think that something else might be possible. "I suppose there were a lot of Americans here in the war," he said.

"I don't know," she said. "I suppose so."

"This one who came back. Did he seem to know your mother?"

She looked at him in surprise. "How could he know her? Mum was just a little girl then."

"I meant, maybe he'd seen her as a little girl and had come back to see how she'd grown up," Moore said. I should stop these questions, he thought. If there are wrong answers I don't want to know them. But he did want to know them.

"I don't know anything about him," she said, "except what Bill told me. Bill said the man had been here in the war and had helped build a bridge over the river. Bill remembered that because the man made some joke about the bridge."

Moore had been trying to keep a door closed against enormous pressure, but now it had swung wide open and he was afraid of what might come through it. Lane had only known two little girls in Wallingford. The battalion had never come back. Gwen must have read his face; she looked at him in a way that told Moore she'd forgotten they were lovers. "Do you know something about him?" she said fiercely.

"I hope not," he said. "What was his name?" But he knew what she would say.

"Lane," she said. "Robert Lane." And then she was suddenly in front of him, her hands on his shoulders. "You know him, I can see you do. Is that why you're here? Did he send you here? Is that why you came to Wallingford? To make peace? To apologize for him now that she's dead?"

Moore took her hands from his shoulders and held them. I'm innocent, Moore said to himself, whatever happened I had nothing to do with it. But his stomach twisted with a feeling that he knew somehow was guilt. "I don't know anything except what happened thirty years ago," he said, and a voice inside him added, *And* what happened tonight. He felt her eyes on him like a physical pressure. "Let me tell you my story," he said, "the one you wanted to hear, the one about the essence of England. That's all I know."

He felt her hands relax in his. "He didn't send you? You didn't know about Mum?"

"I didn't know anything," he said, "and no one sent me. I just happen to be here, I can't say why."

"How strange," she said, but he could see that she believed him. "How strange," she said again, but then she said, "but I know you wouldn't lie to me. I know that about you already." Her anger had left her as quickly as it had come. "All right, tell me about the essence of England. Will it tell me anything about Lane?"

"I don't know," Moore said, and he didn't. He wasn't even sure what it would tell her about himself.

They sat down on the sofa and looked at the fireplace and he finally told her about the pontoon bridge and the Jersey Bounce and the haystack and the two girls sitting on the fence. "It stayed in my memory," he said. "For a long time I thought of it as the essence of England, and then I gradually forgot it. Till I saw the name on the map up in Oxford." He had never had a more attentive audience. He looked at her as he described the young girls. She was crying.

"Mum's name was Nancy," she said. After a moment she said, "So you and he saw Mum together, then, just that once." He nodded. "And then he came back here after all those years." She paused. "And now you've come back. You knew him. Why would he come back?"

Moore shrugged. "I've been thinking about that. I just don't know. We were awfully young. Maybe out of curiosity. Maybe something stuck in his mind the way it did in mine. I really can't remember much about him now except that everyone liked him and he laughed a lot."

"So he came back and found Mum," she said quietly. "And you came back and found me. How odd." Her meaning lay between them, heavy and dark. "Don't worry," she said, "I won't kill myself when you leave."

Moore got up and went over to the fireplace. She had left one of the bitters on the mantel and he picked it up and finished it. He wanted to say, But I won't leave you the way Lane left your mother. It would have been a right and good thing to say, but he couldn't say it. She was right: he couldn't lie to her, and couldn't lie to himself. He wished deeply that he could do both. He turned back to her. She was still sitting on the sofa, her hands folded in her lap, looking at nothing. Her dark hair and the grave face that wasn't Italian still struck him as regal, but the air of composure that had unsettled him so before was gone. She looked smaller and younger. He thought, Maybe I'm living the echoes of her mother and Lane. Maybe she is too.

"And you've never seen him again?" she said, "never heard from him?"

"Not since we were discharged in Chicago thirty years ago," Moore said almost eagerly, protesting the innocence he couldn't feel. "We got drunk that night and I never saw him again."

"Did he ever talk about Mum? I mean about the little girl, Nancy?"

"I don't think so. A lot happened to us after we left here. I think we'd both forgotten about Wallingford by then."

They were silent for a long while. Behind Moore the fireplace made a quiet clicking sound that he hadn't noticed before. Somewhere in another room a clock chimed once. "I've so often wondered what he was like," she said finally. "Mum must have loved him to do what she did. I'm sure it was her only affair." She looked at Moore. "I thought for a minute you could tell me."

"I'm sorry. Maybe I'll remember more about him later, but nothing that will explain why he came back here."

"I suppose it doesn't matter, really. What's done is done. But when I look at what's happened to Dad I hope sometimes that Lane was something special."

"Well, maybe he was," Moore said. "At least he was for your mother."

"Yes, that's what counts, isn't it?" She got up abruptly, and suddenly she looked taller and older again. Standing before him, her hands folded in front of her just below her waist in that posture that Moore had never seen in an American woman, she said, "It's been a strange night, hasn't it?"

"The strangest night of my life," Moore said. They were companionable again, he thought, once again they had shared some troubles the way people do who are close. "The strangest and the most—marvelous."

"Marvelous?"

"I mean except for your father and this thing about Lane. Yes, marvelous, the rest was marvelous."

She put her hands on his shoulders and instinctively his arms went around her. "Do you want to do anything more?" she said.

"Yes, I do, very much."

She turned half away and switched off the table lamp and then turned back to him. Once again they sank by agreement down onto the warm tiles in the reddish light, and as they knelt, Moore, safe from being caught now, slowly and methodically sent his hands over her body from shoulders to knees, then helped her slide out of the pajamas. She lay naked in front of the fire and for a long moment Moore simply looked at her body, so nearly boyish in its thinness except for the little breasts and the roundness of her thighs. For the first time he knew what lovers meant when they said they could eat each other up. His mouth went down her body like some sensitive questing little animal. Lines from Marvell's poem came to him as he kissed her body, and then, having world enough and time, he made love to her again.

For a long while he lay with his head on her stomach while her hands moved back and forth in his hair. Thought came slowly back to him, but not words to say, only a sentence repeating itself like a phrase of music: Out of the fullness of the heart the mouth speaketh. But not my mouth, he thought, my mouth has just spoken, but not words. The clock in the other room chimed twice. She gave his head a little pat that he knew was final and they rolled apart. Silently, she picked up her pajamas and went out. Moore sat for a moment until he realized that he was staring at the rolled umbrella leaning against the wall.

When she came back she was wearing her jean uniform again. "I'll drive you to the George," she said. Her face was as serious and as unreadable as when he had first seen her look at her father in the Fox and Grape.

"Can't I walk?"

"It's too far."

They went out of the house, holding hands. Moore, whose deepest feelings always masked themselves in other men's words, heard Milton telling of another pair walking hand in hand away from paradise, hand in hand "with wandering steps and slow." The late night air hung damp and chilly and the seats of the Morris were wet with dew. Gwen Morgan drove back past the church and the cricket ground and on into the High Street. Two canvas-covered lorries rumbled by, heading for London. Their tailgates said JOHN COURAGE, LTD. TAKE COURAGE. They were the only signs of life in Wallingford. Gwen pulled into the curb in front of the George and stopped. She put the gear into neutral and left the engine running. After a minute she said, "When do you go back to Oxford?"

"I could stay over Sunday," Moore said, "but I think maybe I should go back tomorrow."

She was looking through the windshield down the deserted High Street. "To your wife?"

"No. I was thinking of your father." They sat shoulder-to-shoulder staring straight ahead. Moore thought he had never seen a street that looked so empty. The High Street might have been the main street in a town after an atomic war. I walked down that street this afternoon and out into the country, he thought, looking for something that I thought had a meaning. And I found something that has a meaning and it's too much for me, it's more than I can handle.

"You do have a wife, of course," she said.

"She's coming in Tuesday. I'll be meeting her at Gatwick." She said nothing. Moore looked at her, but it was too dark to see her face, and it probably would have told him nothing anyway. The car engine throbbed on like an electric clock. "I want to say something," he said, "but I don't know what to say."

"You don't have to say anything. You were right. It's been a marvelous night."

"It wasn't just an easy piece," he said, "you know it wasn't."

"No, it wasn't," she said. "But then what was it?"

"I don't know," Moore said, "but I'm not like Lane. At least I don't think I am."

"And I'm not like Mum. At least I don't think I am."

"I could say I love you," Moore said, "and I don't think I'd be lying."

"Perhaps you wouldn't be. But it wouldn't change anything, would it?"

"No," Moore said, "I don't suppose it would." He put his arm awkwardly around her in the cramped front seat and kissed her and for a moment he thought she responded, but then she pulled back and he knew the night was over. He struggled up out of the car to the sidewalk and looked down inside but could see only her hands on the steering wheel and hear the throb of the engine.

"Cheers," she said.

"Cheers." He shut the door and she crunched the car into low gear and he stood watching until it turned off the High Street and he was alone. He went into the George, past the bar with the wicker grating over it, and up the stairs to his room. Lying in bed, more tired than he had ever been, he revisited the Fox and Grape and the firelit parlor like a ghost haunting old precincts. He hadn't even bothered to wash, and her body was still with him in the crusting on his loins and the tang in his mouth, so much a presence that he could hardly believe she was gone. But, settling finally into sleep, it was not her but her words that he remembered and that he took into his dreams. Not just an easy piece. But if not that, then what was it?

CHAPTER 4

Oxford – Part I

R iding back to Oxford on the bus the next morning, Moore had the
feeling that he was leaving the past and coming back to the present,
as if a time machine he couldn't control had taken him to Wallingford and
brought him back again. When the bus finally pulled into the station at
Oxford and he was carrying his bag along the familiar streets back to Corpus Christi, he felt that what had happened the night before in Wallingford
had somehow happened a long time ago, and by the time he got back to his
rooms he was almost nostalgic about the day and night before. He understood well enough what his mind was doing. It was putting troubling things
at a distance.

He sat down at his writing table in the ghastly white sitting room and
looked again at the map that had sent him on his quest, but it meant nothing to him now. It was like looking at a map of Detroit. Maps were for anticipation, and he had nothing to anticipate now. He opened his folder of notes
on Shelley. Monday morning he would have to teach "Mt. Blanc." That was
appropriate, he thought. A man stared at a mountain, was moved by the
experience, tried to determine whether the mountain and the experience
meant anything, thought they did, but finally couldn't say what. He put his
feet up on the table and leaned back in the uncomfortable straight-backed
chair and for a long time stared out the dirty window at the patch of gray-
ish-blue sky above Merton College. The voices of tourists drifted up to him
from the path beneath the window, patterings of French, rumblings of German. After a while, through the window behind him, he heard the clatter-
ing of pans and the whistling of the cook, and he knew it was nearly
dinnertime. But he sat on staring at the little slice of sky until the Merton
bell tolled eight and dinner was long over. Then he got stiffly up and went
out into the hallway to the bathroom and came back and splashed water on
his face in his tiny sink. His body said eat and drink now, he realized; the
body kept going, no matter what. And so did the mind, back here in the present: as he went out the Corpus gate toward the Turf he found himself
thinking of Helen and the trip to Gatwick to meet her.

He went up Magpie Lane to the High Street and, as always, the sight of St. Mary's Church made him stop for a minute. He stood staring up at the Gothic spire while the traffic rushed by in front of him in waves of sound and odor. Newman had preached there, not fifty yards from where he stood, more than a hundred years ago, in a quieter time, when the spire and the street had not been such different worlds as they were now. It had been years since Moore had read Newman, but he had thought of him often here in Oxford. Every time he came out of the lane and saw St. Mary's he thought of Newman's definition of a gentleman: A gentleman was one who never inflicted pain. He thought of it again now, for the first time in relation to himself and to last night. No matter how I measure myself, he thought, I seem to fail.

He waited automatically for a clearing in traffic, but his mind had gone back to Helen again. He would have to walk a long way now, he knew, in order to sleep tonight. Lager alone would not be enough. He got across the street and set a hard pace for himself. He made himself quickstep past St. Mary's and the Radcliffe Camera, on across Broad Street past the White Horse, till he got to what he thought of as the other side of town. He tramped on past Keble College, counting cadence to himself, and rounded a curve that brought him onto George Street, the road leading north out of town. He was tired already, and stopped to rest. Traffic went by toward the roundabout that led either to the carriage way to London or the tiny road to Wallingford. He realized suddenly that he was tired all over. He felt unfamiliar aches in his back and arms and neck. Well, of course, he said to himself, as if he were smiling, after all that action, of course. But in a moment the smiling went away in a surge of shame. It was the smiling part of him that had inflicted pain last night. Today he could wish that he were one of Newman's gentlemen and be sad that he wasn't. But last night it hadn't mattered at all.

He marched up George Street for what he guessed was a mile, then turned around and marched back down. Near the Eagle & Child there was a little restaurant that advertised American food, and on impulse he turned in there instead of going to the Turf. He ate a stringy cheeseburger and chips and drank a cup of tea, like a penitent, he thought, eating tasteless food during Lent. He had a second cup of tea and smoked a pipe while he waited for the food to settle. He wondered what Helen was doing on this Saturday night. It wouldn't be an ordinary Saturday night for her, of course, because she would be flying out Monday night. But then it wasn't even Saturday night for her yet, only mid-afternoon. Right now she was probably at the local shopping mall, trying to think of things she would need at Oxford, wondering whether to take hair curlers along in case the adapter didn't work. She would call Ruthie in Virginia before she left, of course, maybe tonight or tomorrow, and Ruthie would put the baby on the phone to talk to Grandma.

Moore tapped his pipe out in an ashtray and stood up. He was fond of his daughter, and of his granddaughter too, he believed. But now that he was thinking of Helen an old attitude slipped back in and he was half angry. He wasn't fond of Helen as Grandma, and for a long time now there had been too much Grandma and not enough Helen. Walking down to the Eagle & Child, he wondered whether Helen had missed him much these past weeks—or not whether, really, but how. He found himself wishing that she had missed him in bed, but he didn't really believe that. He thought she had probably missed him as a general presence. Or as an old, intimate friend, but not as a lover. He imagined a scene in which they sat in the ugly sitting room in Corpus and he told her that he had had an affair with a young English woman. He could see the hurt in her eyes, the disappointment. But he couldn't see any understanding. He wanted something that he had had with her once but didn't have any longer. But her face showed that she didn't know that; it showed only blankness and pain. He turned the scene off. Maybe it was unfair to Helen; maybe the scene wouldn't be like that at all. But in his heart he was sure it would be. He was sure he would be talking to Grandma. But he would never tell her. It would do neither of them any good.

He went into the Eagle & Child and drew comfort, as he always did, from the dark polished woodwork and the real fireplace with the straw flowers on the mantel. He had begun coming here occasionally because it seemed to have fewer tourists and fewer young people than the White Horse, and it was possible to sit in a corner and think or even read. He had been delighted to find the little copper plate on a wall of the back room, near another fireplace, commemorating the pub as the place where C.S. Lewis and Tolkien and Charles Williams and Owen Barfield had met regularly on Monday mornings. He had never sat in the back room, but it pleased him to think that such formidable minds had also found the pub so appealing. The evening he had found the plate, on his way back to the toilet, he had stared at it for several minutes, trying to imagine some of those conversations, wondering if anyone had ever convinced anyone else of anything that really mattered. Whether on a Monday afternoon anyone had changed his mind about time or God or the limits of human nature.

Now, standing at the bar with his lager, Moore thought that in his own way he was arguing that old problem of human nature in very specific terms. What should a man do to be right? Gwen and Helen, love and loyalty, youth and age. If he were forced to make a choice between Helen and Gwen, he could make a strong argument either way. Both choices seemed right, except that Moore was no longer sure that he knew what rightness was or that you could always recognize it when you saw it. If you didn't believe you could be right by following some kind of system, and if you didn't believe you could be right by following your own feelings, then you probably should conclude that being right was impossible, or that there was no such thing as being right. Moore had felt both ways at different times and had come to both of these conclusions. But the arguments had never really changed the sense that he got up with each day: the sense that there was a right buried somehow at the heart of things, like some obscure law of atomic physics that no one really understood but that in some way gave structure to existence. He thought he knew why he and so many others found Kafka so sympathetic. Kafka told them they were guilty but not able to be innocent, and that was about the way that Moore felt. He ordered another lager and tried to dismiss the problem, because after he had run through all the steps of the argument he had always come to the same answer: to pray to whoever or whatever had this rightness and to do as little as possible in life because all things were suspect. It was an answer that invariably conjured up images of the contemplative life, of a hermit praying before a crucifix in a cell, images that Moore had always found grotesque, even as a boy in a Catholic school.

But the problem would not go out of his mind, because Helen and Gwen were not theoretical possibilities. But then, as if he had caught himself in mid-sentence saying something stupid in class, Moore stopped his thought. Because he had suddenly realized that the problem he was gnawing at really *was* only a theoretical one. Why was he thinking of choosing between Helen and Gwen? Why all the setting up of complex rights and wrongs? He wasn't going to leave Helen: he had already decided he wasn't even going to tell her about Gwen. He had been dramatizing. It would have been more honest to examine his feelings about last night and about Gwen. But if he had done that, he thought, he would have found guilt, like an open sore, and it would have hurt. He scraped his pipe clean in an ashtray, remembering that just twenty-four hours before he had stood at a bar much like this in Wallingford just before Gwen had come back and had asked himself what would keep him from going with her if he got the chance. Fear of looking a fool had been the answer, and it was the same answer now. There was no high moral drama here. If he wouldn't go back to Gwen now it was because sooner or later he would be foolish. Maybe he hadn't been foolish with her last night. No, he hadn't been; he knew that. Last night had been something special for both of them. But that was just it. The nights to come wouldn't be something special. They had shared fear last night, and together they had looked a little into the past and had tried to lift its shroud. But those things wouldn't happen again. Sooner or later she must change for youth, and he felt the quick pain of that fact. He drank his lager and stared at a glass-covered dish of sausage rolls behind the bar. I'm not a gentleman, he thought, not even to myself.

Old Glenn Miller music played quietly from a tape recorder behind the bar, as it had every night that he had been there. It had seemed out of place the first time he'd heard it, but now it seemed to belong. Barfield and Lewis and the others might have argued the imponderables against a background of "In the Mood" and "Moonlight Serenade." He drank his lager, and his mind slid back and forth between sets of images, one real and one imagined, between Gwen as he remembered her last night and Helen as he tried to picture her now. Both sets were unsatisfactory, but after a while they became hazy and not so insistent, and when closing time came at eleven he realized that he had been thinking for quite a long time about Shelley and "Mt. Blanc."

Sunday morning was damp and cloudy and there was a threat of rain. He drank instant coffee in his sitting room, then paged through his copy of Shelley until the Merton bells rang at ten-thirty. Then, unable to sit any longer, he got his raincoat and tramped downstairs and out through the quad. As always, his eyes went to the pelican brooding on its pedestal. This morning its gold looked dingy and tarnished against the gray sky. He walked purposefully, so as not to be stopped for casual conversation, though he didn't know where he was going. When he got to the High Street people were coming out of St. Mary's from the ten o'clock service, and Newman's definition ran through his mind like an old and sad poem. He followed the High Street past Magdalen and the botanical gardens and across the bridge. A few picnickers sat along the banks of the river in sweaters and raincoats. "Under the weather" must be an English phrase, Moore thought; they spend most of their life here in Oxford under a shell of grayness and damp. But they make do, he thought, and I have never seen such beautiful roses anywhere else. When he got to the fork in the road he turned and walked at a good pace along the Iffley Road. He would walk to the old church that he had heard so much about from his students. He was not in a mood for Christ Church Meadows.

For nearly an hour he walked on, past the rows of semi-detached houses and an occasional shop and the neighborhood pubs that were just opening. It began to rain as he reached Iffley and started up a long winding street that he knew must lead to the church. By the time he went around the last curve, past a small hotel with an enormous elm tree stump in front of it, the rain was falling harder. Two cars were parked in the street alongside the church, their windshield wipers going: sightseers who didn't want to get wet. He half ran over the soft ground of the churchyard, over the long stringy grass like the grass on a beach, and around to the front of the church. A man holding an umbrella moved aside and Moore went in.

He stood for a moment, simply glad to be out of the rain, then he peeled his raincoat off and got his handkerchief out and wiped his glasses. Even without them he could sense the oldness: it was in the odor of the place, the reek of dampness and old wood. When he put his glasses back on, the oldness came to him even more strongly. It was a little church, hardly more than a private chapel by Oxford standards. Two banks of uncomfortable looking pews flanked a narrow center aisle that ran up to the altar. The stone walls were blackish gray and Moore knew that if he touched them he would feel grit and dampness. He thought of the chapel at Christ Church, where he would probably go tonight for evensong, where the organist played Bach and where the congregation had to walk around scaffolding set up for cleaning and restoration. He would like to come to a service here, he thought, and then wondered why. Some dim American prejudice against old world elegance? Some literary sentiment about the poor and the old?

He put his hand on the dark stone baptismal font that looked as if it had been carved from a single boulder and looked back at the stained glass window over the front door. It was circular and elaborately ornamented. He stared at it for several minutes, but except for what seemed to be a white bird in its center its symbolism evaded him. He shivered a little in the dampness and walked over to examine the two heavy confessionals just inside the door. The heavy velvet curtains, once apparently red, were worn thin and brownish. A small pile of pamphlets lay on the seat of the last pew and he picked one up and glanced through it. He had stopped reading pamphlets of this sort very carefully. He had seen too many churches this summer and had found that most of them were already running together in his mind, as if he had spent a long time visiting a single church. But he turned the pages: there was the usual plea for contributions and the usual request for reverent silence, and then a page or two of facts. He was in the church of St. Mary the Virgin, twelfth-century Norman Romanesque. Moore had still not gotten used to the fact that all the really old churches he had seen this summer and the really old colleges in Oxford had once belonged to what the British still sometimes called the Old Persuasion. They had once been Catholic, the church that Moore still vaguely thought of as his. He skimmed on in the pamphlet. Something about Chaucer's family tree on the south window. Then a note on the west window. He looked up to get his directions straight. Yes, it was the west window he had been looking at. It was called *Oculus Dei*, the Eye of God. He stared at it again, at the white bird in the center, and then thought, Of course, the Dove, the Paraclete, the Holy Ghost, Wisdom and Knowledge as the center of God's eye, omniscience. He wondered what the window would look like on a fine day, when it would catch the full strength of the afternoon sun. Today it was simply like the rest of the church, old and subdued and dim.

He went to the door and looked out. The rain had slackened to a heavy mist. He struggle back into his wet raincoat and went out and around the corner of the church to the graveyard, and then stopped in amazement. The broadest tree he had ever seen spread over half the graveyard like some monstrous umbrella. He went over to it and stooped to go under its drooping branches. It was a yew, he decided, so huge that it seemed to have survived from some earlier world of giants and dragons. He leaned against the massive trunk as he might have leaned against a house and wondered which had come first, the church or the tree. He stood looking at the thin stone grave markers under the tree, most of them cracked and tilted. Here and there he could make out a letter or number but nowhere a whole name or date. The short and simple annals of the poor, he thought. Gray could have written his elegy here.

He walked back to Corpus in the heavy mist, and by the time he got to his rooms he was soaked through and very tired. He turned on his electric fireplace and stood shivering in front of it. How had they ever done it, he wondered, Sidney and Hooker and Keble and Newman and the rest? How had they written those marvelous things in a place where the winter wetness clung to the walls all through summer and where the winters themselves were unimaginable? He went into the bathroom and ran hot water in the tub and lay in it for fifteen minutes till the chill had gone out of his body. When he went down to dinner he sat between two of his students and made jokes about Shelley and "Mt. Blanc." He pretended to be surprised that they found the poem difficult. The little blond girl, who knew Moore from Detroit, knew he was joking, but the serious graduate student from Arkansas didn't. Moore's jokes were academic jokes. Not funny, really, not intended to be. They were jokes that a teacher made to keep students at a distance, begun when Moore had found himself a decade older than his students, and continued now when the years between them made him uncomfortable. For a moment he pictured Gwen Morgan sitting across the table from him with the students—she couldn't be much older than the Arkansas student—and his mind strayed away to Wallingford. He had met her out of context, he thought; if he had met her here at Oxford nothing would have happened between them. He had stopped being a teacher down there for just a night, as if he had fallen asleep on guard duty for just a moment and had found his position over-run. With an effort he brought his mind back to the dinner table. The boy and girl were looking at him, and he thought maybe they had asked a question he hadn't heard. "It isn't really a hard poem," he said, "you only have to put yourselves in Shelley's place. Try to see the mountains as he saw them. Forget the mountains on the map. Try to see the real ones." They looked at him, trying to see the joke, but there wasn't any joke, and not even any meaning they could recognize.

After coffee he walked down to the White Horse. Ordinarily, with a hard class coming up the next day he would have gone to the Eagle & Child. But he had worked out his stratagems for dealing with Shelley and "Mt. Blanc" because he knew that tonight he would be able to think of nothing but his arrangements to meet Helen on Tuesday. He had noticed often in the past few years that he worried more than he used to about things like this, and he had wondered if it was a sign of age. He didn't feel comfortable any more about a future event unless he was completely in control of it. He had even noticed it in his class preparations; he didn't want to leave anything to chance any more. So he stood at the bar of the White Horse and rehearsed what he would do the next day after the Shelley class. The express bus to London. The walk to Victoria station. The train from Victoria to Gatwick. The local bus to Crawley and the hotel where he would spend Monday night. The bus in the morning back to Gatwick to meet Helen. The train back to Victoria, the walk again with the luggage, the express bus again back to Oxford. He set the bus and train schedules on the bar in front of him and studied them again. He hadn't thought beyond the bus back to Oxford because Helen would be here then. He would simply introduce her to Oxford. He didn't have to plan that, or try to control that. Oxford simply had to be itself and that would be enough. He would tell her some things about it, probably repeat things he'd said in his letters, but those things wouldn't really be necessary. She could see the important things for herself. Anyone could. All you had to do was stand for half an hour in the High Street and look at the spires and listen to the bells and you would know that something great had happened here once, maybe a long time ago, and that some of it had survived.

It wasn't till after the Shelley class the next day, when he had packed his bag and was walking to the bus station that he began to think of how it would be to meet her. As Shelley and "Mt. Blanc" began to slip away from him, he began to visualize the international gate at Gatwick and himself standing there and her coming through. He wondered if she would see something different in him; she knew him so well, after all, at least in some ways. He wondered if somehow he would give off a vibration of infidelity that she would catch. Maybe not just then, he thought, but maybe in a day or a week. Some slip of the tongue, some uncharacteristic act that he could not even imagine now. She had always been very perceptive about him— extraordinarily perceptive, he had often thought; she had always known things about him that he had not known himself until she told him. Or, rather, she had been perceptive until the last few years. She had not been nearly as perceptive as Grandma as she had been as Helen.

On the bus to Crawley, sitting stiffly between two middle-aged women who were going home from London to the suburbs, he thought, One more night alone and then Helen and I will be together again and that night with Gwen will probably seem as if it never happened. Because it happened when Helen and I were separated for the only time, really, in more than twenty years. In two weeks we'll go back home and pick up where we left off and in six months that night will seem like a dream and I'll wonder if it ever really happened. Maybe I won't even think about it, except once in a while, late at night, when Helen is asleep. Pretty soon it will be the old routine again, not really uncomfortable, just kind of dull—maybe more dull now than ever. And the years will go by and before long it won't matter whether it happened or not. I'll turn into Grandpa and after a while they'll bury me in the same cemetery where my mother and father are buried. Helen and I will have a double plot there. But not under a yew tree, not next to a church with God's eye in its window, not where the ragged grass grows over the grave markers. In our cemetery an attendant will come around every holiday and put a floral wreath on our graves; it will be in the contract. Well, he thought, as the bus pulled into Crawley, most people get buried according to the way they lived. That's the way it will be with Helen and me: ordinary middle-class American life, ordinary middle-class American death. It didn't really matter in the long run. If there really was anything like an eye of God it would see you, wherever you were, in whatever kind of grave.

At Crawley he spent the evening in the plush hotel bar, trying to drink enough lager by closing time so that he could sleep, but he was pretty sure it wouldn't work. The bar was full of Americans talking about baseball and the stock market, but Moore talked to no one. He was occupied with the mechanics of Helen's flight. He kept calculating the time difference over and over, as if once he got the arithmetic of it down he would have control over it. At midnight here she would board her plane, and it would be dinnertime there. By about four in the morning here she would be flying over the Atlantic. It would only be about ten at night for her and she would probably be watching the movie. When the bar closed he got two cans of lager from a machine in the corridor and took them to his room. At midnight he finished one and threw it into the waste basket. She should be taking off now. She would have her eyes closed and her knuckles would whiten as she squeezed the armrests. If Moore had been there she would have his hand clutched so tightly that his wedding ring would be cutting into his fingers. At one-thirty he finished the other lager. She should be somewhere over eastern Canada by now, maybe even over Newfoundland. He went to bed then, but the clock in his mind kept running, and at four o'clock he found himself wide awake and thinking, By now she's over the ocean. Then, as if he could do no more to help her, he fell back to sleep. But in his dreams a

DC-10 kept plunging in an endless dive into darkness, and inside it Helen, rigid with horror and disbelief, was screaming his name, over and over, but he wasn't there to help her.

Her plane was an hour late, and just as he was about to go back to the information desk he saw her coming through the doors from customs, and for a moment he thought they must have been apart for years because she looked so different. Her hair was a shade or two lighter than it had been and was cut differently so that her face, always a little round, looked thinner and her blue eyes bigger. She looked trim in a blue pantsuit, and he could tell she had lost the five pounds she had been talking about for so long. She saw him and waved and started to run toward him, her flight bag swinging awkwardly against her legs. For a moment he couldn't move forward because it seemed to him that he was seeing her twenty years before, when Ruthie had been a baby and they had left her at Helen's mother's for a few days. He had gone out to the car and waited and then Helen had come running down the driveway, and they were going to be alone together for the weekend. She had been carrying a shoulder purse and it had bumped against her as she ran. A current of feeling ran through Moore and his legs were suddenly trembling, and when he finally moved and they were holding each other he found that he had no voice, and whatever he had planned to say to her was lost. Her arms were tight around him and she kept saying his name over and over until her voice broke and he realized she was crying. They stood like that until a redcap wheeled her baggage up behind them and stood waiting for his tip. Moore found his hands shaking as he tried to get money from his pocket.

He began to push the baggage cart and she walked beside him, her arm around his waist. "You've lost weight," she said, dabbing at her eyes with a tissue.

"So have you. You look wonderful."

"I wondered if you'd notice."

They were making their way through islands of baggage toward the doors that led to the train platform. "How was the flight?"

"Okay, really. But you know me. I die going up and die again coming down."

"I know. I thought about you."

They rode the escalator down to the train platform and he took the baggage off the cart so that they could each sit down on a suitcase. "There'll be a train along soon," he said, "there's one into London every hour. Now tell me the news from home."

She did, but he only half listened because there wasn't much she hadn't already told him in her letters. They sat knee to knee, holding hands, while she talked about Ruthie and the baby and the last minute shopping, and he simply watched her face. He had almost forgotten how pretty she was, prettier now than she had been a few years ago. Prettier than Gwen, really. If the two of them had walked into a room together he thought most men would look at Helen first. Then he dismissed the comparison angrily. Every once in a while, he thought, I know what women mean when they call us chauvinist pigs.

"I'm so excited," she said. "I can hardly wait to see the deer park and Christ Church and Corpus Christi. And the sitting room. Is it really as ugly as you said in your letters or were you kidding?"

"Not kidding at all. I've lived in it a month and I still don't believe it. But it'll be better with you in it."

Her hands tightened on his. "I've missed you so much. I'll never let you go away again. I didn't know what it would be like."

"I didn't either," Moore said. He hadn't known, and if he had he never would have come. But he hadn't known and he had come, and already he found himself watching his words. I'll never be able to talk to her the way I used to, he thought, I'll always find myself being careful.

"Sometimes when I was feeling low I wondered if you were having an affair over here," she said. Moore looked at her quickly, wondering what his face showed. But it was all right; she was smiling at him. "I mean, I knew you must be lonely, even if you were having fun. At least I hope you were lonely."

"I have been," he said, "more than I can say."

On the train into Victoria she fell asleep on his shoulder, and when they had struggled with the suitcases and finally got on the bus to Oxford she fell asleep again. She woke up once, about half way to Oxford. "I'm sorry," she said. "I've come all this way to be with you and now I can't stay awake."

He patted her hand. "It's the jet lag. Don't try to stay awake. You'll be all right tomorrow." He cradled her against his shoulder and she went deeply to sleep and when they got to Oxford he had to wake her up.

He got the luggage off in front of the bus stop in the High Street and then helped her down. She stepped dreamily off the bus as if she had been doped. "Come on, zombie," he said, "it's not far now." She took one slow look down the street, but he knew she wasn't taking anything in. Carrying her suitcases, he led the way down the cobbled lane that brought them out at Merton. He set the bags down, sweating. "That's Merton. Remember I wrote you about the bells? We're just next door."

She looked blankly at Merton and yawned and Moore, watching her face, found himself laughing. She looked like a tired child being shown something cultural. But the massive gateway and the great double door of Corpus Christi awed her. "So big," she murmured, "so old." They went into the quad and Moore wondered what she would think of the pelican. She looked at it, puzzled, as Moore had been the first time he saw it. "What is it?" she asked him.

"It's the Corpus pelican." She stood staring up at the golden bird perched on top of the obelisk. "It's a symbol of Christ," he told her. "He bites his breast. When you get closer you can see the drops of blood."

She giggled. "It looks tired. Everything looks tired to me."

They went on across the quad. Moore had hoped to get to his rooms without meeting anyone, because nearly everyone in the program knew that Helen was due in today, and he suspected that there had been a lot of jokes among the students about Dr. Moore and his month of sexual abstinence. He didn't really mind as long as he didn't hear the jokes, but now he wanted to slip quietly in. But voices came from the windows in the Junior Common Room: "Hello, Mrs. Moore, Welcome to Oxford, Three cheers for Mrs. Moore." He recognized the faces, most of them his own students, and waved. Helen looked sleepily at them and waved too. "Hello," she called, "and thank you very much." The graduate student from Arkansas appeared in the passageway next to the dining room. "Let me give you a hand with the bags, Dr. Moore." Moore was embarrassed, but the young man had picked up the bags before he could stop him, and so he and Helen followed him across the other quad and up Staircase Twelve to the landing outside the heavy white door.

"Thanks, Mulqueen," he said, and introduced him to Helen.

"My great pleasure, ma'am," Mulqueen said seriously. Mulqueen was always serious. He shook Helen's hand, ready for conversation.

"Thanks," Moore said again, "thanks very much."

"My pleasure," Mulqueen said again, and finally turned around and went down the stairs.

Moore unlocked the door and led her into the sitting room. "This is it," he said. "Did I exaggerate?"

She stood staring at the room in disbelief. "It's just the way you said it was, but I still don't believe it." Her eyes went up to the impossibly high ceiling, then to the dead white paneled walls and to the bizarre furniture. "It's so ugly it's almost beautiful," she said, and Moore felt a sense of old intimacy. Over the years they had grown together in their tastes, and he had forgotten that. She giggled when she saw the cots. "I can see why you're all scholars here," she said.

"Be flattered," he said. "They were end to end till yesterday." He showed her the bathroom just outside their door. "It's almost private; we only share it with the people across the landing. Just leave the door ajar and nip into the bathroom when you have to."

She looked at the ancient tub and the toilet with the long pull chain hanging from the ceiling. "Could I take a bath now? Maybe it would perk me up a little."

"Sure." He turned on the taps and got the water adjusted and put the stopper in. When he stood up from the tub she had gone back to their rooms and when he went in she was opening her smaller suitcase on the double cots. She laid neatly folded blouses on the cot and pulled out a white terrycloth robe and slippers. Already the room seemed less austere, Moore thought, and by tomorrow she would have made it her own. "Your bath is drawn, my dear," he said in a mock English accent, and kissed the back of her neck.

She turned around to him and Moore thought her eyes had never looked so blue. "Don't go away," she said, and kissed him.

She went out into the sitting room and he heard her open the door and leave it just ajar and then heard the bathroom door close and lock. He sat down on the cot and felt himself trembling a little. My love is in my gonads, he thought, and a wave of disgust bitter as acid washed over him. If it was Gwen in there that I was waiting for I'd feel the same way I do now, but I've lived more than twenty years with Helen and only one night with Gwen. Is there really anything to me except this? I lecture on Platonic love and I even think sometimes I believe it, or something like it. I think souls can love souls, whatever souls are. But apparently my soul can't. He sat on the cot and looked out the window at the walls of Merton next door and felt the old familiar tension in his loins, as if all his life and energy were being sucked out of the rest of his body and mind and being drawn down to the bottom of his stomach, narrowing down and concentrating. For what, he thought, for what? But then he felt that concentrated being surging against the crotch of his trousers, and he knew for what, and knew too that part of the power down there came from pride, from that smiling part of himself that kept him from being one of Newman's gentlemen.

He heard Helen come out of the bathroom and back into the sitting room, heard her close the door and heard the Yale lock click, but still he stared out the window at Merton. She came in in her robe and slippers, laid her clothes and towel on the other cot and came and stood by him. He looked up at her and put his arm around her buttocks and laid his face against the soft robe. He could feel her stomach moving as she breathed and felt her hand moving through his hair and he had to remind himself that he wasn't in Wallingford and that if he looked up he would see blue eyes and light brown hair and a face that moved him through familiarity, not strangeness. She pulled the robe open so that his face was against the flesh of her stomach, and he could smell cleanness and a faint perfume. After a minute she turned and sat down on his lap and took his face in her hands and kissed him, and then she said, "Oh my," half laughing, and he knew she had felt him pressing up against her. "Oh my," she said again, and there was excitement in her voice, "this is urgent, isn't it?"

They rolled awkwardly over on the cot and he pulled her robe open the rest of the way. She really had lost weight, his mind noted. Her stomach was flat and her thighs seemed smaller. "Truth time," he said. It was an old joke with them. It meant: Get undressed. His hands were still trembling as he got out of his clothes and dropped them on the floor, and in fact he felt giddy and weak all over except in his loins, as if everything really *had* concentrated there. When he turned back to the cot she was naked and for a moment they stared at each other's bodies and she said again, "Oh my."

He crawled onto the cot and knelt over her and kissed her. "This is going to be historic," he said.

She pulled his face down to her breasts. "As long as that doesn't mean slow." And then a minute later she pulled him down on top of her and hugged his hips with her legs. "No more preliminaries."

They finished as the Merton bell was tolling three, and he lay on her for a few minutes, his face against the pillow, her hair tickling his ear. She kissed his shoulder. "That *was* historic," she said. He couldn't see her face, but he didn't have to. There was contentment in her voice.

"Yes," he said. He was pleased with himself. "We should build a monument to that."

She fell asleep immediately, and he knew she must be exhausted, because ordinarily she would have gotten up and gone to the bathroom, walking like a child who has waited too long, her legs pressed together in a pigeon-toed walk. He watched her for a while. She had always looked younger to him when she was asleep, and she still did. It had been three or four years ago that he had really lost her. That was how he thought of it, as losing her. It was the menopause, of course. He knew all about that, or thought he did. He knew more about the female menopause than Miller did about the male. Body changes, mental changes, emotional changes—hormones and hot flashes. He hadn't often complained when they had not made love for several days, but his pride had been deeply hurt. And every once in a while when they had been arguing over something else he had found himself violently angry with her, and words had come piling out, words that he had known were hurting her even as he said them: listless, sexless, old. Words that he had shot at her like dum-dum bullets, seeing the pain in her eyes and yet not able to stop, sensing even as he spoke the words that they were useless, that she couldn't help herself, as if he were raging at her for having cancer or diabetes. Afterward he had always been ashamed, and had even wondered why she didn't leave him. Leave him for a gentleman, he thought now, who wouldn't inflict that pain. But then there would be a time after his outbursts when it seemed she had turned the calendar back, and for a week or two they would act like lovers together. And then the relapse, when she simply seemed to forget about anything sexual. Not dislike, just forget. He looked down at her now, savoring the last half hour. He thought, If it had been like this or anything close to this in the last four years I would never have spent the night with Gwen because I wouldn't have been in England alone. And he thought, Tonight was like old times, but I wonder how long it will last.

He walked over to the window and leaned on the sill and stared at Merton. If he were a different kind of man, he thought, he would accept things he knew couldn't be different and take things for the pleasure they gave him. He wondered if Lane had been like that, if that had been the secret of his good nature. But Moore couldn't do it. He couldn't accept Helen as eighty percent Grandma and twenty percent lover. And he couldn't accept Gwen Morgan as just an easy piece. What a miserable mixture he was of egotism and American Catholic conscience, he thought. The two things did not fit together at all. But then he thought, Of course they fit together, since they're both part of me. I'm alive and well with both these things working inside me, so apparently they fit. Or not fit, exactly. His mind drifted to the Freudian terms that seemed so natural: man is a meeting place of tensions and opposing forces—the id and the ego, the conscious and the unconscious, and so on. But the terms that explained others to him had never satisfactorily explained himself, and they didn't now. When you named something you put a frame around it and simplified it, he thought, whether you called it an unconscious drive or a sin. We're all too vague to be framed like that, he thought, except by the eye of God, if there is such a thing.

He went quietly back past Helen, got his towel, and went out to the bathroom and sat for a while in a warm bath, trying to think of nothing. When he came back she was still asleep. He set his alarm clock for six-thirty and lay down beside her. Half asleep, he heard the Merton bells toll the quarter hours, and in his half dream he was on a bus riding back and forth between Oxford and Wallingford and between Oxford and London, back and forth, till he couldn't tell whether he was coming or going, or from where to where. All the landmarks seemed the same: all the churches looked alike, and all the pubs had identical signs. All the roads had little cars driving on the wrong side and the woman leaning against him in the bus seat was very dear to him and he held her gently against him so that the swaying and jolting of the bus wouldn't wake her.

He was awake and staring at the clock minutes before six-thirty. He turned off the alarm and waited till he heard it click and then turned to Helen. She hadn't moved. She still lay on her back, her head turned a little to one side on the pillow. He pulled the covers down to the foot of the cot, but she didn't move. She looked like one of the effigies he had seen in so many English cathedrals: a carved figure lying rigidly atop a tomb. Except that the effigies had all been fully dressed, with a knight lying by their side in full armor, and a heraldic animal at their feet. Naked and unashamed, she might have been some pagan sculpture of sensuality, quiescent and inviting.

When he had shaved and dressed she was still asleep, and he woke her slowly and gently. "Rise and shine," he said. "It's time for a little walk by the river and then some dinner. Then you can go to sleep again." He said all this several times while he rubbed his hand across her stomach, and finally she woke up and looked at him blankly. Her eyes went around the strange high walls, then came back to him and she realized where she was. She smiled at him.

"It's just the way I knew it would be," she said.

"What is?"

"Everything. The college, the rooms, this afternoon."

He kissed her. "And don't forget tonight. There's still tonight."

When she was dressed again in the blue pantsuit they went downstairs and across the quad. She looked again at the pelican.

"You always see it," Moore said. "I've found that out. Even when you don't think you do."

They went down the lane beneath their window and down the gravel walk to the river. They sat down on an old wooden park bench and looked at the swans cruising majestically downstream.

"I never thought the Thames was so small," she said. "Back home we'd call it a creek."

"It isn't the Thames here, it's the Cherwell. The Thames comes in a little farther on, but it's just as small. They don't put any stock in bigness over here. The rivers are creeks and the lakes are ponds. If you put Lake St. Clair here they'd think it was an ocean. And the streets are lanes and the shops are closets. But you get to like it." He stopped suddenly because he had been going to say something about expanding inward instead of outward, into miniatures, and Gwen had come into his mind against his will.

"It's so lovely," Helen said, leaning against him. A young couple drifted past in front of them in a punt. The girl was dropping bits of bread into the water behind the boat, and three swans were following. "Somehow it makes me think of Churchill and the Battle of Britain. No wonder they were willing to fight for this."

He knew she wouldn't feel so romantic if she had been looking at Wolverhampton or Birmingham, any more than she would have been romantic looking at River Rouge or Hamtramck, but he didn't say anything. He had been very selective himself long ago in looking for the essence of England. He had never looked for it in Wolverhampton or Birmingham because he had not wanted to find it there.

They went back up the lane and across the High Street and then down the winding streets to the Turf. He told her a little about it as they walked, not what it was really like, just a few guide book facts. Like most of the rest of Oxford, the Turf could speak for itself. And she wasn't prepared for it when they got there; he could tell. He hadn't been prepared either his first time here. Coming out of a narrow alley into a kind of courtyard, you suddenly felt squeezed in and pressed down by the ancient three- and four-storey houses that surrounded you and towered over you and almost seemed to lean together and meet far overhead, like a forest of houses. No act of the American imagination could make probable the lives of the students who had looked out those narrow windows for a moment three-hundred years ago, before they went back to their Latin manuscripts. Down in London a troupe might have been playing *Hamlet*, but up in those garrets, Moore imagined, those pale collegians would not have known it and would not have cared if they had. The sense of the past was very strong for Moore here at the Turf, stronger than it was in more famous places like Tintern Abbey and Westminster. Maybe because he had been living for a month in the musty oldness of Corpus Christi, he felt here at the Turf—so cramped and cave-like—a kind of comradeship with those long dead undergraduates who had peered down from those high windows and who had come in to sit where he and Helen now sat at one of the scarred and massive tables.

They ate bread and cheese and deviled eggs and meat pie, and washed it down with lager. Helen was fascinated by the people around them—students of all ages, none of them British. She listened to the German and French and Dutch and the twangy English of the five middle-aged women from Kansas next to them who were talking about their course in medieval history, then looked at him in dismay.

"I was surprised too, at first," he told her. "They come from all over the world to study here in the summer."

"It's so exciting," she said, "it's like being right in the middle of things."

"That's what they think too. Right in the middle of old things. In the middle of history, I suppose."

She put her hand over his. "You like it here, don't you?"

He nodded. "More than I can say. I don't belong here, but I like it. I'd like to belong here, I think, but if I did I'd be someone very different." It was the first time he had tried to talk about his feelings for Oxford, except in his imaginary letter.

"I don't think you would be," she said. "I think you'd be just the same."

"I'd have to change to belong. As it is, I'm just a tourist."

She stared at the ladies from Kansas for a moment. "No," she said, "I think it's the other way around. I think you're a tourist at home."

He tried to read the expression in her face. Taut with guilt, he was alert for signs of suspicion. He said, "You're being cryptic, my dear."

Her eyes were just slightly glassy. She had had two lagers and she had never been able to drink much. "Maybe I'm being cryptic, darling, but I'm not dense. You were glad to come over here alone. You were glad to get away."

He had the sudden physical feeling of dread that he had had so many times before over the years when something she said had told him that she was about to reveal certain things about him that he didn't know. He had grown quite certain over the years of their marriage that he could understand most of her feelings, though usually in retrospect, but he had never gotten used to the fact that she understood him just as well. Or *had* understood him, until the last few years. Now he waited for the sentence that he would at first reject but then take deep down inside himself and gnaw on until he found that it was true. Because she was always right about him, he had found, and usually what she told him was what he had already suspected about himself in a way but had dismissed as unimportant. She always gave him a new perspective, and generally an unpleasant one. The minor flaw always emerged as a major one, a serious defect in himself that he was forced to deal with. It was like being driven by God into rigorous self-scrutiny. Marriage was in many ways a terrible thing. The familiarity bred knowledge so intimate and so accurate that it was a wonder anyone ever stayed married at all, he thought, or at least it was a wonder that any love remained at all.

"I was glad to get away?" he said. "Get away from what?"

"Not just from me," she said, "though I'm part of it." She wasn't looking at him; she wasn't looking at anything in particular. "You're a tourist over there," she said again. "You've never been comfortable. You've always been the off-ox in our families."

"I don't know what you mean," he said, and he didn't, but he knew he would, and it wouldn't be terribly surprising. Unexpectedly, she put her hand on his. "I know I must sound as if I'm starting a fight," she said, "but I'm not, really I'm not. I'm not even angry. I'm awfully glad to see you—I guess I showed that this afternoon. Maybe it's just this place and the beer.

Some things I've thought for a long time are sort of falling into place. They don't mean I don't love you."

"Well, I'm glad of that," he said. He knew she hadn't said the real sentence yet. She really *wasn't* angry, he thought. That meant that what she was going to say really was true. Something about him was true, and had been true for a long time, and in a moment he would know what it was and at first reject it and then, as if he had been injected with a drug, he would begin to feel its effects.

She was looking out the low doorway into the walled garden where tables were set up under umbrellas with the names of beers printed on them: Skol and Whitbread and Guinness. Just beyond the walls were shadows where the other walls of the ancient houses began. Moore, looking where she looked, had again that feeling that he always had at the Turf, of being in a small, lighted, present place at the point where the dark, towering past began. Only tonight it was not just the general past shrouded in shadow outside the garden but his own as well.

"Maybe I'll be sorry I'm saying this," she said. "You've been a good husband and a good father and all the other things. I have no complaints. I'm not complaining now. No one has any complaints about you. Not my parents. Not Ruthie. Sometimes I don't think you know how much Ruthie cares for you. But I know something they don't. You don't belong, you never have belonged, you've always been playing a part. I think you always wanted to be like the rest of us and you couldn't be, but you gave a good imitation." She pushed her empty half-pint over against his. "We're out of beer, honey."

He took their mugs up to the bar and waited while the bearded young man filled them. The sentence had been partly said, he thought, and more was to come. But already the words she had said were sinking down inside him and dissolving and spreading through his system. Change was coming, change in what he knew about himself, or what he wanted to know. He would be like an aging actor whom someone forced to look in a mirror without his makeup. He took the drinks back to the table.

"You look so sad," she said. "I'm sorry."

"Why wouldn't I be sad? You seem to be telling me I've been living a lie all these years."

"Not a lie," she said, "more like a double life."

"And where was this other life? This summer is the first time we've ever really been apart."

"I don't mean that. I mean you weren't ever really—" She paused, looking for words. "Part of you wasn't ever really with the rest of us. I don't know where it was. Or I didn't until this summer. Till your letters."

"What about my letters?"

"The were contented letters. Happy letters. I read them over and over. I was glad you were happy, but something about them bothered me. I thought about them all this last month and finally decided what it was. It was just that they were so happy. It finally occurred to me that I'd never heard you talk like that before, not ever. It didn't seem to matter what you were writing about. Churches, plays, Tower Bridge. The happiness just came through. You were away from all of us for the first time and you were happier than you'd ever been before. It was as if you'd come home. That's what I meant about you being a tourist back there."

So he hadn't had to write his letter about his love affair with Oxford. She had known anyway. He might have guessed it. "You're making a lot out of a few letters," he said.

"No, I'm not. I know you, dear. I've always known you were a tourist at home. Only I never called it that till tonight. It wasn't ever that clear to me till this summer, till you went away and found something better."

"But I haven't found anything better," he said. At least nothing that makes any sense, he thought, nothing lasting, nothing tangible. Gwen is the only tangible, and that's already over.

"Maybe you haven't. But one night I put your letters in order and read them all through. And the only thing I could think was, He'll never be content back here now, he'll be unhappier than ever."

He looked at her. The blue eyes were wide, as they always were when she was excited and was talking as thoughts came to her, but her eyes were getting a little vague in focus from the lager and the jet lag. It must be that combination that's bringing this truth out of her, he thought, because she isn't angry, just in some rare moment of tiredness and alcohol when truth comes spilling out and damn the consequences. He tried honestly for a moment to decide whether he had been seriously discontented back home before the past few years, but only a jumble of images passed without connection through his mind. The familiar classrooms and the cluttered office. Exit signs on the expressway. Quiet meals in the breakfast nook with the FM radio playing music neither of them really heard. The front lawn in early spring when the last snow had melted, brownish-gray with patches of yellow snow burn. The eleven o'clock news on television that usually ended their day. The artificial Christmas tree in the attic that they were going to throw away each year but didn't. The folder of notes in the desk in the den that weren't ever going to become the books that would finally explain Whitman and Blake and Shelley. Would he be unhappy going back to these things?

"I don't think happy and unhappy are the right words," he said. "I'm not unhappy back there. And I'm not happy here."

"All right," she said, "they're not the right words. But you're more alive over here. Your letters showed it. You showed it yourself this afternoon in bed."

Now that's all wrong, he thought, now damn it, that's all wrong. That happened because we'd been apart for so long and because she's lost weight and looks better than she's looked in years, and because she seemed eager for the first time in a long while. That was a perfectly natural thing. Besides, I've been alive all along. She's the one who hasn't been alive. Words boiled up in him, but then he caught himself. I won't be angry, he said to himself, or at least I won't let it show. This once at least I'll be a gentleman, I won't inflict pain her first evening here.

"Old sad-face," she said, looking at him. "Don't look so solemn." She put her hand on his knee under the table and rubbed it. "What I said was old news, honey, I just never said it before. Besides, I didn't say you were wrong to be different. Maybe I wouldn't have loved you if you hadn't been different. Maybe you'd have never loved me. I can't imagine that."

"Neither can I. We wouldn't be here now. And Ruthie wouldn't be anywhere at all." He was pleased that he was able to put his anger aside.

"I suppose I would have married someone else," she said dreamily, still rubbing his knee, "probably someone a lot like you, if I could have found him. I really didn't mind your being a little different, you know. It made you more interesting than most other men I knew. I didn't mind it till just this summer, when you were so glad to get away."

"I wasn't—" he began, but she stopped him.

"I mean when I found out there was something over here that you didn't have at home. But now that I'm here I guess I can see what it is. It's just England, isn't it? Just all this?" She gestured vaguely with her hand to include everything around them. He nodded. "And the college and the river and everything." He nodded again. "Well, I guess I can't be jealous of England," she said. "I suppose I should be glad you didn't find it sooner."

But he had found it sooner, Moore thought, more than thirty years before. If he had come back then to find the essence of England he might even have stayed. An odd thought flickered in his mind. He might even have married Nancy. For a moment his mind sparred with the old problem of hypothetical other lives. Helen wouldn't have existed for him if he had come back, Gwen and Ruthie wouldn't have existed at all. That would have left only Nancy. Or would it? What if Lane had come back in this other life? For an instant Moore saw himself as Nancy's husband, feeble and full of hate, a pathetic figure at the Fox and Grape. This life was better, he thought with a kind of shudder, any kind of real life was better than the unknown.

"You're not listening," Helen said and squeezed his knee hard.

"I'm sorry."

"I said I haven't been here very long, but I like it too. Maybe I'll be more alive over here too."

"You mean like this afternoon? You were pretty alive then."

She giggled and took a long drink of lager. "Maybe you should get a job over here, honey. Maybe we'd both grow younger. Maybe we'd start over and have a lot of babies." She giggled again, but this time it was different and Moore looked at her closely and found himself smiling at her. When she giggled like that, with an odd little quaver in her voice and a quick intake of breath that was almost a hiccup, it meant she was tipsy. Tipsy was his word for her on these rare occasions; it had never seemed to him to fit anyone else. He looked closely at her again. Yes, her eyes were a little more glassed over now and the blue seemed a little lighter than usual. The lager and the jet lag had done the trick. She would be light-hearted now for the rest of the evening, Moore thought, and he was delighted. She had turned a corner and come to a stage that everyone who ever drank wanted to reach and almost never did. She was in a state of pure enjoyment. He watched her as her eyes went around the room and he knew that whatever she saw delighted her. It was pleasure for him to see her this way; it always had been. But tonight it was a relief too, because he was sure now that serious talk was over until tomorrow. It was as if a psychotherapist had gone on vacation and the patient could stop digging at himself for a while. She was ready to forget his being different, she had said, had even said it was not important. But it was important to him, and he didn't want to think about it for a while. He wanted to join her in her fun, wanted to be part of it. He knew he couldn't match her special state of mind. That kind of exhilaration he had really felt only once, as a sophomore, when for a week or so he had thought he knew what Aquinas meant by Being, and for that week everything was mystically interesting, and people and places had stood out from their backgrounds with their own peculiar light. He envied her for the unheard music she danced to at times like this.

She finished her lager and set her glass down with a flourish. "I want to see those other places you wrote about," she said, "especially the White Horse and the Eagle & Child." She stood up and smoothed her jacket as if she really were heading for a dance floor and the music was running through her mind.

"You're an argument for alcohol," he said, getting up. "If we were all like you there wouldn't be any alcoholic wards or WCTU."

"Don't talk philosophy," she said, "just take me to those wonderful places."

So they went hand in hand out of the Turf and through the yard, and just before they got to the dark alley that led into the street she stopped and looked back at the incredible houses that rose over them into the darkness. "Maybe we could live up there in one of those," she said. "That would be so romantic."

"You mean when we'd gotten younger."

"Of course. And before the babies came."

They went down Broad Street to the White Horse and stopped in front and looked through the street-level windows, pulled down at the top for ventilation. It was crowded, and smoke and voices came out to them and Moore could already feel the heat inside.

"Oh, I like it," Helen said, "it looks so homey."

Inside, he managed to wedge a place for them at the bar and ordered a pint and a half pint. The blond barmaid was not here tonight, he noted automatically. They stood pressed together as he and Gwen had stood a few nights before, drinking their lager, and Moore felt the pleasure of her hip against his, but not the intense pleasure that he had felt with Gwen. The forbidden against the familiar, he thought, what chance does the familiar have? But then an answer came back out of some almost forgotten class in ethics: Don't blame your vices on human nature unless you are willing to let human nature take credit for your virtues too. I shouldn't be thinking that the sexual instinct is perverse, Moore thought, I should be thinking that *my* sexual instinct is perverse.

"You're not listening again," he heard Helen say. "What's a scotch egg? What's a sausage roll?" She was reading the signs over the bar.

"Pub grub," he said, "snacks."

She laughed delightedly. "Pub grub," she said, running the words together, "pubgrub. It sounds like the monster in a fairy tale."

The owner's wife came down the bar to be introduced to Helen and in a few minutes they were talking about children and houses. Moore looked past them and out the windows. Across the street were the busts of the philosophers in front of the science museum, though he couldn't see them now. Next door was Blackwell's bookstore. All the best things in life were here in this little place, he thought, in this little area of the globe, the best things of mind and body: knowledge, lager, love. He looked at Helen tenderly. She and the owner's wife were comparing pictures of their children. All around them eager young people were drinking beer and Moore heard again the scattered phrases that went with literature and philosophy and love. It was the best of all possible worlds, Moore thought again, may it never end. He didn't belong here because he was too old and had come too late, and Helen didn't belong here either. But she had sensed it too, this thing he felt. Neither of them knew what to call it, and so they called it Oxford, or England, and they talked about being young here in this old place. Maybe it was because people had been trying to get at truth here for five-hundred years, Moore thought, and you could sense that in the spires and in the bells and even here in the White Horse. Truth was important here, even Helen's small personal truth about him. It was a part of the larger truth and it had grown with her for a long time, and it wasn't the same truth here in Oxford that it had been back in Michigan. He was still the off-ox, or at least she thought he was, but that was a more complicated truth than she had thought it was back home. She was probably right about him; she always had been. And already he felt that what she had said somehow matched what he had always known but had never been willing to put a name to. As he thought of it now, it was, very vaguely, a sense of incompleteness. Yes, she was probably right, but not wholly right. Newman might have said that her truth was still evolving, from simple to complex. Oh, yes, Moore thought, I'm very complex, I'm different in ways she hasn't thought of yet. He stared hard out the windows toward the invisible philosophers' busts and thought, Here amid all these monuments to truth I'm committing myself to a deception, and only three nights ago I drank a toast with Gwen to full portraits and honesty, and I seemed to mean it then.

Helen and the owner's wife had their heads close together over the bar. The owner's wife was drawing a diagram of something, probably a house, and Helen was following the diagram with close attention. In a half hour she and the owner's wife would know more about each other's house and children than Moore would have known or revealed in a month. The gift for easy conversation, Moore had often thought, was the greatest of all social blessings. He didn't have it, of course, and he was pretty sure that Gwen hadn't either. She was too intense. For a moment he imagined her standing there at the bar next to Helen in her jeans and jacket, taller than Helen, darker, not talking easily to the owner's wife, her face serious—Helen chatty and still blond and vivacious, Gwen balky and dark and carrying an old grief like a weapon. Scenes from an old Alec Guinness movie came into his mind. The captain of a ship that sailed regularly between Gibraltar and Africa had had a proper English wife in Gibraltar and an exotic mistress in Africa, and he had lived a successful life with both of them until something had happened—Moore couldn't remember what—something had happened that had destroyed the balance. *The Captain's Paradise*, that was the title. Something had happened and the captain's paradise of two different loves was lost. It was a freakish accident or a bizarre coincidence. It was very improbable; it shouldn't have happened, but it had. Moore remembered that it had been a very funny movie until the incident, whatever it was, but he had a vague idea that the story ended sadly.

He watched the clock move on to eleven and then turned to watch Helen as the owner's drill sergeant voice boomed "Time!"

"My God," she said, "what was that?" Her hand was pressed flat against her chest in that odd gesture of fright or surprise that women have, as if they were keeping their hearts from leaping out.

"The voice of judgment," he said, laughing at her. "It only means they're throwing you out. But not you personally. All of us."

"I don't believe it," she said, looking around at the young people finishing their drinks, "it's only eleven o'clock."

"You remember early closing. I wrote you about it."

"But it's so early. You never wrote me how early eleven o'clock was. What do people do now?"

"They go home."

She gave the special giggle and leaned against him. "And then what?"

"They go to bed."

"And then what?"

"If they're not too old and too drunk they make love."

"What a lovely custom," she said. "Let's go home and find out if we're too old and too drunk."

"Even finding out should be fun," he said.

She looked at him, her eyes as glassy as before, but still only tipsy, he thought, not drunk. "Everything's fun over here, isn't it? That's what you found out, isn't it?"

"Yes," he said, "that's the secret. But it's more fun now that you're here."

They went up the steps from the White Horse and into the warm heavy air. She held out her hand for him to take and they went along the shortcut past the Radcliffe Camera to the High Street. She bumped against him as they walked, partly from the lager but partly because she was trying to look upward as she walked. "I'm rubbernecking," she said. "What's that?"

"The Radcliffe Camera, but it isn't really a camera."

"Don't be so superior, Professor. I know what it is. You wrote me about it. What's that?"

"The spire of St. Mary's."

He put his arm around her and as they went down the High Street he tried to look upward too, to see Oxford as she was seeing it, and they lurched along like two companionable drunks. Turning off the High Street, he led her down past St. Aldate's and into the lane that ran behind Christ Church. The Christ Church bell tolled the quarter hour as they went past the Bear. "One of the oldest pubs in Oxford," he said before she could ask him. "It's kind of the Corpus pub." The door to the Bear was closed, but young people still lounged at the picnic tables outside, nursing their final beers.

"Backward we go in time," she said, as if she were saying a line from a song. "Every day in every way we get younger and younger." She giggled. "Pretty soon we'll be like them and always wear jeans." When they came out of the lane by the carpark next to Corpus she said, "Are we back at the Turf?"

"No, we're home at Corpus."

"Too bad. I'd like to go up into one of those high old houses and spend the night with you there."

"Corpus is just as old. It's a lot nearer too."

"Okay, Corpus will do. Good old Corpus." When they got to the gate and he was unlocking the wooden door she said, "Corpus, Corpus Christi. That means Body of Christ, doesn't it?"

"Yes."

"But you just call it Corpus. Just body. Just corpse."

"It's just a nickname," he said.

They went across the quad past the pelican—"Tired old Corpus," she said—and up the sagging staircase to the second floor. In the moonlight the heavy white door to the sitting room looked more massive than ever. Moore unlocked it and pushed it open. "Remember what I told you about the lock," he said, "remember to leave the door ajar when you go to the john." He touched the wall switch and the cavernous sitting room came into sight.

"You told me all that," she said. "Doors bore me, Professor. Let's get on to better things." She put her arms around his neck and pulled his face down to hers.

He kissed her. "You're a sexy old woman," he said.

"I know that. I want to find out how sexy. And how old. And how drunk."

He turned on one of the table lamps and turned off the overhead light, and the high white ceiling dissolved into vagueness. He took her hand and they went into the bedroom. "Don't turn the lights on," she said.

He leaned against the wall, a little drunk, watching her undress. Pale moonlight came in the single window facing Merton and softened the monstrous wardrobe and the ugly little dresser and the leprous walls. Nymph undresses by moonlight, he thought, because she really looked like a painting, or a sketch for a painting. She pulled back the covers on the cots and got into the one nearer the window and lay looking at him. Her back was to the window and he couldn't see her face. "I'm waiting," she said softly.

He undressed quickly and got in beside her. Her arms and legs came around him in a double embrace and for a moment they lay like that while the Merton bell tolled. Then, without speaking, they began the movements that over the years had pleased them most. When the Merton bell tolled again they finally rolled apart. Moore, with his hand lying loosely on her stomach, felt her body quiver a little and knew she was laughing. "Backward in time we go," she said in a little singsong, "hand in hand like Jack and Jill."

He rubbed her stomach. "If you get any younger I won't be able to keep up with you."

"Oh, yes you will. We're going back together. Just one of us going back wouldn't be any good at all." She was silent for a while and he thought maybe she had fallen asleep. But then she said, "Oh damn, I've got to go to the john." She kissed his shoulder, then got up and pulled her white robe around her and felt for her slippers.

"Remember about the door," he said drowsily.

"I remember."

He listened to her go through the sitting room, heard her set the latch, then heard the sound of the bathroom door close. The good sounds of home, he thought, already she's made it like home, as if we'd lived here for years. She's already domesticated this bachelor's attic just by being here for a day. She hasn't moved a thing, but all of a sudden it's not my place any more, it's ours. It's a gift she has, like making easy conversation. Half asleep, he remembered what he had said to her once on their honeymoon. "You make every hotel room a love nest. You're a remarkable woman." He couldn't remember now whether it was in Quebec or Montreal, but they were lying in bed looking out at city lights, and they had just made love. "I hope that's a compliment," she had said, and he had replied, "Oh, yes, you're the perfect blend of sexuality and domesticity. I think I've married the perfect wife." Tonight had been like that, he thought, like a second honeymoon. And then, as if he had tossed a ball into the air, it came down and he was thinking, I wonder how long the honeymoon will last, I wonder when the vacation will be over. He felt himself drifting into sleep, but he ordered himself awake until she came back. You can go back, he said to himself, yes, you can, you really can turn back time. But it's only for a little while. It's like holding your breath; you can't do it for long. But what if they could hold their breaths over here? What if they simply didn't go back to the old life? What if he could somehow manage to keep them in England? But it wouldn't work, he knew, even as he thought it. She was magnetized; she was a mother and a grandmother, and the magnet was in America. I'm a father and a grandfather, he thought, but apparently I'm not magnetized. Yes, he thought, she was right about him, as usual, and he had always really known this about himself, but not very clearly. He was a tourist at home; he was different. If I stayed here, he thought, I wonder if sooner or later I'd be a tourist here too. And then he remembered Gwen's face in the firelight and he thought, I'm already a tourist here.

He heard the hall door shut and the lock click and in a moment she came in. She went over to the window and leaned on the sill. "What is that next door?" she said. "I know you told me, but I've forgotten already."

"Merton College."

"Yes, Merton," she said. "I remember you wrote me about Merton. And about Oriel. You said you lived between them. You said you lived between—" she stopped. "I don't remember the rest."

"I said I lived between Shelley and Newman. It was a don's joke. Shelley went to Merton and Newman went to Oriel." He could remember writing that mild joke, and wondering even as he wrote it why he put it in the letter, because it really was a don's joke and Helen wouldn't understand it, even though she had heard of Shelley and Newman. He had finally left it in, though, because it had seemed to place him so neatly between Shelley the atheist and Newman the Catholic. And then something rang wrong in his mind, as if he were looking at a column of figures and suddenly found a mistake in addition. Shelley hadn't gone to Merton; he'd gone to University. The private joke had been a wrong joke.

She said, "And the deer park. I remember you wrote me about the deer park."

"That's at Magdalen, just down the High Street. We'll see it tomorrow. And Christ Church Meadows. And a church I didn't write you about, at Iffley."

She repeated the names slowly, half aloud, and then she was silent for a while. He looked at her hunched over the window sill. There was nothing for her to see except the black wall of Merton, and he knew she was lost in thought. Then she said, "Honey." For twenty-five years she had been saying that word to him, and he had come to know what was to follow by the way she said it. What was coming now was a question. "Do you remember when we went to see the Plains of Abraham and Mount Desert Island?"

"You know I do," he said. They were places they had seen on their honeymoon. "No one ever believed us when we told them how we leaned against the fog." The fog had been so heavy at the top of Mount Desert that they couldn't even see the ocean and a brisk wind was blowing onshore. They could never understand why the wind had not blown the fog away, but it had not, and when it had gusted they had actually leaned into it and put their weight against the moving fog.

"But I mean, do you remember how interested we were in those places before we ever went to them? Remember how exciting they seemed?"

"Yes, I remember."

"We saw lots of places after that, but we never got as excited again." She turned and half sat on the windowsill, but her face was in shadow.

"We were on our honeymoon," he said, "we took our excitement with us wherever we went."

He thought she nodded. "That's the way I feel now," she said, "that's the way I feel about Magdalen and Christ Church Meadows and Iffley. I can hardly wait for tomorrow." She came over and sat on the edge of the cot and stroked his shoulder lightly. "It really is like a second honeymoon," she said.

"It's better than that. It's more like a first."

"The first one lasted two weeks."

"Well, that's what we have left here, two weeks. Let's repeat it."

"Tonight I really think we could," she said, sliding her hand down to his stomach. "How can a place so old make me feel so young?"

He reached up and touched her breast affectionately, but he was thinking seriously about her question. "Because nothing is dead here," he said. "I mean, everything is old, but everything is alive. The past is alive here."

"That sounds grand, even though I don't really know what you mean."

Moore tried hard to be clear, because he was trying to say something he had felt ever since he had got to Oxford; he was trying to say what he had partly said in his imaginary letter. "I mean the best of the human spirit has survived here," he said. "That's what all the monuments are for. They aren't built for something dead. They're built to celebrate something that's still alive."

"What's still alive here, honey?"

"Truth," he said, "or at least the search for truth. Remember the Rhine castles we saw, and the fortresses, that summer? Well, they were monuments too, but they were monuments to love or pride or courage or things like that. Here the monuments are to truth. Every college and every church is a kind of argument."

She didn't say anything for a moment, then she said quietly, "I liked the monuments to love. Like that church in the Vienna Woods that they built where Rudolf and his mistress committed suicide. Or was it Rudolf?"

"I think so. You mean Mayerling." He hadn't said what he wanted to say. Maybe he couldn't. Maybe he really didn't know what he thought. Or maybe he wasn't the one to be talking to her about truth.

Her finger played absently with his navel. "I suppose it's because I'm a kind of monument to love myself."

Moore looked up at her, not sure of what she had said, "What do you mean?"

She sat back from him and patted her hair. "Isn't that why you were so glad to leave, really? Because you thought I'd become a monument?" The lightness had disappeared from her voice.

"Hey, wait a minute," he said, "wait a minute. What is all this?" He sat up and tried to put his arms around her, but it was too awkward and so he simply put his hand on her knee. "A minute ago we were talking about our second honeymoon."

"I know," she said, "I'm sorry, I don't want to spoil it." She turned toward the window and he could see that she was crying. Nothing in her voice showed it, but in the gray light from the Merton window he saw the tears. She made no motion to wipe her eyes, as if she wasn't really aware she was crying, or didn't care.

He swung his legs over the edge of the cot so that he could sit beside her and put his arm around her. Something he had learned in the last twenty-five years kept him silent, though he wanted to ask questions. In a minute she said again, "I'm sorry. I'm sure it'll be a wonderful second honeymoon. But it'll be by accident, won't it?" She turned to him. She still hadn't touched her face. "People go away on their second honeymoon together, the way they did their first one." Moore said nothing, only tightened his arm around her waist. "But you didn't go away so we could meet over here. You just went away."

"I thought we'd settled all that back at the Turf," Moore said. But I must have known even then we hadn't settled it, he thought hopelessly, we'd only put it aside for a while.

"Honey," she said, and again he knew a question was coming. "Honey, I'm forty-eight, not twenty-eight. Maybe I can be twenty-eight over here for two weeks. Maybe we can go back for two weeks. But then we have to go home. What will it be like when we go home?"

If only she had gone to sleep after they had made love, Moore thought, if only the lager hadn't worn off, we wouldn't be talking like this. "You're so intelligent, but you're so stupid," she said. She was crying harder. "You don't know you're fifty, you think you're Peter Pan."

I don't have to wonder what it will be like back home, Moore thought, it will be just like this. Except that the words that would have made him angry at home didn't make him angry now. He only thought again, I wish the lager hadn't worn off, I wish she could have stayed tipsy. But she had been nursing that hurt for a month—or for years?—and a chance word of his had brought it out and surprised him. Maybe it had surprised her too, like an old muscle sprain that unexpectedly aches in bad weather. But it would have come out tomorrow or the next day, he thought, if it really hurt that much. At the Turf or Christ Church Meadows. Sooner or later the time and the place and the chance word would have interlocked, would have put just the right amount of pressure on. And afterward they would have been sitting as they were sitting now, looking at nothing.

He stood up and patted her shoulder. She had stopped crying at least. He picked up his pajamas from the other cot and put them on. She didn't move. He went into the sitting room and felt around on the writing table for his pipe and tobacco. When he went back she was in bed, in the cot nearer the window, lying on her back with her hands locked behind her head. He went over and stood by the window while he lighted his pipe and tamped it and relighted it. He had to speak. He couldn't let their first night in Oxford end like this. He knew that the first words after a long silence were the hardest, and if he could once get those out the rest would be easier. He even knew that what he said wasn't really important, because there weren't any words that would heal what had happened to them in the past few years. He knew that, and he was sure she did too. What mattered was to say something that would give them both a chance to show they were sorry and didn't want to quarrel any more. The tone was more important than the words. And yet he fumbled for the words. Though he didn't seem angry to himself, he knew it must be partly anger that made him delay. Finally it was a kind of courtesy that made him speak, a vague feeling that he was the host here and she was the guest, and that at least he owed her hospitality.

"I guess we agree about Oxford," he said. "I mean, what a fine place it is."

"Yes," she said. Her voice was very small and a little choked. He knew it wouldn't take much to make her cry again.

"Let's see it together then. Just the two of us. We always had our best times when we snuck away from the tour guides, remember?" It was an old joke of theirs. They had slipped away from guided tours at the Alhambra and at Notre Dame and at the Schonbrunn Palace in Vienna. When one of them raised an eyebrow in a certain way it meant, Slip away to the nearest cafe or beer-hall. Sipping their drinks, one of them would say solemnly, "I suppose we're missing a lot of interesting facts," and the other would reply, "We'd have forgotten them in a week anyway."

"All right," she said. Her voice was a little clearer.

"Remember how we snuck out of the Alhambra and found that place with the great red wine?"

"I remember," she said, and then, "I suppose we missed a lot of interesting facts."

Moore's heart turned over with relief. "We'd have forgotten them in a week anyway," he said. He went over and sat on the edge of the cot and ran his hand through her hair.

"I guess I'm awfully tired tonight," she said.

"Me too. We'll both feel better tomorrow."

"Can we go back to the Turf for dinner tomorrow? I'd kind of like to start all over."

"That's a great idea. I would too." He leaned down and kissed her and felt her arms come up around his neck. Now we've both finally said we're sorry, he thought.

"Let's not talk any more," she said, "let's go to sleep."

"That's a great idea too."

He crawled over her and onto the other cot. The cots were still made up as single beds and they had to reach out of the sagging centers before they could hold hands. In a minute Moore could tell she was asleep, but he kept his hand in hers even after the awkward position had put his hand and arm to sleep and he could feel nothing. We have patched it up one more time, he thought, covered it over one more time, and now we can play As If. With luck we can play it for the whole two weeks. As if nothing were wrong between us, as if there were no bitterness, as if. There was a lot to be said for As If. She wanted it as much as he did. Because the alternative was unbearable. The alternative was the open warfare, the hurt that raged to hurt back, the cruel names, Grandma and Peter Pan. As If was better, but hard to keep up. You had to be as careful of it as if it were truth, maybe because it was more important than truth.

Moore pulled his hand away from hers carefully and flexed his fingers until he could feel them again. The Merton bell tolled once, and the bell from Christ Church echoed it a moment later. Merton, Christ Church, Oriel. Arguments for truth I called them. Monuments to truth. But Helen prefers the monuments to love. She doesn't want truth any more, she wants As If. I'm the great admirer of truth. I really meant what I said about Oxford and truth, but I will never tell Helen the truth about Gwen. I wonder what that makes me. A hypocrite? A moral schizophrenic? He stared up at the dim white ceiling, and the grand words from Sir Thomas Browne tolled in his mind like the Merton bells: Not every man is fit to be a champion of truth, or worthy to take up the gauntlet in the cause of verity. He drifted into sleep thinking of Newman's gentleman again. How do you keep from inflicting pain? And again logic operated, even in sleep. You isolate yourself; you live the hermetic life, sealed off from contact with other people, not because they are germ-ridden but because *you* are; to live with others is sooner or later to inflict pain. And after that there is no healing, not in words and not in silence.

In his dream he stood at the bar in a pub with Helen on one side of him and Gwen on the other. They pressed against him with their hips and looked at him demandingly. Gwen wanted him to speak and Helen wanted him to be still. I can't do both, he told them pleadingly, but they kept demanding without words. He prayed for the closing time bell.

The Merton bell was tolling three when Moore's bladder drove him back to consciousness. Very aware of Helen next to him, he got carefully out of bed and padded quietly out of the bedroom and through the sitting room. Automatically, he set the door ajar and went into the bathroom. He made a pass or two with his hand in the darkness until he found the string for the light. A fly buzzed loudly on the window pane as he stood urinating. He pulled the overhead chain and the toilet flushed with a long groaning sound that followed him back into the sitting room. He shut and locked the door and went on into the bedroom. In the gray light from the Merton window he saw that Helen had turned over and lay on her side now, facing the window, her right arm dangling down from the side of the cot. She looked uncomfortable, and when he had gotten into his cot he reached over and pulled her gently over onto her back. Her right arm flopped over and lay across his stomach at an impossible angle and his hand and forearm felt as if he had rubbed them in warm jelly. He stared stupidly down at her. There were black splotches on the gray sheet. Ice formed in his stomach and raced on up to his fingers and up into his hair, and he hung frozen over her. Then something made his rigid hands move and he clawed at the sheet and pulled it down. Her chest was washed in black, as if someone had poured a can of paint on her. His mouth opened to say her name, when a voice said, "Fucking Yanks, fucking Yanks, fucking Yanks," over and over like a stuck recording, and he half turned his head and the absurd figure he had seen before came out of the darkness by the wardrobe with his right hand upraised. There's no umbrella, Moore thought, where is the umbrella? He rolled himself to one side, as he had been taught to so long ago in the army, and he felt the warm wetness of Helen's chest on his, and then a strange sharp thrill in his back as if he had been injected with a monstrous needle.

CHAPTER 5

Oxford Part II

He swam languidly in dark gray-green water. Dim light filtered down from above, and occasionally, if he got close to the glass walls, he could see blobs of white faces pressed against the walls from the other side. But they did not interest him, and he swam slowly away from them. From time to time he wondered what kind of fish he was, but mostly he was content to swim slowly for a while, then sleep. Unlike most fish, he closed his eyes when he slept, or he supposed he did, because the light and the faces went away then. He swam slowly because his back hurt if he moved too fast. Other than that pain, there was not much difference between swimming and sleeping.

Then one time when he was sleeping he knew somehow that he wasn't a fish and that if he woke up this time his life in the aquarium would be gone. He didn't know what would replace it, and he didn't want to wake up, but for some reason he had to. The first thing he saw was the foot of a bed. He was lying in a bed, and it was clearly a hospital bed. The first thing he felt was an odd tightness across his back. Some part of his mind watched another part begin to move, ever so slowly, like the workings of an old and rusted clock. He was in Oxford, his mind said, and he was obviously sick, so he must be in the Radcliffe Infirmary. Probably the sickness had something to do with the strange feeling in his back, though now he felt a tightness across his chest as well. A heart attack? Pneumonia? His hands crept up under the covers and under whatever he was wearing and found bandages. He was wrapped tightly from his armpits almost down to his waist. Tentatively, he moved his right leg, and sharp pain radiated across his back. Afraid, he lay quiet and closed his eyes, ready to sleep again. But sleep didn't come, and in a moment he opened his eyes again and looked around him. The walls of the room were a pale green. There was a window to his left with vertical venetian blinds pulled nearly closed. Beyond the foot of his bed and to his right was a wide hospital door, varnished darkly, that stood halfway open. A nurse came in, a tall woman in white with heavy horn-rimmed glasses. She seemed to Moore to be almost running, and he had trouble keeping his eyes on her. She stood beside the bed and looked down at him.

"So you've finally come back to us," she said, and put her finger on his right wrist. Moore could think of nothing to say to that; his mind was occupied with what she was doing. Finally he decided that she was taking his pulse, but he seemed to know that from memory, not from any facts that he could put together at present. She went out, and almost at once a short, wiry man of about forty-five came in. He was wearing a white hospital coat, and something dangled from his coat pocket that Moore's memory said was a stethoscope.

"I'm Dr. Harker," he said. "How are you feeling?"

Moore didn't really know how he was feeling and tried to shrug his shoulders, but the pain in his back stopped him.

Harker came over and laid his clipboard down and took both of Moore's hands in his. "Squeeze," he said. Moore squeezed weakly. His hands felt like putty. Harker pulled down the bedclothes and put his hands on Moore's thighs just above the knees. "Try to raise your legs." Moore tried and gave a gasp at the pain in his back. Harker pulled the bedclothes back up and stood staring at Moore critically. "Talk to me," he said. "Say something."

"Say what?" Moore asked. His voice was reedy and thin. "What do you want me to say?"

"Just that will do," Harker said. "There's no need to recite." He wrote on his clipboard, then looked back at Moore. "You're doing well," he said. He had a crisp, no nonsense way of talking, Moore noted, and felt slow-witted in his presence. "You had us a bit up in the air, but you're doing well now. I was quite sure there'd been no muscle or nerve damage, but it was important for you to wake up, and you've obliged us by doing that. Now it will be a matter of recuperation."

"Recuperation," Moore repeated. The word was almost too hard for him.

"Time and rest," Harker said briskly, "easy steps for little feet."

Slowly, and with enormous effort, Moore's mind formed a question. "Recuperation from what? What's the matter with me?"

Harker looked at him closely. "Why, from the stab wound, my dear man." He frowned at what he saw in Moore's face. "I say, Professor Moore, what's the last thing you remember before waking up here just now?"

Moore stared back at him, his mind turning over slowly like a car engine on a cold morning. The last thing he remembered. "The Turf," he said finally, "the old high houses by the Turf. And the Merton bells."

"Nothing after that?" Harker's voice was very quiet.

"The argument," Moore said, "the argument."

"What argument?"

"With my wife. Not an argument, really. A misunderstanding." He could feel his mind beginning to quicken a little. "No, not really a misunderstanding. Sort of an old quarrel." Somehow that didn't seem the right description either, and he was going to make another distinction when Harker broke in.

"You've no memory after that?"

"After the quarrel she went to sleep. I mean, after we patched it up she went to sleep." Now that he had mentioned Helen he wanted to ask about her. About why she wasn't here when he was sick. Only something wouldn't let him. Something bad would be the answer, he sensed. It was like when Gwen had said a name.

Harker pinched his chin between his finger and thumb, frowning at Moore. "I think you've blocked out a memory, Professor Moore, a very painful one. It will hurt a great deal to bring it back, but I think you'd better do that now, if you can. It will never be any easier."

"It's about Helen," Moore said, and Harker nodded. Moore could feel his heart begin to pound under his bandages. He almost knew what Harker was going to say. Almost. But he hung on to a last second of ignorance, because to know would be to assent.

"Yes, about your wife." Harker waited for Moore's question, but when Moore wouldn't ask it, he said, "I'm afraid she's dead."

A part of Moore's mind exploded into images of grayish-white and black like an old movie speeded up, and he felt his hands jerking up to his chest, feeling for the warm stickiness. I knew then it was blood, he thought, and then he thought, If only I could have stayed swimming in the tank, if only I could have stayed asleep.

Harker's voice came through to him, flat and direct. "It's coming back?" Moore nodded. His mind was bursting with a kind of wild energy now, but he couldn't speak. "That's good," Harker said. "It's no good trying to hide it. Now you can begin to deal with it."

But it dealt with Moore instead. Time and place collapsed against each other in his mind, and he was back in that other shadowed room, he was walking again through the bedroom doorway, hearing the Merton bells, seeing Helen in that ungainly sprawl so unlike her. Again he got into bed and reached over and pulled her gently onto her back and her arm flopped over onto his stomach. The lisping voice came again out of the darkness by the wardrobe, and with a groan he rolled toward Helen and onto her and felt again the sticky warmth on his chest. His back muscles screamed with pain, waiting for the sharper pain to come.

And then Harker had him by the shoulders and was pulling him onto his back, gingerly. When Moore opened his eyes again it seemed to him that he had been away at Corpus for a long time, and he was surprised to find that Harker was still in the room.

"Easy does it, Professor," Harker said, "or you'll tear yourself open all over again."

Moore lay still until the pain in his back eased. The tall nurse came back in and stood next to Harker, and together they looked at Moore. The nurse had a tray with a syringe on it.

"Where is she?" Moore said. He could hardly hear his voice.

"She was taken to the mortuary, Professor Moore," Harker said.

"How long have I been here?"

"About forty-eight hours. That's why I said it was past time for you to wake up." He nodded to the nurse, and she took Moore's arm, kneaded it, and he felt the sting of an injection. When she had left, Harker said, "You were awake off and on, actually, or I should have been more concerned than I was."

Forty-eight hours, Moore's mind repeated. Then it must be Thursday. His mind rejected that passage of time. Only a moment ago it had been Tuesday night and he and Helen had been quarreling. That was what stuck in his mind now, not the other part that was too much of a dream to be real. The tears and the patching up of the quarrel were what was real. It was Thursday now, and he had lost Wednesday, and they had lost Magdalen and Christ Church Meadows and Iffley.

"A police inspector has been waiting to talk to you," Harker said. "And your daughter is here."

"Ruthie here?" Time was baffling Moore again, and for a moment he thought that Helen and Ruthie must have come over together.

"Your colleagues at Corpus called her, I believe," Harker said. "Do you feel up to seeing her now?"

Moore nodded, too muddled to speak. It seemed impossible that Ruthie should be here, and when she came through the doorway his first feeling was surprise, and then, as she came toward him something broke inside him and he began to cry. He could feel the tears on his cheeks running down onto the stubble on his chin. She looked so much like Helen: the blue eyes, the hair, the way she walked. She put her face down to his and he put his arms around her and they cried together in long heaving breaths.

When they had finally cried themselves out she stood up and got a handkerchief from her purse and wiped his face, then her own, and leaned back down over him and held his hand. "I can't believe it," she said. Even her voice had always sounded like Helen's; he had never been able to tell them apart on the phone. "I still can't believe it. I can't believe she's dead."

He patted her hand. "I know, I know," he said hoarsely. I will have to comfort her, he thought, but how? He looked at her and was surprised, as always, to find that she was not still eleven years old. She was twenty-two now and married and had borne his granddaughter, but still he thought of her as eleven, having trouble with arithmetic and not much aware yet of boys. He patted her hand again.

"Dr. Norton called us," she said. "It was so late, but I suppose it was early morning here. I caught the first plane out of Dulles. We didn't have time to make arrangements about the baby, so Jim stayed home."

She was doing what people always do when someone has died, Moore thought. They tell how they heard about it. I suppose it helps somehow, eases the death into their lives. Maybe I'll be able to do that some day, but I don't believe it, I don't want to accept it like that, not ever. Then he felt his hand on Ruthie's and said, "And you've just been waiting here?"

She nodded. "They've been very nice to me. But they wouldn't let me see Mom. They said to wait till you woke up." She lifted his hand and kissed it. "I don't know what I would have done if you hadn't come to pretty soon. I felt like an orphan."

"I'll be all right now," he said, "you're not to worry about me." He patted her hand again. She looked so tired. There were deep shadows under her eyes and her khaki-colored pantsuit was wrinkled. Moore felt tears behind his eyes again but held them back. He wanted terribly to say something comforting to her, as he had sometimes been able to do in the living room of the old house, when she really had been eleven, so she could go upstairs now and go to bed. But that time of easy comforting had gone.

"It's like a nightmare," she said. Her voice was jumpy and a little hoarse, and the words came pouring out. "I still don't know what happened or why or anything. Dr. Norton said on the phone that there'd been a terrible accident and that Mom was dead and you were seriously hurt. So I thought it was a car accident or something like that. Then when he met me at the plane he said that some crazy man had done it, but he didn't know anything else. Someone who'd followed you, he said, but he didn't know why."

Moore took in her words like a man eying a great weight that had to be lifted, and the mere thought of it exhausted him. There was a truth that he had to tell Ruthie, but it was a truth that had to be carefully said. His mind knew that, but his mind could not hold the truth in focus. Some things had to be said, he knew, and some had to be held back, but he could not hold the two groups separate in his mind. I have to rest, he thought, I have to get control. "I don't understand it all either, honey," he said. "I'm sorry, but I can't stay awake any longer. I think they've given me something." And he really couldn't stay awake any longer. Ruthie's face was starting to disappear and reappear like the face of a ballerina slowly pirouetting in front of him. "We can talk tomorrow. You get some rest too, honey."

She leaned over him and he felt her kiss his forehead and felt her hand on his cheek. His eyes opened for a moment and he tried to smile. There were tears on her cheeks again. Tomorrow, he thought, tomorrow when I feel better I must begin to comfort her somehow. "Good night, Dad," she said. He nodded at her, too tired to form words out loud. "I'll see you in the morning," she said, and he nodded again. "I love you," she said, and he nodded again and formed the words "I love you too," but he couldn't tell whether he said them aloud. When he opened his eyes again for a moment she was gone. Someone had turned out the overhead light, and the room was dark except for a triangle of light that lay just inside the door. He stared at the lines of the triangle and for a few seconds his mind was clear, and he said to himself, I must get organized, I must get my story straight. But then the triangle disappeared, and he slid into sleep. He dreamed of a room full of filing cabinets. He stood in front of the one labeled M, but he was afraid to open it. The room was very cold and brightly lighted, and the filing cabinets were arranged like the spokes in a wheel. He stood in the hub of the wheel, shivering.

Voices in the corridor woke him in the morning. Then outside his door was the clatter of crockery that he had grown used to at Corpus: morning tea was coming. A short, stocky woman in the usual shapeless smock brought it in, hot and milky. "Good morning," she said, like a bird chirping, "and how are we feeling today? A bit foggy this morning, but it'll clear off later on." She reminded him of his scout at Corpus who had always been impossibly cheerful in the morning, and his spirit automatically lifted a little. When she had gone he inched himself to the edge of the bed and made himself sit up very slowly. The pain in his back spread around to his stomach, but after a minute it eased. Carefully he put his feet flat on the floor and gradually stood up. The pain came back with a rush, and he could feel sweat on his face and under his arms. Humped over, his legs wavering, he made his way across the room to the toilet. He had things to think about, and he was determined to begin by handling his toilet functions. He must have had a catheter until he had shown signs of waking up. He didn't want that again, nor a bed pan. He had to act well for Ruthie whether he felt well or not.

The light over the bathroom mirror was merciless. He saw a lined face stubbed with beard, gray thinning hair and hollow eyes. There's no one here named Peter Pan, he thought, and a surge of pain went through him that had nothing to do with his back. Grimly he pushed images of Helen into a different compartment of his mind. He knew that if he looked at them he would do nothing else; he knew without thinking that in the days to come he would look at them carefully, over and over, and that he wouldn't be able to help himself then, but he had to control that now. He managed to urinate, and then very slowly he got soap and water on his face and neck and brushed his hair up off his face. If he could only straighten up, he thought, he would feel better, but he couldn't—the pain frightened him when he tried. When he got back to his bed he lowered himself onto the edge and sat and drank his tea. As if he were preparing for a class, he began to outline in his mind what he must say to Ruthie, and more important, what he must not.

And then suddenly he remembered what Harker had said about a police inspector waiting to see him. The unbelievable thing that had happened to Helen was murder. Gwen's father was a murderer. And Moore was not only the husband of the victim, he was the only witness to the murder. If that shambling, lisping, absurd man went to prison or to the gallows it would be because Moore testified against him. He had an image of a courtroom, with Gwen's father sitting at a table with authority figures around him, Moore himself in the witness box, and Gwen in a front row of people, her eyes never leaving him. He set his cup down, his hand shaking violently. It was too much. It was too much, and his mind tried to shy away from these things but couldn't: Helen dead, Ruthie to be lied to, Gwen to be protected, and now Gwen's father.

Gwen's father. The image of the courtroom came again, but this time Gwen's father was in the witness box and he was telling in that voice that would haunt Moore forever what he had seen in front of his fireplace. Moore stared at his teacup in despair. There was no protecting Gwen from that scene, and there was no lie that would keep that truth from Ruthie. It wouldn't even matter if both he and Gwen denied it. That lisping voice would ring true for everyone because the man had no reason to lie. They might find him insane, but they would never believe he had hallucinated that scene. Moore could feel the weight of the imagined eyes on him and Gwen as the scene slowly evolved, but worse were Ruthie's eyes that he didn't have to imagine. He couldn't even deny that Gwen's father had done it because everyone seemed to know that already. Harker knew it, and so did Ruthie. He could lie about Gwen and him and hope she would lie too if asked. He thought she would. He thought she would do that for Ruthie, as one daughter to another. But it wouldn't do any real good. They would be no match for the truth that came out of that tortured and twisted mouth.

His mind went wearily back over the past few days; he had an absurd feeling that events could be changed if he could find a mistake somewhere, a break in the chain. But from the time he had seen the name Wallingford on the map until now everything had proceeded as if one thing had simply begotten another. He remembered Sam Johnson's remark from somewhere: everything looks fated and predestined if you look at it after the fact; seen backwards, everything looks caused and inevitable. Moore looked back over the past few days and nights and could find nothing but interlocking causes and effects. And the next cause would be his and Gwen's lying to make life possible for themselves and for Ruthie, to leave some doubt in the public mind, he thought, even to make it possible for Ruthie to lie to her daughter about her grandfather, and for Gwen to lie to the children she didn't yet have. To tell the truth now would prevent the saving lies needed in years to come. Yes, he thought, we'll play As If, as if what we say is true. What else is there to do?

A nurse brought in a tray and set it on the table next to him and said something cheerful, but he hardly noticed her. But then he hunched over the tray and began to eat methodically. He would need strength to carry off the lie, to guard it and repeat it over and over, because all of his instincts told him to give it up and—what was the phrase?—throw himself on the mercy of the court. On the mercy of Ruthie, rather. Only one flicker of light shone for a moment in his mind: that Helen was out of it. But since he had no real religion any more, he was not even sure of that, was tortured for a moment by some primitive fear that the dead could still be harmed.

"Ah, Professor Moore," a voice said from behind him. He turned to see a middle-sized man about his own age in a dark pinstripe suit. The man came around in front of him and extended his hand, and Moore automatically shook it. "I'm glad to see you looking so fit," the man said. "I'm Inspector Broderick. You've given me quite a wait." He pulled a chair over in front of Moore and sat down and crossed his legs comfortably. "May I offer my condolences? A horrible thing. We hardly know what to make of that sort of thing here in Oxford."

"I hardly know myself," Moore said. Now it starts, he thought. He wished deeply that he were dressed and shaved and at least able to sit erect. It seemed terribly unfair to have to argue his lie to this urbane person when his own feet were bare and his body stank of sweat.

"I've had the pleasure of meeting your daughter, " Broderick said. "A lovely young lady, sir. You should be proud of her. She's holding up well under the circumstances."

"Yes," Moore said vaguely, "thank you." But he thought, How well will she hold up under the circumstances you want me to talk about?

"I need a statement from you," Broderick said, taking a notebook out of his inside jacket pocket. "An informal statement, of course. For our own satisfaction, really. You can make a formal statement later on."

"All right," Moore said, "what do I say? Where do I begin?"

Broderick looked down at his notebook. His graying hair was parted neatly on the side, his white shirt collar was starched and trim, and his black shoes were glossy. Moore looked at these things and felt grubby and afraid. Like a prisoner at Dachau, he thought, being examined by a spit and polish commandant, except that this wasn't a movie and the prisoner didn't even have the right on his side. "Actually, it's mostly verification, up to a certain point," Broderick said. "Up to the point of the actual—." He paused. "The actual homicide." He turned the pages of the notebook backwards. "You went to Wallingford on the afternoon of July twenty-first, from Oxford." He looked up at Moore. "Had you ever been there before?"

"Once. During the war."

"And why did you go there that afternoon?"

"Out of curiosity. To see what it was like after all those years."

"You'd been in Oxford for a month by that time, Professor. Why did you wait so long to go back?"

"I didn't realize I was so close. I saw the name on a map."

"You knew no one there, then?"

"No, no one." It was strange, Moore thought, he had told nothing but the truth so far, but somehow it rang false to him. If he were Broderick he probably wouldn't believe it.

"You had never met Edward Morgan?"

"I don't know the name."

"He was the man you sat with in the pub, in the Fox and Grape."

"No, I'd never seen him before."

"Had you ever met Gwendolen Morgan before?"

"You mean his daughter? No, I'd never seen her before that night."

"I see," Broderick said. He looked down at the notebook again. "Please tell me if the following information is accurate. You sat with Morgan at the Fox and Grape. You talked with his daughter when she came to take him home. Later, after she had taken him home, you and she joined each other at the bar. After closing, she drove you to your hotel, the George. The next day, July twenty-second, you came back to Oxford by bus." He looked up at Moore. "This is information given by patrons in the pub and by Miss Morgan. Is it accurate?"

So Gwen had lied about them. Because she knew I would, he thought. He could almost see that grave face as she worked out their options as he had done, and found there was only one. But it must have been even harder for her, he thought for the first time, because she'd have to call her father a liar and a madman when she knew that only one of those things was true. No matter what they did with him, she would have to see him again, and live with what she had said.

"Yes," Moore said, "it's accurate." It isn't so hard to lie, he thought with surprise, maybe because I began it with Helen. Or did I begin it with Gwen?

Broderick made a note in his book. "Beyond this point it's not so clear," he said. "On Tuesday, July twenty-fifth, Morgan was at the Fox and Grape at about noon. Several of the regulars saw him there, and saw him leave shortly thereafter. This was unusual. As you probably know, he didn't get around very well by himself. He bought a bus ticket to Oxford; the man at the bus stop remembers him. At about seven that evening he appeared at Corpus Christi, at the porter's lodge. He inquired about you. That is, he inquired about an American professor. The porter told him there were several American professors there. He didn't know your name, apparently, but he described you, and the porter told him where your rooms were. After that we have no information until six the next morning, July twenty-sixth, when the porter raised the alarm. Except that the previous afternoon his daughter reported him missing from Wallingford. But of course the police down there simply looked around town for him. It wasn't till after the homicide, after he had been identified here in Oxford, that anyone thought to check at the bus stop down there." He looked up from the notebook. "So we know how he got here, though we can hardly imagine his getting here at all in his condition. But we don't know how he got into your rooms, and we don't know the most important thing. Why. This is where we hope you can help us, Professor."

"I can tell you how he got in," Moore said numbly. "I left the door ajar when I went to the toilet. He must have gone in then." Moore hadn't thought about that before. Morgan must have been on the landing when he went to the toilet, or maybe the next landing down, where the stairs turned. But how had he known that Moore would come out? He couldn't have known. Maybe he had simply hoped for good luck. Maybe if Moore hadn't come out he would have gone away, in the morning. Moore felt his stomach rising into his throat and he was afraid he was going to vomit. If I hadn't come out, he thought, if only I hadn't come out.

"I see," Broderick said again, "so that's how he got in. We thought it must be something like that, since the door wasn't forced at all. But that raises another question that puzzles us very much."

"What question?" Moore was trying to imagine Morgan somewhere on the landing, hunched in the shadow, waiting for luck.

"If he saw you come out onto the landing and go into the toilet why did he go into your rooms and—do what he did? Let me put it this way, Professor:

we're not clear about his motive for attacking you, but at least he had seen you. But he had never seen your wife. He may not even have known she was there. The porter can't recall whether he mentioned your wife to him. But even if he did, why should Morgan go in and kill her? Why didn't he wait for you outside the toilet?"

"I don't know," Moore said. "I haven't really thought about these things. I only know he must have gone in when I left the door unlocked." He thought for a minute. "Wouldn't he have to go in then? Wouldn't he know I'd lock the door after I went in again?"

Broderick brushed the questions aside. "I'll tell you what we believe, Professor Moore," he said. His words had increased in tempo, and Moore thought stupidly, He's really interested in this; it's a murder case for him. "We believe he came here to kill you and that he found out from the porter that your wife was here with you and decided to kill you both. Perhaps he didn't know how he was going to do it. But you made it possible for him when you went out and left the door unlocked."

"Yes, I see, I made it possible," Moore said, "yes, I see." Yes, I see, he thought, woe be to him by whom evil cometh. But even in his sense of guilt his mind labored at what Broderick was saying. He's playing a game of some kind, he thought. Why all these questions about what Morgan did and how he did it unless Morgan had denied everything? Or unless he's too mad to make sense? Or unless they don't believe him? What was Broderick trying to make him say? "Wait a minute," Moore said, "what do you mean when you say I made it possible for him to do it?"

Broderick looked at him without any expression that he could read. "Not intentionally, of course," he said. "I meant that you made it possible for him to act out his motive. It's his motive that we don't really understand."

So either Morgan hadn't spoken or Broderick was lying. Moore wondered whether British police were allowed to lie under certain circumstances. Well, Moore would keep it simple for himself: he would lie only about his involvement with Gwen.

"What was your impression of Morgan, Professor?" Broderick's term of address was beginning to grate on Moore; so was Broderick's insistence on pluralizing himself, as if he were royalty. Moore sensed malice behind the innocuous words.

"I only talked with him for a few minutes. But he hated Americans. I found that out very soon."

Broderick nodded. "Yes, it was a joke down there, I gather. His daughter has told us of some of the reason—the Yankee lover, her mother's suicide, and so on. But what we're puzzled about is why he should have singled you out—or you and your wife. Why should he track down a man he'd talked with for only ten minutes and try to kill him?"

Moore shook his head, as if he were puzzled too. "He wasn't right in his mind, you know."

"True enough. But he did remarkable things for a man in his condition. He could hardly walk by himself, ordinarily. Yet he got up here to Oxford by himself, apparently, got from the bus depot to Corpus Christi, climbed those stairs, and—did what he did. All alone, apparently. He must have been remarkably motivated. We all know stories—don't we—of cripples running from burning buildings, for example. But that's in order to save their own lives, isn't it? But he hadn't that motivation, did he? So what was the remarkable cause of all he did?"

"Well, he didn't see many Americans," Moore said, praying for plausibility. "His daughter told me that. I suppose I happened to be the one that—" He couldn't find the word he wanted.

"The one that set him off? Yes, that's possible." Broderick cleared his throat. "I must ask you, Professor, if you said anything or did anything that might especially have antagonized him?"

So this is finally it, Moore thought, the big lie. "No," he said, "nothing."

"You didn't—" Broderick paused. "I'm afraid this is rather a brutal question under the circumstances. You didn't show any special attention to his daughter that he might have found offensive?"

So he's told them what he saw, Moore thought, and Gwen has denied it. Or maybe Broderick is lying, and they're testing me. He ordered his words carefully. "I never talked to her in his presence," he said, "except for a minute or two in the pub before she took him home."

"The two of you spent time together in the pub later on."

"But he wasn't there then."

"I don't mean to be indelicate, Professor, but several people in the pub said that you and she seemed very interested in each other. There were several toasts, I believe. And a kind of conduct that seemed to the regulars to be—would 'romantic' be the word?"

"We found each other interesting," Moore said. "But only briefly. It had nothing to do with her father." He tried to look directly at Broderick. God, how I hate him, he thought, how I wish I could meet him on his own grounds: neatness, security, rightness.

"Is it possible that something happened later on between you two that might have upset Morgan?"

The voyeur, Moore thought angrily, he wants me to talk about it, that's the reason for the cat and mouse game. "No," he said, "nothing. Miss Morgan drove me to the hotel. That's all."

Broderick's eyes stayed on Moore while he moved his notebook over to his other knee. "May we go back for a moment to the actual homicide, Professor? Are you able to talk about that?"

"Yes, I suppose so."

"Then tell me as carefully as you can what happened." Broderick moved his ballpoint pen back and forth on the notebook as if to make sure it worked.

Moore thought, It will be a relief to tell the truth, whatever he may make of it. He told what happened. He told it as briefly and as precisely as he could, but he had the feeling that it was taking him a very long time. Toward the end he forgot that he was telling it to Broderick, because the persistent feeling came back that what he was saying was really all a dream and that Helen was still alive and that tomorrow or the next day they would see Magdalen and Christ Church Meadows. When he finally stopped, Broderick said something, but Moore missed it. "I'm sorry?" he said.

"I said, did Morgan say anything while he was in the room?"

"Yes," Moore said, still back in the Corpus bedroom and not thinking whether he should lie or not. "He said 'Fucking Yanks.' I think he said it several times."

"When did he say that?"

"Just as I rolled over. Just before I felt the pain."

"When you rolled over on your wife to protect her, you mean?"

Moore had been looking off somewhere, but now his eyes came back to Broderick. "Rolled over to protect her?"

Broderick looked at him oddly, Moore thought. "It's the opinion of the Home Office physician that your wife must have died almost instantly from those multiple wounds. But you couldn't know that, of course. So naturally when you saw Morgan with the knife you rolled over on her to protect her. You couldn't have saved her, but you may have saved yourself. So the Home Office man said. Stab wounds in the chest are more likely to be fatal than stab wounds in the back. Something about the angle and the possibility of the blade being deflected. That's apparently what happened with you, you know. The blade deflected off your shoulder blade." He had kept his gaze on Moore while he was talking. "Do you find that a strange explanation, Professor?"

Moore said nothing, and he was hardly aware of Broderick and his tricks. In his memory he was rolling over onto Helen, the sticky warmth on his chest and the nightmare presence behind and above him. But he was trying to get behind that memory, and he couldn't. The figure had come out of the shadows with the arm raised, the flat metallic voice had said those words, and Moore had rolled to his left onto Helen, as he would have rolled a second later in front of the fireplace in Wallingford if Gwen had not moved first. When you were down and someone came at you, you didn't try to get up, you rolled. It didn't matter which way, but you rolled. That was what they had taught him in infantry basic training at Fort Benning thirty years before, and every day for two weeks he had rolled in the red clay while his buddies had lunged at him with real bayonets. That Tuesday night in the Corpus room with Morgan coming at him he had rolled. He had rolled left, onto Helen, but he couldn't say why. Over and over the sequence went through his mind like a film re-run. Like the films of the John Kennedy assassination that showed again and again the blood spurting and Jackie moving but never showed, and never could show, what she was thinking as she moved.

"Well," Broderick said, "I suppose we shall never know what the man knew. Or what he thought he knew."

"Why not?" Moore said angrily. He had finally had too much of the cat and mouse game. "Why don't you ask him what he knew or thought he knew? Why all the theorizing? Why all the amateur psychoanalysis?"

Broderick's face showed surprise that seemed genuine. "Why, I thought you knew," he said. "Morgan is dead."

"Dead?" Moore said, "dead? How? When?" He stared hard at Broderick, smelling a trick. Broderick might be lying. Why not? It seemed easy enough to Moore. And even if it was true—Moore would not let himself be trapped—what had Morgan said before he died?

"At the base of the pelican, in the quad," Broderick said. "You haven't seen the papers? They're calling it The Pelican Death. The porter found him there last Wednesday morning. That's why they raised the alarm and went up to your rooms."

Relief washed through Moore's body like an interior wave. If the newspapers didn't have the truth, then Morgan had died without speaking, and Ruthie was safe now, safe from the truth, and safe from the lies he would have told her. And he and Gwen, they were safe too. A dead man couldn't be tried for murder. But then the relief began to drain away. He and Gwen were safe, but they weren't safe like Ruthie. They had gotten away with something and maybe they wouldn't be caught now, but they would never be safe as Ruthie was safe.

"I really thought we were talking from the same premises," Broderick said, and for the first time he seemed angry. "How could you not know he was dead? The doctors didn't tell you? Or your daughter?"

"No," Moore said. Everyone knew but me, he thought, they forgot I was a fish swimming in a tank until last night.

Broderick closed his notebook and put it back in his jacket pocket. "I don't suppose you would have answered my questions any differently if you had known he was dead, Professor?"

"No," Moore said. And he wouldn't have, he thought. The lie was the same either way. But now the only man who could have exposed it was dead, and probably in the same mortuary as Helen. "At the base of the pelican," he said. "Why there?"

Broderick shrugged. "There's been a good deal of rubbish written about that already, and I expect there'll be more. One view is that he tried to climb it."

"That's crazy. No one could climb it."

"Of course not. But he *was* crazy. Perhaps he thought he could. He'd already done remarkable things. Whatever he was doing there, the Home Office physician ruled that he died of heart failure. Perhaps he was simply leaving, and that was as far as he got. We shall never know that, I suppose. We can hardly even guess. As for why he came to Corpus Christi and did what he did, we shall probably never know that very clearly either. Though there we can at least theorise."

Safe from Morgan now, Moore let his anger come out. "Why don't you tell me what you theorize, Inspector?" He tried to say "Inspector" as Broderick had been saying "Professor," but it didn't come out with the proper venom, and he wasn't sure that Broderick even noticed it.

Broderick's voice when he answered was smooth, and his words seemed as carefully chosen as ever. "A policeman develops certain instincts, Professor, or he spends his career as a constable walking a beat and checking shop doors to see if they're locked. I've talked to Miss Morgan, and I've talked to the people who saw the two of you together in the pub, and now I've talked to you. My instincts tell me there was something between you two. Something that Morgan discovered. Given what we know about him, nothing else could have made him do the impossible things he did."

"You just said he was crazy," Moore said. He had a passionate desire to score some small victory over Broderick. "If he was crazy he might have imagined anything."

"There's no evidence that he was mad except on a single subject, Professor: Yanks. More precisely, the Yank who seduced his wife. And you, the Yank who—" He wasn't at a loss for words, Moore knew, but he didn't finish the sentence.

"Go ahead," Moore said.

"No." Broderick stood up and looked down at him. "My official business here is over."

"Is it the official view that there was something between Miss Morgan and me?" Moore wished he could stand up and shout these words at Broderick, but he couldn't do either one.

"Shall we say that it's the official view that the criminal activity in this matter was carried out by Morgan? Whatever you and Miss Morgan may have done was not criminal activity, so far as we can see. A policeman's job is criminal activity, Professor."

"But you have a private view as well."

"Of course, but that's—what's your American phrase?—'off the record.'"

"And what is your private view, off the record?"

Broderick's mask of courtesy dropped away, and even his language changed. "My private view, Professor? You wanted a bit of the young stuff. It's as simple as that. It was too chancy here in Oxford, so you went somewhere else. You got it in Wallingford. By luck, I should say. Perhaps she was bowled over by the American don business. Perhaps she had a pint too much and would have gone home with anyone, and you happened to be there. Anyway, two people are dead from your bloody bit of fun, and I hope you think it was worth it. Was it worth it, Professor, your bloody little bit of uncriminal activity? Did you get something you couldn't have got at home?"

Moore found himself on his feet somehow, but he couldn't straighten up, and his voice was too shaky to carry the anger he felt. "You moralistic bastard," he said. "You've got a notebook full of times and places and the imagination of a priest. You look at arrivals and departures and then you make a moral judgment on the people who come and go. I suppose you're married. Go home tonight and tell your wife about the dirty people you've had to deal with. You don't know anything but outsides. You don't know anything at all."

Broderick's mask went up again, and his face was as smooth as his accent. "You're understandably upset. Who wouldn't be, with three women to account to? Or one to account for and two to account to?" He smoothed his jacket and gave a look around the room and then stepped past Moore and out of his vision. Moore heard the neat click of his shoes across the room, then heard them stop at the door, but he didn't turn around, and Broderick's last words came from behind him. "That's always the final plea of criminals and sinners and madmen, isn't it? 'You don't understand me.' Perhaps there isn't really much to understand, Professor."

Moore was silent. In a moment he heard the click of the shoes in the corridor and he knew that Broderick was gone. To talk to Ruthie? To hint urbanely to her what he had finally said outright to Moore? You could never trust a moralist. A moralist was not a gentleman; a moralist never worried about inflicting pain. Moore knew this because he had once been like that himself. I dislike him so much, he thought, because he's so much like me. Or so much like the way I was once, shooting from the hip like a western gunman. Moore sat back down on the bed, shaking. The stupid bastard, he thought, he's my age, but he hasn't grown at all, he hasn't learned you can't judge people that way. Except yourself. Yourself is the only fair target. He wished Broderick were back so he could say that to him. But then he thought it wouldn't have mattered. You couldn't score a victory over a moralist by saying something like that. Moralists were secure, and they were neat and tidy, like the part in Broderick's hair and the knot in his tie. But sometimes they changed, Moore thought, and they became like him, uncombed and baggy in his hospital gown. As to why they changed, Moore thought, echoing Broderick's words, there was no official view. His anger at Broderick faded. If Broderick talked to Ruthie, well, then he talked to her. Moore's lie had to be the same.

The papers, he thought suddenly, The Pelican Mystery. Ruthie would have seen the papers by now. She wouldn't be safe from the papers. American

Don's Wife Slain By Wallingford Man. Police Seek Motive. She would be reading something like that, or seeing it on the television, reported by a BBC type in that BBC tone that implied reluctance at having to mention the tawdry side of life. Well, the lie would have to handle that sort of thing as well. Moore had nothing else to turn to. It had been foolish to think Ruthie safe because Morgan was dead. He couldn't talk, but the rest of the world could.

"Someone brought these things over for you, Professor," a voice said behind him. He turned slowly; a plump blond nurse was just going out the door. On the foot of his bed was his old brown overnight bag. He zipped it open. His green bathrobe lay folded on top, and when he pulled it out he saw his razor, toothbrush, slippers, and tobacco pouch and pipe. He hunched himself into the robe and put on the slippers, wishing he had had them while Broderick was there. He lighted his pipe and sat for a moment savoring the aroma and taste. When the pipe went out after a minute he reached automatically into the pocket of his robe for matches and instead brought out a clutter of folded papers. A bus schedule with the times from Oxford to Wallingford circled. A note to himself to compare Shelley's "Mont Blanc" with the twelfth book of Wordsworth's *Prelude*. A leaflet on Oxford pubs and the kinds of beer they sold. The scraps were all familiar, but they all seemed very old to him, as if he were looking at mementos that his grandfather might have kept.

He heard Ruthie's voice say "Hi, Dad," and he turned around to watch her come in. She looked better this morning, he noted with relief. She had changed her clothes, and when she came closer he could see that her eyes looked less haunted. "Hi," she said, and kissed him. Her voice wasn't as brittle as it had been the night before. "It's so good to see you sitting up and smoking your pipe. You looked so sick last night."

"Oh, I'm much better," he said, and again he thought, I can't have her worried about both Helen and me.

She put a paper bag on the table and brought out two plastic cups of coffee. "The coffee's so awful," she said, "but I brought us some anyway."

"If you stayed here very long you'd switch to tea. Where are you staying?"

"The Eastgate Hotel. Dr. Norton got a room there for me."

"Good. That's a nice place. Corpus is just down the lane from there."

"I know. I walked by there this morning."

Something in her tone made Moore look at her sharply. "You didn't go in?"

"Oh no, just inside the gate, to see—" She stopped.

"The pelican?"

She nodded. "I was hoping you hadn't seen the papers."

Moore almost laughed. "I was hoping *you* hadn't seen them. Broderick told me a little of what they're saying."

"The Pelican Murder," she said, and her voice shook a little. "I see that and hear that on the TV and I think, It's Mom they're talking about. It's bad enough thinking about her without all that." Moore took her hands in his and patted them. He didn't trust himself to speak because he knew his voice would shake even more than hers. "I'll never go up to that room," she said, "not if I stayed here for a year. But I've read some of the descriptions of what they think happened. Dad, I think of the pain, and the shock, what she must have felt in those few seconds." Her voice broke more, and he gripped her hands harder. "That quiet woman who never hurt anyone in her life." Her voice broke completely and she put her head down on his knees and cried. He got one of his hands free and stroked her hair, over and over.

"She was asleep," he said hoarsely, "she couldn't have known anything, and the doctors say she went immediately. There couldn't have been any time for her to think or be afraid." God, how he hoped that was true! He found himself praying now that there had not been one split second when she had come to consciousness for the last time in an ecstasy of pain and fright. Not one split second when her deepest silent voice had said his name and he had not been there.

Ruthie sat up and rubbed her hands over her eyes, then got up and went over to the window and stood with her back to him. She took a handkerchief from her jacket pocket, and he knew she was dabbing at her eyes and trying to force herself to stop crying. And he knew she wouldn't turn back to him till she had got control of herself. She's so much like Helen, he thought, but she's so much like me too. She won't turn around until she's organized again. Looking at her was like looking at both Helen and himself. Yes, Plato was right, he thought, you have your immortality in your children.

She came back and sat down again and picked up her coffee cup. "It's so strange," she said. Her eyes were red and puffed, but her voice was even again. "All the way over on the plane I thought Mom had been killed in an accident. And then when I got here they said a madman had killed her, but it was still like an accident. Like the people who got shot by that man in the tower down in Texas. They just happened to be going by and he shot them. He didn't know them, he would've shot anyone who went by. And then I found out this man knew you and followed you here from somewhere else. It was like going up a flight of stairs and finding something new on every floor. Now I know it couldn't have been an accident, and that makes me feel even worse."

Moore felt suddenly hollow, as if something had sucked his body clean of energy and blood. It was time to take his evasive action now, to shuttle back and forth between truth and lie and somehow save them all: Helen and Ruthie and Gwen and himself. He didn't feel up to it, he hadn't really prepared enough, but he couldn't wait any longer. Ruthie was waiting, watching him with Helen's eyes, but she would be listening to him with something like his own mind. It would be like lying to himself, and he had never been adept at that.

"I think I know what you mean," he said. "It was better as long as it was just bad luck."

"Yes, it was awful, but it was better."

"But it *was* just bad luck, honey. That man had never seen your mother; he didn't even know she existed. She died because she just happened to be here when he came. Just as if she walked past that tower in Texas and that man shot her. He didn't come here to kill her. He came here to kill me. At least, I suppose that's why he came."

"But why, Dad? What had you ever done to him?"

"It wasn't what I did to him. It was what another American did to him. And to his wife. Do you know about that?"

She nodded. "I know what the papers are saying. That his wife had been seduced by an American and had killed herself, and that he'd hated Americans after that. And that he'd had a stroke."

"More than one stroke, Ruthie. Let me tell you what his daughter told me about that affair her mother had with the American." He hadn't meant to mention Gwen at all if he could help it, but he was carried along now on the current of his evasion. "It was in that same pub where I met him that that other American had met his wife. That was where it all started. Later on, he discovered the affair and discovered that his wife was going to leave him for the American. Except that the American had gone away by then. That was too much for him. And when his wife killed herself, he broke.

That's when he had the first of his strokes. That's when his mind began to come apart." So far, he thought with surprise, I haven't lied at all. Maybe the trick is to tell nothing but the truth but not all the truth.

She had been listening to him intently, and now she said, "You mean when he saw you it brought back all that business with the other American? That's sort of what the papers are saying. Except that they keep hinting that maybe you paid some attention to his daughter and that was what set him off. That he saw the same thing happening all over again."

"I *did* pay some attention to his daughter. I talked with her while some-one took him to the men's room. In fact I helped her get him on his feet. Do the papers mention that she came back after she took her father home?" She nodded, and he thought he could see pain in her eyes. "What do they say about that?"

"Oh, a lot of things. But mainly that you and she were interested in each other."

Moore reached down for his last truth. "We *were* interested. Let me tell you why. I knew the man who seduced her mother." Her eyes went wide in astonishment. "I know it sounds crazy, but it's true. After she told me some things about this man I realized that he and I had been in Wallingford together in the war. I said his name to her, and it was the right name." Tell all the truth but tell it slant, Success in circuit lies—the lines from Dickin-son came easily into his mind, as they might have done in a class, but then shamed him. She hadn't meant lies, only poetry.

"My God," Ruthie said, "what a coincidence!" He could almost see her mind working. "Did her father know you knew this man?"

I could say yes, Moore thought, and it would be helpful. But he hadn't yet directly lied to Ruthie, and he had a wild hope that maybe he wouldn't have to. "I don't think so," he said. "He wasn't there when we were talking about it."

"No wonder you two had so much to talk about," Ruthie said. "Are you going to tell this to the papers? Maybe they'd stop all their dirty speculating."

He thought he could sense the relief in her voice. She was so eager to vindicate him; he could imagine her rushing into a newspaper office with her defense of him and an editor saying, like Broderick, "The regulars thought they saw romance, and weren't there several toasts?"

"I don't think I can do that," Moore said. "I don't think they'd believe it, unless I named the man. And I couldn't prove it anyway. I suppose I'd be open to a law suit." That might even be true, Moore thought, but felt grimier than if he had lied outright.

"I suppose that's true." She put her hand on his knee. "I'm glad I said what I did to that policeman. Broderick."

Moore felt himself tighten inside. "What was that, honey?"

"It was just before I came in just now. I asked him why he thought that the man had done what he did. He said, 'Some men will go to great lengths to protect their daughters.' And I said, 'Either you don't know my father or you're a filthy-minded bastard.'" She smiled a little at the memory.

Moore had somehow never got used to young women using what he still thought of as army language. "You shouldn't swear like that, honey," he said, but then he added, "Although it was a well-turned phrase."

"Not as good as what you would have said."

"Better," Moore said, thinking of his skirmish with Broderick, "much better."

They sat silent for a few minutes. Moore was thinking that he really hadn't know what he was going to say to her when he began but that it had worked out pretty well. He hadn't lied, at least not in the letter, though God knew he had lied in the spirit. But at least he hadn't inflicted pain.

"How awful all this must be for his daughter," Ruthie said. "She must feel a lot like me, losing a father."

"Yes, I suppose so," Moore said. It was a side of the situation he hadn't really thought of yet. I've been mired in my own suffering, he thought, as if Gwen had no existence apart from me.

"If I were going to be here longer I think I might go see her. Though I suppose it would be awkward. Maybe you'll see her, Dad."

"I don't think so," Moore said quickly. "I imagine she's trying to hide from all the publicity."

"I suppose so. What is she like?"

Moore's heart gave a jump of fear, but then he decided that Ruthie was simply curious. "Quiet. Fond of her parents. Serious." He thought he would find it hard to say what Gwen was like, even to himself.

"I've been thinking," Ruthie said, and he knew her mind had gone on to something else. "We have to decide what to do about Mom."

"What do you mean?"

"I mean about a funeral and everything."

Of course, Moore thought, angry with himself. These are things I should be thinking about; Ruthie shouldn't have to worry about them. But he hadn't thought about those things at all, because some part of his mind refused to believe that Helen was really dead. Even while he had lied to Broderick and evaded the truth with Ruthie it had been the vague notion of somehow protecting Helen that had kept him going. But now that Ruthie had said the word *funeral* an image came back to him of the high dim ceiling in the Corpus bedroom, and Helen lying asleep next to him, and the promise of Magdalen and Christ Church and Iffley.

"Dr. Harker says you can't travel for quite a while. Ten days. Maybe two weeks. I think I should take her home."

"Home?" Moore said. The low ranch house with the attached garage and the wide driveway came to his mind like something out of another life. But then he realized that Ruthie meant to take her home to be buried. "You mean, have the funeral without me?"

"What else can we do, Dad? We can't leave her in the morgue for two weeks. It just wouldn't be right."

No, it wouldn't be right, he thought, it would be obscene. It would be as if no one had claimed her, as if she were some anonymous body dragged out of the river. But something deeper than decency wrenched at him. It was as if Ruthie were telling him he couldn't be present at his own burial. Something of himself would be going underground: all of Helen that he had made his own or that had sunk into him over the years. He looked at Ruthie, seeing the ghost of Helen. Something would be going underground, something of himself.

"Jim and I will do what you would do, Dad. People will understand."

"I suppose so," Moore said. "I wasn't thinking of that."

They talked about the funeral arrangements, hesitantly. He knew she was being as careful with him as he was with her. If one of them slipped now they would both backslide into tears, so they played a game of roundabout, almost as if they were planning an excursion. In a half hour they had settled everything that could be settled. But one thing Moore insisted upon. He would see to the business of having Helen released from the morgue and taken to the plane. He had no clear idea of what that might involve, but he had a hollow feeling that someone would have to make a formal identification, and he meant to do that alone. He wanted Ruthie out of that.

"Does that mean I won't see her?" Ruthie asked.

"I don't know. I just don't know. If I think it's all right I'll tell you."

"All right," she said, very quietly. "I suppose Dr. Norton will help me with the plane arrangements."

"Sure he will."

She stood up. "I'd better let you have a little rest. You look tired. I'll come back this afternoon."

Moore was indeed tired, so tired it was an effort to keep himself from trembling as if he had a chill. But with a last surge of energy he said, "Honey, why don't you try to see a little of the town? You may never come back here."

"All right. Where shall I go?"

"Almost anywhere. But there are three places I'd especially like you to see. Magdalen College, the Christ Church Meadows along the river behind Christ Church, and a little church called St. Mary the Virgin in the far south end of town in a section called Iffley. Anyone can tell you how to find them."

"All right, I will. What's special about them, Dad?"

Moore took a long breath. "They're places I promised to take your mother."

"Okay," she said and kissed him and went hurriedly out. He knew she would be crying by the time she got into the corridor, because she was so much like him, and he was crying now.

After a while he swung his legs carefully up onto the bed and lay back on the pillows. He was so tired he thought he could easily sleep forever, but his eyes would not stay closed. The words he had said in the past two hours kept coming back and he found himself saying them over and over again, some to Broderick, some to Ruthie. He found it hard to remember which words he had said to which person. Their faces stared at him as he spoke, Broderick's stony with disbelief, Ruthie's intent, believing. But of course she had wanted to believe. It was an act of faith. He wondered if in some time to come the faith, the thing hoped for, would give way to the thing feared. But he had no control over that. He hadn't inflicted pain, at least; maybe she would see that too in time to come. Finally he slept.

He woke some time later when a male nurse wheeled in a cart with two plastic basins on it and a pile of towels folded neatly on a shelf below. "Bath time," the nurse said cheerfully. Moore obediently pulled himself up and let himself be sponged all over except on his back and chest. "You might feel better if you shaved," the young man said. He handed Moore an electric razor and a small mirror and Moore pushed the razor back and forth over his stubble. It did make him feel better, though he wouldn't feel clean till he had shaved with a blade. He looked better too, and that was important, because he had to ask Dr. Harker to let him go to the morgue. When he finished he asked if he could see the doctor.

He was sitting on the edge of the bed smoking his pipe when Harker came in a few minutes later. "Well, aren't you the chipper one," Harker said, "sitting up smoking and waiting to join the foot race."

"I really do feel much better," Moore said.

"You look better," Harker said, "relatively speaking." He gestured for Moore to put his pipe down, then put his stethoscope on Moore's chest and then on his back. "All right," he said, "now lift your arms over your head." Moore did, and hoped the pain in his back didn't show in his face. "Put your legs straight out." Moore did, but only for a second before the pain in his back dragged them down.

"You're very fortunate." Harker said, "or did I mention that yesterday?"

"Why fortunate?"

"A half inch one way and you'd have been dead, a half inch the other and you'd surely have some paralysis. I suppose the real luck was that you were struck only once. You probably wouldn't have been so fortunate a second time."

"How many times was my wife—" Moore couldn't finish it.

"I didn't do the examination. But several times, I believe."

"So she had no chance to be fortunate."

"I suppose you could say that." Harker lowered his head and looked at Moore over his half spectacles.

"I wonder why," Moore said.

Harker was still looking at him over his glasses. "I meant the medical odds," he said. "The medical odds were against her."

"Yes, I know," Moore said, watching Harker write something on his clipboard. "My daughter tells me I'll be laid up here for some time."

"Yes, I told her that. Your wound is very clean but very deep, and you've lost considerable blood. The primary healing is most important. You must stay immobilised for at least ten days, I should think. If you break the primary scar there will be considerable danger of infection, to mention only the most obvious problem. Even at best you must expect to have a very stiff back for some time. A month or more. There's tissue deep down that must knit itself."

"I don't have to be persuaded, Dr. Harker. I don't feel like going anywhere, except—" He stopped, looking at Harker's neatly trimmed hair and the pencil line mustache and the half spectacles, stopped because something had broken into his thought. "Dr. Harker," he said, "Dr. Jonathan Harker."

Harker's narrow face broke into a smile that seemed almost too big for it, a smile of pure delight. "Not Jonathan," he said, "but, yes, Dr. Harker."

For just a moment Moore forgot Helen and Gwen and Ruthie in the sheer remembering of something else that had given him great joy. "You wrote those marvelous letters about Count Dracula in the beginning of the book, and the last thing you wrote was that Dracula was crawling down the castle wall head downward, like a gigantic bug."

Harker nodded, still smiling. "They *were* grand letters, weren't they? And then I died, of course."

"I remember thinking that you weren't really dead. I was sure you'd come back somehow. I was sure of that till the very end."

"You can imagine how disappointed *I* was that I didn't come back," Harker said. He sat down in the chair by the bed and took off his spectacles. "You know, you're only the seventh person who's ever caught the name. I've kept careful count. It's an odd thing to have the name of a minor character in fiction. It becomes quite a personal thing. It makes one think of symbolism and coincidence, or at least it made *me* think of those things. From the time I read the book when I was twelve I never seriously considered any profession except medicine, yet I don't believe I'd ever given any thought to medicine before I read the book. The day I began my internship I remember thinking, 'Well, there really is going to be another Dr. Harker.' I suppose that's why I've never believed in coincidence as mere accident."

Moore looked at Harker sitting so companionably across from him, so clearly eager to talk about a pure concept. He felt an almost physical need to shed the shuffling and evasive part of himself that had dealt with Broderick and Ruthie and to be once again the Professor James Moore who could discuss pure concepts. An old pride of mind made him put on his old identity as he might have put on his jacket and straightened his tie before going into a graduate seminar. For something like a fifty-minute class he would put aside the shabby American don of The Pelican Affair and be who he really was.

"I've thought about that a little lately, as you might expect," he said. He can't imagine how much I've thought about coincidence, Moore thought, but he's thinking about himself, not me. "I suppose I think, like most people, that some coincidences are meaningful and others not." And some are tragic, he added to himself, but that doesn't make them meaningful.

"I don't believe that view will hold up, though," Harker said with animation, and Moore guessed that Harker had been over this ground many times; he had the air of a man whose arguments were ready to hand. "Meaningful coincidence implies pattern."

"I don't see that at all," Moore said. "I don't see that it implies anything more than mathematical probability. Given a certain sequence of events or a certain sequence of anything else, the probability is that there will be a certain number of matchings. I mean that some few will be significant, but most won't be." I'm arguing about a pure concept, Moore told himself, but my life keeps getting in the way.

But Harker went on. "Oh, of course coincidence is mathematically describable, but that's hardly what we're talking about. When I say 'pattern' I don't mean mere mathematical pattern. I don't mean coincidence but the *result* of coincidence. In my case the coincidence was that I should read a book in which a character had the same name as mine. But the result of the coincidence is that I became a physician. You might meet someone tomorrow whose name was Moore, but that would be a merely mathematical coincidence, unless somehow your life was affected by your meeting him, or of course unless his life was somehow affected by his meeting you. And, generally speaking, we look at the coincidences we know of only from our own point of view. How a matching of some sort affects us, I mean, not how it affects someone else. We think of ourselves as what you might call receivers of coincidence, but surely there are times when we are agents for someone else's receiving. Probability would surely argue for that."

"I suppose that's so," Moore said, "but when most things seem to happen by accident I don't see that occasional meaningful coincidence implies anything like a pattern." He tried not to recall his sense that coincidence had been the law of life in Wallingford that night. That suspended probability had put Morgan on Stairway Twelve on the chance that a door would open. Helen had died because of coincidence, he had told Ruthie, and it was true. But all that was over now. You couldn't call that a pattern, maybe only a brief run of bad luck.

"Well, I think we make out own worlds, Professor. If we're inclined to believe in pattern, for whatever reasons, we shall see coincidence and symbolism everywhere. If we're inclined to see mere chaos we shall see considerably less, and we shall discount what little we do see."

"You mean that the evidence can be read either way?"

"I mean that what you call evidence is the next thing to infinite, and no one can possibly look at enough of it to make a purely rational decision. The evidence lies in every moment of every life of every person who was ever born. I regard it as insanity to think that we can evaluate on the basis of evidence. Whether the world is ordered or disordered, we shall never know on the basis of evidence. Except of course that even in the microscopically small samples of human existence that we know, we see some evidence of coincidence, meaningful coincidence, from which we may infer that human life is not totally chaotic. If we cannot infer total order, at least we cannot infer total disorder. I believe that's as far as the evidence can take us." Harker put his spectacles back on and looked at Moore over them. "I'm sorry to go on about coincidence. I was forgetting your situation. I get rather carried away when I meet someone who knows the coincidence of my name."

"Because it may be a meaningful coincidence that I recognized the coincidence?"

"Yes, of course. And I shall be wondering now which of us is agent and which is receiver. I suppose we shall never know, until it doesn't matter to us, when we're preoccupied with something more important."

Moore didn't ask what something more important might be, because he was thinking: agent and receiver—Nancy, Lane, Gwen, Helen, Morgan, myself—who was doing and who was receiving? But in a moment he began to feel as if he had been staring at a geometrical figure too long and had lost the sense of its primary shape. And then his other urgent need came back to him. "That's all very interesting," he said, "but I'm afraid my mind is really on something else. I need your help with something more immediate than metaphysics."

Harker peered over his spectacles at Moore. "Nothing is really more immediate than metaphysics, but we needn't go into that now. Tell me what you want."

Moore outlined the plans that he and Ruthie had made, and when he had finished Harker simply said, "They seem sensible arrangements. How can I help?"

"I want to see my wife before she leaves." Moore had meant to say "before they take her away," but those words had refused to come out.

"Of course," Harker said. He appeared to think for a moment, then said, "Actually, either you or your daughter will have to see her." He paused. "For identification."

"I want it to be me," Moore said. "I know I'm not supposed to move, but I want it to be me. That's where I need your help. And I don't want my daughter to see her unless I give the okay. I suppose I need your help there too."

"I haven't seen your wife," Harker said. "You're concerned about facial marks?" Moore nodded. "I could find that out easily enough."

"No," Moore said, "I want to see her no matter what. But I don't want Ruthie to see her unless I say so. I don't care where they have to take me to see her. I want you to help me with that."

Harker sat down in the chair again. "I shouldn't think you'd need much help, Professor Moore. Very likely she's here."

"Here?" For a wild moment Moore didn't know what Harker meant. The word was like a sudden gunshot.

Harker said hurriedly, "I mean here in our mortuary. She would have been taken to the Central Police Station for the post mortem. After that, if a delay occurred for some reason, she would likely have been brought here to Radcliffe."

Moore felt deflated. "I thought I'd have to be taken somewhere by ambulance or something." He had envisioned a long ride and pain. Something theatrical, he thought now with disgust. "I suppose I can be just wheeled there on a cart?"

Harker nodded. "Quite easily. I'll just check to make sure she's here." He got up and went out. Moore sat staring at his feet till Harker came back. "She's here," he said. "When do you want to go?"

"Now."

Harker nodded and went out again. In less than five minutes he was back again and said, "It's arranged."

"Thanks," Moore said.

Harker stood in front of him, toying with his stethoscope. "I have a last thing to say about coincidence," he said. "It's about Jonathan Harker."

Moore, his mind full of Helen, was not ready for more talk about coincidence, but he said perfunctorily, "What about him?"

"Only this," Harker said. "He wasn't a physician. He was a solicitor, what you would call a lawyer. He was arranging for Dracula to buy a house in England. That's why he went to Transylvania."

Moore thought for a moment. "That's right," he said, "I remember now. It's odd that I made him a doctor. I suppose because you're a doctor, and there was the coincidence of names."

"What's even more odd is that I made him one too," Harker said. "Of course, I was only a boy when I read the book, and I never read it again as an adult. I suppose I may have skimmed through a lot of the detail. Perhaps I wanted to be a physician even before I read the book, and so I made someone with my name into what I unconsciously wanted to be."

"Yes, I suppose so," Moore said. "That would explain it."

"But it wouldn't explain why we both made the same mistake and were thus led to a discussion of coincidence, would it?" Harker smiled. "It rather looks as if our meeting here is marked by coincidence, doesn't it?"

"Yes, I suppose so," Moore said again. He felt vaguely as if he had made a foolish mistake in some parlor word game that he didn't want to play any more.

Harker waited for a moment, then when Moore was silent, said quietly, "Someone will be along to take you to see your wife," and went out.

Fifteen minutes later the man who had given Moore his bath appeared with a wheelchair and helped Moore into it. Moore felt himself pushed out of the room and into the corridor, then around a corner and past a high counter where a nurse was talking on a telephone, and then they were in front of an elevator door. Moore was suddenly cold, and shivers ran through him that he could not control.

"Here now, we can't have that," the attendant said. He went back around the corner and in a moment reappeared with a blanket. He draped it over Moore's shoulders and down over his legs, and Moore clutched it to him. Like an invalid, he thought. The movement of the elevator was so smooth that Moore could not tell whether they were going up or down, and he didn't think to look at the indicator till he was being wheeled out into the corridor, but he had a sense of being down. The wheelchair moved again and they went smoothly past laboratory doors and past doors marked Clinic and Unit and Section until the chair stopped in front of the door marked Mortuary.

The attendant reached over him and pulled the metal door open and pushed him inside. The room was large and brightly lighted and cold. One wall, the only one Moore noticed, was like the wall in a safe deposit vault except that the drawers were over-sized. He felt his chair move forward. A small man in a tight fitting white hospital suit came from somewhere outside of Moore's vision and took hold of the handle on one of the drawers and the drawer slid silently out from the wall. Except that it wasn't a drawer at all when it was open, only a flat slab with no sides. On the slab was something under a white sheet. It had no shape, Moore thought, it could have been anything. His chair moved forward again until he was at the far end of the slab, the end against the wall. Then the man in the white suit leaned over and very precisely pulled the sheet down about fifteen inches, to the base of the throat. He stood holding the end of the sheet in both hands like a magician doing a trick.

Her eyes were closed and her hair was only a little mussed. There were no marks on her face or neck. Framed by the white sleeves of the man holding the sheet, her face and neck hardly stood out at all. They would change that in the funeral parlor back home, Moore thought, they would give her some color. And people would stand in front of the casket and say she looked as if she were asleep. But here she didn't look asleep. She looked dead. Staring at her as if hypnotized, Moore thought of the dead he had seen in the war, the only truly dead he had ever seen, the unadorned dead. They didn't look as if they were sleeping. They looked dead, dead and gone, and after you stared at them for while you had trouble remembering who they had been. Helen looked like that.

"That's my wife," he said.

The man in the white suit nodded and smoothly pulled the sheet back up. Moore felt nothing. What was being covered up was not Helen, only a facsimile, something he could identify. He felt the wheelchair turning around and going back to the door. They might as well have showed me a picture, he thought, or a negative.

Back in his room, the attendant helped him into bed and went away. A minute later a girl in white brought in a tray of food and put it down on his table. He stopped her as she was starting to crank up his bed so he could sit up.

"I'm not hungry," he said, "but could you do me a favor?"

"If I can," she said, "but you really should eat."

"Tell Dr. Harker that my daughter is not to see the body. Not. Okay?"

"Okay."

"And could you see if someone has brought my wallet to the hospital?" She looked puzzled. "My pocketbook."

"All right, but try to eat."

"I will."

She went out. Maybe Norton had thought to send the wallet over. Moore hoped so. There was a picture of Helen in it, in color.

It was nearly dinnertime when he woke up and saw Ruthie dozing in the chair. He reached over and touched her hand and she woke up. "Why didn't you wake me, honey?"

"I thought you needed the sleep," she said, "and I did too." A nurse brought in two dinner trays. "They're letting me eat with you tonight because I'm leaving in the morning."

"So soon?"

She nodded. "Once we'd decided to do it I thought we should do it right away."

"I suppose that's best."

They ate the broiled fish and the inevitable chips. When they were drinking their coffee she said, "I had a message from Dr. Harker when I came in. I'm not to see Mom?"

"Not here, honey. Maybe when you get home. I mean at the funeral home."

"Is she—"

"No, nothing like that. She's all right. It's just that—" He looked hard for the words he needed. "I don't want you to see her here in the morgue." He touched her hand. "There's just no need, honey. Please."

"All right, Dad." She lighted a cigarette. "I'm not sure I really wanted to. I've never been in a morgue."

"It isn't bad," he said quickly, "it's just, you know, impersonal."

Neither of them spoke for a while. Then she put out her cigarette and said, "I went to the places you told me about. I can see why you were going to take Mom there."

"I knew you'd like them."

"The deer at Magdalen are so scruffy, aren't they? I fed one of them an apple through the fence. Then I walked along the river behind Corpus

Christi all the way to Christ Church Meadows." She paused for a moment. "I tried to see it all the way I thought Mom would have seen it with you."

"You probably did. You're a lot like her, you know."

"It was getting late after that, so I took a cab to Iffley. I looked at the church for a while, but I spent most of my time in the cemetery, just sitting. Thinking about Mom."

"I spent some time there too. Under the yew tree."

She nodded. "Is that what that tree is? Then I took a cab back here. I felt better. Only I wish you were coming home with us."

"Yes, I do too. But I'm glad you could see those places before you went." He cleared his throat because his voice was getting husky. "They may not be the best places in Oxford, but they were the special ones."

He could see the tears standing in her eyes. She said, "You and Mom loved each other so much, didn't you? You always did. It was the one thing I could always count on."

Yes, we did, Moore thought, yes, we always did. Even at the end, when we were going to play As If here in Oxford and maybe for the rest of our lives. I really believe we were going to do that because we loved each other, because we didn't want to inflict pain.

When he kissed Ruthie goodbye at ten o'clock he said, "You and Jim are in charge now. You do what you think best. Just call me when it's over and you're back at the house. I'll be waiting."

"I will. Take care of yourself now. Come home soon."

And then she was gone, and Moore sat for a long while, thinking, Now I know how old folks feel in a nursing home when their children have come and visited for a while and then have gone home. A nurse came in to take his temperature and blood pressure, and he asked her for a sleeping pill. When she came back with it she had a message from Harker. "He thought you might be worried about the arrangements for your wife," she said. "You're not to be concerned. The mortuary just rang up and told us that the hearse has just left for Heathrow. She'll be there long before flight time."

"Thanks," Moore said, and took the pill eagerly. He lay back and waited for it to work, as if he had just been given Novocain in a dentist's chair. So now even the slab down below is empty, he thought, and I really am alone. Alone as Jonathan Harker in Dracula's castle, stealing down to discover the coffins filled with consecrated earth that had to be shipped with Dracula wherever he went. Moore tried not to think of the coffin in Heathrow, set apart from the other luggage in a corner of some storage shed. But when the sedative finally eased him into sleep, he and a dark haired woman whom he seemed to know were searching in some high-ceilinged place like an airplane hangar for the coffins they had to find and sit beside until the sun came up.

He woke early the next morning, long before flight time. He drank his tea and nibbled at his breakfast and made the long slow trip to the bathroom. If the flight left on time it left when he was crouched on the toilet, the pain in his back straining against the pain in his bowels. After that he made his way to a chair by the window, and there he sat for the rest of the day with the crossword puzzle from the *Times* spread open on his lap. He could see a patch of lawn and a massive gray building beyond it. Occasionally people crossed the lawn, perhaps to go into the building. He couldn't tell, because he couldn't see the door. A nurse came in from time to time and scolded him and wanted him to go back to bed, but except for two painful treks to the toilet he sat stubbornly in the chair till dusk. Then he knew it was afternoon at home and Helen and Ruthie had landed. That was how he thought of them: Helen and Ruthie going home, not Ruthie taking Helen's body home. He knew that Helen was dead, of course, but still some part of his mind thought of them as simply going home together, leaving him alone over here, a tourist. "Helen and Ruthie have gone home." No image accompanied the words; they were simply a set of sounds he repeated over and over to himself, a kind of incantation.

He had his dinner in the chair and then sat on till bedtime, long after it had grown too dark even to see the grass and the building. By then his back had stiffened so much that a nurse had to help him into the bathroom and then into bed.

"Do you need anything to help you sleep?" she asked him.

"Yes," Moore said, "the strongest thing you have."

He lay waiting again for the drug to take hold. It had been just twenty-four hours since he had lain like this the night before, but he had no sense of time having passed, only the same bitter sense of aloneness that had come with the message that Helen's coffin was gone. Helen and Ruthie have gone home: it was as if someone beside him were saying the words to him again and again. Soon images began to form themselves in his mind: the funeral home, where his mother had been laid out; the cemetery where she and his father were buried; the house. The funeral would be like his mother's funeral, and like his father's, except that the mourners would be coming back to his and Helen's house. He saw the contributed dishes of potato salad and cold cuts on the dining room table, the cars in the driveway and along the street. Then he saw the tree, the slender locust sapling he had planted between the sidewalk and the street two years before. It had never taken properly. He would have dug it out after the first year, but he had planted it just before Helen had gone into the hospital for surgery on a lump on her shoulder. The lump had been benign, and Moore from then on had associated the tree with Helen's recovery. He had never told Helen this, nor anyone else: it was too sentimental. But he had pruned the tree carefully and coddled it and fertilized it, and it had survived two hard winters, but just barely. He saw it now, thin and reedy and hardly any taller now than when he had planted it. I wonder how it's doing now, he thought, I wonder if it knows it's time to die.

The sleeping pill was working now. His bones seemed to be turning into warm water. The last thing he saw, though he saw it in a dream now, was the funeral. The procession of cars wound slowly around the gravel drives to the gravesite. He could see the canopy set up over the grave and the cloth runner that stretched from the grave down to the road. And he could see the quiet people ranked around the open slit in the grass. He could feel a breeze and smell the scent of flowers. But he wasn't there; it was like watching it all on some marvelous television that transmitted odor and feeling as well as sight and sound. The images faded as he slid into deeper sleep, and he felt the light pressure of his watchband against his wrist. He would have to calculate the time difference very carefully so that from here in Oxford, in this place that he and Helen had talked of as the place of might-have-been, he could send his mind to be present when they lowered the coffin that held so little of Helen and so much of himself.

CHAPTER 6

Oxford - Part III

The next morning after breakfast Harker came briskly into the room. After he had examined Moore he sat down in the chair and said, "I'll allow you to have visitors now if you like. How does that strike you?"

"All right, I suppose." Moore was not eager to see anyone from Corpus, but he knew he should; they would be leaving for home in a few days. Norton would certainly come, and perhaps one or two of his students.

"Reporters have been waiting to see you for two days now. I've told them no, of course. But if you may have visitors now, you'll have to deal with them."

Oh, God, Moore thought, I forgot about them. *The Pelican Mystery*. Of course they've been waiting. "All right," he said, "I suppose I might as well see them now."

"You're not compelled to, you know. I said you had to deal with them. You can send them away if you like."

Moore looked at him. After their talk about coincidence he had come to think of Harker as almost a colleague. But that was because Harker had said nothing directly about Moore's situation; Moore had no idea what Harker thought about it, or about him. He wanted Harker to think well of him. If they had met differently they might have had good talk about coincidence and probability, perhaps in the Eagle & Child, when Moore wouldn't have taken Harker's notions so deeply into his own life. "No," he said, "I'll see them. Ruthie told me some of the things they've been writing. I'd like a chance to say a word back."

Harker shrugged. "I'd say you couldn't win with people like that. They have the last word, you know."

"Even so," Moore said.

"All right. I'll leave word they're permitted."

When Harker had gone Moore sat for a moment and decided he was being foolish. He hadn't really any desire at all to say a word back to them, but it had seemed like a brave thing to say to Harker. Well, he was committed to seeing them now, and he had no plan except to tell them as much of the truth as possible and to admit nothing about Gwen. He wished now that he had read the papers these last two days, and again he felt as if he were going into a critical class without preparation. Ruthie had been eager to believe the best, but these people wouldn't be; they would be more like Broderick.

There were three of them: a thin young man from an Oxford paper, a rather gentle looking man about Moore's own age from one of the wire services, and a woman from a London tabloid. At first glance he thought she was a man too. She was a squarish, stocky woman of about thirty-five in a pantsuit and necktie and low-cut shoes; her sand-colored hair was cut short like a man's. Moore assumed she was lesbian. A cameraman came in with them, a tall man with his camera slung around his neck. They pulled up chairs close to his bed and sat down, except for the cameraman, who kept moving slowly around the room, checking light and angles. They asked Moore first about funeral arrangements, and he told them the exact truth.

"Have you seen your wife's body since the night of the murder?" The question came from the London woman.

"Yes. To identify her so she could be released for burial."

"You mean at the mortuary?" the Oxford man asked.

"Yes."

"How did you get there?" He seemed surprised.

"They took me in a wheelchair."

"To the Central Police Station?"

"She was brought here to the mortuary. But I would have gone to the Central Police Station if I'd had to."

"Really?" said the London woman. "That would have been quite an excursion for someone in your condition."

"I suppose it would have been."

"Why didn't you want your daughter to identify her?" she asked.

"I was afraid of what she might see."

"So you could have made the trip across town, but you felt you couldn't make the trip to the States for your wife's funeral."

"That was the doctor's decision, not mine. Maybe I couldn't have made the trip across town either. Maybe they wouldn't have let me."

"I see," she said. "So it was fortunate for you that you could see her here. What did you feel when you saw her?"

"Oh, really now," the wire service man said, and the Oxford man looked uncomfortable.

Moore stared at her, but she returned his look, unembarrassed. "I can't describe that," he said. "I suppose you might call it grief." No one spoke for a minute. Moore had the uneasy feeling that the cameraman had taken several pictures. The camera had no flash.

The Oxford man cleared his throat. "Is it really true, Professor Moore, that you had never seen Morgan or his daughter before you went to Wallingford?"

"Yes."

"And that you never talked to Morgan except for those few minutes in the pub?"

"Yes."

"And that you never saw his daughter except in the pub?"

Moore remembered Gwen's statement to Broderick that she had driven him to the George. "We talked for a while outside the pub and in her car when she drove me to the hotel."

"But did you see her in the hotel?" the London woman asked.

"No. She dropped me at the door."

"Oh, come now, Professor," she said. "She's an attractive young woman. You obviously found her interesting and she obviously returned the favor."

"Really? Who says so?"

"Everyone who saw the two of you at the pub, that's who."

"Well, then, I'm flattered. I'm old enough to be her father, you know."

"January and May," she said, "it's an old story. You and she drank together at the pub and she liked you enough to drive you home, but she dropped you at the door." Her voice was heavy with sarcasm.

"That's right," Moore said. He looked at her, then at the other two. None of them believe me, he thought, they all believe she came up to my room; they can see the lie even in the truth.

"How disappointing for you," the London woman said.

Moore disliked her enormously. "No, for you," he said, and then knew at once that he had made a mistake because her eyes glittered at him with malice.

"Professor Moore, what prompted you to go down to Wallingford?" It was the first question from the wire service man.

"I'd been there in the war. I was curious to see it again."

"Did you meet anyone there that you'd known in the war?"

"No, not that I know of." I never knew anyone there except Nancy, he thought, and the other little girl. I wonder whatever happened to her. Maybe I passed her in the street.

The Oxford man cleared his throat again. "We've heard a lot about how much Morgan hated Americans. From Wallingford people and from his daughter as well. Did you have any sense that he disliked you particularly?"

"No. It seemed a general dislike."

"Tell us," the London woman said, "do you see yourself as the victim of a mad killer?"

Moore couldn't hold back his anger. "No, I see my wife as the victim."

The Oxford man was clearly annoyed at the woman's interruption. "What do you make of the pelican business, Professor?"

"I don't make anything of it."

"Did Morgan express any religious views to you? Did he mention Christ at all? More particularly, did he ever use a phrase like 'the suffering Christ'?"

"Oh, for God's sake," the London woman said, "what about the suffering Christ?"

The Oxford man glared at her. "The pelican is a Christ symbol. The pelican's breast is bloody because he pecks at it, wounds himself. Morgan was found at the base of the pelican, you know."

"I know that," she said. "To use an Americanism, so what?"

"The suggestion has been made by someone here at Oxford that in some mad way Morgan may have been religiously motivated. That he saw himself as a kind of Christ figure. That he went to the pelican after the killing to—to report, as it were. Perhaps to pray."

The London woman stared at him unbelievingly. "I've never before heard such dreary nonsense," she said.

"What do you think of that notion, Professor Moore?" said the wire service man.

"I think he was unbalanced," Moore said. "If he was, anything is possible."

"Rot," the London woman said, "rot and balls."

"Why rot and balls?" the Oxford man said angrily. "People have been killed before this for religious reasons. And died for them too."

"I don't deny there are religious fanatics," she said, slapping her note-book down into her lap. "But I'm from London. That's the real world, you know. Down there they kill for money or drugs or sex, and generally you don't have to look beyond those things."

"But if those things don't apply?" the Oxford man said.

"Then you go beyond. But they almost always do apply. You're dream-ers here in Oxford. Go by the statistics and you'll be right nine times out of ten. Show me sex or money or drugs and I'll show you a motive, nine times out of ten."

The three men looked at her, and Moore thought he could see his own dis-taste reflected in their faces. She hates us all, he thought. She doesn't hate me any more than she does them, but I'm the vulnerable one, I'm the one she can get at. The hate comes off her like body odor, and they can smell it too.

The wire service man stood up. "I think that's enough," he said, and the Oxford man nodded and stood up too.

"I don't think it's enough," the London woman said, "I don't think it's nearly enough."

"I'm sorry," Moore said, "but I'm very tired."

The London woman looked at Moore, then at the other two. "I see," she said, "suddenly you're all very tired." She stood up and stuffed her note-book into her jacket pocket. "Well, I'm not tired. Come along, Jack." The cameraman came away from the window he had been lounging against and the four of them left, the London woman marching ahead alone.

It had been stupid to see them, Moore thought. They believed now what they had believed before they talked to him. He had given them noth-ing new to write about, and he had not given them any reason to change what they had already written. He had proved nothing except that with luck and evasiveness you can keep from telling an outright lie. And Harker was right, of course. They would have the last word. He hardly dared to won-der what the London woman's last word would be.

He was moving slowly over to the chair by the window when George Norton came in. He and Moore were not really old friends, but they had worked together for ten years and their wives had gotten to know each other at department parties. They shook hands solemnly.

"What can I say, Jim?" said Norton.

"Nothing, George. There's nothing anyone can say. Thanks for all you've done for us, especially for Ruthie."

Norton brushed the thanks aside. "Anyone would have done it." He leaned against the windowsill and watched Moore carefully sit down. "You look as if you might break if you moved fast."

"I don't think we'll find that out unless I fall out of bed."

"I wired the university. Everyone sends condolences and so on. I imagine you'll be getting a lot of mail in a few days. The dean wired back that he'd put you on sick leave for next term."

"I hope to be navigating before then, George."

"Take the time anyway. You've got more to recover from than a sore back."

"Yes," Moore said, "that's so. It might be better to be working, though."

"Maybe you should travel around a little. Go south for a while. Go down to Ruthie's for Christmas."

"Yes, I suppose I'll do that at least." Old habits of responsibility stirred in him for the first time. "What's been happening to my class, George?"

"Don't worry about it. We made do. Your kids did a lot of research in the Bodleian. It's okay. They understood."

"What are they saying back at Corpus, George?"

"They're not saying anything, Jim. Except how sorry they are. They don't believe the rot they read in the papers. Some of them are outside now, waiting to see you."

Moore leaned stiffly back in the chair. Norton seemed wholly sincere, but Norton was a very bland person. He always said exactly what was expected of him, and yet he always seemed to mean it. "When do you all leave for home?" Moore asked.

"Saturday. What can I do for you before we go?"

"Send my clothes and suitcases over, I guess. Could you just ship the books and other stuff home?" Norton nodded. "Maybe you could send my big anthology over."

They talked for a few minutes more, then Norton got ready to leave. He held out his hand formally to Moore and Moore shook it. "I want to say I'm sorry, Jim. I want to say it for myself and for the other people in the program who aren't here. I really do speak for all of them."

Moore was sure he did. He could almost see Norton calling a meeting in the Junior Commons Room and telling them all he was going to Radcliffe and wanted to speak for all of them. With someone else it might have been a gesture, but not with Norton. He might be bland, but he was a gentleman.

As Norton left, Mulqueen and the blond girl came in. Moore shook hands with Mulqueen. "It's good of you to come," he said. He was surprised to hear his voice quiver, and he knew they noticed it. They pulled chairs over and sat in front of him, so that it was almost as if they were all in class together, and they talked small talk about the course and what they had been doing at the Bodleian.

After about ten minutes the blond girl, whose name Moore could not for the life of him remember, said, "Just the two of us are here because we thought the whole class would be a bit much for you. So we had a kind of election."

Mulqueen nodded. "We thought about finding something appropriate to put on a card or something. I mean something from the course. You know, about death and immortality. But we couldn't agree on anything. So I just want to say how sorry we all are." The blond girl nodded her head in agreement. She looked as if she might cry.

"Thanks," Moore said, "thanks, thank them all for me." He groped for words, but no words came. He put his hand out and Mulqueen shook it earnestly. "I'm glad you came instead of sending lines from somewhere." He started to say something more, but his voice wouldn't let him. He just sat there and nodded at them for a moment, and then they left.

Moore sat for a while, until the tightness had left his throat. He looked at his watch. It was not quite noon yet, but he was terribly tired, and the pain in his back seemed to be spreading up into his neck and shoulders. When his lunch came he ate a little of the crust off the shepherd's pie and drank a cup of tea and was dozing in the chair when Harker came in with a nurse.

Harker eyed him sharply. "You look done in."

"Too much company, Doctor."

"You mean the reporters? Well, you wanted your word with them. I expect you got more than you bargained for with the woman, though." He put out his hands to Moore and when Moore took them he pulled Moore slowly to his feet. "We're going to have a look at your back. I want you sitting on the bed for that." When Moore was settled on the edge of the bed Harker went behind him and in a moment Moore heard the snip of scissors. He felt the harness loosening across his chest and back and then he felt air on his back and shoulder blades. Harker's fingers touched here and there on his back, all around the spot that was numb yet kept sending out pain.

"Good," Harker said. "All right, Sister, let's wrap up the package again," and in a minute or two more the harness was back in place again. The nurse went out and Harker sat down in the bedside chair. "Yes," he said, "a tiresome person, that London woman. I must say she had devilish persistence, if that's what it takes to make a reporter. You can't imagine the questions she asked me about you."

"No," Moore said, "I'm sure I can't."

"You must have antagonized her somehow, though I shouldn't think it would take much to do that. She asked me if it was possible that your wound was self-inflicted. I told her that in my opinion such a thing was anatomically impossible. Then she wanted to know if it was medically possible for you to have gone down to the quad after you were wounded and then have gone back up to your rooms. I said it was so unlikely as to be impossible, or the next thing to it."

"My God," Moore said, "what was she getting at?"

"I've no idea, really," said Harker. "She seems a most bizarre woman. Lesbian, I should say, of the most aggressive sort. Very likely hates men on principle. Generically, as it were."

"I wonder what she'll write."

"Something monstrously unpleasant, I should think. Something a centimeter this side of libel." He looked at Moore, lowering his head to look over his spectacles. "Isn't that rather what you wanted?"

Moore was startled by the question. "What do you mean?"

"I mean only the most obvious thing in the world, Professor Moore. It doesn't take a psychiatrist to see that you've been punishing yourself ever since you came back to consciousness here. You could have delayed seeing Broderick, but you didn't. You were clearly disappointed that seeing your wife didn't involve discomfort and pain. You needn't have seen these reporters, but you did."

"There could be a lot of other reasons for these things," Moore said.

"No doubt there are. I'm talking about the main reason. The reason that is so obvious to an attending physician. Guilt over the death of a loved one."

Moore tried to keep his face impassive, but Harker's words stabbed into him as surely as Morgan's knife had done, and he thought, What smallness and grubbiness he must see in me.

But Harker's face showed nothing and his voice went quietly on. "May I say something to you about guilt and self-punishment? I've seen a good deal of guilt, Professor Moore. I spent a year in an emergency ward in London. I saw a good many deaths from car smashes and fires and other kinds of accidents. When a wife or husband was killed, the surviving spouse always blamed himself or herself for the accident. Sometimes in the most bizarre ways. It seemed to be a natural reaction. They almost always got over the guilt, though, on reflection. They generally came to see the accident as simply an accident. I was interested enough in the phenomenon to go to the case studies. At the time I agreed with them. I regarded the guilt as medically unhealthy. I think differently now, as I suggested yesterday. About accidents, I mean."

Moore looked at him. "You mean, no accidents, no coincidences, I suppose."

"I mean I think now that their feeling of guilt was a kind of awareness of the pattern of connection we were talking about. But it was an awareness that they lost. For whatever reasons."

"You can't mean you think it would be better for them to stay feeling guilty? Or better for me?"

Harker waved his hand as if a little impatient. "Words, words, Professor Moore. If the feeling of guilt leads to an awareness of pattern, then surely it's a good thing. If something is so, surely it's a good thing to know it."

"But you said yesterday that no one can know pattern on the basis of evidence."

"Words, words again. I said you couldn't infer pattern on the basis of evidence. I didn't mean you couldn't know it if you saw it, or saw part of it. I think that in the state of guilt after a death one is given a chance to see— to *see*, not to infer. The people I'm referring to had their chance to see and let it pass."

"And that brings us to my case," Moore said. "My guilt is my opportunity?"

Harker nodded. "One is never more aware of pattern than when one is able to look steadily at the marriage relationship, because that is the most subtle and interlocking of all human relationships. And I believe no one is better able to look at the marriage relationship than someone who has just had it taken away, like you. Your world has ended, you feel. But why? Because that relationship formed the basis of your whole existence. Everything was related to that, everything vibrated when that string was touched."

Moore did not say anything. It was as if Harker were probing at the wound in his back when he talked so calmly about the end of a relationship and the end of Moore's world. Moore felt pain he could hardly bring himself to bear. Finally he said, "If she had to die, I wish it had been some other way, some other place. A car accident back home, maybe. Something that didn't involve me so directly. Something I didn't really cause."

"Allow me to tell you that you would not feel significantly different if that were so," Harker said quickly. "Believe me, the feelings of guilt and responsibility would be the same, because the feelings come from seeing part of the pattern. From seeing that one is totally involved with the marriage partner, so that anything that happens to one partner must have its connections with the other. It's like the A and B of mathematics. Multiply A and B and you get AB, a single substance. Nothing can happen to A without there being a connection with B, and vice versa. The marriage union is like that multiplication."

"The two become one and so on," Moore said vaguely.

"No, I don't mean the biblical view of marriage," Harker said. "That's another dimension. I mean only the natural relationship between two people who have been married for some time. It's a remarkably complex and far-reaching relationship. It really is a total world. That's what I mean when I say that at in those rare moments when we can see into that world, we see something like the larger figure in the carpet. Marriage is the miniature of the larger world. And I don't even mean what is called a happy marriage, necessarily. A miserable marriage is just as intimate and just as good a model. The web is just as much there."

"All right," Moore said, "I feel guilt, I feel involvement, I feel I don't know what. Loss, I guess. Yes, you're right, I've lost my world."

"No," Harker said, "you've lost your model. You may have found your world. That depends on you."

Moore looked at him wearily. "You don't think I should be like those people in the emergency ward. You don't think I should get over my guilt. Is that it?"

"I'm not talking about should and shouldn't," Harker said quietly. "I'm talking about is and may be. You've had an experience. You've seen something. What you make of it is up to you."

"So I may be just a guilt case, like the people in the emergency ward, or I may be a different kind of case? I've never thought of myself as a case of any kind."

"We're all cases of one sort or another, Professor Moore. None of us is unique."

"You're an odd sort of physician, Dr. Harker."

"No more than you're an odd sort of don. We may both be odd sorts of men, of course. We're men first, you know, before we're anything else."

"Yes, so Newman said. Men first. Gentlemen first, if possible. Men who never inflict pain. You know the definition?"

Harker nodded. "Oh, yes. A good definition, as far as it goes. And of course Newman only meant it as the height of natural courtesy. He didn't mean there was nothing better."

"I don't know about that," Moore said. "It's been a long time since I read him." He sat silent for a while. Then he said, "I tried to convince my daughter Ruthie that her mother's death was an accident. I thought it would be better for her. Less painful, I mean."

"Yes, of course," Harker said. He didn't seem surprised at Moore's shift of thought. And it really *was* an accident," Moore said, "I mean an accident in the usual sense. No one plotted to kill her. It was just a combination of things. Part of your pattern."

"You're in rather an odd position," Harker said. "In most cases of accidental death it's the members of the family who try to show the survivor that he wasn't at fault. He has the luxury, as it were, of wallowing in his guilt feelings. You've been denied that by the—ambiguous nature of your wife's death."

It was the closest reference Harker had made to Helen's death, and again Moore wondered what Harker really thought of the whole affair. In all that Harker had said in the past few days there had nowhere been a personal note. After a moment Moore said, "Maybe that's why I don't see the pattern that you say people in my position see."

"I don't mean to press the point," Harker said, "but you *do* see the pattern. That's what your feelings of guilt mean. Or feelings of responsibility. That's really a better word." He stood up. "I think it's time you had some rest. You've had rather a full morning."

Moore sat on the edge of his bed staring down at his bare feet. "I loved my wife," he said. The words jumped out of him unexpectedly, and the past tense startled him.

"I'm sure you did," Harker said, and then he went out.

But not enough, Moore thought, not enough. Not enough to see her through her menopause, not enough to stay away from crotches for a month, not enough, just not enough. Guilt, he thought, oh, yes, I feel guilt. And then he thought, Harker says the guilt means seeing the pattern. All right, what pattern? He lay back in the bed and propped his head on the pillow and stared at the window. Guilt, responsibility, involvement. A and B, AB. How am I involved with her death? But the answer was simple, of course. Broderick and the London lesbian had already said it. What Helen couldn't give him he had gone elsewhere to find, and finding it he had found Morgan too, and Morgan had found Helen. And behind that simple pattern was the other pattern of coincidence that had dovetailed into his and Helen's pattern. The pattern of Morgan and Lane and Nancy and Gwen. It was as if a writer had lost his grip and told two of his stories together instead of separately. If I hadn't been dissatisfied with Helen I never would have come to England alone, much less gone to Wallingford alone. And Morgan's hatred of Americans would have stayed dormant, because he would never have seen what he saw. Oh, yes, there's a pattern, Moore thought, a set of interlocking events. For want of a nail a shoe was lost, and a horse lost, and a battle lost, and so on. It started with two girls sitting on a fence outside of Wallingford thirty years ago. Or at least that's where I pick up the pattern. And that's what the world is like, Harker says, a web of interlocking personal patterns.

He closed his eyes, very tired. I wonder why Harker is so pleased to discover a pattern like that, he thought. I believe it, or half believe it, but I don't find it comforting at all. In fact, he thought, opening his eyes in surprise, I don't really find it even meaningful; it still seems only mathematical to me. And again he thought of Johnson's remark: everything looks connected if you look backwards. The trick is to know what's connected if you look forward. History is easy, but whatever is the reverse of history isn't. He fell asleep trying to determine the reverse of history but finally gave it up and dreamed of the capital letters A and B. Abel, Baker, Charlie, Dog, he said in his dream. And then Abel, Baker, Abelbaker, Charliedog, and down through the alphabet to HJ. Helen, James, he thought, Helenjames, but the combination seemed odd even in his dream. And yet they were next to each other. An odd coincidence, he said to Harker in his dream, but only mathematical, not meaningful. Just a matter of luck.

Just before he woke up an hour or so later he dreamed that he was in the front Corpus quad, naked and cold, standing before the golden pelican. From beyond the massive front door he heard a chatter of sound that he finally made out to be voices. A moment after that he realized that they were shouting his name, and then the great door began to open. He ran behind the pedestal of the pelican to hide, though he was sure that it would only be a minute or two before they found him. When he awoke, shivering beneath his blanket, he knew he had been thinking of the reporters, and for the first time it became real to him that he was a news item, that strangers were actually writing about him and that other strangers were reading about him. He felt slightly sick to his stomach and yet strangely excited, as if for some reason he had agreed to spend a night in a haunted house. After a while he rang for a nurse and asked her for a cup of tea and the local paper, but then before he opened it he wondered if reading it would simply be more punishment. He couldn't decide that.

A glance at the front page showed him that his story was still news. He hadn't caught any of the reporters' names, but after a line or two of the story he was sure it had been written by the diffident Oxford man who had interviewed him. The headline to the story read "Corpus Christi Enigma Darkens," and the story began, "A new dimension was added today to the mystery of the Corpus Christi deaths." The new dimension, which the writer thought might well be symbolized by the ancient golden pelican with its bloody breast, was the possibility suggested by a "well-known authority" that Morgan had been moved to murder out of religious motives. The well-known authority suggested that the murder might have been sacrificial, a kind of ritual killing, though of course at the moment the reason for such a sacrifice was obscure. One of the most puzzling aspects of the case, the writer noted, was the incredible strength and energy required for a partially crippled man to do the things he had done. "But remarkable physical feats are regularly reported from around the world and are ascribed to religious beliefs." The writer cited the cases of Indian shamans walking in fire and lying on beds of nails.

Morgan's body, he reminded his readers, had been found beneath the effigy of the pelican. "Why there?" he asked rhetorically, "Why there of all possible places?" He hinted at the possibility that Morgan had intended to die there beneath the pelican. "Although he did not technically commit suicide, it is just possible that he felt his work was finished and that it was therefore time to die. The literature of religious hysteria lists many instances of self-induced death. Indeed, certain North American Indian tribes regularly practised voluntary death when old age or illness threatened." Of course, the writer had to admit, on the basis of what they knew of Morgan's life there was no evidence that he was a religious man. Friends of the dead man could not remember when they had last seen him in church. His daughter, when asked about her father's religious views, had replied that he had not been to church since his wife's funeral three years before.

Moore's hands holding the paper began to shake at this point. He smelled danger. But as his eyes leaped ahead he saw that the Oxford man, intent on his religious thesis, had missed the connection between the dead wife and Helen. The connection between the dead wife, he thought suddenly, and the other dead wife. Moore let the paper drop into his lap and stared at the wall. It was an accident, he had told Ruthie, and it *had* been. Helen had been killed because she happened to be there. But suddenly Moore was sure that she had been killed because she was his wife. "I will be even with him, wife for wife": Iago's words burned in his mind. Morgan had come into that dark room to wait for Moore, and had found a woman he knew must be Moore's wife, and he had evened himself with Moore, wife for wife. Or evened himself with Lane, it didn't matter which. Moore felt tears streaming down his face. Morgan had found Helen by accident, but he had not killed her by accident. He had killed her to punish Moore. He hadn't stabbed Moore when Moore came into the room. He had waited till Moore had lain down next to Helen and had pulled her over onto her back and had seen the arm flap and knew she was dead. Then it was complete for him, Moore thought, when I knew. That was when he came after me. When I rolled onto Helen. When I knew she was dead.

When the crying spell was over he lay for a long time, till the tears dried on his face. Then he picked up the paper again and read, "But though there is no overt evidence of religiosity in Morgan's life, the deepest religious feelings, whether orthodox or fanatic, exist in the hushed life of the soul." Moore put the paper down. Maybe in some oblique way the reporter was right, he thought, more right than he knew. Something had certainly gone on in Morgan's soul, something that had wanted Helen and him dead. An eye for an eye, a tooth for a tooth. Why not call it religious motivation? That was as good a name as any other. It was even possible that Morgan *had* gone directly to the pelican for some reason. Maybe just to sit down and rest on the step, Moore thought. He must have been very tired. Maybe just to wait until Helen and he were discovered. He must have known he couldn't get away, if he even wanted to. It must have been getting almost daylight by then, Moore thought, and maybe he had sat there, or lain there, or stood there, thinking "I've killed them, I've killed the fucking American, and now I'm even." Or something like that. And then the stroke had hit him, or the heart attack, whatever it was, and it was all over, and he was out of it, and Nancy was out of it, and Helen was out of it. I wish we were all out of it, Moore thought, but he knew he didn't really mean that. He stared at the venetian blinds as if they were bars in a prison window, stared at them until they half hypnotized him and he fell into a doze. But he kept seeing the pelican, and Helen looking at it and saying "Sleepy old pelican, sleepy old bird," and he could see the blood on the pelican's breast and it was Helen's blood.

He woke up and rubbed his face where the tears had dried and stiffened, then got slowly out of bed. Picking up his pipe and tobacco, he saw his poetry anthology on the bedside table. Norton must have sent it over and someone had put it there while he was asleep. He picked it up and went over to the chair by the window. He knew what he wanted to read, and he knew what Harker would say about it. He wanted to read "The Rime of the Ancient Mariner." He had never really liked it as well as some other Coleridge poems, but he wanted to read it now. Like calls to like, he thought, or was it deep calls to deep? He wanted to read it again because it was about a man who had committed what seemed to be a small sin and was visited with an enormous punishment.

Moore read the poem slowly and carefully, as if it were a coded message, but at the end it remained as cryptic as ever. The mariner had killed the albatross for no reason and had been punished for it in a way that defied logic. Moore could say no more about the poem now than before, except that now he phrased his conclusion differently. The mariner had inflicted pain. He was punished because he had not been a gentleman. But then Moore recalled his retort to the London reporter: I am not the victim; Helen is. It seemed the height of egotism to believe that he was being punished when he was alive and she was dead. Harker was right: he was punishing himself, and not only for a specific act but for the general failure of his life. When he had taken his sedative and finally got to sleep that night he dreamed of Newman. He saw a tall spare man with an ascetic face who came out of the archway of Oriel College and went around the curve in King Edward Street past Corpus Christi. He turned down the path between Merton and Corpus Christi. When he got beneath Moore's window he looked up and said something that Moore could not hear. Then the man went down to the river and sat down on a bench. When the swans came drifting by he raised his hand over them in a kind of benediction.

The next morning he asked the nurse who brought him breakfast for the London papers. This time he did not wonder whether he would be punishing himself by reading what the London woman had written. He assumed he would be. But he had a driving curiosity to fill out the picture of himself as others saw him. It was as if he had been a kind of settled substance at home, a mixture but a rather familiar mixture, because no one had seemed to look at him carefully except himself. But since he had come to Oxford he had been walking in a kind of fun house of mirrors. It seemed to him that for the first time he had been made to look at himself from the outside, as Helen saw him, and Gwen, and Broderick, and Ruthie, and Harker, and Norton, and Mulqueen. And even Morgan. It was an urge for completion that made him page through the London papers. Sitting in the chair by the window, he dropped the *Times* on the floor without looking at it and skimmed the tabloids.

The London woman's story was in the second one he looked at. The headline read "A Detective-Story Look At The Corpus Mystery." The author was H. J. McCardle. The sub-heading of the first paragraph was "Facts Presented But With Misdirection." The story began, "A standard ploy in detective fiction is to present basic facts with an implied interpretation of these facts which the reader does not notice. The reader is led to accept as facts things that really are assumptions by witnesses. The basic facts are never allowed to stand alone, because if they did the reader would at once make the right interpretation." She cited Poe's "Murders in the Rue Morgue" and other examples from Conan Doyle and John Dickson Carr. "As an exercise in critical thinking, let us look at the Corpus mystery as if it were a bit of detective fiction. Let us see if we can dissociate fact from the interpretation of fact by witnesses." She went on to tell the whole story as it had come to be accepted, what she called the "authorised standard version" of the story. An aging American don went down to Wallingford from Oxford, met a local man who hated Americans, spent some time with the man's daughter, went back to Oxford. A few days later the don's wife arrived in Oxford. That night she was murdered by the Wallingford man, who also wounded the don. The murderer then left the rooms and died of heart failure near the Corpus pelican.

"Now the accepted interpretation of this sequence of incidents is that the Wallingford man, his mind dimmed by a series of strokes, somehow came to Oxford and madly vented his hatred of Americans on the don and his wife. But what are the unadorned facts, especially the facts of what occurred at Oxford?" The facts were, she said, that the Wallingford man had been seen by the porter and had asked the way to the don's rooms. That the don's wife had been stabbed to death and the don wounded. And that the Wallingford man's body had been found in the quad near the pelican effigy. "Is there no other interpretation of these facts?" she asked. "It has been assumed that Morgan committed the murder because he came into the college and because he was found dead with the murder weapon beside him. But is there a witness to the actual murder? There is, of course. The don. But let us look at the facts without presuppositions, the facts only, as they exist without the colouring judgement of witnesses. What do we actually have? We have a man and his wife in a room and the wife murdered. Who is the logical suspect? The husband, of course. Who generally kill wives? Husbands. Nine times out of ten." Motive, method, opportunity, McCardle went on, they were the sacred triad of detective fiction. And who was the most likely suspect on the basis of this triad? The husband, of course. Motive: simply that he was the husband; statistics showed that husbands were most likely to have murderous motives in cases where their wives were murdered; that was why they were always the primary suspects. Additionally, the husband in this case had spent an evening a few days before with an attractive young woman who, just coincidentally, was the daughter of the alleged murderer. That was an unadorned fact open to a number of possible interpretations. (Moore could almost see the London woman's eyes glitter at this point; no reader could miss what she meant by "possible interpretations.") As for Method and Opportunity, who had a better opportunity or an easier way of doing the murder? The husband's wound and the death of the Wallingford man could be explained in a variety of ways. There was no need, for example, to assume that the wife's murder and the husband's wounding had occurred at almost the same moment, and that the two assaults had been carried out by the same person. Suppose that the don had stabbed his wife and then met Morgan and was stabbed by Morgan as the result of some sort of an argument in the quad. The attending physician had said that the don could not have gone from his rooms to the quad and back again in his wounded condition. But suppose he had been wounded in the quad? That would have cut his trip in half. There was more: the possibility of collusion between the don and Morgan, or between the don and someone else, with Morgan as the scapegoat (what the Americans call "the fall guy"). When she had exhausted these other possibilities, she concluded: "In brief, if we look at the facts as facts, we see that other interpretations are possible, some of them even probable." The story ended with an ironic disclaimer, perhaps because of an editor's fear of the libel laws. "This is, of course, only an exercise in detective story logic. Readers are invited to supply their own interpretations of the facts."

It was a clever piece, Moore thought. It was the kind of thing you could write if you didn't care anything about the people involved. He found himself echoing Harker: if you hated one of them generically, if you didn't know that you were somehow connected to those people even if you didn't know them. It was an ugly piece, an exercise in malice, and he was glad that Ruthie would never see it, though Gwen might. But Moore was not moved by it, not shaken as he had been by the Oxford man's story. He could find no accidental truth in it. Perhaps wives who were killed were killed by their husbands nine times out of ten, but he couldn't even imagine himself killing Helen in order to be with Gwen, as the story clearly suggested. He might not be unique, but here at least he escaped statistics. If Helen was dead it was not because he had wished her dead, not even in the darkest and foggiest part of his mind. Maybe I'm beginning to come out the other side of my guilt feelings, he thought. But then he had a momentary vision of the years to come. He saw himself carrying his secret sorrow tinged with guilt like a lone pilgrim with a heavy knapsack. The man whom people finally stopped inviting to parties because he gave off gloom. The man who maneuvered his life so that he was always alone. The man who spent whatever years were left to him remembering and reliving a single incident and what had preceded it. The man who found himself endlessly interesting long after everyone except perhaps his daughter had forgotten him. The man whose obituary notice in the paper would surprise the people who used to know him, because somehow they thought he had died a long time before. The vision was gone in a moment, but he thought it was a true vision, not a distorting mirror, and the vision disgusted him.

Then it was the day of the funeral and Moore awoke early. He made his way to the bathroom and for the first time seriously washed and shaved. He found his pajamas and robe in the closet and put them on and had his breakfast in the chair by the window. He meant to stay there until Ruthie called him after the funeral.

"You can call it punishment if you like," he told Harker when Harker came in, "but it will make me feel a part of it."

Harker only shrugged. "As long as you're aware of what you're doing," he said. He glanced at the London tabloid from the day before where Moore had left it on the window ledge.

"You've read that?" Moore nodded. "Nasty," Harker said, "but I should think she'd be finished now. I can't imagine what more she could find to say."

"It doesn't matter," Moore said, "I'm finished with them now. Finished reading them and finished talking to them."

"Good," Harker said. "Concentrate on important things."

When Harker had gone Moore wrote letters mechanically, thanking everyone who had sent condolences. He did this until noon, then dawdled through his lunch. From then until four o'clock he sat with a crossword puzzle in his lap, but mostly he stared out the window. Then it was ten in the morning back home and he sat up straighter in the chair and turned his mind to the funeral home: the rows of folding chairs, the heavy odor of flowers, the hushed voices. He didn't try to visualize faces, nor the casket at the front of the room. He wondered whether Ruthie had asked to have the casket closed. At four-thirty he imagined them leaving for the cemetery, and he followed the procession along the route he knew they would take. He didn't know what to do about the weather, so he made it warm and clear. At five-fifteen he tried to visualize the burial, but couldn't. He could see the canopy, but only from the outside, as if from the gravel road. Helen going under the earth was unimaginable for him. At five-thirty he thought it must be over and he got up stiffly and went over to the bed near the phone. He was finishing his dinner when the phone rang at ten past six.

"Dad? Dad, this is Ruthie." The connection was good and her voice was clear and natural. "How are you?"

"I'm fine, honey. How did everything go?"

"Everything was okay, Dad. We've just come back to the house. Everyone sends regards."

"What kind of day is it there, Ruthie? I mean the weather."

"It's bright and sunny. There were so many people there, Dad, you'd hardly believe it. Lots of people from the university."

"That's nice," Moore said. He'd gotten several questions ready beforehand to ask her, and he was thinking of them. "Was the casket closed?"

"Yes, Dad. You told me to decide. I thought it was better."

"Good. Ruthie, there's a little tree that I planted out in front. How is it doing?"

"Tree? What tree?"

"Out in front. Beside the driveway. You can see it from the front room."

"I'm in the kitchen, Dad. Just a minute." She must have turned her head away because her voice was fainter. He heard her say, "Jim, go look at the little tree out by the driveway." He heard Jim's voice say something and then she said, "Dad wants to know how it looks. I don't *know* why." In a minute her voice came through clearly again. "Jim says it looks fine, Dad, a little scrawny but okay."

They talked for a few minutes more, small talk. Names of people who were there. What the priest had said about Helen. Moore was relieved that Ruthie seemed in control of herself. It wasn't until just before they hung up that her voice quavered. "I'll write you more about everything," she said. "Jim and the baby and I will be leaving for Virginia in a day or two. I guess we'll just shut up the house."

"It'll be all right."

"I hate to go away from here so soon," she said, and he knew now that she was at the edge of tears. "But there's nothing more I can do."

"No, you go, honey. And give my love to Jim and the baby. I'll be home soon, maybe two or three weeks. Don't worry about anything. Just go home." It was very important for her to go home and resume her own life. She would have to do without Helen now. It was better for her to get out of that house that was so much Helen's house, where very table and dish and knick-knack gave off Helen's presence.

"Write me, Dad." She was crying now. "Write me."

"I will, I will." His own voice was beginning to shake and his eyes stung. He hung up and sat down heavily on the bed. He hadn't realized he was standing. It was over. But of course it wasn't really over at all. All that evening while the sky darkened over the building he could see from the window he kept seeing the canopy and kept looking at his watch and kept thinking, Now she's been buried for two hours, four hours, six hours; the canopy must be down by now, and the grave filled in. Again he asked the nurse for a sleeping pill and that night, when he finally slept, he dreamed of open places, wide places: the parking lot at the local shopping mall, the outfield at Tiger Stadium, the river under the Bluewater Bridge at Port Huron where it opened out into the vastness of Lake Huron.

The next several days went quietly by, identical. He had no visitors now except Harker, who told him every day that the healing was going well. Harker said nothing more about coincidence, or responsibility, or guilt. Perhaps he was waiting for Moore to bring those things into the open again; in fact, the more that Moore thought about it the more he was sure that that was the case. Harker had not been merely chatting about these things; he clearly believed them to be important, and he just as clearly believed that what he had to say about them was true. It was hard to dispute with a true believer when you believed in so little yourself; Moore told himself he was keeping an open mind about Harker's notions, but he knew it was more complicated than that. The truth was that sometimes he believed and sometimes he didn't, and for the present he preferred to be as nearly mindless as possible, to muffle his mind almost completely except when he was asleep.

He could feel strength coming slowly back in his arms and legs, and he directed his consciousness to those parts of himself; he spent a good part of the days walking, first in his room and then later in the corridor, reveling in his physical strength as if he were training for a decathlon. He read letters from friends, but casually and without real attention, since he knew they could have nothing important to say about Helen's death, and once in a while in the evenings he walked down the corridor to the television room and watched British situation comedies, but never the news. He didn't read the newspapers at all. At night he dreamed of Helen, although almost never directly. Mostly he dreamed of change, change of all sorts, but usually the change of seasons. He had never been aware of trees and flowers except in the most general kind of way—or so he had always thought—but now often in the mornings as he stared out at the bleak building across the way from him he found himself remembering dreams of the flowering fruit trees that lined the streets of the bland neighborhood that had been his and Helen's. He dreamed of them in their first flowering in May, the plums and quinces and crab apples with their clouds of soft pinks and whites and lavenders, and he dreamed of the lilacs and the forsythias, as they were in May, before their summer green, as if his dreaming would prevent the change. But most often he dreamed of the lake and the river. When he had taken Ruthie as a child to watch the freighters from Windmill Pointe to Belle Isle he had only been repeating his own childhood in her, repeating his own father in himself. Now he dreamed of the first freighters of the season, in April, heading upriver to Duluth or Superior. He dreamed of the ice forming in the fall and early winter, thin in December, solid then until late March. He dreamed of standing at the foot of Woodward Avenue in the last days of winter, watching the ice breaking up, seeing the ice islands carried downriver by the current, under the bridge that led to Canada. He dreamed of telling Ruthie again what his father had told him: every drop of water you see here will find its way to the Atlantic, a truth that he had always felt to be somehow symbolic. Twice he dreamed of the locust tree he had planted. Once it seemed to have grown incredibly, and once he was sure it was dead.

Two weeks after the funeral Harker told him he could walk outside. When he went out for the first time he spent most of the day sitting on a bench, simply watching the traffic on the Woodstock Road. The next day he walked a little farther, around the wing of the building his room was in. The building he had been staring at for so long was the Eye Hospital. Slowly he explored the grounds of the Infirmary, a little bit each day. At the end of a week he could walk more than a mile, he judged, without tiring very much, though he still could not walk naturally. The harness of bandages kept him stiff-backed now, so that he strolled the grounds like a military cadet on parade.

He found himself thinking of Gwen quite often now. Since he no longer read the papers he had the impression that the publicity had faded and he wondered how she had survived it all. Because that was what they were, he thought, survivors. He wondered how she passed the time, and even how she measured the time passing. He could measure it by his medical progress, but she hadn't even that to go by. He tried to see her tidying up the parlor and tending the roses, but he couldn't. He wondered if she ever stopped at the Fox and Grape any more, or whether that was closed to her now by conversations that stopped when she walked in and faces that turned away. Perhaps she went anyway, out of balkiness, Moore thought. One night he decided to write her. He didn't know her address, but he thought a letter addressed to Ms. Gwendolen Morgan, Wallingford, would reach her.

He wrote, Dear Gwen, then sat for a long while staring at the page. Finally he threw it away. It isn't that I can't find words to say what I want to say, he thought, it's just that I don't know what I want to say. Maybe I don't want to say anything at all. Maybe she doesn't either. He wondered if she had tried to write him, sitting at the roll top desk in the parlor, staring at the fireplace. He thought perhaps she had, and had given up, like him, thinking, After what's happened, what good are words?

Two weeks later, on a heavy morning of damp sunshine, Harker told him he was to be released. They had gone through the ritual examination again and Harker had reduced the harness of bandages to a kind of bandolier that extended from Moore's back over his right shoulder and down under his arm. His chest, scrubbed clean by a nurse, felt raw and chilly where the bandages had been for so long.

"Yes, I think we shall let you go in a day or so," Harker said. "I shall get up a record of what we've done here and you can pass it on to your own physician at home. There's no medical reason for your staying here any longer."

"I suppose I should be glad," Moore said, "but somehow I'm not." They were sitting in their usual positions, Moore on the edge of his bed, Harker in the chair. "I guess I've grown to like it here."

"Grown used to it, rather," Harker said. "Convalescing people are much like children, Professor. They become accustomed to routine, and it makes them feel secure. Later on, when they're well, they're able to face the variety of life outside. Leaving a hospital is a good deal like growing up."

Moore nodded. "I suppose that's it. I feel as if I'm going out into the big world for the first time. In a way I suppose I am."

"Yes. There will be a period of adjustment, no doubt. Perhaps you'll be like an awkward juvenile for a bit. I can give you something to ease you over the worst times if you like."

"You mean tranquilizers?"

"That's a vague term, Professor. What I give you will be designed to ease the muscle tension in your back, which fatigue and anxiety are sure to increase. But no doubt it will work on your mind as well. Very likely I could prescribe something directly for your mind that would ease your back as well. You're convalescing from a psychic as well as a physical wound, after all. They're obviously connected. As a matter of fact, for all practical purposes they're a single wound."

Moore said nothing for a moment, staring down at his feet in the shabby old slippers. Then he said, "I've had the feeling for some time now that they were connected. I mean connected in more than the usual way. It seemed too freakish to talk about though."

"Ah, but they're not connected in more than the usual way. If anything is unusual it's that you see the connection. Your wife's death and your back wound occurred almost simultaneously. You might say that you were doubly traumatised, in mind and body. I prefer to say simply that you received a single shock, part of which your body took in and part of which your mind took in. What you lost with your wife's death was after all part physical and part spiritual. Your reaction to that loss is on both levels. I can only guess, of course, but I should say that if somehow you hadn't been wounded, you would have found some way to wound yourself, as a way of registering the physical part of your loss."

"I don't mean with a knife, necessarily. I mean that you might well have developed a physical ailment of some kind. A heart attack, a stroke, something of that sort. It's not at all uncommon. Grieving people nearly always grieve physically as well as emotionally."

"It's a strange combination, isn't it?" Moore said. "I mean the combination of body and mind."

"Yes," Harker said, "and one of the things that makes it strange is that we talk about it always in the wrong terms, as we're doing now as a matter of fact. Body and mind, soul and body, and so on. Always sets of oppositions."

"The joke they used to teach in logic classes," Moore said. "What is mind? No matter. What is matter? Never mind."

"Exactly. As long as we continue to use those oppositions we're bound by them. You're only puzzled by your so-called connected wounds because you think of them as oppositions. How can your back hurt your mind?

How can your mind hurt your back? If you could think of your mind and your back as simply aspects of a single entity you would see that they are intimately related, and that if one is changed the other is necessarily changed with it."

"You're not a Christian Scientist, I suppose?"

"If I were, Professor, I shouldn't have treated your wound at all. I should simply have prayed for you. And needless to say, I shouldn't be a physician at all. No, I treat physical ailments because they are obviously real. But it's become clear to me in recent years that they are never simply physical. And the reverse is true as well: mental wounds are never simply mental."

A term had been floating in Moore's mind just out of his reach and now he grasped it. "Holistic medicine," he said, "is that what you're talking about?"

"I'm associated with it, for want of something better. It's a step in the right direction, because it insists on the mind-body relationship, but it doesn't pretend to understand that relationship; it's purely pragmatic. And it's still mired in the old sets of oppositions, the ghost in the machine and so on. It hasn't discovered the truth that man *is* a ghostly machine; it can't make that identification; it could rid itself of the oppositions by compounding them, but it won't. It won't call water water; it insists that it's part oxygen and part hydrogen."

"But what happens when you compound the oppositions?"

"Then you see man as a single substance. A great deal follows from that."

"A single substance," Moore repeated. "You mean monism, I suppose. Everything is either all spirit or all matter?"

"I do indeed mean monism, Professor, but I don't mean either-or; I mean both. The water isn't either hydrogen or oxygen; it's both. It follows that no illness can be either simply organic or simply psychic, nor any wound, for that matter. An illness is an illness of the substance, whether it manifests itself in cardiac arrest or hallucinations."

"I suppose I can understand that as a theoretical concept," Moore said, "but I can't visualize it, and I can't see how it would mean anything in a practical kind of way."

"Perhaps not," Harker said. "And yet your whole life, and everything that you call practical, is governed by a theoretical concept, the theory of oppositions. The very grief you feel for your wife is shaped by that theoretical concept."

"I don't know what you mean by that."

"Wouldn't it be true to say, Professor, that you feel you didn't love your wife spiritually enough, that you were too much preoccupied with her body?" He held up his hand as if to prevent Moore from speaking, but Moore had not meant to speak. "Forgive me— I'm not referring to anything you may have done or not done with the young woman in Wallingford whom the papers have played up so much. I'm referring merely to a feeling that most men have when they have lost their wives."

"Yes," Moore said, "I feel that, I feel that very much."

"Well, there you are," Harker said. "The oppositions again, body and spirit, mind and matter."

"But what difference could it possibly have made if I'd thought differently? What if I *had* seen her as what you call a single substance? What then?"

"I can't say, Professor. I'm not a magician or a clairvoyant. I only say your life might have been essentially different."

Moore was silent for a long moment. Then he said, "Are you married, Doctor?"

"Oh yes," Harker said.

"Then you'll understand what I'm going to ask you."

Harker nodded. "You want to know if I see my wife as a single substance and whether there is any practical difference between you and me."

"Something like that. I don't mean to be personal."

Harker took off his half glasses and tapped them gently on the arm of the chair; when he began to speak his eyes were wide and seemed to be looking at a point somewhere above Moore's head. "I'm not sure that anything I say will be very meaningful for you. One may live according to a concept different from other men's concepts and yet his life may seem no different from other men's lives, from the outside. I doubt that anyone I know marks me as much different from anyone else. The difference is interior. Let me put it his way as a partial example. For my wife and me there is nothing in our lives that is specifically erotic or sexual, but at the same time nothing in our lives that is not generally erotic or sexual. We don't confine our sexuality to specific acts. By the same token, the specific acts of intercourse are never merely sensual. As far as possible we involve ourselves totally in all our activities. By choice we live in very small quarters so that we are nearly always together, and we touch a great deal. We are almost always within reach of each other. We never talk to each other without touching, and we are never simply silent during intercourse. As a matter of fact, we've discovered that that's perhaps the best time to pray together. That surprises you, I see."

Moore had been on the point of laughing, but something—something about Harker, he supposed—stopped him. "Yes, it surprises me. More than surprises me. Forgive me, but it seems almost grotesque."

"I'm sure it does. It would have seemed grotesque to me as well before I got beyond the old sets of oppositions. Now it seems to me the most natural thing in the world," Harker said.

Moore took in Harker's matter of fact tone and found himself stung by old premonitions and half thoughts. He might think Harker's notion of prayer grotesque, but he had only his own life to set against it as an argument. I don't like to abandon myself to sexuality, he might say, I sometimes flirt with the notion of a kind of Platonic love, I believe my love is more than sexual, or at least someone else does, and I want to think she's right. But all he finally said to Harker was, "No offense, Dr. Harker, but I don't think you and I mean the same thing by sex."

"No offense taken, Professor Moore," Harker said, "but I don't think you and I mean the same thing by prayer. Prayer isn't just words, you know, any more than charity is. That's why we have rituals. Words alone won't do. Prayer is movement, of the mind or of the body, ideally of both."

"Well, I suppose I'd agree that lovemaking is a ritual," Moore said. "People even buy manuals to improve their rituals."

"People buy manuals about mechanics, you mean," Harker said. "But lovemaking isn't mechanics, unless you insist on isolating the body and concentrating on it. When the mystics tell us that the union with God is a sexual union you surely don't imagine that they're talking about mechanics? Surely they could use the image only because they had experienced lovemaking as more than mechanics." He paused for a moment. "Love is action of the single substance."

"Well," Moore said, "I've never thought of the mystics as very much like us. Or at least like me."

"But then what *are* they like?" Harker said patiently. "They're human, like us. If we share a human nature we surely share it for better and for worse. You don't think you share a nature with Hitler or Stalin, but of course you do. If you're proud to be of the same lineage as Shakespeare, you must admit kinship with the people who dropped the gas pellets at Auschwitz. If you didn't believe they were much like yourself you could hardly condemn them. You don't condemn a cat for torturing a mouse."

"All right," Moore said, "I agree about kinship, assuming there is such a thing as a common human nature. But we seem to have gotten away from prayer and sex."

Harker smiled. "Well, Professor, you've just proved my earlier point. The very terms you use show that you can't think of prayer as anything but spiritual and sexuality as anything but physical. Hydrogen and oxygen again, not water."

"All right," Moore said again, "I see that. Maybe I even understand that. But it's still an ideal."

"Exactly," Harker said, "an ideal. An understood ideal. Understanding is what makes the ideal possible. Once you've seen the ideal realized, you can't un-see it. As the lawyers say, you can't un-ring the bell once it's rung. Once you have knowledge you can never be ignorant again."

"That's so," Moore said, "but there's another side to that. You may know yourself well enough to know you can't ever reach the ideal. Then you're only committing yourself to pain."

Harker shook his head. "If there's an obverse to the sin of pride, Professor, you've just described it. Failure to try is surely worse than failure to succeed. By comparison, failure to succeed is a kind of victory. May I cite one of your countrymen? 'I am defeated all the time, yet to victory am I born.'" He looked at Moore in surprise, because Moore had suddenly found himself laughing.

"I'm laughing at your genius for coincidence," he said. "I was thinking of Emerson as you talked. The party of memory and the party of hope. And then you quoted him."

Harker smiled. "Perhaps you're like me. You go to Emerson for what you Americans call 'a pep talk.' But if there's a genius of coincidence I think we may safely say his name is neither Harker nor Moore."

Moore was silent for a while. He felt like an undergraduate again talking to a major professor except that he was not sure he wanted to know what the major professor had to tell him. "These oppositions," he said, "these wrong oppositions of body and soul, how did you ever get beyond them? Surely you were trained in that old concept, just like the rest of us?"

"Of, course, very rigorously. And clearly one does not simply replace one concept with another as if one were changing parts in a machine. The only way to truly accept a concept is to live by it, as we do with the old. To accept it as the ground on which we stand as we try to answer all questions. We do that by habit with the old set of oppositions. With the new concept it is necessary to discipline oneself, to be much more conscious of the concept than one ever was with the old. It involves training oneself in consciousness, training oneself to be constantly attentive to the concept and its implications. It's rather like having to speak a new language that is different in grammar and syntax from the old one; you must be careful not to slip back into the old easy language."

"This discipline, this constant alertness," Moore said slowly, "this applying of the concept—you talk as if these things were part of a religion."

"Of course," Harker said, "the most important part. The central theological concept of Christianity, the simple identity of body and soul. The meaning of the Incarnation, if you like."

"It's not the Christianity I know," Moore said. Then he added, "Or knew."

"No, it's not the large public Christianity of the churches. What I was taught—and you as well, I expect—was a rather jumbled version of the concept. I'm not scholar enough to know why it was lost, or even when. Somewhere in the early Middle Ages, I've been told, when most of the Fathers were Platonists. Whenever it was that the doctrine of the oppositions of body and soul became the dominant doctrine. I've heard it called a kind of modified Manichaeism, and I know that Aquinas tried to scuttle it. Or perhaps the doctrine of the oppositions always was the dominant doctrine, since it's a much easier doctrine to understand."

"And easier to live by, surely?"

"Are you so sure of that, Professor? Did it comfort you when your wife was killed?"

"You think your concept would comfort you if your wife should die?"

"Not the concept, perhaps, but the knowledge that one had tried to live by the concept. I can't say what I should feel. Grief, certainly, loss, the usual things. But I don't believe I should feel guilt, except the sense that I might have done better. But not your sort of guilt, the helpless feeling of having done wrong without the true knowledge of what it would have been to do right. One can't love simply with the mind, yet that's what one feels one should have done when one has loved much with the body. You were doomed by your concept to be guilty. I'm not."

Moore, his mind full of Helen, said nothing, and after a minute Harker stood up. "I've gone on too long, I think. I don't usually discuss these things. I thought perhaps in your circumstances you might find it worth thinking about. I can give you a few book titles if you like. Most of us began by reading them, usually by accident. Though as I've said, I don't believe in accident, or coincidence."

"I don't like the occult very much," Moore said. "And I'm sorry, what you've said seems occult to me."

Harker shrugged. "Everything we know was once occult," he said, "but I suppose you mean the secret societies and the spirit rappings and so on. I've no use for them either. But what I've been talking of isn't occult. It's only difficult."

"Anyway, it's too late for me," Moore said, "even if I were to believe it and try to practice it."

"Perhaps you'll have another chance," Harker said.

"Not with Helen."

"You really should read the books, Professor. People are not as separate as they seem to be. Perhaps on some level they're not really separate at all."

"What do you mean?" said Moore.

"I mean only that metaphysically we all participate in each other, or all participate together in something or someone else—or perhaps both. I think it very possible that we also participate in each other—at least on occasion—on the existential level as well. I believe my wife and I have experienced that participation. I know other people who say they experience it quite regularly—in fact have come to accept it as normal for them."

"That seems eerie to me," Moore said. "It's like saying we can change our identity, become someone else."

"It would be more accurate to say that we can merge our identity with another temporarily in order to participate in a much different identity. These experiences, I believe, are hints of a unity that will ultimately come to pass. We are plurals now, but we shall one day be a singular. We see plurality everywhere, but there is really only a single model with many variations: Adam, if you like, and all his varying descendants. The mystics have told us—haven't they?—that in the eyes of God all men are one man."

"Yes," Moore said, "but only very holy people have ever believed them."

Harker shrugged. "That may be so, but that wouldn't make it any the less true. Only particle physicists understand subatomic reality, but we accept their findings."

Moore was silent for a minute. "A single model," he said. "The same basic identity repeated with variations. Something like endless reincarnations?"

"Not of specific persons, no. But reincarnations of a basic nature, yes. Surely that is what the biological evolutionists tell us: a basic element that evolves and varies until you have a bewildering multiplicity and yet an underlying common marker that shows a common heritage. All biological life is related. I make the same assertion about mental and spiritual life. What is true below is true above. I believe that what is metaphysically true generally manifests itself on all planes of existence, rather like a family resemblance. That's really what we mean when we talk of human nature, isn't it? A family resemblance that makes us one in spite of our individuality?" Harker toyed with his glasses for a moment, then polished them absently against the sleeve of his coat. "But we were talking about love and selfishness a moment ago," he said. "Surely the notion of participation in one another has some bearing on that. Consider, Professor: every human activity we hold to be laudable is self-sacrificial except the general notion of romantic love, which is almost wholly self-gratifying. Patriotism, martyrdom, parenthood: all of them imply the giving up of oneself for something else. Only love is different. Only love is purely self-directed, like one's personal hunger for food. Surely there's something odd and wrong about that. Either love is not laudable or it's different from all other laudable things. Unless, of course, we have been practising it wrongly."

For a moment Moore had an image of himself thirty years before, in Germany, when he had driven all night in the frightening darkness and had found out the next morning that he had taken the wrong road. So much energy expended, so much care, all of it misdirected. "All right," he said to Harker, "I'll read the books, but I don't think I'll believe them. I know myself pretty well."

"You know the way you were," Harker said. "You may not know what you are now. You're starting out new, you know." He wrote several things on a prescription pad and folded the sheet over and handed it to Moore. "Go home slowly," he said. "Go to London for a few days as a first step. Try to relax, and take the medication I send along with you."

They shook hands formally. "I appreciate all you've done," Moore said, "and all you've tried to do. I'll look up the books."

"I'm sure you will," Harker said, "when you're ready."

When Harker had left, Moore went over to the window and stared for a long while at the Eye Hospital and the patch of grass in front of it. If I had my way, he thought, I'd stay here indefinitely, just walking the grounds and looking at the traffic and not thinking. I don't really want to do anything but stay here and not think. Harker says I'll grow up on the outside, but I don't want to go outside, I prefer to stay unborn here in the womb.

He sat down in the chair by the window and filled his pipe and lighted it. Then he took out his wallet and pulled out the paper Harker had given him and looked at the titles. It was an odd list, he thought. He had thought it would be all occult things, but it wasn't. There was C.S. Lewis on courtly love. Charles Williams on the theology of romantic love. Vladimir Solovyov on the meaning of love, Philip Sherrard on Christianity and Eros, Dante's *Divine Comedy* and *Convito*. Aquinas on the relationship of the body and soul. Moore felt like a student being given a summer reading program. He tucked it back into his wallet. It was a formidable list, but that was not what bothered him. If those books might make him think like Harker he was not sure he wanted even to look at them. But he knew he would look at them sometime, out of deference to Harker if nothing else. What Harker had said still seemed grotesque to Moore, and yet Harker himself was not grotesque. Moore tried to visualize himself and Helen praying as they made love, or himself and Gwen, but he found it impossible. But even the attempt to visualize it made him feel very odd and at sea, as if he had been told to write a sentence with no words. The image of Gwen's body in the firelight came back to him and he tried to remember what he had been thinking as he looked at it. But no memory returned. All he could be sure of was that whatever he had been thinking, it had nothing to do with prayer.

That night as he lay in bed waiting for the sleeping pill to work he watched his mind fill up with Helen and Gwen, like a pail held under hot and cold faucets at the same time. At first they were perfectly distinct, but after a while they began to slide back and forth and blur into each other. He would be sitting in the breakfast nook in Detroit talking to Gwen about going to Oxford and then he would be looking down at Helen's body in the firelight at Wallingford. He made an effort to order his mind, but as the pill took him nearer to sleep he found it impossible to keep them apart. He met Gwen at Gatwick and listened to her revelations at the Turf, and he watched Helen leave the Fox and Grape with Morgan and saw Helen's buttocks as she steered her father away from the hearth in the parlor. Finally, drifting into sleep that he was glad to feel coming, he knelt beside a cot next to the baptismal font in the Iffley church. He could hear the rain outside and smell the oldness that came out from the walls, and he knew he was being watched through the window by the Eye of God. He stood up naked beside the cot, saying the "Our Father," and as he lay down on the cot the woman beside him reached out to him and in the dim light he could not tell whether it was Helen or Gwen or someone else. Let us pray, he said to the naked figure, and looked hard to see if the woman was laughing.

But when he woke in the morning he was thinking of Gwen, clear and distinct from Helen. Now that he was leaving he knew he should have seen her, or talked to her at least by letter. He felt as if he were suddenly dying and had forgotten to put a favored person in his will. Standing at the window, drinking his tea, he thought, I'll write her a note, I can at least do that. But then he thought, What will I say? Goodbye, I suppose. It's better than nothing at all. He imagined her opening the letter in the parlor, taking in those few meager words, perhaps turning for a moment to look at the hearth, the way people look at places that have once been important to them.

He was still standing at the window when the nurse came in and laid his mail on the table next to him. He looked down at the four or five envelopes there. He was looking at them upside down, but suddenly he was very sure that one of them was from Gwen. No, he said to himself, no, that would be too much of a coincidence. But what shook him was not the thought of coincidence but a deep fear that it would be Harker's kind of coincidence— no coincidence at all, something meaningful. Slowly he turned the small pile around until he could read the writing.

Hers was the second letter, a small envelope addressed in large firm handwriting. He didn't want to open it. He didn't want to go home and he didn't want to open the letter. He only wanted to stay here safe at Radcliffe, walking the grounds a little bit more each day, taking in only small and easy information like the name of the Eye Hospital. A long and easy rehabilitation with no limit set to it, a semi-permanent and pleasant invalidism—that was what he really wanted. He didn't want to know what was in the letter, because whatever it was would mean pain and energy to be expended, and thought, and perhaps even a kind of meaning. And as if Harker were standing next to him, he heard Harker's words in his mind: *Yes, no doubt it will be an adult thing you're called on to do, whatever it is.* Ever so slowly Moore opened the envelope and read the letter.

> Dear Jim,
>
> I have tried to write this letter several times but I haven't been able to. It's hard for me even to write 'Dear Jim' because I don't think I ever called you by your name. I have called the hospital several times to inquire about your condition but I've never left my name. I know you will be leaving soon. I'd like to see you before you go, if you would like to see me. I don't know how you feel about everything that has happened. I'm not sure how I feel myself. Sometimes I think we should talk, other times I think not. I suppose I'm writing this because if I don't talk to you about what has happened I shall never talk to anyone. I'm afraid that rather frightens me. But I'll understand if you don't want to see me.

There was a telephone number at the bottom of the page and then simply the signature, Gwendolen Morgan.

Moore stared at the note so carefully understated, and like a man who has bumped himself on a sharp edge he waited for the pain to begin, the thought. After a moment of dullness it did. *Once again she's made the first move,* he thought, *but this time it isn't just attraction, it's courage; or maybe it was courage the other time too. How strange: we were together for only one night and now if we don't talk to each other we're shut up in ourselves forever.* And then he found himself thinking of the lesbian reporter. He knew what she would say if she knew he had phoned Gwen: "Ah, the don's going back to his little piece now that wifey's conveniently out of the way. Sex, nine times out of ten. Put high-sounding words on it if you like, Professor, but it's still just sex." But that wasn't true, Moore thought. Gwen had a claim on him that had nothing to do with their bodies, or at least nothing to do with their bodies now. But then his mind shifted back to the coincidence, if it was a coincidence, that he had gotten the letter today. He remembered what Harker had said about the books: you'll read them when you're ready. Perhaps he was ready to phone Gwen now and that was why her letter had come. But he didn't feel ready to phone her; he didn't feel ready for anything. But now that she had written he knew he would answer; he couldn't imagine deciding not to respond; he could only decide when. After a moment he picked up the phone and asked for the Wallingford number.

She answered. He knew her voice. "Gwen," he said, "this is Jim Moore. I just got your note."

"Oh, did you." Her voice was guarded, like her note.

"I'd like to see you. I tried to write you, but I couldn't."

"I thought you probably had. I know how hard it was for me." Her voice was warmer now.

"Can you come up? I'm still not very mobile."

"Yes. Whenever you like."

"How about tomorrow?"

"All right. Shall I come to your room?"

He thought for a moment. "I've been walking outside. Can we meet on the grounds somewhere?" He wanted to be somewhere in the open with her in case Broderick or the reporters should reappear. He didn't know exactly why.

"Anywhere you say."

They arranged to meet near the Woodstock Road. Moore thought he remembered a bus stop near where he had sat a few days before. She had a bus schedule by her. The bus from Wallingford would bring her into Oxford at nine-thirty and they could meet by ten.

"Are you all right?" he said.

"About as all right as you are, I expect. Nervy. Sick of lying."

"I know the feeling."

"I need to talk to someone I don't have to lie to."

"So do I, I guess."

"It's like belonging to a secret society, isn't it?" she said.

"Yes. Secret and small."

There was a pause. "Well, I'll see you in the morning then," she said, and rang off.

Moore sat for a long while staring out at the Eye Hospital. He had a sense that a wheel had started to roll again, and that he had helped to start it. But now that he and Gwen were going to come together again, like two beads on a string that had been randomly broken, he found he needed a perspective of himself, an angle, a point of view to counteract the lesbian woman's and Broderick's point of view that kept recurring to him. He imagined a scene in which he reduced them to meek silence with his righteous anger, but the scene had no words. He imagined a more realistic scene in which he tried to explain to them that he and Gwen had a kind of claim on each other like the sole survivors of a shipwreck, but in this scene they merely nodded their heads knowingly and leered.

Finally he put his pipe and tobacco in his jacket pocket and went down to the place where he was to meet Gwen and sat on a bench and smoked. A dozen times or more he saw himself the next morning walking down the slope to meet her when she got off the bus, but no matter how many times the scene ran before his eyes, like the opening of a play, he saw himself as if the London woman and Broderick were in the audience with him: it was his scene, but they seemed to have written it. That wasn't true, of course. It really was *his* scene, but he couldn't shake their view of him. Because the view was half right, he thought, half true—but not *all* right, not *all* true. I despise them, he thought, but anger doesn't make them less right. Surely there's more to me than what they think, but I can't say what it is.

He stood up stiffly and walked slowly along the slope parallel to the road. The traffic came by in clusters from a stoplight around the bend—lorries, buses, cars, motor bikes. All had stopped for a red light a moment before and then had surged forward on the green, all obedient to a pattern. And inside the vehicles or on the bikes the drivers were following other patterns as well. When they stopped at the light they were following one pattern, but what was going on in their minds followed another pattern. High patterns and low ones, Moore thought, easy ones and hard ones. He remembered Malebranche's maxim: if you refuse to follow the higher pattern you are doomed to follow the lower. If you reject the pattern of rationality by drinking too much you will be doomed by the pattern of gravity to fall into a ditch. Harker would agree with that, Moore thought. If you can't abide by the pattern of the single substance, or if you don't know it, you're doomed to abide by the pattern of the false oppositions of soul and body. You'll live by the body, and so you'll die by the body; you've taken the easy way, the lower pattern. Moore imagined a brief scene in which he said to Broderick and the London woman, "The only thing I'm guilty of is not following the doctrine of the single substance, but you see, I didn't know anything about it." But they only sneered and said, "Balls to your high-sounding words, Professor," and he knew he couldn't refute them.

Because as he thought about it he knew that he had known the doctrine, or could have known it, but had dismissed it a long time ago. He suddenly knew why listening to Harker was so disquieting: it was because what Harker was saying was what Moore had believed when he was very young. Order, pattern, meaningful coincidence, even prayer during intercourse: Moore wouldn't have thought these things so absurd when he was a boy. They wouldn't have been ideas for him then. They would have been softer things: wishes, hopes, the unexamined things that young people live by. They went with acne, and trying to catch your profile in a mirror, and wondering if you looked like John Wayne and Gary Cooper when you walked. Soft things, not yet hardened into ideas. Like water, Harker might say, not separated out into oxygen and hydrogen. Moore remembered with a start that the world had once been almost a seamless thing for him—when sliding into second base and thinking about a girl's breasts and going to Saturday afternoon confession had all run together, when Jesus and sexuality and the feel of the dirt under you at second base all ran together like the currents of a river. There had been a time in his life when centerfield and Jesus and a certain girl's breasts beneath a blue sweater had lived as images in his mind with no anomaly or friction, because somehow they had not been separate things. If they had not complemented each other, at least they had not denied each other. But that was long ago. And after that time Moore had been taught that to be an adult is to recognize complexity in the world, to respect differences. Now Harker seemed to be saying to him that unless you saw unity you were following the lower pattern. But I grew up, Moore thought, and I put away the things of the child; I recognized complexity; it's Broderick and the London woman who are still children: they don't recognize the complexity of human motives. But again he heard their voices in the theater of his mind: "Balls to your complexity, Professor. That's where your complexity is, in your balls."

He went back to the bench and sat down and thought of what Gwen had said in her note: if she didn't talk to him about what had happened she would never talk to anyone. I hope she doesn't want answers, he thought, because I don't have any. Maybe it will be like a class. There are varying interpretations of that, Gwen; I suggest you consult the sources—Harker and Broderick and the London woman. I only pass on what the authorities say. There's much to be said for all views. No, I have no view of my own. I'm absolutely open on the subject. At the moment my research is incomplete.

He was waiting at the bench by the Woodstock Road by nine-thirty the next morning in case her bus was early, but it wasn't. He sat on the bench as he had the day before, staring at the segmented flow of traffic, seeing himself still as he knew Broderick and the London woman saw him: the aging sensual man back for another go-around with his bit of young fluff, the follower of the lower pattern. And again he thought stubbornly, There's more to me than that, and then as an afterthought, Or at least there used to be.

It was a typical Oxford summer morning, warm and damp. The dew was still on the bench and the branches of the trees hung limp with moisture. Even the traffic in the road before him seemed to move sluggishly in the heavy air, and the odor of engine exhaust moved up the slope to Moore in a slow tide. It was nearly ten-thirty before a bus stopped. Two women and a man got out, and then behind the man a slender tallish woman in dark slacks carrying a mackintosh over her arm. No one else. So that's the meaningful coincidence, Moore thought, feeling hollowness in his stomach, not that she comes but that she doesn't come. But when he looked back again he saw that the woman in the dark slacks was Gwen. In the morning light she looked older, her hair not as dark, her face broader. How strange, Moore thought, if I had first seen her walking down a street in Wallingford or Oxford I might never have noticed her at all. He waved and she saw him and started up the slope with the deliberate stride he remembered. Even at that distance he could feel her eyes on his face, and he thought, I must seem strange to her too, someone she would have passed by in the street without a second look if we hadn't met just the way we did.

They met midway on the slope and stood awkwardly facing each other for a moment, not touching. Really, we are strangers, Moore thought again, except for that single night. She looked at him gravely. "You look thin. Are you really all right?"

"Yes. Or I will be before long."

They went up the slope to the bench and sat down. "I want to talk," she said, "but I don't know where to begin."

"I know," Moore said, "it's almost too big to talk about at all."

"I wonder if anyone has ever been in our position before. Do you think so? It doesn't seem real to me even now. My father killed your wife and nearly killed you. I can hardly make myself say it like that, even now, but that's what happened. That *is* what happened, isn't it?"

Moore looked at her in surprise. "What do you mean?"

She didn't answer for a minute, staring down at her hands folded in her lap. Then she said, "Everyone says my Dad did it—the papers, the television, everyone. Only no one saw him do it, did they? That's all I mean. We know why he might try to kill you, because we saw him try to do it once before. But why would he kill your wife? I know he wasn't in his right mind, but I want to believe he couldn't have done that. Is it possible he didn't?"

What a powerful thing hope is, Moore thought, reason and probability mean nothing to it. "Well," he said, "one reporter hinted that I might have done it."

"But you didn't," she said, "I know that. No, I mean—isn't it possible there was someone else in the room, someone hiding?"

Moore picked his words carefully, but he knew he would be inflicting pain. "Gwen, the room was empty when my wife and I came in, and the door was locked. The only time it was open was when I went out. But the thing is," Moore hunted for easing words, "I saw him come at me." He saw the hope drain from her face.

After a moment she said, "All right, he did it. I suppose I really knew he did. I wish I knew why."

To get even, wife for wife, Moore thought. But I don't know that, and there wouldn't be any point in telling her even if I did. "We can't know his mind that night," he said. "We can't even imagine it."

They sat for a while, silent, staring ahead of them at the traffic going by. Somewhere behind them a bird called in a long rasping sound—a crow or starling, Moore thought.

"Was it awful that night?" she said. "Was it as awful as the papers said?"

Moore knew she was trying to save what was left of her father. "They think Helen died immediately," he said. He said it quickly, so that the sense of black jelly and inky sheets would not have time to get back into his mind. "And I went under as soon as I was wounded. It was all over in a minute or so."

"Thanks," she said. She stood up abruptly and walked away from the bench twenty yards or so and stood with her back to Moore. He sat and watched her. The sun was getting higher, but the dampness still hung in the air like invisible fog, and Moore could feel sweat trickling down between his shoulder blades and onto the bandage on his back. She turned around and came back to the bench and stood in front of him, looking down at him as she had that night in the parlor after she had put her father to bed, but Moore felt no impulse to put his arms around her legs and pull her to him.

"I thought you might hate me," she said, "but I see you don't."

Moore looked up at her. "Why would I hate you?"

"Because I caused your wife's death, in a way."

"So did I, in a way. So did Lane, in a way."

"Lane?"

"He started it all. If we hate anyone it should be him."

"I did hate him," she said, "for a long time. Three years. That's a long time to hate."

"He was the one American you hated," Moore said. "That was almost the first thing you told me."

"I think I could have killed him once, just after I got home and found out what had happened with him and Mum. But that passed. After a while I suppose I just wished him bad luck in anything he did. Now I don't even wish him that." She sat down beside Moore. "I stopped hating him the day of Dad's funeral." She took a cigarette from her purse and lighted it with a lighter before Moore could get his matches out of his pocket. "It was after the funeral. We'd gone back to the Fox and Grape. I'd had them set up a bit of lunch there for the mourners. There weren't many of them. Mostly old neighbours of Mum and Dad. People made allowances for Dad, but they didn't make any for me. I made my appearance and then went home. I had a drink in the parlor all by myself and cried. I don't cry much ordinarily. I don't believe I cried at all when I was divorced. But I cried that day. I think I was crying over everyone. Dad, Mum, your wife, your daughter, you and me." She stopped for a minute. "And then I sat there for a long while, all wrung out, and I went back over it all, over and over. Mum's death, Dad's stroke, you and me, and then that night at Corpus Christi. And I thought like you about Lane, the bastard that started it all. If only he hadn't come back." She looked at Moore and he found himself wondering what she looked like when she cried; she seemed so in charge of herself. "We wouldn't have met if he hadn't come back. Mum would still be alive and I'd still be in Edinburgh."

"Or you might have come back anyway and we might have met there in the pub," Moore said, caught up for a moment in her game of might have been, "and Helen would still be alive."

"Yes, and you would have gone back with her," she said, "like Lane."

"Yes, I suppose like Lane," Moore said.

"That's what I mean," she said, "you would have done what Lane did. In fact we all did what Lane did, Mum and you and I. That's what I finally thought that day of the funeral, that's why I stopped hating Lane. I would have had to hate you and Mum and me as well. We all went after something we wanted and we didn't mean to hurt anyone. Those other things just happened."

Not if Harker is right, Moore thought, if he's right nothing just happens. Harker, if he were listening to Gwen, would say that Lane and I and maybe Nancy had followed the lower pattern, the pattern of body only, or one-sided love only, whatever you called love that wasn't love of the single substance. Maybe Gwen had followed that pattern too, up in Edinburgh, shedding no tears at her divorce. Maybe they had all chosen to abide by the law of gravity and that was why they were in the ditch now, Nancy dead, Gwen and he poking at pieces of a jigsaw puzzle. But though once again he found himself thinking in Harker's terms, he once again realized that he was arguing with them even as he echoed them. If they had all been wrong then they had all paid for it one way or another, if only through knowing they had been wrong. All of them except Lane, Lane presumably alive and well somewhere in Wisconsin, knowing nothing of what he had begun. "There's one difference between Lane and us," he said. "We know about those other things that just happened, if they did just happen."

"I suppose that's so," she said, "but what difference does that make?"

"I don't know exactly. But if we're all playing the same game we should be playing by the same rules. Your mother paid her price, and we're paying too, in a way. He isn't paying anything."

"We don't know that," she said. "But I don't care anyway. I told you I don't wish him bad luck any more."

Moore looked hard at her. "You mean if you had the chance to talk to Lane you wouldn't tell him what happened after he left?"

"I suppose I would," she said quietly, "but not to make him suffer. There's only one thing I would want to say to him." Moore waited for her to finish, and as he waited he saw her again as he had seen her that night when they had come out of the pub and were standing together in the dark street, remembered what she had said to him, and guessed what she would say now. "I'd ask him if he was in love with Mum," she said.

"But what would it matter what he said? He left her."

"You would have left me," she said. "Because you were married. I think Lane must have been married too. I think that's why he left. But I wouldn't have hated you if you'd left, so I can't hate Lane either. I think Lane must have loved Mum or she would never have had an affair with him."

Once again hope, Moore thought, it must be the strongest thing in the world. Reluctantly, he said, "But she killed herself after Lane left."

"Mum wasn't a strong person," she said. "Dad was the strong one. I take after him, I suppose. He was too strong for her, I think. She should have waited it out, like me. But I suppose she couldn't, not with Dad."

"But waited it out for what?"

"I don't know. But waited it out or been satisfied that what she had with Lane was a good thing."

"But you weren't there," Moore said, "you don't know anything of what went on between them."

"No, I don't."

"You're just taking our case and projecting it onto theirs."

"Yes, I know. I hope they had what we had. I think they did. I believe they did."

Moore stood up from the bench, forgetting his back, and pain surged through him, but he discounted it. "If they were like us, then it was all okay?"

She looked up at him. "I don't know about okay. But it was real, it was genuine, it had a meaning."

In the morning sunlight it was hard for Moore to realize that he was talking to the same woman he had spent a night with in the softer light of the Fox and Grape and her parlor. Only her seriousness seemed the same, a kind of bridge. "You put a lot on that one night," he said. "You want it to justify not only us but them too."

"I don't have to justify us," she said. "I know about us. I hope for them."

"You have a lot of faith in love," Moore said. "I'm not sure any longer I even know what it means."

"That's because it's a word with you," she said. "You live and die with words. Maybe what I'm talking about isn't love. Maybe I only call it that. It doesn't matter. We came together that night, we shared something that wasn't just sex." She stood up next to him, nearly as tall as he was. "I know that," she said, "I know that here," and she put her hand just above her left breast, "and I know you know it or you wouldn't be here now."

Yes, Moore thought, the heart has its reasons. The feeling in her voice moved him as well, so that even her gesture didn't seem theatrical because it came to him as genuine. He looked beyond her at the windows of the Eye Hospital. Someone looking at them from up there would see a middle-aged man and a young woman engaged in serious conversation, perhaps a father and daughter. And then for the first time since Gwen had gotten off the bus he thought how it would look to Broderick and the London reporter: a fig leaf of words over his genitals and Gwen's.

"All right," he said, "that night was something special. I thought so then and I still think so. But I can't say what it was."

"You don't have to say what it was," she said. "Just leave it alone."

Yes, Moore thought, just leave it alone. No matter how hard you tried to say things right they came out bent and caused pain. "I tried to tell Helen what Oxford meant to me," he found himself saying, "that night not long before she died. I talked about arguments for truth."

She waited for him to go on, and when he didn't she said, "And what did she say?"

What did she say? Moore thought. The good old times and monuments to love. Just before she began to cry. "She said she preferred love," he said.

"Most women would have said that," she said. "She must have said that to you a thousand times, one way or another."

"She said I was a tourist at home," Moore said. "She thought I'd found something over here that satisfied me. We even talked of staying over here, starting over, but we knew we couldn't do it."

"You could do it now," she said. "We could go anywhere you wanted. There's nothing to stop us."

"Only time," Moore said. "I'm too old for you. I told you that once before."

"I know, and then you proved yourself wrong."

"That was one night. Over time it couldn't work out. I'm old enough to be your father."

"So that's it," she said, as if in surprise, "you're afraid."

"Afraid?" Moore said. "Of course I'm afraid. Afraid of being old and foolish."

"Well, I'm afraid too," she said, "afraid of being alone and wrong."

"Wrong about what?"

She had been sitting straight backed on the bench, but now she seemed to square her shoulders even more. "I think I could have endured it if you'd gone away with your wife, or back to your wife, like Lane. I could have endured it better than Mum. But if you were to go away now, with nothing to go back to—" Her voice trailed off, then picked up strength. "Then I'd think perhaps I was wrong about us. I won't believe that, not until I have to."

"You'd stay in Wallingford, hoping you were right about two Americans?" Moore said. "Is that it? Two Americans, one that you never saw and one that you spent a single night with? Is that what you'd do with your life?"

"You can make it seem silly if you like," she said. "But is it, really? Doesn't everyone try to make sense out of their life? I'm gambling on two things, on two little parts of my life. I suppose you could say I'm gambling everything on them."

"You're young," Moore said, "you have years ahead of you to live over these things if you have to."

"That's not true," she said quietly, "you know it's not. You and Lane both came back to find out about something that happened to you a long time ago. You didn't live over it, neither of you."

Moore touched her for the first time, taking her hand, and they walked slowly away from the bench. Traffic sounds came up to them from the road: the startling buzz of a motor bike, the whirring of tires.

"I have to go home," he said. "There are things I have to do."

"I suppose so," she said. "Yes, I'm sure there must be."

"I'm not even sure what things," Moore said, "but I have to go and do them. Things about my wife and daughter. And Lane. I have to see Lane."

She stopped, and so he had to stop too. "You wouldn't do anything foolish?"

"No," Moore said, "I'm too civilized for that, even if I believed he was to blame for everything." But just for a moment an image floated into his mind of someone in a dirty GI winter uniform lying at his feet, and the muscles in his arms tensed, all on their own, as if he were ready to strike with something—a club or a bat or a rifle. Or an umbrella, he thought. What a wild delight to abandon everything except physical action, he thought, a delight so exciting it was almost sexual. Not unravel the knot but cut it, not study the cancer but cut it out. But then what? "No," he said again, "I only want to talk to him. I want to know why he came back after all those years."

"Then ask him my question too," she said.

"All right." They walked on again, then turned and went back toward the bench, as if not to get too far from home. They sat down again and stared straight ahead of them at the traffic flow like two people watching a movie. "I don't know what things will be like back there," Moore said. "Right now I feel cut off from everything, but I suppose I'll get involved with things after a while. With the teaching and everything that goes with it. What will you do?"

"I shan't stay in Wallingford. I suppose I'll go to London. I'm quite a competent stenographer and I know computers. I shall catch on somewhere."

They sat silent for a while, close but not touching. There was movement in front of them, and from behind them and around them the occasional country sound of birds. The sun was almost directly overhead now and Moore could feel the damp warmth like a soft weight pushing down on him as if he were a hatching egg.

"So we're both afraid," he said finally, "but not of the same thing."

"I think it's the same thing," she said. "It's just love, isn't it? Or whatever you want to call it. Aren't we both just afraid it won't be enough?"

Again Moore could almost hear Harker's voice speaking inside him: You're right to be afraid, because if it's not love of the single substance it can't be enough. It can only be the same old carousel, and some time, sooner or later, the carousel will stop. "I don't know when I could come back," he said.

"I didn't ask you for a date."

"It isn't just Helen. It's other things too. I have to think."

"All right."

"It's my way. I can't see things as simply as you do."

"All right."

"I'll come back when I can."

"All right."

Moore looked at her wonderingly. "You don't ask for anything?"

"Yes," she said, "I ask for everything, even if I have to wait for it."

"I wish I knew what everything is, and I wish I could give it."

"Just don't think it away," she said, "just come back." She stood up and put her mackintosh over her arm, then sat down again. "We'll be writing, I suppose. We should exchange addresses." She took a pen and a little leatherette notebook out of her purse and wrote her address on a sheet and gave it to Moore. "I'll write you my new address when I move." She handed the notebook to Moore and he wrote down his address and handed it back. She stood up again and this time Moore stood up with her.

"It seems as if there should have been a lot more to say," he said.

"I suppose there is, but perhaps it will keep." She put her free hand on his cheek and kissed him on the mouth, a quick dry kiss. "Don't be too hard on Lane, if you really do see him. And take care of yourself."

"You too."

She turned and walked quickly down the slope of lawn to the bus stop, not looking back. He wondered if she was crying. When the bus stopped a minute or two later she turned back and waved and Moore waved back. Then the bus slid into the flow of traffic and Moore thought, We both have to go home and visit graves and think. But even as he thought it he knew it was only half right. They both had to visit graves, but only he had to think. She knew what she knew, or what she hoped. Moore wasn't sure what he knew, and could hardly imagine what he should even hope for.

CHAPTER 7

London

The next morning Moore was formally discharged from Radcliffe. A nurse gave him a large envelope containing his medical records, helped him pack his few clothes and books, and gave him a plastic bottle of tablets Harker had prescribed for him. Moore sat down gingerly on the edge of the bed and looked around the room for the last time. The morning wasn't warm yet, but he felt sweat beneath his arms, and his hands shook a little as he lighted his pipe. He wished Harker would come in and examine him and tell him that he really wasn't well enough to leave, that he should stay on for another week or so. But he knew that Harker was in surgery and that even if he did come in it would only be to say goodbye.

"You're going to London?" the nurse said. Moore had never learned her name, but she was the one who had brought him his wallet when he had wanted to see Helen's picture.

"Yes, for a day or two."

"Where will you be staying?"

"I don't know," he said, "I haven't thought about it."

"You should phone ahead," she said seriously. "Really, you shouldn't just go into London and wander about. It's quite crowded, you know."

"I thought I'd try to stay somewhere in the West End." He and Helen had stayed once at a small place near Paddington, but he couldn't recall the name now.

"I've a friend at the Charles Dickens," she said, "just off the Bayswater Road. Shall I ring her up?"

"That would be fine," Moore said gratefully. I really am like a child going out into the world, he thought, I don't even know how to make travel plans.

The nurse went out and Moore sat fidgeting with the handle of his overnight bag. Perhaps there wouldn't be any place available in London. Perhaps he could just stay on a few more days in Oxford. But then he thought, Any place outside of this room is outside, so what's the difference?

When the nurse came back a few minutes later she said, "You're in luck; they can put you up there." She handed him a slip of paper with the address. "Shall I call you a cab?"

"No," Moore said, "I'll just walk down and catch the bus."

"All right," she said, "but remember you're not to over-tire yourself. You really have been quite ill, you know."

"Yes, I know," Moore said, and thought, I'm still quite ill, in ways I don't even understand.

She shook hands with him formally and said, "Good luck. I hope you'll come back to England again. I mean, in spite of everything."

"Thanks," he said, embarrassed, because he had kept up the fiction to himself that the hospital staff was not really aware of his situation. "Maybe I will."

He picked up his single bag and walked slowly out of the room and then turned back and looked at it for a moment from the corridor. He had never seen Harker or Broderick or the reporters except in that room. Whenever they came back into his mind, as he knew they would, they would be as he had seen them there, as if they had never had any existence outside of the Radcliffe Infirmary, as if they had been created only to be there in that place when Moore was there. As if I were Adam, Moore thought, and the creation was patterned around me. What monstrous egotism to think that. Yet he thought he could hear Harker saying that there are no accidents, that we are all centers of our patterns, but that the patterns overlap. In some other patterns Harker and Broderick and the London reporter and the others were centers and Moore's pattern had overlapped theirs. Everyone was unique, so no one was unique. Everyone was special, marked in some peculiar way. Easier to see this if there weren't as many people as there seemed to be, he thought, remembering Harker's words about plurality. Everyone special, a kind of elite unit of one. Perhaps even a test unit. The thought chilled him; and what chilled him even more was the sense that it was becoming harder for him to distinguish his own thoughts from those of Harker. It was as if Harker's words were sprouting silently inside him, like seeds growing in a greenhouse, all on their own, untended. Thinking of Gwen, he knew his decision to go home was his own, but he wondered if his promise to return was Harker's.

When he had walked down the slope to the bus stop where he had last seen Gwen he turned and looked back up the gentle green rise. The windows of the

Eye Hospital were drab and opaque in the morning sunlight. If anyone was watching him he couldn't feel it. But it didn't matter, he thought. He would be taking Harker with him, and Broderick and the London reporter too, and Gwen. He had internalized them all, taken them into his mind, and they had settled there. Whatever he had been when he came to Oxford, he was now that and something more, or less. But maybe that's not right, he thought, maybe I'm just the same, maybe I'll shed these experiences, maybe they'll just run off me like water off a duck's back and I'll still be the same old duck's back. Again he was chilled physically for a moment in the heavy damp sunshine, as if a doctor had just told him he was going to die. Because whatever that same old duck's back was, something deep inside him said it wasn't very good, or not good enough, or not as good as he had once hoped it would be. At the age of fifty, he thought, I want to change, but from what to what I can't really say.

He rode the bus to the central bus depot, past the Randolph Hotel and St. Mary's, and King Edward Street that led down to Corpus, and Carfax: a tourist leaving places that in a short time had leaped into tenderness and familiarity, places that he knew he had also internalized, had taken into that moving mass of impressions and memories and ideas that he had thought of as the essence of England. He watched them as they slid by, but not carefully, because he knew that nothing that he saw of them now would change what they already were for him.

At the central depot he waited only ten minutes for the express bus to London, and then in a few minutes more he was on the motorway. Already he was more tired than he usually was by late afternoon back at Radcliffe, and he closed his eyes for a moment and dozed. But when he did that he found he was riding into London to meet Helen, and he jerked himself back to consciousness and stared at the bland passing countryside, trying to make his mind equally blank and bland.

London loomed ahead of the bus, the post office tower off to the left, then the high rise apartments, and then on the right the long low gray roof of Paddington Station, and Moore's mind began to register again like a computer accidentally touched. Paddington for Moore had always meant Holmes and Watson. The first time he had ever walked into that mammoth structure that was half inside and half out, the sunlight glinting dimly through the dirty skylighted roof, he had simply stopped short and stared for a long moment. Because it was like other train stations in Munich and

Vienna and Paris, and yet it wasn't. The lines of people were like other lines of people, the trains butted up just beyond the entrance gates were like other trains, even the sooty sunlight sifting down from the roof was like other sunlight. But Paddington was different. He had stood there and looked at the signs that said Southampton and Weston-super-Mare and Brighton and he had forgotten where he was going. In his imagination was a cluttered room, full of books and scruffy easy chairs and ashtrays with half burned gobbets of tobacco, and a tall lean man was saying to a shorter stouter man, "We've just time to catch the eight-twelve from Paddington, Watson. Hurry! The game's afoot!" It was from Paddington that Holmes and Watson had followed the pattern of the Baskerville hound and the king's mistress and the mystery of the speckled band. Or so it had seemed to Moore that time as he stood there, excited beyond reason at a mere place that someone had written about.

Now he watched Paddington slide past him and he thought, I distrust Harker's occult patterns, but the patterns I've always found the most exciting—the Holmes patterns—were like his. They were improbable, yet I believed them. They were better than what I knew, they were more interesting. Except that they weren't frightening—like Harker's talk of marriage as a model of the universe—you could always close the book on them. And that's what I'm trying to do with Harker's patterns: I'm trying to close the book on them because they're disturbing. I don't want a world of overlapping circles, or at least I don't want it now. There was a time when I would have welcomed it, when I thought better of my own circle. Moore stared at the crowds lining up outside Madame Tussauds wax museum, barely seeing them for what they were, except to note that they were probably symbolic, probably meaningful to him if he could put his mind to them. But he was thinking now of Gwen.

It had seemed absurd to him that she should believe what she did about him and Lane on so little evidence, yet he couldn't at the moment say how he differed from her. She believed what she had to believe—what she saw. He disbelieved what he had to disbelieve—what he didn't see. But somehow her way seemed admirable and his shabby. She left herself open to anything and everything; he was only trying to close any door that might open into his own small life. He felt suddenly dishonest. Paddington had saddened him because in his present mood he saw that Paddington meant fiction to him, and he felt that he had betrayed it. For more than twenty years he had praised fiction as a serious imitation of life, as the writing more than any other kind that caught what James had called the strange irregular rhythm of life. For more than twenty years he had insisted that the fiction writer's imagination perceived pattern not perceptible to the ordinary view. And now it seemed to him that Harker was a kind of silent novelist and that when he denied Harker's imagined patterns he gave up James and all the other heroic imaginers, gave up Holmes and Watson, and Dracula and Jonathan Harker, and quite suddenly in the middle of teeming London Moore's world seemed empty and chaotic, only ordinary life without meaning.

He felt not only lame and stiff but very old as he got off the bus at the depot near Victoria Station. When he carried his bag out into the street to the cab stand he willed himself not to remember that walk from Victoria to the bus depot with Helen on that morning that seemed so long ago, but the image of her walking next to him as the suitcases banged against his knees came back in a rush of pain. Helplessly, he had to recall the bus ride to Oxford with her asleep on his shoulder, the called greetings in the quad, the lovemaking on the lumpy cot. Like a man condemned to watch a slow-motion film in its entirety, he saw the high shadowy houses at the Turf, the umbrellas with the beer names on them, heard her giggle there and again at the White Horse, watched again their lovemaking in the ludicrous high ceilinged room at Corpus, listened again to her sobbing at the wrong words he had said, lifted her in his arms again when she was sticky and dead. He stood until the reel was finished and he was free to move again.

Slowly he walked the long two blocks to Victoria and joined the queue for taxis. He thought he could get to his hotel by bus or tube, but suddenly he found himself too tired and too listless to take the trouble. For twenty minutes he stood behind a middle-aged American couple, half listening to their Midwestern accent that seemed broad and strange to him, though it was his own. They had just come in from Gatwick and were in that exalted state of fatigue and excitement that Moore knew so well. They went over and over their plans, like children going on a picnic, and Moore, invisible to them in their excitement, tried not to listen but had to. The hotel reservations in London, the train reservations to Edinburgh, the bus reservations for the Highlands.

"I'm so excited," the woman said, "I can hardly believe it's really happening."

"But it is," the man said, laughing, "all just the way we planned."

"I'm so happy it's almost sinful," she said.

"So am I," he said, "but it's not sinful. We've worked a long time for this."

She reached over and squeezed his hand, and Moore suddenly found himself picking up his bag and going back to the end of the queue. Then he felt foolish and hoped they hadn't noticed his leaving. He wished them well, but he couldn't listen any more.

Finally it was his turn for a cab and he settled gratefully into the back seat of the box-like black Austin. "The Charles Dickens Hotel," he told the driver.

The driver was charcoal black, Jamaican or West Indian, Moore guessed. "You mean the Charlie Dickens," the driver said and laughed as if he had made a marvelous joke. "Are you in a hurry?"

"No," Moore said, "why?"

"Because I am," the driver said and flashed a gleaming smile of white teeth and gold fillings. "I'm always in a hurry."

The smile was so genuine that Moore found himself smiling back, and it occurred to him that he couldn't remember when he had last smiled at anything or anyone. "Time is money, you mean?"

"Oh, yes," the black man said, "most assuredly time is money." The rhythm of his words was singsong and the accents fell oddly on last syllables. "Most assured*lee* time is mon*ee*. But I am forever in a hur*ree* any*way*." He put the cab in gear and Moore fell back in his seat as the car jumped away from the cabstand and into traffic. They went booming down the Buckingham Palace Road, the driver with his right hand out the window making a non-stop series of signals to other drivers—thumbs up, thumbs down, hand up, hand down, like a band leader—and then they were in Park Lane, skirting Hyde Park in a mad convoy of other cabs.

"Why are you always in a hurry anyway?" Moore shouted.

The cab suddenly crossed two lanes of traffic to turn at the Marble Arch and the driver gave a thumbs down to someone on his right. "Because slow is so bor*ing*," he shouted back. He changed lanes again, cutting off a double-decker bus, and swung into the Bayswater Road. "Slow is for the old in rock*ing* chairs." Moore looked at the gold and white grin again in the rearview mirror and found himself smiling again. He wished he had someone to share the driver with. Helen would have been delighted.

"Where are you from?" he shouted again above the traffic noise.

"Jamaica," the black man shouted back over his shoulder.

"How do you like it here?"

"Marvel*ous*. Everything is so in a hur*ree* here. Pubs close fast, shops close fast, everything is bang-bang. Marvel*ous*."

"But how about the weather?"

"Marvel*ous*. In Jamaica everything is very warm, very slow." He made a sudden right turn and then a sudden left. "Charlie Dickens is straight on," he said, and in a moment, with one final rush, he pulled up in front of the hotel.

Moore got slowly out of the cab and put his bag down on the sidewalk. The driver took off his cap and leaned out the window. In the sunlight his hair was like blackish-gray steel wool. Not a young man, Moore thought with surprise, but he likes the hurry here in London. Maybe he doesn't think about his age. Moore paid his fare and added a good tip.

"Thank you, *sir*," the driver said. "It's a love*ly* day, don't you think?" He gestured up toward the sky. "The air, you know?"

Moore nodded. "Yes, a fine day." The driver gave him a wave and the cab went away in a leap. Moore picked up his bag. The day really was fine, he noticed. He stood in the bright sunlight and felt a light breeze against his face. He couldn't remember ever feeling a breeze in Oxford. It was if he were in a higher place here in London, though he knew he wasn't. He turned toward the hotel. It was simply a part of one solid block of squarish Georgian building, four storeys high. Across the street was a nearly identical block of building whose front doors must face on the Bayswater Road, and he knew it must be a hotel too, or more than one. These buildings had once been private apartments, he supposed, bought up after the war by real estate people and turned into tourist hotels. He knew what the Charles Dickens would look like before he went into it. And he was right. When he got to his room he could tell at once that the tiny bathroom was a late addition and that the wall behind his bed had been built to cut the room in two. The window, which looked out on nothing, was peculiarly near the new wall, and he knew that just beyond that wall was the partner window of the original room. Fifty years ago someone had lived in a spacious and elegant apartment here. Moore guessed that if he were to go into the room next door he would see the vestiges of a fireplace, plastered over and bulging out a little from the garish wallpaper that covered the walls of his own room. All this is part of the hurry that the cab driver likes so much, Moore thought.

And then he thought, I should have told him to go to America, to California or Texas. With just a touch of homesickness, Moore thought, They're in a hurry there too, but at least they're building new, they're not tearing down the old or trying to hide it. For just a moment he had a sense of what America must have meant to people here in the Old World four-hundred years before: endless emptiness, space, an infinite new canvas to paint on and an infinite range of colors to work with.

He took off his jacket and lay down on the bed and in a few minutes he was dozing lightly. In his half dreams he went backward to Oxford and forward to Detroit. And then, as if it were a football game, the positions changed at half time and he went forward to Oxford and backward to Detroit. He was sometimes a boy and sometimes a middle-aged man and sometimes he was both, like the cab driver, and he couldn't discover where he belonged or what age was his real one. Whichever way he went he found himself on the same street, which he knew but couldn't name or place, and there was a man he was looking for somewhere in that street whom he had to put a question to. Only he wasn't sure he would know the man if he found him, because sometimes he thought the man would be wearing a mackintosh and rain hat and sometimes he thought he would be wearing army suntans and combat boots.

When he awoke an hour later it was to the sound of a vacuum cleaner in the corridor outside his room, and he knew he was in a hotel but for a moment couldn't remember where. Then he sat up and waited for the mixture of pain and stiffness in his back to ease. He washed his face in the little bathroom and took the lift down to the lobby. A ruddy-faced girl behind the desk was arguing with a party of Japanese about room reservations. Moore wanted to ask her where there was a pub that served lunch, but after a few minutes he gave up and went out. To his left, the way he had come, there was nothing but a stretch of classical facades as far as he could see, and he knew they meant only more Charles Dickenses, so he went the other way and around the corner. Halfway up the block he found his pub, the Leinster Arms, and went in. It was larger than the Oxford pubs he was used to, a long wide high ceilinged room with cushioned booths and a long bar with racks of wine glasses hanging upside down over it. There were glass cases on the bar with sandwiches and sausage rolls and meat pies. The room was crowded, about evenly divided between whites of various kinds and Indians and Orientals. He ordered a lager and a sandwich and took them over to a little counter that stood by itself in the middle of the room. He ate the sandwich, and then because his back was still bothering him more than it had for a long while he took one of Harker's pills and washed it down with lager.

He finished his lager and went back and got another. Automatically he noted that it was nearly two, afternoon closing time. He drank the lager quickly, waiting to see what the medication did for him. For his body or soul, he thought, or both of them together. After a few minutes he began to feel oddly detached, not only from the Leinster Arms and the people in it, but from his own body as well. He tried to put a name to the sensation. I feel like a free-floating idea, he thought with interest, an idea drifting free, without mooring, not confined to anyone's mind. He lifted his glass to finish his lager but found that he had already finished it, so he walked, or drifted, to the door and out. He moved lightly past the street the hotel was on and past another block to the Bayswater Road. Just across the road was a gate to Kensington Gardens, and when the traffic light changed he crossed the road and went through the gate. He kept on the path that led from the gate, walking without effort and with almost no sensation. In a few minutes he found himself walking alongside a stream, and a London map appeared in his mind and he knew where he was. He was walking along the Serpentine River. After a while he came to a boathouse. Punts were drawn up on the shore in front of it and more of them were stacked like timbers behind it. Swans swam slowly back and forth just off the shore. He sat down on a bench, though he didn't feel at all tired. A few children threw bits of bread to the swans and shouted, but their voices came to Moore as if from far away.

He sat for a while and simply looked at this river, another small and neat river like the Cherwell or the Thames at Oxford. Somewhere in this modest stream Harriet Shelley had drowned herself after her husband had left her for a more attractive and more talented woman. It might have been just here, he thought, a century and a quarter before. Languidly, his imagination pictured a young woman in a long full skirt walking out into the water past the circling swans, walking and walking until after a while she wasn't walking but floating, and then she went under, and the swans continued to circle, not bothered by the intrusion. Gwen's mother had gone under the water too, he thought, but the water had been within her. The pills would have acted like rising water in an enclosed room. She would have risen with the water until it reached the ceiling, and then the last breath of consciousness like the last breath of air. Then blackness and darkness, and then nothing.

More knowledge than she could bear, he thought, and he meant both Harriet Shelley and Nancy Morgan, more knowledge than she could live with. And Gwen's father, too, he had more knowledge than he could live with. And himself and Gwen: they were carrying a burden of knowledge too. Only Lane was free, Moore thought again. Dreamily he saw Lane come and sit beside him on the bench, tall and lanky in the suntans of thirty years before, hardly more than a boy. Dreamily Moore talked to him about pattern while the children shouted dimly and the swans circled silently. When Moore had finished, Lane stood up and turned his face away, toward the river, and stood for a moment, and Moore knew he must be taking in the pattern. Then slowly Lane walked down to the shore and into the water. Moore watched while Lane, stiffly erect, walked slowly out from shore. He was very tall and he had to walk out a long way before the water was up around his armpits, then he simply laid himself down in the water, arms at his side. Moore watched this with enormous satisfaction. But a moment after Lane had left his feet Moore knew somehow it was not right. Vaguely, something Gwen had said and something Newman had said flowed through his mind, though he couldn't recall their words, and he stood up and shouted at Lane to come back. But Lane didn't hear him.

Moore stood up from the bench and turned back the way he had come. A swan sailed in toward him, but Moore had nothing to give it and it sailed away again. Moore walked slowly back to the gate and found another bench and sat and watched the traffic on the Bayswater Road for what seemed a long time. Then he finally stood up to go back to the hotel he was aware of his back again, and he knew that Harker's pill must have spent itself.

He went back to his room and took a bath. At seven o'clock he went back to the Leinster Arms and ate a shepherd's pie and drank some lager, but long before closing time he found himself very tired. Tomorrow he would walk around London a little, he told himself. He had done enough for today, his first day out in the great world.

The next morning he got a bus schedule and a subway map from the desk clerk and took them with him into the dining room. The room was full of tourists, the tables were littered with dirty dishes and bits of breakfast buns, and Oriental waiters and waitresses, who seemed angry to Moore, moved slowly with trays of tea and coffee. The tourists snapped at the Orientals and the Orientals snapped back in languages only they understood. It was all very unpleasant and disorderly and if Moore had known where else he could have gone for coffee he would have left. He sat for a while at an empty littered table, then finally went back to the urn that the Orientals were drawing coffee from and drew himself a cup of coffee. A waiter said something to him angrily and Moore, caught up in the general air of dislike, replied "Same to you," and took his coffee to his table.

London was not new to Moore and there was no particular sight that he wanted to see again, but on this one day he had before his flight home he felt he should try to involve himself somehow in the life of London, if only by riding a bus or subway. He spread the subway map on the table while he sipped the tepid coffee and after a few minutes decided simply to make for the Thames, near Westminster Bridge. The river was the heart of London for Moore, not Oxford Street or the theatre district. He supposed the feeling came from having been brought up on the east side of Detroit, where people always described their neighborhoods as either near or far from the Detroit River or Lake St. Clair. He left a shilling on the table and went out of the dining room. He walked two long blocks to the Lancaster Gate tube station and went down the stairs to the white-tiled waiting platform. He stood for a moment in front of the enlarged subway map on the wall and checked his connections, but he wasn't really worried. He understood the subway maps, he felt in control of things. At Oxford Circus he changed trains and by ten o'clock he was at the river.

He stood for a while watching the crowds lining up to go through Westminster Abbey, then walked down along the river toward the Houses of Parliament. He sat down on a bench near Churchill's statue and let his eyes travel slowly over Big Ben and the spires of Westminster Cathedral. All around him the tourists surged, with bags and knapsacks and cameras. Plunging into the public heart of England, he thought, snapping pictures of the spires and statues and doors and windows that spelled out England's history. And it was a history like any other history, Moore thought, full of heroism and glorious deeds and ringing words, but full of shame and dark deeds too—murders and thefts and betrayals. And full of ambiguous situations and unfathomed people that the passage of time had cast a kind of glow over, or a kind of enameled surface, so that the question of good or evil in connection with them seemed hardly to matter. Part of the sweep of history, he thought, the charm of time: all lying open here for all to see and try to understand. He felt a sudden love of openness, for lack of secrecy, for things thrown open to public view and the judgment of time. I would like to have our stories told in the open, he thought, Nancy's story, and Morgan's, and Gwen's, and Lane's, and Helen's, and my own. I would like them to be laid out in all their complexity and ambiguity for the world to see. But not yet, he thought, not quite yet, because Ruthie is part of that world. But some time long after Ruthie is gone and her children are gone, maybe when Westminster Abbey is another century older, I wish our stories could be laid out in the painting on a window or the carving on a door or in the faded pages of someone's diary, so that some small segment of the people to come could look and say, Yes, how interesting that all was, and how sad, before they passed on to some other story. Not making judgments as they looked, just nodding their heads and saying, Yes, that's just how it all happened, how interesting. Just as they looked now, these tourist crowds, at the river where Elizabeth had ridden on the royal barge, and at St. Paul's, where Donne had preached, and at the Houses of Parliament, where Pitt and Gladstone and Churchill had spoken out their versions of the truth. Not making judgments, he thought again, or at least only judgments that are softened by time. The harder judgments we can make for ourselves, while we're still alive.

Moore walked slowly along the Embankment past Westminster Bridge and on downriver toward Waterloo Bridge. Earlier in the summer on another trip to London Moore had left the Oxford group and had gone off on his own on a marathon walk along the river, crossing and re-crossing Westminster Bridge, then going along the Embankment to Waterloo Bridge and crossing that. He'd had lunch at a pub near the Royal Festival Hall, then had walked past grimy warehouses all the way to London Bridge and across that. By that time he had been so tired that he had been looking for a cab when he had rounded a corner and had a sudden vision of St. Paul's at the end of a narrow street, almost as if he had seen it at the end of a tunnel. He had stood there for several minutes in the light rain, tired and missing Helen enormously, simply staring up at the ball and the cross so suddenly revealed to him.

He would not be walking that far today, he knew. Already his back was beginning to shoot out pain, and he began to set modest goals for himself: to get as far as Waterloo Bridge and try to find the pub across the river where he had had lunch that other day. Ahead of him was the grotesque shape of Cleopatra's Needle and he made for that and sat down on a bench near the little fence that ran around the base of the obelisk. A shameless monument to English thievery, he thought, as open and public as if it immortalized something better. He lighted his pipe and felt for Harker's pills. He would like to take one now, but they were large hexagonal tablets that he didn't think he could get down without something to drink.

Suddenly someone stood in front of him and a high-pitched London voice said, "Have you got a light?" For a moment he thought he was looking at a teenage boy in jeans and tight jacket, long-haired and fingering an unlighted cigarette. But as he reached for his matches he realized it was a girl. Her eyelids were a startling blue and as his gaze went downward he saw that the skin-tight jeans ended in impossibly high spiked heels. He got his matches out and lighted one and she leaned over him and cupped both hands over his hand to light her cigarette.

"Thanks," she said, and took a long drag on the cigarette, tilted her head back and blew out a long plume of smoke. It was a gesture Moore was sure he'd seen in the movies. "You look so lonesome," she said, and took a step forward so that her leg was against his knees. A whore, he thought, and no more than seventeen. He started to say something, but straight ahead of his eyes was the tight crotch of her jeans and for a moment he had to envision the boyish thighs open before him in some drab room near Waterloo.

He made himself look up to her face and said, as if he were talking to a child, "No, there's nothing for you, my dear."

She stepped back and said, "You can't imagine what you're missing, you know." But Moore shook his head no, and she turned away and walked in a stilted wig-wag gait away from him down to the Embankment railing, not looking back. He watched her as she stared out over the river, wondering what she was seeing. After a few minutes she looked back the way Moore had come and stepped away from the railing and walked a few steps along the Embankment. A heavy-set man in a white mackintosh came along toward her and stopped as she stood in front of him with another unlighted cigarette. He looked foreign to Moore, dark-skinned, with black hair flattening down in the light rain that had begun. He was carrying a rolled newspaper. When they had talked for a moment he laughed and with a quick movement stuck the newspaper between her legs and pulled it back and forth several times. The girl jerked back, and Moore thought she said something, but her face was turned away from him and he couldn't tell whether she was angry. The dark man laughed again and gave her a hard pat on the buttocks and came on past Moore, still smiling. When Moore turned his eyes back to the girl he could only see her back as she went in her wig-wag walk away from them both.

Moore sat for several minutes, staring across the river but seeing nothing. The lower pattern, he thought, how ugly, and how painful. Unless you were involved in it. Like the flatlanders, he thought, recalling some dim analogy, the people who lived on a single plane, in the single dimension of horizontal movement, knowing nothing of vertical movement. But what if you knew of the other dimension but chose to stay a flatlander? That was the key, of course. But how could you know the other dimension in anything like the way you knew the lower? Wouldn't the vertical dimension always seem vague and mythic by comparison with the one you lived on? But he thought he knew what Harker would say: you had to live the higher one just as you lived the lower one; it wasn't a question of knowledge but of doing.

He stood up and pain throbbed through his back. The light rain was beginning to soak through his trouser legs and as he began to walk it ran off the brim of his hat and down inside his collar. He went along the Embankment to the Waterloo Bridge and on across it, walking as fast as he could. At the end of the bridge he looked down and could see the pub sign that he remembered. He went down a slippery flight of steps alongside the Royal Festival Hall and in a few minutes he was in the pub. Like the Leinster Arms, it was more elaborate than Oxford pubs. One long room was a bar and another room next to it was a restaurant with a steam table and a man behind it serving hot dishes. Moore took a lager over to the restaurant side and hung his raincoat over a chair and sat down at a table. He shook one of Harker's pills out of the plastic bottle and swallowed it and washed it down with lager. A jukebox, the kind that had been popular in the States twenty years before, played in one corner of the room, and Moore listened to records by Sinatra and Crosby that he had almost forgotten. By the time he finished his lager the pill had begun to work. He half floated up to the steam table and got a plate of mashed potatoes and peas and baked beans and a piece of crusty bread and went back to his table. Pabulum, he thought, baby food, but it presents no problems. He ate it and drank his lager while Crosby sang "I Surrender, Dear" and Sinatra sang "I'll Walk Alone." Moore listened dreamily, for a few minutes eighteen years old again and untested by war or love.

At afternoon closing time he left and went without effort back up the steps and across the bridge. The rain had stopped now and he walked with his coat slung over his shoulder, back along the Embankment to Westminster Bridge. At the foot of the bridge one of the excursion boats that went up and down the river was moored at the stone pier and a crowd of young people waited along the stone path to board it. Another crowd had formed along the Embankment to watch, and Moore stopped to watch too. The boat, long and narrow and double-decked, swung easily at its moorings. Inside the upper cabin, which was nearly at eye-level to the crowd on the Embankment, long tables had been set up, neatly covered with white cloths, and white-coated waiters were carrying in trays of sandwiches and cakes and ice buckets with wine bottles in them. The lower cabin was set with smaller tables, with a space left in the middle of the room. Moore guessed that it was some sort of graduation cruise. The young people waiting to go aboard were conspicuously dressed for a great affair, the girls in long filmy dresses, some with bouquets at their wrists, and the boys in dinner jackets. They stood in little groups, self-conscious, half embarrassed, half pleased at the attention they were drawing. An afternoon and evening cruise, with sandwiches and champagne above and dancing below, while the boat slid past London Bridge and Tower Bridge and perhaps as far as the mouth of the Thames.

Moore, still in his semi-detached condition from Harker's pill, stared at the throng of young faces as if they were a pageant arranged especially for him. It was impossible not to feel the happiness they gave off like an aura, and Moore did feel it. And then along with the feeling came the thought of the patterns again, the high and the low. Those young people now hurrying up the narrow gangway were hurrying into one pattern or the other, they were at a moment of choice, but they wouldn't know that now, not if they were like Moore thirty years before. It would be years on from now when they had met someone like Harker, either outside themselves or inside, or they had lost someone like Helen, that they would realize, or have the chance to realize, what choice they had made. In his odd state Moore saw their young forms as soft and malleable and saw them dashing up the gangway into a mold that would close them in, and for a wild moment he thought of trying to stop them. But even in his dreamy state something like

Harker's voice said, The choices are interior and the chances are everywhere. Turning away, he thought he saw the face of the young whore in the crowd along the embankment. But he was mistaken; it was some other young enameled face staring at the excursion party, a face blue-lidded and without expression, like the face a child might draw on an Easter egg. It was hard to believe that behind that face was an interior of any kind at all, except an intense wish to be on that boat, but then in a pang of shame he thought, I'm judging her from the outside, the way Broderick judged me; how can I know the truth of what she really wishes?

He waited with the rest of the crowd while the boat filled up and then cast off and swung out into the river. The sun had come out now in the low damp sky and in its watery light Moore and the others watched as the boat churned slowly downriver until it reached Waterloo Bridge and then rounded a bend and was gone. The faint sound of dance music came back to them along the water for a moment or so even after the boat itself was out of sight.

The crowds broke up and drifted away and Moore drifted away with them. He joined a queue at a bus stop, not really caring where the bus was going, and rode it past Lambeth Bridge until he saw the familiar face of the Tate Gallery. He got off and went in and for a long time he passed lightly back and forth in front of the Blake drawings and the Turner paintings. He couldn't have said which he thought were the more magnificent, the marvelous firm outlines of Blake or the explosions of diffuse color in Turner. If only you could put them together, he thought, but he couldn't imagine them together. Though in a way they were already together, since they were both visions of the same thing. They were together, he thought, only not together enough for him.

It was early evening when he finally left the Tate. Harker's pill had worn off by now and he walked slowly and heavily across the Millbank Road to catch the bus. When it came he rode it back to Westminster Bridge and got off for a last look at the river. He walked to the middle of the bridge and leaned on the railing. The sky had lifted and the air had cooled and the prospect downriver was one you saw on postcards. The setting sun glittered on the water, painting the grayness purple and flashing white. He let his eyes follow the river as far as the bend where the excursion boat had disappeared and then his eyes lifted and St. Paul's was there, around the bend and looming over the river that he couldn't see, the ball and the cross gilded in the western sun, sharply defined against the blueness of the sky and burning with a color like golden fire. As if painted by Blake and Turner together, he thought. For a moment he couldn't catch his breath and he had to look down at the water and squeeze his hands hard on the railing until he felt his breath coming normally again. When he looked back up it was like looking through a window in the rain and he realized he was crying. He knew why, but he couldn't find words for it, or not his own words. The words that he found in his mind now were Aquinas' words, and not even Aquinas' real words, because he could remember only a rough translation. Knowledge is always of the first order, Aquinas had said, but when it comes to God, then it is better to love than to know. Moore bowed his head and felt his tears drop onto the backs of his hands. Suddenly it seemed to him that everyone around him had known this secret that wasn't a secret at all. He felt like a child who hasn't been invited to a party. They all knew, he thought, Helen and Harker and Gwen. They all knew but me. Or me and Lane, the two Flatlanders, the one-dimensional men.

After a while he found himself staring down at his hands, no longer crying, the pain in his back asserting itself again. He felt as he had felt after his mother's and his father's funerals, as if everything had been sucked out of him and he was as shapeless as a wet sack. He turned away from the railing with only a short parting look at St. Paul's. Already some part of him was thinking of the Leinster Arms and a shepherd's pie and lager. Already some part of him was thinking, I've been devastated before and I've survived and haven't changed, this is a mood that will pass after a while. Behind him on the river he thought he could hear the faint dance music from the excursion boat, but whether the boat was coming back or he was only imagining the music he couldn't tell.

CHAPTER 8

Detroit

It was exactly four weeks from the night of Helen's death that Moore went back home. He had shipped nearly everything on ahead of him so that when he stepped off his flight at Metro Airport he was carrying only a flight bag. The international terminal seemed unfamiliar, as if he had been away for years, not months, a tourist coming home after long travel. From the airport limousine that took him into Detroit he watched the traffic with almost a foreigner's interest, marveling at the over-sized cars driving on the wrong side of the road. The limousine let him off at a motel on the far east side of town, about a mile from home. He went into the motel bar to call a taxi, then instead sat down at the bar and ordered a beer. He stared at the television, fingering his housekeys in his pocket. A sportscaster was reading the baseball scores, and Moore realized that for the first time he could think of he didn't know how the Tigers were doing. They had lost tonight, but someone whose name meant nothing to Moore had pitched well. Moore felt the old need for more facts, the hunger for standings and statistics. He wouldn't really be home until he had those things.

Commercials came and went on the television, but Moore hardly saw them. He was feeling the old pain of a Tiger loss. It was a familiar pain, one that linked his childhood to the present. He had never tried to analyze his feelings about the Tigers; they were too personal. The earliest Fourth of July he could remember had had nothing to do with fireworks. He had spent it at the ball park—Navin Field then—with his father, in the bleachers, under a broiling sun. He could still see Gehringer dancing to his left into the hole for a ground ball, so graceful he hardly seemed to be moving at all. And in the years that followed there had been Greenberg and Newhouser and Dizzy Trout: he couldn't say even now how important they had been. But now he thought, Something in me that never came out for Helen and Gwen, something they wanted from me, had come out easily for the Tigers. It had come out in a kind of second life where good and evil were clearly designated, Home Team and Visitors, and where it seemed natural to yell with happiness and boo with anger. He had read somewhere that it was healthy to think of life as a game, and now he wondered if he had sometimes thought of a game as life. He tried to dismiss the notion because it caused him real pain. And yet, he thought, I was a tourist at home for Helen, and Gwen is waiting even yet for me to speak. Maybe someone will write on my tombstone: He was a poor lover but a good baseball fan.

He called a taxi and then went outside in the hot August night to wait for it. He had to go home now. He had to get that over with. He had to walk into that haunted house and stay the night there. And then tomorrow he had to go to the cemetery. He hadn't thought beyond that.

The taxi headlights touched for a second on the little sapling as they turned into the driveway, and then the headlights settled on the garage door. Even from the cab Moore could see that it wasn't closed tightly; it had never come down just right and he had always meant to fix it, but he knew he wouldn't bother now. He paid the driver, and when the cab had left he went over to the tree and looked at it in the dimness of the streetlight. He had pruned the top branches off because he had been sure they were dead, and now the tree stood only a little taller than himself. It looked the same, no better, no worse. The new branches he had hoped for had not come, but what there was of the tree looked healthy enough. He went in through the garage, between the Olds and the VW. He wouldn't need two cars now. The VW would do for him. But he knew it would be a long while before he got rid of Helen's car.

The bedroom and the kitchen were the worst, as he had known they would be. Whatever she had touched most often gave off her presence like a physical aura. Moore thought of ghosts, the kind that haunt places where they have spent their earthly lives. He had read that they never left until the structure of the building was changed and made strange to them. Moore believed something like that. In the bedroom the bed waited to be turned down by her, the clock waited to be set. The closet door stood ajar as if she had been looking for something there. He didn't look inside. The clothes would be too much. In the kitchen, on the counter, the coffeemaker, the electric can opener and the breadbox looked back at him. They might as well have had soft neon lights on them that said her name. Everything was neat, as Ruthie had left it after the funeral. Not a coffee cup in the sink, not a cigarette in an ashtray. He opened a door under the kitchen counter and crouched and looked at cans of tomato soup and packages of salad croutons and a can of coffee. The refrigerator was nearly empty. Ruthie must have cleaned out all the perishables. There were two cans of beer, a can of diet soda, bottles and jars of mustard and ketchup. It was like coming into a cottage where the former tenants had left a few things out of politeness.

He opened one of the cans of beer and went into his den and sat down at the desk. He touched nothing, only sat like a visitor. The desk top was tidy. Helen would have seen to that before she left. He got up and unlocked the windows over the desk and opened them. He knew he should open windows all over the house to air it out, but he sat down again. He would do that tomorrow. He sipped at the beer, strong and over-carbonated after the British lager. In the deep drawer of the desk, he knew, were the Blake and Whitman notes. Helen wouldn't have touched those. But he felt no interest in them. Or in anything else, he thought. If I had come home and found the house burned to the ground I wouldn't really have cared, except that I wouldn't have known where to go. Yes, he thought, a good fire might have been a mercy: the past was dead; why not cremate the body? Then I would have come back to a check from the insurance company; that would have been my only reality in the new life.

He sat for a long while at the desk, finishing the beer. Then he moved over to the easy chair and sat in that. He was very tired, but he knew he wouldn't be able to sleep in the bedroom. He leaned back in the chair and stared at the print on the wall between the den and the bedroom. It was a sentimental farm scene that Ruthie had given him for his birthday when she was a small girl. When he had been working late in the den he had often found himself looking absently at it while he thought of something else and half heard the soft mutter of Helen's radio in the bedroom. Now as he stared at the print there was no noise except the buzz of a fly against the screen over the desk. It must have been caught there between the screen and the window when Ruthie closed up the house. He stared at the farm scene and listened to the slight irregular noise and finally fell asleep. Lying back in the chair, he dreamed that he and Helen were flying somewhere to the south, toward Gibraltar or Greece. When he looked out the plane window he saw blue water and white sand etched in brilliant sunlight. Look, he said, look, and turned to her, but her seat was empty.

He woke early the next morning, chilled and uncomfortable. His back had stiffened in the chair overnight and he had to raise himself slowly and stand erect for a while until feeling came back. He went into the kitchen and made coffee and while it was dripping he went quickly through the house, opening windows. From somewhere down the block came the summer sound of a power mower. He opened the front door to get the morning paper, then realized there wouldn't be one. It was a fine morning, warm already, warmer with a different kind of warmth from that of Oxford: harder, drier, more intense. He drank his coffee, then showered and shaved. His face in the mirror looked thin to him and more lined than he remembered it. But it wasn't the face of a man devastated by a catastrophe, he thought, it was only in the movies that people changed like that. He went into the bedroom for clothes, carefully not looking at anything except the closet where his own things were, dressed quickly and left.

The VW started without trouble; Ruthie's Jim must have run it a few times to keep the battery up. He backed out of the driveway and pulled away without looking around. He wasn't ready for neighbors yet. He drove slowly toward the cemetery. It was in an older part of the east side, near the old city airport. His parents were buried there. He drove the winding gravel roads until he got to their graves, then stopped but didn't get out of the car. He hadn't visited their graves very often. He probably wouldn't visit Helen's grave very often either. His father had visited his mother's grave almost daily for months, but Moore had hardly gone at all. Moore had thought a good deal about it at the time, and he had thought about it again when his father had died and when again he hardly ever went to the cemetery. He had finally decided that people went to the graves of loved ones because they still felt a presence there. But Moore had never felt that. If I want to visit Helen, he thought, all I have to do is go into the bedroom. She was still there in the things she had made her own, but she had lost that power of imprinting herself on things in the seconds it took Morgan to kill her.

He drove on, recalling the directions Ruthie had written him. Two curves in the road past Grandma and Grandpa, by the red cross, between Lewandowski and Benvenuto. He saw the cross and stopped the car and went up the little slope. Lewandowski was to the left, Benvenuto to the right, both upright markers. Between them was Helen's stone, flat in the ground, as he had told Ruthie to put it, already looking as if it belonged there. The ground in front of it was perfectly flat—somehow he had thought it would still be mounded—but he walked carefully to the side of it and stared down at the stone. Helen Thomas Moore, wife and mother, 1927-1976. Nothing more. No RIP, nothing. We are quiet and ordinary people, he had told Ruthie, when we die it's important only to us, leave the ornamentation and rhetoric for kings and counselors. He looked away from the stone and let his eyes travel over the cemetery. Beyond Lewandowski and Benvenuto it stretched out flat and uniform like Detroit itself, an endless billiard table of markers and miniature American flags and wilted flowers in grass-green plastic vases. He thought of the Iffley churchyard and the Eye of God and the gigantic yew tree. I'm not sentimental about burials, he thought, but I wish Mother and Dad and Helen were buried at Iffley, in that smaller place that seems to have more meaning. But then he thought, as he had thought that day at Iffley, you lie dead where you lived; if anything is appropriate, that is. They don't belong at Iffley; they'd only be tourists there. And when I die they'll put my body here, or my ashes, four feet away from Helen's, and the marker will say James Lee Moore, husband and father. Not bad husband or erring husband. Just as Morgan's stone probably said the same thing. Not murderer: just father and husband. Just the primary facts, just the life in miniature, the bad forgotten and the good probably not worth recording.

I'm thinking death thoughts, graveyard poetry, he said to himself. Death is too big for us; it always turns our brains to water. He looked down at Helen's headstone again and at the flat empty patch of grass in front of it and wondered for the first time if he should have brought flowers. It was, after all, what other people did. But after a moment he decided that the gesture would have been an empty one for him, and thus for Helen as well. He had almost never brought her flowers in life. If he brought them now it would be for other people. She had known him so well—perhaps somehow she still did—and if she did she would know that. If, he thought, if she bothered to think about little things like that, wherever she was and however she was. There was nothing he could bring her now that would be meaningful, except himself and his tangled lines of desolation and self-pity.

He drove slowly out of the cemetery, without conscious thought, like a cowboy giving his horse its head, and in a little while he found himself at the entrance of Windmill Pointe Park. He remembered Helen's standing joke: when the car goes out of the driveway it automatically heads for the river, like an old milk wagon horse that knows only its old route. He drove into the little nondescript scrap of ground that no one ever seemed to take care of. The usual vans and stripped-down cars were lined up in the asphalt parking lot, the booming of rock music and the odor of marijuana filled the summer air, and several long-haired young men wearing only jeans were sailing a frisbee back and forth. They were always there—or others like them—winter and summer, but they had never bothered Moore much because they never went near the river, never even seemed to know that the river was there. They stayed in the parking lot with their music and their dope and their frisbees and seemed contented. Moore parked as far away from them as he could and walked across the road to the shabby park. Now, in mid-August, the old elms were dusty and tired looking and the grass was burned brown and dry. The wire trash baskets had long ago overflowed, and beer cans and soda bottles and paper wrappers and pizza boxes lay everywhere. A few people, mostly black, were picnicking at the old wooden tables, and Moore walked through waves of charcoal smoke and the smell of scorched hot dogs. The cinderblock lavatory had been freshly painted white since the summer before, but already it was covered with East Side gang names spray painted on the walls in a welter of misspellings and apostrophes and assorted obscenities: the White Hood's, the Black Knight's, the Erol Flyns. Down at the water's edge the cement walkway put in a few years ago was already cracking, and a thirty-foot section of railing had been torn loose from the pavement and never replaced. The usual assortment of fishermen sat on milk cases and camp chairs, cans of beer cooling in buckets beside them; their rods leaned against the railing and pointed out over the water, with little warning bells tied to the ends. Every few minutes a bell would tinkle as a rod bent and the fisherman would reel in and untangle the clot of seaweed he had caught. Moore had always thought it odd that the fishermen hardly ever talked to each other. It didn't seem to have anything to do with age or race, though some were old and some young and some were black and some white. They simply paid no attention to each other, and Moore had finally concluded that what they were doing required no special skill; they weren't like trout fishermen comparing lures; they were city fishermen simply passing time.

Moore found an empty place along the railing and leaned against it and looked out over the river. Directly in front of him was the low green slice of land that was Peche Island and that visitors always took for Canada. But Canada was just behind it, a mile away, the high-rise apartments of the Windsor riverfront towering up fresh and clean looking in the afternoon sun. Downriver a mile or so the Edison smokestacks curled white smoke into the intense blue sky, and around the point of Belle Isle Moore could see the white prow of a lake freighter coming up-river. He waited for it with the anticipation one feels for old pleasant recurring sights. It came silently, like a dream ship, till it was a quarter of a mile away, and then he could hear the quiet beat of the engines coming across the water. When it came abreast of him he could see that it was a Canadian Steamship Lines boat, a self-unloader riding deep in the water. A man in a blue tee shirt came out of the aft cabin and leaned against the rail and waved and two or three of the fishermen waved back. The freighter slid slowly by, past the park and the Senior Citizens' Center that had once been a coast guard station, past the nearly abandoned Marine Hospital that now housed only a substance abuse clinic, and out of sight, bearing away from the American shore and out into the channel in Lake St. Clair. As it disappeared it sounded its horn in three long blasts, and Moore knew there must be another ship downbound and not yet in sight. In a moment he heard its answering horn and in a few minutes it came by, an ocean freighter, German, out of Hamburg, bristling with unloading masts, moving faster than the lake freighter, riding with the current. He watched it till its stern swung nearly at a right angle to the shore as it made its turn to go around the Belle Isle point.

Moore hardly ever saw the downbound boats after they got past Belle Isle, but he knew that when he drove home along the lakeshore he would see the upbound boat, or one like it, far out in the lake, almost invisible in the heat haze, like an idea at the edge of the mind. He leaned against the railing, savoring the warm air and the sunlight on the water, feeling for the first time that he was really home. He was old enough now to understand something of the strange pull of the familiar, even when the familiar was partly ugly and corrupt. This was his home, this dirty and neglected park, this polluted river that still looked so beautiful, these silent ships that measured the seasons for him and always had. If he had been somehow a different person, tiny and picturesque Oxford would have been his easy and comfortable ground, his reservoir of comforting and familiar things, but he was not that different person, and this drab and decaying stretch of America along the Canadian border had been his nursery and forever his point of all comparisons. He doubted that he would have changed it even if he could. And yet he had only been a tourist here, Helen had said, and if he was a tourist here, where would he be anything else?

He went back to the car. The long-hairs were still sailing the frisbee and the air was still full of marijuana and acid rock. He drove out of the park and past the Marine Hospital and onto the lakeshore drive. Out of the corner of his eye, over the glittering blue of the water, he saw the upbound Canadian boat, and suddenly he was thinking of Lane. Not just Lane. Robert F. Lane. The full name came back to him as part of a picture he had long forgotten. It was Lane himself who had stressed the full name. Moore had been sitting with Lane and someone else at a cafe table somewhere in Germany after V-E Day, with Lane and this other person and three German girls, young girls wearing wooden clog sandals. "My name is Lane," Lane had said, "Robert F. Lane. Guess what the F stands for." Moore couldn't remember much about the girls except their clog sandals and their brown bare legs. They hadn't known much English and it was a long while before they caught the joke and laughed. Lane, tall and lanky, and with a way with the girls. The picture faded. Moore had no memory of anything that had happened after that moment in the cafe, but he was glad that he had not remembered that cafe scene in Gwen's parlor when she had asked him about Lane. Moore found himself wondering what Lane had looked like when he went back to Wallingford, what Gwen's mother had seen that night when the American stranger had walked into the Fox and Grape and set the pattern for so many people. Had she recognized him after thirty years, as if time had stopped that morning by the haystack and only picked up again when he had walked into the pub? No, Moore thought, only in the movies. In real life when you looked at a thirty-year-old picture of yourself you could only identify the person because you knew who it was. No, she must have seen only a man—American, from the cut of his clothes and his accent—but what else? Had she seen something at once that made her prefer him to her husband, had there been an almost instant recognition of some quality, some charm, that she had waited all her life to find? Or had it been gradual, something that grew, something that perhaps she had resisted for days or weeks, something that Morgan had never had, or had had once and lost?

Moore made a U-turn around one of the islands on the lakeshore drive and headed back toward downtown. He had been to the cemetery and he had been to the river, and now it was time to find Lane. He drove faster than he should have, past the Ford estate, past the black nannies walking with lit-tle white children, past the older men and women in expensive summer togs strolling with manicured poodles and Yorkshire terriers, and as always they ground at his middle-class spirit, but this time he knew it was Lane he was really thinking about, knew that he was trying to find a focus for the anger he felt. He had to find Lane. He had to ask him Gwen's question: Did you love my mother? But he had to find him for his own reasons too. He had his own questions to ask: Why did you go back? What were you looking for? Do you know anything about the pattern you began? If you know, does it make any difference to you? You must know about Nancy, but do you know about Morgan and Helen? Moore drove on, words tumbling around in his mind. There were things Lane must be told; he owed them all that much.

At the main library Moore found the city directory for Madison, Wis-consin. There were several Lanes, and three Robert Lanes, but only one Robert F. Lane. Moore wrote down the address and put it in his wallet. He drove home by way of the lakeshore drive again, but more slowly now. Far out in the shimmering lake an ocean freighter was upbound, trailing lazy smoke, and closer in a lake freighter was downbound. They were too far apart to have to signal each other with their horns.

At home that night, in the den, Moore got out his road atlas and checked the route to Madison. It was simple enough. Detroit to Chicago, Chicago to Madison. About seven hours. He turned on the radio. The Tigers were losing again, in Boston: good pitching but no hitting. Moore went into the bedroom and set the alarm for seven and turned down the bed. Now that he had the Madison trip in his mind he thought he could sleep here tonight. He took underwear and socks from the highboy drawer that Helen had made his. Above it was the shallow top drawer: he looked at it but couldn't remember what was in it. He pulled it open. There was an old belt there, his, and two or three of Helen's headscarves. In the far back corner there was a black lump. As soon as he touched it he remembered it. He lifted it out carefully—the army had taught him to be careful with guns—though he knew it wasn't loaded. He sat down on the bed and took it gently from the holster. A P-38, the German enlisted man's ersatz Luger. He slid the clip out of the handle—empty—and checked the chamber—

empty. He couldn't remember when he had seen it last. It looked dry. He had never bothered to oil it regularly. He had fired it once at a firing range out of curiosity and found he couldn't hit anything with it. It was just a souvenir. But it was a souvenir that Lane would remember. Moore had bought it from someone at the embarkation point in Belgium just before they had come home. Lane had been there. He had bought something too—Moore couldn't remember what—a knife or a corkscrew, but he had wanted to buy the gun and Moore had gotten it first.

He put the gun back in the holster and dropped it into the bag he was taking with him. Just a souvenir. Maybe he would show it to Lane. He imagined a scene in which he produced the gun and said, "You remember this?" He imagined the look of fear in Lane's face, and savored it. He went to bed and slept lightly. The scene with Lane kept repeating itself in his dreams. Lane's face, still fresh and nineteen, kept crumbling in fright as he looked at the gun. Moore said things to him that made his face crumble even more, and then, over and over, Moore's finger tightened on the trigger. In the dreams the gun was oiled and worked smoothly and was loaded.

CHAPTER 9

Madison

B y eight the next morning Moore, driving Helen's car, was out of
Detroit and nearly to Ann Arbor. It was a bright, hot morning, and by
ten o'clock he had to close the windows and turn on the air conditioner. He
listened to the local radio stations as he went past Battle Creek and Kala-
mazoo and St. Joseph. Outside of Chicago, on the Indiana Turnpike, he
stopped for gas and a sandwich. It was just past noon and the sun beat down
on the cement apron by the gas pumps. He walked stiffly around while the
tank was being filled, feeling a little lightheaded. The sun in Oxford had
never been this hot, and somehow in two months that was the sun he had
become used to.

He got directions for the best way through Chicago, but he made a
wrong turn somewhere off an expressway and found himself on Lakeshore
Drive, so he followed it north for several miles. He had not been in Chicago
in years and had forgotten that remarkable long stretch of the city that
fronts on Lake Michigan, the endless hotels and high-rise apartments on
the left, the endless Lake Michigan on the right. Somewhere in that long
span he had come with his parents to the 1935 World's Fair. He could
remember a parking lot baking in the sun and frightening cable cars and
posters of Sally Rand.

Lakeshore Drive finally put him on the route north to Wisconsin and by
four o'clock in the afternoon he was coming into the outskirts of Madison. He
had no idea where Lane lived, so he headed into the center of town down a
broad boulevard that led to the capitol. He drove around the capitol square
until he found a parking space. A Walgreen drugstore was only a block away
and he walked stiffly toward it, his back throbbing from the drive. He needed
one of Harker's pills. He hadn't taken one before because he had to drive, but
now he knew he couldn't have much farther to go. In the drugstore a boy
behind a cigarette counter told him where Lane's street was: out along the road
past Lake Winona in a new subdivision called Lakeside.

Moore found a Coke machine in the back of the store and got a can of
Coke and took a pill. He went back to the car and half leaned and half sat

on a front fender, waiting for the pill to work. In about fifteen minutes he began to feel the familiar sense of lightness, as if his body was made of gossamer, and he got into the car and circled the capitol and headed out along the road past Lake Winona. He found the three-way intersection the boy had told him about, turned into a winding road and in a few minutes stopped the car in front of a comfortable looking tri-level house with Lane's address. The house was in a cul-de-sac, a circle of eight houses set around a miniature park with young maple trees and a children's slide and some swings and a carousel, the kind that children sit on and move with their feet. All new, all upper middle-class, Moore thought. This was where Lane had come from when he had gone to England and had for some reason begun that series of falling dominoes that Harker refused to call coincidence.

Moore sat for a few minutes, his hands on the steering wheel, trying to bring his mind to bear on the meeting with Lane. He had rehearsed this meeting in his dreams the night before, but now he was here with his empty gun and his questions and the whole thing seemed suddenly slippery. It seemed to him that Harker's pill was having more than its usual effect, and he put this down to fatigue. But there was something else as well. He took the gun out of the overnight bag on the seat next to him and slid it out of the holster. It's empty, he said to himself, I'm only bringing it as a symbol. Maybe I'll even give it to him, because he wanted it once. I think Gwen would like that. I'll leave it here and then come back and get it for him.

But when he took the holstered gun out of the overnight bag on the seat next to him and looked at the initials scratched into the holster—WFA—he could think only of death. If the gun was a symbol of anything it was a symbol of death. Gwen had forgiven Lane. She had said that, and Moore believed her. But as he hefted the gun in his palm he felt his hand trembling and he remembered that in his dream the gun had been loaded. I will forgive him, he said to himself almost as a continuation of his dream, but not yet. He stuffed the holstered gun in his jacket pocket and got out of the car and went up the walk to Lane's front porch. I come announcing death and guilt, he said, forgiveness will come later. The words seemed eloquent and kept time with his steps.

Standing on the porch with the gun heavy in his pocket, he thought of the old Sergeant Friday television series: Friday and his partner knocking on a door and Friday saying to the suspect who opened the door, We only want to ask a few questions, we only want the facts. If Lane answers the door,

Moore thought, he won't know who I am, he won't recognize me. I'll be a strange man standing on his porch saying very calmly, Hello, I just want to ask you a few questions, I only want to know some facts. Maybe for a moment he'll think I'm a policeman.

Suddenly he was cold. He reached to turn up his jacket collar and looked up for the cloud that was blotting out the sun. There was no cloud. The sun beat heavily down on him, but without warmth, suddenly an arctic sun. He looked down at the peony bush beside Lane's porch. The purple and white blossoms looked frigid, like flowers in a florist's refrigerator. He shivered, and then he felt accompanied. Without turning to look, he was sure that Broderick and the lesbian reporter were there beside him, waiting with him for Lane's door to open. The three of us, he thought, three judges with ice in their hearts, waiting to condemn. He shut his eyes and turned completely around so that when he opened them he was looking at the little park across the street. A small boy was perched on top of the slide and two more small boys and a girl were sitting on the carousel seats, scuffing their shoes in the dirt to make it move. Moore watched until the boy slid down and the carousel had made one full slow circuit and then he felt the warmth of the suburban sun again and knew he was alone. He turned back to Lane's front door, a trickle of sweat inching down between his shoulder blades, and pushed the doorbell button.

The door opened and he was looking at a girl of about twenty in blue jeans and blouse. Her light brown hair was frizzed in the current mode that aped the twenties. Moore could see nothing of Lane in her face. "I'm an old fiend of Mr. Lane's," he said. "I suppose you're his daughter?"

"Yes," she said, but she looked at him carefully before she answered. Moore wondered if somehow he looked odd to her, if there was something in his face that wasn't friendship. A woman appeared behind the girl. Moore, peering out of sunlight into shadow, could only vaguely make her out. "It's someone about Dad," the girl said to her, "an old friend."

The woman stepped forward and Moore could see that she was slight, with heavy graying hair. She wore slacks and a white blouse with the sleeves rolled up. A pair of glasses hung from a thin chain around her neck. She put the glasses on and looked through the screen door at Moore. "I'm afraid I don't know you," she said.

"I was in the army with Bob," Moore said. This had to be Lane's wife, the betrayed woman. Moore wondered whether she knew she had been betrayed. She was about Helen's age, he thought, but she looked older. Too old to be Lane's wife, he thought, but then he caught himself: he was still thinking of Lane as nineteen.

"Oh, I see," she said, "please come in." She opened the screen door and Moore stepped in out of the sunlight and took off his sunglasses. He was on a landing. Stairs on his left went down into a living room and stairs on his right went up to another level. She went in front of him down into the living room and he could feel the girl following behind him. The room was dark and cool; vertical slatted blinds were pulled almost shut against the afternoon sun and he felt the sudden coolness of air conditioning. The two women sat down together on a massive tan couch and he lowered himself into a matching easy chair across from them. The carpet between them was grass green and thick.

"I'm sorry," Lane's wife said, "did you mention your name?"

"Moore."

"I'm sorry, Bob's not here, Mr. Moore," she said. "He's away for the afternoon. This is our daughter, Betty." The girl nodded and smiled.

"I can come back later," Moore said, "it's not urgent. I'm just passing through. I thought maybe we could talk over some old times for a while." He wasn't sure whether he was relieved or disappointed that Lane was not here.

"Did you know my dad very well?" Betty asked eagerly. "Did you and Dad go through the war together?"

It seemed to Moore that Mrs. Lane was looking at him with more than casual interest. He wondered how much she knew of Wallingford, or whether there had been other Wallingfords. "I suppose you could say that," he said to the girl. "What we saw of the war we saw together."

"I remember some of the places he mentioned," Betty said. "It was a long time ago when he used to talk about them, but I remember. The Saar River, Lunéville, Neckarsulm. Were you with him in those places?"

Moore nodded, caught up for the moment in the magic of the old names. "Yes, and Saint-Avold and Colmar and Saarbrucken."

"I remember those names," she said, "don't you, Mom?"

"Yes, I think I do," Lane's wife said. Then she turned quickly to Moore. "Have you come far, Mr. Moore?"

All the way from Wallingford, Moore thought, but he said, "From Detroit."

"Honey," Lane's wife said to her daughter, "I'm sure Mr. Moore would like some coffee. Would you make some?"

"Sure, Mom." Betty got up and gave her mother one quick look as she went out, and Moore was sure she knew she was being sent away, and guessed that she knew why. He and Mrs. Lane were going to have adult talk now, the kind you keep from children if you can, even when they're grown up.

Lane's wife sat for a moment, toying with her glasses. Moore shifted in his chair and felt the gun move against his hip. He waited for her to speak, feeling as he had that night in Gwen's parlor, that bad things were coming.

"Were you in England with Bob, too, Mr. Moore?"

"Yes."

"Weston-super-Mare?"

"Yes."

"Wallingford?"

"Yes."

She got up and went over to a cherrywood desk against the wall, opened the middle drawer and took out a small key. She unlocked one of the side drawers and took something out that Moore couldn't see, put on her glasses and looked at it for a minute, then took them off again and turned to Moore. "Have you been back to Wallingford since the war, Mr. Moore?"

"Once," Moore said.

She looked at him gravely. "You too," she said. "What a remarkable little girl she must have been."

"Who?" Moore said, thinking, I don't know whether to lie or not; I wanted to tell the truth to Lane, but I wasn't counting on his wife.

She came over and handed him a photograph. "Nancy Morgan," she said. "Don't you know her?"

Moore looked at the picture. It was black and white, a studio portrait of a woman of forty or so in three quarter profile. The face was not Gwen's face, but in fifteen years Gwen might come to look more like it. The eyes were the same, dark and level, and the serious expression was the same. Nancy Morgan, he thought, the girl who once sat on the fence by the haystack, part of the essence of England.

"I knew a little girl named Nancy once," he said, "but I never saw her again."

Lane's wife looked at him, then back at the picture. "You never saw her grown up?"

"No."

"I was hoping you could tell me something about her. A wife is curious about her rivals."

"She isn't a rival any more," Moore said.

"I know she's dead, if that's what you mean. Someone sent a newspaper story—we never knew who. But she's still a rival. Maybe more than ever."

"You know about her and Bob?" Moore said. "Then what more is there to know?"

"Only everything," she said. She took the picture from Moore and went back to the desk and put it away and then turned back to him. "I only know the facts," she said quietly, "I don't know what they mean." She sat down on the couch again and stared at the green carpet. In the shuttered room she looked almost girlish in her jeans and shirt because the gray in her hair hardly showed. After a moment she said, "I don't know you, Mr. Moore, and I probably won't see you again, but you're my only contact with something that's very important to me. May I talk to you?"

"Of course," Moore said. The gun dug into his hip and he thought, I didn't plan on this, I didn't make any provision for this, I only wanted to talk to Lane, clean and simple.

"He went to London on business," Lane's wife said. "It was nothing unusual—he'd gone there before. But when he came back this time I knew something had happened, but I didn't know what. He was restless, moodier than usual, quieter." She stopped, still looking vacantly at the carpet. "After a while the letters came, from England. I didn't read them—they were addressed to him. It seemed to me he was drinking more than usual and spending more time in his den upstairs. And he—" She paused. "He didn't pay much attention to me." She paused again. "I mean, even less than usual." She put her hands, palms down, on her knees and stared down at them, and Moore thought she might be looking for age spots or wrinkles, touches of time that a husband would have seen a long time ago. I was a husband, Moore thought, I noticed things like that. "I tried to talk to him about what was wrong," she went on, "but it wasn't any good. He just wouldn't talk about it." She got up and went over to the window and adjusted the venetian blinds up, then down, then back the way they had been. "Then one morning I went into his den to clean a little. He'd been in there late the night before. There were open letters on his desk, and that picture. I looked at the picture, and then I read the letters, all of them. That night I told him what I'd done. He wasn't upset. I think maybe he wanted me to see them. He just said he was sorry and it was over and he was trying to forget it and he hoped I would. He said he'd understand if I left him but he hoped I wouldn't because of Betty. He left it all up to me. He said nothing like that would ever happen again. Only he wouldn't talk about Nancy Morgan, he'd only say it was over and done."

"Her letters," Moore said, "didn't they tell you something about her?"

"Not really. They were just love letters—love notes, really. Any woman might have written them. They didn't say much—they were like little reminders that she was there."

"He never answered them?"

She shook her head no. "He swore he never did. I believe him."

"And then you got the newspaper story?"

"Yes, about a month after she died."

"What did it say?"

"That she'd died from an overdose of sleeping pills. There was a coroner's inquest. They called it accidental death."

Moore was silent, thinking, No accidents, no coincidences. Somewhere on the upper level a phone rang and he heard Betty's voice answering it.

"Maybe it *was* accidental," Lane's wife said. "I hope it was. But Bob didn't think so. He never said that, but I know. He thinks he caused it, I know he does. But he won't talk about it, or at least not to me." She stopped for a minute, then said, "But he's got to talk to someone about it, because I think it's killing him." She came across the room and stood in front of Moore. "You wonder why I'm curious about Nancy Morgan, Mr. Moore? My husband saw her once thirty years ago and then again for maybe two weeks, and now she's dead and he's drinking himself to death over her. I want to know what was so special about her, and no one can tell me. I've got a few of her love letters and a picture of her and that's all, and my husband can't forget her." She put her hands to her face and began to cry, quietly, and Moore knew she was afraid Betty would hear her, and he felt useless and irrelevant, like the gun in his pocket. He stood up stiffly and put his hand on her arm. She looked up at him; she wasn't wearing makeup, and her face was raw with tears. "You were his friend and you knew her, you at least saw her. Will you talk to him? Or will you get him to talk to you?"

"Of course I'll talk to him," Moore said and patted her arm again. "I don't know what I can do, but I'll try." I came to punish Lane, he thought, not his wife. But it was like the A and B in mathematics, as Harker had said, what affects A affects B. "Maybe I can help," he said. "Tell me where to find him."

"The Badger Athletic Club, by the stadium. He'll be with his friends there, watching the ballgame." She wiped at the tears with her index fingers and took a long breath. "I'm sorry to be crying."

"It's all right," Moore said, "I understand. I'll find the place." He turned away from her, shifting the gun in his pocket, heavy with the feeling of Helen crying in that other darkened room, and again finding no words of comfort. When he went up the stairs Lane's wife was still simply standing, looking down at the chair he'd been sitting in. He went down the hallway and was at the front door before he realized that Betty was behind him.

"You're not staying for coffee?" she said.

"I'm sorry, I'm afraid not."

She came out onto the front porch with him into the bright sunlight. "You're going to see Dad?" she said. Now that Moore looked at her again he thought she looked like her mother, and yet there was something in her face that made him think of Lane as he remembered him.

"Yes, I think so."

"It's about the woman in England, isn't it?"

"You know about that?"

"I know something," she said, "not everything. More than I want to know."

She looks so young to know these things, Moore thought, what a pity she isn't even younger, playing on the swings across the street, not knowing anything at all. "Nobody knows everything about these things," he said vaguely, "but give it time. Time smooths out everything." He knew the words were meaningless, but they were at least a ritual, the sort of thing people said at funerals.

But she didn't hear him, or didn't pay any attention. "If you see Dad," she said, "will you tell him something for us?" Moore nodded. "Tell him we love him," she said, and turned and went back inside.

Moore went down the walk to his car and stood for a moment looking at the little playground, but he was seeing the two women standing together in the cool darkened room trying to comfort each other. After a while they would have a cup of coffee, because it was made, and then they would go on doing the things they usually did on a summer afternoon while they waited for Lane to come home, hoping he would be the way he used to be. Mrs. Lane was clearly not a New Woman. If she'd read Gloria Steinem and Betty Friedan they hadn't affected her. She was the old-fashioned wife, patient Griselda. Moore, seeing her again in the neat living room of the tri-level house, remembered the tall houses that ringed the harbor in Port Huron, the houses where captains of the lake ships had lived a hundred years ago. The top stories had a balcony where the wives could stand and look out past the harbor entrance to the lake and wait for their husbands to come back from the autumn storms. They called the balcony the Widows' Walk.

He got into the car, the gun bumping again against his hip, and when he got a block away from Lane's house he stopped and pulled the gun out of his pocket and put it in the glove box.

Near the capitol he stopped at a gas station and got directions to the Badger Athletic Club. It was a block from the stadium, one of a row of old red brick buildings, most of them with glass store fronts: a convenience store, a coffee shop, a pizzeria. The Badger A. C. had obviously been a store once too; it still had the large windowpanes on either side of the door and there were still display counters behind the windows. But the counters were covered now with red and white cloth and the products on show now were rows of pictures of Wisconsin athletes, some of them studio portraits but most of them enlargements of action pictures taken from newspapers. There was a picture of Crazy Legs Hirsch catching a pass, one of George Paskvan bucking into the line, and one of Earl Averill posed rigidly at bat. Moore stood looking at them, wondering what to say to Lane if he found him. Still fueled by Harker's pill, his mind lazily addressed his responsibilities: to speak and to listen for both Gwen and himself, yes, but somehow for Helen and Nancy Morgan and Gwen's father. And now Lane's wife and daughter as well. He would be representing both the present and the past. He thought, I'm a kind of ambassador at large for all the world I know.

He went inside and found himself standing at one end of a long narrow room with a bar along the left wall, tables crowded in the rest of the room, and a giant television screen against the back wall. The place was packed with men, most of them wearing tee shirts or nylon athletic jackets, and the air was heavy with beer and cigarette smoke. Everyone was watching the ballgame on television. Out of habit Moore watched too until he knew who was playing: Cincinnati and Pittsburgh; he recognized Bench and Rose and Stargell. He looked up and down the bar and then at the tables, one by one, wondering whether he would recognize Lane. He found him easily. He was sitting with two men in tee shirts, men in their forties. Lane wore a red nylon jacket with the word Badgers on the front. He didn't look much different to Moore than he had looked thirty years before. His blond hair was still thick and curly, though it might be graying a little in better light, and his face still had the rounded ruddy look it had had when he was nineteen. If he stood up he might show a paunch, but Moore doubted it. Lane seemed to be one of the elite who weather well. That's the man Nancy Morgan saw walk into the pub that night, Moore thought; I wonder if that was part of the charm for her—that he could come from so far out of the past and still look so young, as if somehow he had evaded time.

Moore got a stein of beer from the bar and made his way over to the table and stood there while Bench threw out a Pirate trying to steal second to end the inning. A beer commercial came on and Lane and the other two men turned away from the screen and saw Moore.

"Mind if I sit here?" Moore said.

"Always room for one more," one of the men said, "as long as you bring your own beer." He filled the three steins on the table from a nearly full pitcher.

Moore put his beer on the table and sat down. Lane glanced at him with no recognition. When the next inning started and they were all looking at the screen again Moore leaned over to Lane and said, "You're Bob Lane, aren't you?"

Lane looked at him. "That's right. Do I know you?"

If I had the P-38, Moore thought, I could take it out and lay it on the table in front of him. That would have been fun, watching the shock, then watching him start to remember. But games like that have been taken away from me. "I'm Jim Moore," he said. "Remember Bristol and Weston-super-Mare and The Jersey Bounce? *That* Jim Moore."

Lane stared at him. "Oh my God," he said, "Jim Moore, you old son of a bitch." He looked hard at Moore again. "It really *is* you. My God, I would have walked past you in the street. What in God's name brings you here? How did you know me?"

"It's a long story," Moore said. "I was just passing through and looked up your address. Your wife told me you'd be here."

"I'll be damned," Lane said. He turned to the other two men. "This is my old army buddy, Jim Moore. We haven't seen each other in thirty years." The two men shook hands with Moore and said their names and turned back to the ballgame. "Let's get away from the TV where we can talk a little," Lane said, and stood up. Moore noted that he'd been right about Lane: he was nearly as lean now as he had been thirty years before. Moore followed him back to a table near the door and they sat down beneath a picture on the wall of the 1937 University of Wisconsin football team. "Now," Lane said, "how can we fill each other in on thirty years?"

"I guess we can't," Moore said, "but I've seen your wife and daughter and they fill in a lot."

"Yes, they're fine," Lane said, "I guess they're as good as they come. How about yourself? How much family?"

"I've got a daughter too, but I lost my wife just last month."

"Oh damn," Lane said earnestly. "I lost someone not long ago too. It tears you up." He pushed his beer stein back and forth in front of him. "Of course it wasn't my wife, but it was someone very dear to me. A bad business."

I might as well get to it, Moore thought, though I really don't know what I want to say, or what I ought to say, or whether I should say anything at all. "I just got back from England," he said. "I came up here mainly to tell you that Nancy Morgan is dead, but your wife told me you already knew that."

For a moment he thought Lane hadn't heard him, but then Lane slumped back in his chair and looked away toward the television. When he turned back, for the first time he looked older to Moore. The beery friendliness had gone out of his face as if some interior light had been turned out. He had always looked boyish when he smiled, but he wasn't smiling now. "She told you that?" he said. "Then I suppose she told you the whole thing."

"She doesn't seem to know the whole thing," Moore said, "only a kind of outline. Just that you had an affair and Nancy Morgan is dead."

"And I'm going down the sewer?" Lane said. "She must have told you that too."

"Something like that. No details."

"Well, this is the sewer she meant," Lane said. He waved his hand to take in the entire room. "All these guys here are going down the same sewer if you believe their wives. But we wouldn't call it a sewer. More like a home away from home." He finished his stein of beer. "It's weird seeing you like this. We were good buddies once, weren't we? Now we're like strangers. I suppose we told each other a lot of things about ourselves back then, but I don't remember any of it. Do you?"

"No, I don't," Moore said, "but it's been a long time. You just remember bits and pieces."

Lane nodded. "Odds and ends. Funny things. Some names. Crapping in a snow bank. The guy who got run over by the truck. What was his name?"

"I can't remember. An Italian name. Russo?"

"Maybe." Lane fingered his empty glass. "Do you remember Wallingford very well?"

"Yes," Moore said. Oh, yes, he thought, I remember Wallingford.

"I didn't," Lane said. "I mean, not till I went back. Then I remembered a lot." He pushed his glass back and forth on the table. "Now I remember it a lot more." He looked around the room again and then back at Moore. "Do you plan to see my wife again? You're not going to report to her, are you?"

"No," Moore said, "I'm just passing through." I'll report, he thought, but not to her.

"It's funny," Lane said. "I see you now and I remember that we had a lot of fun over there, didn't we? I mean, in spite of the bad things. Sometimes I think those days were the high point of my life, I mean the most interesting part. You know, I started out as a lit major here at U of W after the war. I took some courses in creative writing because I thought I had a lot of good stories to tell about the war. The classes were full of vets like me and they all had stories to tell too. We all passed the courses, I guess, but none of us turned into Hemingways. I remember what the prof wrote on one of my stories: "You have the gift of gab; now you should learn the craft of fiction." I guess I was too lazy to do that. But maybe he was right about the gift of gab. I'm a good computer salesman." He stopped. "Shall we talk over old times a little? That's what old buddies do, isn't it? I'll get some beer and you can tell me why you went back there and I'll tell you why I did. If you want to hear it."

"I want to hear it," Moore said. Yes, he thought, we all want to hear it, all of us whose lives overlapped yours.

Lane got up and went to the bar. Moore watched Rose triple and come home on a sacrifice fly by Bench. Lane came back with a pitcher of beer and filled their glasses and sat down. He took a long swallow and then said, "You went to Wallingford?" Moore nodded. "Why? Why did you go back there? To see Nancy?"

"No," Moore said, "mostly just to see the place. I happened to be near there. I suppose I went there out of curiosity." Without surprise, he noted that he was speaking the truth but only the minimal truth, and it occurred to him that he would probably never speak openly again to anyone but Gwen, that everyone else had to be either deceived or protected.

"How did you find out Nancy was dead?"

"I met her husband by accident. And her daughter."

"Her daughter?" Lane said. "Yes, I knew there was a daughter. I know her name is Gwen, but I never saw her. And they told you?"

"The daughter did."

"I would have supposed the husband did," Lane said. "He was a quiet one, but I'm sure he knew what was happening."

"Maybe he would have told me," Moore said carefully, "but he was half crippled when I saw him. From a stroke. Not really all there. He died while I was there."

Lane was silent for a moment. Then he said, "I'm sorry to hear that. I didn't think he amounted to much, but I wouldn't wish that on him. I mean, along with everything else." He finished his stein and refilled it. "What was the daughter like? How old is she?"

"In her twenties. Quiet. Serious."

Lane nodded. "Like her mother, probably." He looked away from Moore, then back at him. "I suppose she hates me?"

"I think they both did, but I think she's got over it now."

"Well, I suppose I'm glad," Lane said, "not that it matters much now." He drank from his stein, then lighted a cigarette. "So Marion told you I'm on the road to hell. Well, why wouldn't she? She's told everyone else."

"She didn't say that. Only that you've been moody and not yourself. Blaming yourself for Nancy's death, she thinks."

"I *am* myself, though," Lane said, "but she doesn't understand that. There's a lot she doesn't understand. Because she's a woman." He leaned back in his chair and half smiled at Moore. "You're not a psychiatrist, are you?"

"No, anything but," Moore said.

"Marion's been after me to unburden myself to someone. Preferably her, I think. She thinks I'm suffering from pent-up guilt feelings. But I don't have pent-up guilt feelings. I just know something that every man here knows but won't tell his wife. The Wallingford thing isn't a special case, except that someone died. I'm as sorry about that as a man can be, but I didn't mean that to happen." His voice was suddenly hoarse. "No, I didn't mean that to happen." He cleared his throat and took a swallow of beer. "I don't deny it's been on my mind, but not the way Marion thinks. It's in my mind like a story that taught me something I should have known all along. But it's a story I wouldn't tell to Marion. If I tell you it's because you were there at the beginning of it and now you're here at the end of it. Here's the way it was."

Lane began. It took him about twenty minutes, and Moore listened to him for himself and for all his constituency while in the background the game went into extra innings.

Lane said: It was in October. I was in London and the weather was beautiful. I'd just closed a computer deal in two days that I thought was going to take two weeks and all of a sudden I had nothing to do except come home. I thought I'd give myself a treat, so I rented a little Morris and headed out of London. I was going to drive down into Devon or maybe Wales—I didn't really care which. But I got mixed up in a roundabout and before I knew it I was on a carriageway going the other way, heading north. So I thought, all right, I'll go north—what's the difference? After a while I saw some signs for Oxford, but I didn't want to go there, and then I saw a sign for Wallingford and the bells started to ring. I remembered The Jersey Bounce—I hadn't thought of that in years—and I thought, why not go to Wallingford for a day? It might be fun.

I drove over to the road by the river and all kinds of memories started coming back. The Morris had a four-speed gear shift with the H pattern, and I remembered that our truck had the same pattern and that was the first time I'd ever seen it. Only now I was shifting with my left hand in the Morris, and everything was backwards. That's the way I felt about everything as I drove along—it was kind of familiar but somehow different. I tried to find the place where they built the bridge, and I think maybe I did find it, but I couldn't be sure. Remember how dark and wet it was and how glad we were to get the pontoons off the truck? I drove along the road toward town and tried to pick out the farm where we bunked down—remember the haystack?—but I couldn't find it. I thought about you that day. No offense, but I hadn't thought about you in years till then. And I thought about the little girls who woke us up and I wondered what had happened to them.

I drove into town and took a room at a little hotel and wandered around for a while and was kind of bored. That evening I went to a pub with one of those strange English names—The Fox and Grape—and that's where I met Nancy Morgan. Of course I didn't know who she was at first. I just saw this good-looking dark-haired woman sitting with some other people at a table. There were some other women in the pub, a lot of them younger than she was, but she's the only one I remember. I don't know why she stood out for me, but she did. She knew right from the start that I was looking at her, even though I tried not to be obvious, because I was sure one of the men was her husband. I looked at her and she looked back and I had a feeling something was getting started. She told me later she'd had the same feeling. Right from the start it was as if we knew it was us against the others, as if we were spies, or secret agents. Maybe that sort of thing has never happened to you, but let me tell you it's the most exciting thing in the world, because it's secret and because it's dangerous. Us against them, us against the world. I know what you may be thinking: we wouldn't have been starting something like that if we'd been happier at home. But that's understood, isn't it?

I was standing at the bar and after a while one of the men at their table came up to get beer—his name was Bill, I remember—and he and I talked a little and then he invited me over. I went over and sat down with them, across the table from her, and introduced myself. They were all nice enough, even her husband. You know the way the English are. They were interested to find out that I'd been there in the war—they all remembered the Americans. We chatted on about that, and I could feel Nancy looking at me. I still didn't know who she was, of course, but she knew me. She told me afterward that as soon as I said I'd been there in the war it clicked for her. It's remarkable, that she'd remember my face after all that time, but it's true. I didn't remember her, of course, I just remembered two little girls.

We all stayed on till closing time and then we all split up and left. She went off with her husband, and we hadn't really even said anything to each other at all. I went back to the hotel and sat and stared at the wall for a while, trying to decide what to do. Finally I decided I'd stay another day and night to see if I could see her in the pub again. I didn't know what else to do, except leave, and I didn't want to do that, I *couldn't* do that. I've fooled around a little since I've been married, but it was never serious, never important, mostly just boredom. But this was serious and important—I just knew that, though I don't suppose I could have said why if someone asked me. I thought then it was something that had never happened to me before and I couldn't walk away from it.

Well, the next morning I'd just finished drinking my tea in the room when there was a knock on the door, and there she was. She said, "Hello. You don't remember me but I'm one of the girls who woke you up in the haystack." Just like that, as if it had happened the day before. She had this cool direct way of talking, as if she never said anything unless it really mattered. And then she said, "I can show you where it was if you like." She had a bike outside and she borrowed another one from the hotel clerk and in ten minutes we were pedaling out of town on these rusty old bikes that people must have been riding when you and I were there thirty years ago. I rode behind her, and I remember how thick and dark her hair was, blowing in the wind, and how straight she sat up on her bike. I would have followed her anywhere that morning. We went down the highway for a mile or so and then I saw a rail fence, old and rotting away, and back from it was a stone barn with the roof fallen in, and behind that the skeleton of a stone house; it was burned out, and only one wall was still standing, and about half of the stone chimney. She turned into a pathway there and stopped. She said, "That's where it was," and she pointed to a place about thirty yards away, near the fence. It seemed as familiar to her as if it was a monument. We walked over and looked at it. I didn't know what to say; nothing looked familiar. But I wasn't thinking about the place anyway, I was thinking about her. She told me the owner of the farm had died not long after the house had burned down and whoever owned it now only farmed a little bit and let the rest go to rot.

Did I say what a great morning it was? The sun was getting high as we stood there and it was almost as warm as summer. But better than summer, really. There was a kind of edge in the air that made you feel kind of brisk and alive. We walked over and looked at the barn. There was grass growing inside the walls and birds up in what was left of the rafters. I remember how quiet it was, just the birds chirping, and how warm the sun felt on my back, and all around us that quiet green countryside. I remember thinking, It's like being alone with her on an island.

And then she said, "We used to come here so often, Gwen and I. We were just silly girls then. We used to come and sit on the fence and talk about the handsome Americans and how some day they might come back to us, and how romantic that would be." She said that even after the war, when they were growing up and going out with boys, they would still come back there once in a while. She said, "You can't imagine the stories we used to spin about you and the other soldier. You had sweethearts here, if you'd only known."

I didn't know what to say, so I asked her what had happened to Gwen. She told me Gwen had finally got married and moved away and she didn't see her any more. But she had named her daughter after her, years later. And then she said what I was thinking. She said, "It's so strange you've come back now. It's as if the stories we made up were really true, only we didn't wait long enough for them to happen." And then she looked at me in that odd, direct sort of way and she said, "In our stories you were always *my* beau. We agreed on that from the start. So it's right that I should be the one still here and that you should be the one to come back." And then she put her hand on my face and she said, very quietly and very seriously, "I want to think you remembered me and came back. Am I being very silly?"

And I thought, My God, maybe she's right. Because I *had* remembered her, and I *had* come back, even though I hadn't meant to. And then we were making love, on the grass inside the barn, in a shady place by the wall. Afterwards we talked a little. No big love speeches. It didn't seem as if they were necessary. She talked about her husband and daughter and I talked about Marion and Betty. We didn't hide anything from each other. It was as if we were just talking about people we knew who weren't really very important. Background people. It was like telling each other what we did for a living or what kind of car we drove. Nothing seemed very important next to just sitting there in that ruined barn and feeling the sun on us. Did I say it was like being on an island?

We went on like that for more than a week, meeting somewhere every day and then seeing each other again at night in the pub, with her husband and the other people, playing secret agents those nights. We went back to the barn twice more, I think, and a couple of other times we took my Morris and drove around the countryside. I'd rent a room for an hour or so, then go on. Once we even found a haystack and made love there. It's funny, but I didn't think anyone knew what we were doing. I don't know why I thought that, because we weren't especially careful. I don't think she really cared if anyone knew. I'm not really sure I cared very much either. I think maybe I had some wild notion that what we had was so good that no one would even blame us if they knew. Now I think her husband knew almost from the start but didn't say anything. He was such a quiet, dull man—going to his stationery store every day for twelve hours, coming home, spending his hour at the pub in the evenings. Maybe he was afraid she'd leave him if he made a fuss. But of course she was going to leave him anyway. That was understood from the start. We didn't make plans, but we were going to stay together. That was settled after that first day in the barn.

I know what you must be thinking: how could it be settled if we hadn't talked about it? But I tell you we didn't need to talk those first days. But finally we did talk, of course. I'd decided to stay over there, in London. I thought my company would agree to that—most of our accounts are in England and Scotland. So I thought I'd just stay over there with her and leave the whole stateside scene behind. I wish I could tell you how she looked when I told her that. She looked so happy at the idea of being with me that it made me feel as if I was something special. I remember what she said: 'We'll just go down to London and start over, we'll just forget the last thirty years.' And I said, well, there'd be the divorce business that we'd both have to go through. She thought about that for a while, and then she said, 'You don't have to be divorced. I know it would be hard for you. I don't have to be married to you. I'm married to someone now and it doesn't mean anything.' She didn't care about legalities. Or maybe she was afraid of the legalities and that was why she said, Let's just walk away from everything, we've lost so much time already. And God knows I wanted to do that too, but it couldn't be that simple for me. I told her we couldn't do that, that we had to make our break legally, because of money and taxes and property and all those other things. And as I spelled out all these things I began to get a funny feeling in my stomach, almost as if I was going to be sick. Because as I talked about all those things we'd have to face—the letters to Marion and Betty, the lawyers, the explanations to my company, the trips to London looking for somewhere to live, the worries about money, everything like that—I began to have just a hint of a feeling that maybe, just maybe, it wasn't worth it. The more I talked the more complicated it got, and after I'd gone on for a few minutes I realized she wasn't saying anything at all, just listening. Yes, I think now she wasn't afraid of the legalities but she was afraid I was. So finally I stopped and I said, well, we could work out the details later, and she just nodded. And then we put it all aside for the rest of that day.

But that night, back in my hotel room, after I'd left her and Morgan in the pub and everything seemed all right again, I thought for the first time what everyone would say about us, or think about us. The world's opinion, I suppose you could call it. The world would say, Look at the trouble they went to and the hurt they caused—and at their age, too—just to change partners. And I thought, they won't condemn us for being sinners, they'll laugh at us for being fools.

But the next morning that mood had passed, and we had a marvelous day together. Morgan had gone to London for a meeting—a John Menzies stationery meeting—and he was going to be gone all that day and that night. We drove up to Oxford and rented a punt in the afternoon and fooled around on the river with all the undergraduates and their girlfriends. We fed the swans and had supper at an old place called the Turf and then came back to Wallingford and went back to her place and made love on the sofa in the parlor. It's the only time we were ever alone there. And then she turned on the electric fireplace and we sat on some cushions on the floor and drank beer. Everything was perfect. And then all of a sudden the mood came back on me. She saw in a minute that something was bothering me, and in another minute she guessed what it was. Why is it women always seem to know what you're thinking? She said "You're having doubts."

I said no, but that I couldn't help seeing us as other people would see us and that it bothered me. She didn't say anything to that. She just looked at me in that way she had. You never saw her grown up. She had dark eyes that moved over your face point by point as if she was sort of assessing you, sort of weighing and considering. I said, "Don't you ever look at us that way, from the outside?"

And she said, "Yes, sometimes, but that doesn't matter, as long as you love me."

I said, "You know I love you. Maybe even *they* will know I love you, but that won't change what they think."

She said, "That only means they don't understand, or they've forgotten."

I said, "They won't see us as anything special."

And she said, "That won't matter, as long as we do."

And that was all we ever said about it to each other. I didn't want to say anything more. I didn't even want to say the things I'd already said. But nothing I said and nothing I ever could have said would have given her the doubts I had. Everything was open and shut for her. She just believed.

And yet it was still all right for me. I hadn't talked myself out of it or anything like that. I thought, Well, I'm just being more realistic and practical than she is. I see problems she doesn't, but that's all right, I'll take care of them, that's what a man is supposed to do. So I drove back to the hotel. It was late and everything was shut up and dark and the streets were empty. I was brushing my teeth in my room when something happened. I can't explain it very well. One minute I was brushing my teeth, not thinking about anything, and the next minute I was looking at myself in the mirror and—I wasn't *thinking* anything, but I had this sudden strong feeling that I was doing something I'd done before, that I was re-living something. I never knew what deja vu meant till that night. The feeling was so strong I think I forgot where I even was and I just stood there staring at myself with my toothbrush in my mouth. And then I began to shake all over, as if I had the palsy. Remember how we lay there in Bitche shaking when the Germans had us lined up with the 88's? It was like that, so scared you shake all over as if you were going to have a fit. I stood there like that for maybe a minute and then the shaking stopped and I rinsed out my mouth and went and sat down on the bed. I just sat there, sort of feeling my body, waiting to see if the shaking came back, but it didn't. And then I got that feeling again, only not so strong, that feeling of re-living something. Only this time I knew what it was. Because it was like being at a movie. I saw Marion and me on our honeymoon in New York City. I saw us on the Staten Island ferry with our arms around each other, and I saw us at Nick's down in the Village, holding hands. But mostly I saw us in our hotel room, making love, and then sitting by the window, looking out at the harbor and the Statue of Liberty and feeling as if we were at the center of the world. And then I almost cried, sitting in that little hotel room, because it was like remembering the good times you had with someone who was dead now. Because it hadn't lasted, it had gone away little by little until it was just something I was remembering. And all of a sudden I knew this thing with Nancy wouldn't last either. Because it was the same thing. That's what shook me up so. It was just the same thing, not anything new and different at all. Nancy wasn't any different than Marion, and I was still me. And then I knew why I'd been thinking about all the problems Nancy and I would have to face: I'd been just easing myself toward this fact I didn't want to admit. Nancy and I were at the center of the world, yes, but I'd been there before and I couldn't stay there. Nobody can. I suppose you could say I had a kind of revelation, if a revelation can tell you something that everyone else already knows. I had to get the shakes to find out the law of gravity. But you have to understand that I was scared too, not scared of dying, the way we were at Bitche, scared of doing something bad. You have dreams where you're on the edge of a pit and one more step will take you into it and then you wake up, and that's the way I felt, as if I'd woke up just in time. I'd been just at the point of doing something bad, starting the same merry-go-round ride with Nancy that I'd been on with Marion, and at the end of it Nancy would be left where Marion is, sitting home somewhere wondering how to nurse something back to life that died a long time ago. I thought I could at least spare Nancy that, and I did. I packed and got out of there. I left a note at the hotel. It took me most of the night to write it, but it was just a little note in the end. I said goodbye in it and I said I hoped some day she'd under-stand why I was leaving. And I did hope that, God knows. I don't think I ever believed it, but I hoped it. I thought at least she'd survive, like Marion and most of the other women I know. I suppose you could say I was abandoning her, but I didn't call it that. I thought it was better to leave early than late. And I still think that. I had two bad choices and I made the one I thought less bad. Maybe I was wrong. I've gone over it more times than I can tell you since I heard she was dead. All I can tell you is that I thought I was right at the time, or maybe not right, but less wrong. But now that she's dead it can't make any difference to her, can it?

I read her letters, but I never answered them. I kept them along with her picture in my desk. I spent a lot of dark hours with them, but I was never even tempted to write her. I knew by then that what I had started with her over there was wrong, but there wasn't anything I could do about that except not go on being wrong. I thought, Maybe she'll keep up her day-dream about us, but at least I wouldn't help her do it. Then Marion found the letters and the picture. That was a mistake, I should have been more careful, I should have known how hard she would take it. I guess I was so busy thinking about Nancy surviving that I forgot Marion had to survive too. I told her as much as I had to. I couldn't tell her everything. I couldn't say, I left Nancy because I knew it would end the way it ended for us. That would have been too much for her. I'm not sure she would have believed that anyway. She would have thought she could revive it, she thinks that anyway. Like Nancy. She must have thought that same thing all those weeks and months.

And then I got the news story about her death, and I showed it to Marion. It said accidental, but I knew that wasn't true, even though Marion tried to convince me it was. I knew what had happened. She'd come to her senses, just as I'd hoped she would. She'd seen that the world was right and she was a fool and so she walked away from that. I never thought she would kill herself, but I was forgetting she was a woman. You see, Marion survives because I'm still here, and as long as I'm here she doesn't have to admit that what we lost a long time ago is really lost. But Nancy didn't have that, so she had to face what Marion and most of the other women I know don't have to face. And I think she did face it. She was a remarkable woman. I think she found out that the world's opinion about love is right and she decided she didn't want to have anything more to do with it.

And the world's opinion is that love is bullshit if a man tries to prolong it or repeat it. It serves a function and then it's over, and if you're lucky it leads to friendship. Women are able to believe it lasts, and I suppose that serves a function too. A man shouldn't believe what a woman believes, and a woman shouldn't believe what every married man knows. That's the world's opinion, the wisdom of the race, and that's what I finally learned. Only I learned it too late for Nancy Morgan. But at least it won't happen again. Marion is safe. As long as I'm here her pipe dream is safe. And at least I'm being honest. When I'm down here with the boys watching the ballgame I'm telling her that I think her view of love is bullshit, but I'm telling her that in a way she can accept, like all the other wives. She doesn't have to worry about me straying any more, and I think she knows that. There won't be another Nancy for me.

Lane finished and took a swallow of beer. It had gone flat while he talked, but he didn't seem to notice. On the television they were showing a slow motion replay of the wild pitch that had let in the winning run. Sanguillen tore off his mask and turned after the ball, then slammed the mask down in disgust as Concepcion loped across the plate. Moore was hardly aware for a moment that Lane had finished. A long while before he had forgotten that Lane was talking at all, because so much of what Lane had been saying had seemed to Moore to be welling up from his own mind. He stared across the table at Lane as Lane had stared at himself in the mirror in Wallingford, with something of Lane's feeling of repetition. Before I got there, he thought, my story was acted out, and after he left his was repeated. Harker's pill and the spell of Lane's story conjured up for a moment that nagging sense of doubleness he'd felt back at the White Horse, that persistent sense of being more than himself that Harker had hinted at in his talk of shared identities. I didn't have to come here to get his story for Gwen and the others, Moore thought, I could have just told them all my own. Except for Gwen's question: Did Lane love my mother? I've been looking in the mirror, Moore thought, but the mirror doesn't tell me how I answer my half of the question: Do I love Gwen?

The television was blank now, but Lane was still looking at it as he said, "I come away from this looking shabby, don't I? I come off a bastard. I wouldn't argue that. But you know, I didn't mean to go there and fall in love with Nancy. That just happened. After that I couldn't do anything right. Whatever I did was bound to hurt someone—her or Marion. I was bound to be a bastard either way in the world's opinion, and in my own too. I'd like to think I'm less a bastard for coming back here though. But there isn't much comfort in being a bastard at all."

But the world's opinion was a peculiar thing, Moore thought. The wisdom of the race was cool and cumulative, but the people who judged you in your own time were people like Broderick and the London reporter, and he thought he knew what they would say to Lane. Not wrong to go back, Mr. Lane, no, afraid to go back, afraid of the gossip, afraid of starting out in a new country, afraid of the demands the woman might make on you. Balls to your right and wrong, Mr. Lane. You were afraid of all the embarrassment and nastiness and discomfort of divorce. Not high morals, Mr. Lane, just low cowardice. You'd had your fun, why should you stay on when things got sticky? And Moore thought again what he had thought after talking to Broderick: We should only judge ourselves, because there's no stopping us once we start to judge someone else; we're like prosecuting attorneys, there's no act or thought we can't find a poisoned cause for.

So he simply said to Lane, "Well, you tried to be a gentleman. You tried not to inflict pain."

Lane looked at him curiously. "I don't remember you well enough to know whether that's supposed to be a joke. I suppose it is."

"No, it isn't," Moore said, "it's just something I remembered when I was in England. I applied it to myself, but I always came up short too."

"Well, thanks for the sympathy, if that's what it is," Lane said. "I've never told anyone else the whole story about Nancy. I never thought I would. And then you showed up out of nowhere and it seemed natural to tell it to you, because you were there at the beginning of it all. Makes you think about coincidence, doesn't it?"

Moore nodded, thinking, Yes, it makes you think of coincidences until your mind is ready to burst with them. I look at Lane and I see what Harker must have seen in me, a man whose mind has been teased open by coincidence, a door left just ajar so that something could enter that had never entered before. I promised his wife I'd help him if I could, but what do I have to offer him except what Harker offered me?

But he knew he couldn't say what Harker had said the way that Harker had said it. He couldn't have Harker's quiet assurance, the air of talking somehow from the inside of an experience. He could hardly frame Harker's views for himself, and he knew that he believed them only now and then, not continuously, like a light bulb burning bright and dim as the current fluctuates. He thought, All I can do is tell him my story the way he told me his, with all the coincidences, all the odd overlappings. If I do that maybe he'll come to where I am now: a man in a dark room who's been told of a way out into the sunlight, except that the sunlight may not be the one we know, may be like the sunlight on some other planet closer to the sun, too hot and intense for us. But at least it's a choice, and if he's like me that's more than he has now.

So Moore leaned back in his chair and began. "You said you learned something in England. Well, I did too. At least, something was told to me, while I was agonizing about being a gentleman."

"Let me guess," Lane said. "It had to do with a woman."

"Yes. Two women. Three, really," Moore said, because Nancy Morgan had always been there, a presiding presence shaping all their lives.

"Three women?" Lane said, "better and better."

He wants to hear a funny story, Moore thought, he's had enough serious talk for a while. But he pushed on. "It was after I lost my wife." Lane's face became grave again, and then Moore stopped abruptly, thinking, What am I doing? I didn't come here to hurt him. I left my gun in the car. My story will be too much for him. He's barely surviving Nancy's death. He'll see the pattern of coincidence all right, and it will show him that when he left Nancy Morgan he set something in motion that finally killed Helen and Morgan as well as Nancy. I wanted him to know that once, but I don't now. I can't send him back to his wife knowing that. Only an enemy would do that.

So, as a friend, he chose his words carefully, once again telling a guarded and selective story. He knew as he began that it was a halfway measure. He could never convey Harker's truth to Lane as a doctrine, only as part of a story that he couldn't completely tell because of what he hoped was charity. But somehow he found it harder to lie out of charity than it had been to lie out of self-interest. He had no lie ready at hand to explain Helen's death or his stay in the hospital. He remembered Ruthie saying she'd first thought there had been a terrible car accident, and he improvised on that, reminding himself that he was lying in a good cause. But he almost couldn't do it. The little stretch of time he had shared with Helen and Gwen and Morgan wasn't an era or an epoch that the world would care about; it was only a dot on the infinite line of time, but it had a meaning, maybe even a truth, and he had an ugly sense of falsifying history, even a sense of betrayal. He hurried on to the parts he could tell truly: his depression after Helen's death, the doctor who had sensed his feelings, the discussions of coincidence that had led to the doctor's other views. No coincidences, no mere accidents, a pattern behind everything. A glimpse of that pattern when a loved one dies. A chance to act on that glimpse rather than forget it. The hints that people are not really separate but parts of each other, or replicas of only a few models. Thus the hint of a chance to redeem an inferior love by replacing it with a superior one, loving another woman who would be not exactly the dead woman but not exactly another woman either.

Moore stopped here, knowing that he was garbling Harker's message because Lane's face showed something between amusement and puzzlement. So Moore added, "There's more to it than I can tell you, things that happened in a certain way that made me listen to him. He was telling me that I had a chance to learn from my mistakes, if I was willing to take that chance. Because of Helen's death, you see. It was a terrible thing, but it could be used. As if when she died she opened a door for me. I think he might have told you the same thing, because of Nancy Morgan's death."

They sat silent for a moment, and Moore realized again that they were really strangers, not old friends who might easily talk of personal things. Only their pilgrimage to Wallingford connected them.

"A doctor said these things?" Lane said. "He sounds like a spoiled priest."

"He's married," Moore said.

"You mean he practices what he preaches? What does he do that we don't do?"

"I don't know exactly." Moore hesitated. "He told me he and his wife are very close. He said they pray together when they make love."

Moore had expected Lane to laugh at that, but Lane didn't, though for the first time he seemed genuinely interested. "Do they really?" he said. "I knew a man once who used to argue with his wife while they made love. About all kinds of things—politics, the kids, money. I thought that was pretty bizarre, but your man beats that." He lighted a cigarette and stared around the room. "It takes all kinds, I guess."

"He's not a fanatic," Moore said. "He didn't mean just words. He meant the act itself was a kind of prayer."

"Maybe he's not a fanatic, but people like that are on the edges," Lane said. "People like you and me are in the center. We're the norm, we're the average. Those people are wired differently."

"But what if the center isn't good enough?" Moore said.

"Good enough for what?" Lane said sharply. "People like your doctor friend are always trying to square the circle, and when they've done it they don't have a circle any more. They have something different. If the doctor and his wife want to pray while they make love that's all right with me. But most people don't do that, and most people wouldn't want to because it would spoil something good. It would be like making love in front of a third party. The world goes on with people like you and me, not with people like your doctor and his wife."

"People like you and me inflict a lot of pain," Moore said.

"I know that," Lane said, "I can testify to that. I think we could be better than we are, but I don't think we can be different than we are. I'm trying to be better, but I can't be different. I don't even *want* to be different, like your doctor." He drew circles with his finger on the table top. "I'll tell you what I think. I think it's too bad you can't stay in love the way you are in the beginning. But that's not possible, so you have to deal with that. You can't change the rules of the game or there isn't any game. You have to face the facts. Your doctor's invented a new game. Maybe it's fun for him, but it's not the game I know."

"No, it's not the game I know either," Moore said.

"Let me ask you something," Lane said. "You've lost your wife and now you're involved with another woman, isn't that right?"

"Yes."

"You've fallen in love again? You know, like Nancy and me—all the excitement, all the thrill? All the feeling of the world be damned?"

"Yes, I guess so," Moore said. For one night at least it had been like that.

"So this time you want to make it different," Lane said, "this time you want to make it last, this time you don't want to blow it."

"Yes. At least this time I want *me* to be different."

"Then you're a fool," Lane said harshly. "You're making my mistake. I should have known better and so should you. I can see why you'd listen to your doctor. You want to believe you'll be different the next time. But the only way you'll be different is if you're a freak like him, if you square the circle. And if you do that you may have what the doctor has, but it won't be anything that you and I would recognize. It'll be something that people out on the edges have." He shoved himself back in his chair and stuck his hands in his jacket pockets, then took them out again and leaned forward and put them flat on the table. "You can dream that your new woman is really your old one if you like, but that can't last, you know in your heart that's not true. They're like each other, that's all. Dogs are like each other too. If your spaniel dies you get another spaniel because they're so much alike, but they're not the same dog. Only the breed is the same."

"You and I are much alike," Moore said after a minute.

"Yes, we come from the same breed," Lane said, "but that's all."

"Let me ask *you* something," Moore said. "You were in love with Nancy Morgan. Isn't there anything about that experience that you could transfer to Marion, anything that would make her happier than she is?"

"I've told you what I can transfer," Lane said, "and it's nothing mystical. We're old companions who were in love once in that special way that can't last. We'll go on like that, her wondering why it didn't last and me knowing it couldn't. Just like other people. And we'll get by with that. Most people get by with that. That's the game, and it's the only game. Even the women know that, in some way. That's how they survive." He stopped, and Moore knew he was thinking of Nancy Morgan. "Or at least most of them do."

Yes, Moore thought, there are always exceptions to the rule. But there seemed no point in saying that, or anything else.

Lane seemed to know too that it was time to leave. They stood up together and Moore followed Lane out of the bar. It was still bright and hot outside after the cool dimness of the bar, and they stood on the sidewalk squinting at each other. Two aging investigators of love, Moore thought, how absurd we'd seem to someone listening to us. But then he thought of Harker's remark that there is nothing more important than metaphysics, and he thought, We're no more absurd than other thinkers, we're simply investigating the universe from a certain angle, the only angle we seem to know anything about. He looked with a surge of compassion at Lane's narrowed eyes and the crowsfeet around them as he sometimes looked at himself in a mirror. "I almost forgot," he said, "your daughter gave me a message for you. She said to tell you they love you."

Lane turned a little, away from the sunlight slanting into his face. When he answered, his voice rasped. "She has all this coming," he said, and he gestured back toward the bar, "all this we were talking about. All the pipe dreams. You can't stop them. You can't pass on what you know." He turned back to Moore and put out his hand and Moore shook it. "I won't ask you back to the house, under the circumstances."

"I couldn't come anyway," Moore said, "I've got to leave."

"Remember the things I told you," Lane said very quietly.

"I will," Moore said. He watched Lane walk away, squaring his shoulders in the shiny athletic jacket. He was going home, and Moore didn't want to think about the two women waiting for him there, hoping that something Moore had said would send him back restored. Lane reached the corner and turned back and gave a mock army salute and Moore returned it. He stood for a moment in the hot Midwestern sun, beginning to sweat beneath his jacket. Nothing I could have said would have restored him, he thought. They think he lost something at Wallingford, but he thinks he found something.

Moore walked back to his car, peeled his jacket off, and got in and rolled down the windows. Then he sat and stared at the fortress walls of Camp Randall Stadium. After a while he thought, He's home by now. He's gone into the house and his wife has looked at him and she knows by now that nothing has changed, the long shot of the old army buddy hasn't paid off. And now she's probably thinking again, What was so special about Nancy

Morgan? But she'd never know, because Lane was determined to be a gentleman if he could. He'd never tell her the secret: that there was nothing special about Nancy Morgan at all, that she was just like his wife.

Moore put his hands on the steering wheel, but it was too hot to hold. He took out his handkerchief and folded it around the steering wheel, started the car, and moved out into the street. He headed back toward the capitol, looking for road signs for Chicago. He thought of Lane trying to go south to Devon or Wales but going north to Wallingford instead, by accident; and he thought of himself looking at the Oxfordshire map and finding Wallingford there, by accident. If there was such a thing as accident. They hadn't meant to go to that quiet town so far in the past, but they had gone there as surely as if they had been sent. And now, Moore thought, what we found there, or lost there, we can't forget.

CHAPTER 10

Detroit

The morning after he came back from Madison, Moore sat down in his den to write Gwen what he thought of as his report on Lane. He sat for a long while staring at the blank sheet of notepaper, no words coming to him. He and Gwen had said they could talk openly to each other but to no one else, and that was true, but still he couldn't begin his letter. Lane's story, and his own reaction to it, seemed a shorthand version of everything that had begun in Wallingford thirty years before and had now moved into the present. To tell Gwen everything Lane had said would be to tell her also what he himself had felt in listening to hm. It was as if he and Lane were identical twins whose shared minds and souls doomed them to predictable ends, but Moore could not believe that. Sooner or later, he would pour this all out to Gwen, but not now, not on paper, but at some unforeseeable future time when they were not three-thousand miles apart.

So he wrote, "I've seen Lane and his wife and daughter. His wife thinks that he's torn with guilt over the affair with your mother, and she's right. I had a long talk with him. I think he was in love with your mother but couldn't handle all the obstacles to their being together. We said we wished he could feel some of the pain we think he caused us all, and that has happened to him. I think we should feel sorry for him now. I'll write more soon. Love, Jim."

August moved on into September, fiercely hot and freakishly damp. Every third day or so for what seemed like weeks to Moore a storm front moved in from the west, usually late at night, and lashed the city for an hour or two before it passed out over the lake. Labor Day came and went, and for the first time he could think of Moore watched it pass with no feeling at all. He had no classes to prepare, no texts to order, no meetings to go to. He lived passively in a world that was small and insulated. He tended the lawn and did odd jobs around the house: puttied a window, replaced a washer in a faucet. He wrote Ruthie once a week and phoned her twice. And twice he went to the cemetery and sat for a while by Helen's grave, waiting for feeling, as a bird watcher might go to a special place where a rare bird had been reported. But as usual he felt nothing that he did not feel more strongly at home at odd moments when he had forgotten for a while that Helen was dead: when he mowed a certain patch of back lawn and looked up and was surprised that she wasn't in the back doorway holding a cup of coffee; when the phone rang three or four times and he waited for her to answer it. Those were spears of pain, raw and real. By contrast what he felt in the formal setting of the cemetery was dull and decorous.

Most evenings he listened to the Tiger games on the radio, sometimes in a folding chair in the backyard but more often down by the river at Windmill Pointe. He didn't have to take his own radio there. He could hear the game from a dozen radios among the fishermen and the late picnickers. He simply found a bench by the water and listened while he watched an occasional freighter slide by. Behind him most nights would be the rumble of thunder and now and then a flash of lightning, and in front of him, across the river, the late sunlight would finally leave the tops of the Windsor high-rise apartments and the water would deepen from dark purple into black.

It seemed to him that Gwen and Lane and Helen and Harker were in his mind those nights, and most other times as well, but rather like tenants who lived in the same apartment building with him. They were always there, but he saw them only occasionally, and when he did see them they were more like neighbors than like thoughts, though he knew he must be thinking of them in ways unknown to him. It was as if his memory kept presenting a film of them as he remembered them best: Gwen in the parlor at Wallingford or looking at him outside the Eye Hospital in Oxford; Lane staring at the television in the Badger A. C. and talking of Nancy Morgan; Helen crying in the dimness of the high white room in Corpus Christi; Harker peering over his glasses in the hospital room and talking quietly of love and the single substance. They were always there for him. All he had to do was turn his attention in their direction and the film would start. And in his sleep too, he knew. He awoke every morning feeling that he'd been with them again all night and had only left them when the morning sun woke him.

One rainy morning he went to the main public library—he was staying away from the university campus—and got the books on Harker's list, took them into his den and put them neatly on his desk and stared at them. He felt like a graduate student assigned a crash reading program by a major professor. Except, he thought, there'll be no one to examine me on them but myself.

He sat for a while, then went to the window and looked at the rain puddling in the backyard in the low places by the maple tree. All right, he finally said to himself, the old graduate school tactic: hard ones first, easy ones second, and fifty pages a day come hell or high water. Segment the assignment, cut it down to size. But he wasn't a young graduate student any longer, and the exam to come was one he couldn't imagine. He went back to the desk and began sorting the books: Aquinas' *Summa Contra Gentiles*, hard. But then he stopped, thinking, I really should be sorting them as unknown and known-but-forgotten. Solovyov would be unknown, yes, but the others? All of them known in some degree or other. He had read these others: Aquinas, Lewis, Williams, Dante. If there was a special truth in them, how had he missed it? But as soon as he phrased the question for himself he knew the answer, and the answer saddened him. The answer, as nearly as he could put it in words, was that he'd gotten too old for them, not in years but in experience. All he knew now was that at some indeterminate point in his life they had become irrelevant, to be recalled only nostalgically. He could still argue their Christianity intellectually, as he had done with Harker, and he could still be moved by such things as the church at Iffley or Milton's evocation of Eden. But once he had been able to read Aquinas and Lewis with partisan delight, yes, and Chesterton too, and Newman, and now he could only read them as opinions. But if he had dismissed them, he hadn't replaced them; they clung to him like a mark of baptism. They had spoiled him for anything else. If he was skeptical of them now, he was skeptical of everything else as well. If at odd moments only a phrase from Newman or Aquinas seemed to say what Moore couldn't say for himself, the phrases were only fragments recalled like the faces of old friends long dead. It embarrassed Moore to remember now that at one time he had thought of himself as a soldier in the war for truth and that he had even thought of Newman and Lewis and Aquinas and Chesterton and Dante as comrades in arms against the forces of error. But he *had* thought that, and now even though he had concluded that the war was lost he still felt something like loyalty, like an old soldier on Armistice Day. A year ago he would have said he had outgrown them, but now he wasn't sure of that. Was it growth or drift? Harker had said Moore would read the books when he was ready for them. It had seemed a cryptic remark to Moore then, but now he wondered if in the past he hadn't been ready for them, and if he was ready for them now.

He put the known-but-forgotten pile aside and turned to the Solovyov book (blessedly small), put a marker at page fifty-one and began to read. He read far into that night and went to bed exhausted. He finished Solovyov the next afternoon and almost without stopping went on to the sections of Aquinas that Harker had listed. A day and a half later he had worked through Williams' book on Dante and the two Lewis books—the long essay on medieval courtly love and the short book on Eros, agape, and friendship. Like a hound following a single scent, he read selectively, on the hunt for the page or paragraph or chapter that would reveal what Harker had sent him to find. But there had been no startling epiphany, no sudden flash of truth. He turned to the pages of notes he had so meticulously taken. He knew himself well enough to realize that his notes had often been merely hints and signals, that the real work of thought had to come later. In an undergraduate philosophy class years before a teacher had told an anecdote about Peter Abelard. Abelard was supposed to have said, "What others do by long labor I do in a moment by an act of genius." Moore had taken the anecdote to heart, and still did. He had never over-estimated his own intelligence, and in darker moments had even wondered whether that self-knowledge had made him a literary person, comfortable only with the softer forms of truth.

So now he turned to his notes, page after page on a yellow legal pad, and went over them scrupulously. They were good notes, he thought, they recorded accurately what he had read. They were knowledgeable. He could have lectured from them. But they were of no help to him. He stared at the painting of the farm scene on the wall of his den and then went over the notes again. There was a sameness about all the books, he decided. They didn't exactly repeat each other, but they were like variations on a single theme of music. The theme was the existence of the triangle formed by the two lovers and God. True love brought the two lovers not only close together but close to God. That was the conclusion all of them came to in various ways. That was the answer, the meaning of the term "romantic love." But for Moore the answer was like the answer given at the end of a mathematics text; the answer was stated, but not explained. That was the process that led to that remarkable conclusion? That was where the variations began.

For Solovyov, true sexual love marks the high point in man's long ascent from his animal past. Coition is no longer simply a necessity for the propagation of the species. For some few humans it is the completion of human nature as God intends it to be. In true love man and woman fuse into a single nature, a nature made "in the image of God." They create the condition required for the planned union of mankind and Christ in the Incarnation. Moore, never comfortable with theology and intensely mindful of his own experiences with Helen and Gwen, wondered if only these happy few lovers became immortal, as Solovyov seemed to suggest, if only these rare lovers received the blessings of the Incarnation. If the true lovers were the sheep, then Moore was sure that he and most other people were the goats. But even if he was not reading Solovyov correctly he was still left with the question: How do the elect in love become the elect? What do they do, and how do they do it?

He found himself asking the same kind of question as he read Aquinas and Lewis and Williams. There too the theme was clear but the variations troubling. Aquinas: Man is "a compound of body and soul;" thus man's actions should come "from the complete substance"—Harker's insistence on the doctrine of the single substance, of course. One should love not merely with the body but with the soul as well. But I've always known that, Moore thought, always been ashamed of mere sensuality, but I've never known how to love with the soul, and I still don't. Maybe very old people, people past the age of sexual passion, could love with the soul, but that wouldn't be love alongside of passion, only love without the possibility of passion. And Lewis, praising the love poetry that idolized the loved woman, assumed that as one ascended the ladder of love one did not exactly desert the body but somehow superseded it, loved with what Aquinas called the soul. But how did one ascend that ladder? And Williams, too, assumed that the highest kind of romantic love led to what he called "the Beatrician vision," borrowing the experience from Dante's *Paradiso*: Dante, having traversed both Hell and Purgatory, is led into Heaven by Beatrice. But, Moore thought, Beatrice and Dante were in Heaven, in the very presence of Christ. Earthly lovers were just that: earthly and earth-bound; no one led them into Paradise. If those lovers read Aquinas and Lewis and Williams and Solovyov as he was reading them now, they would find that if they loved properly, loved with the spirit as well as the body, they would be transported into the divine presence. But no matter how much they read they would not discover how to practice that higher love. All answers, but no way of finding the answer for yourself, Moore thought. That's what I gave Lane: the thing to do but not how to do it. I couldn't tell him that because I didn't know it, and

I still don't. Counsels of perfection. Answers from the outside, none from within.

Only Dante was left in what Moore had come to see as his assignment. He looked at the two books in their separate pile—the *Vita Nuova* and the *Divina Commedia*—and for the first time felt a need to call off the hunt for a while. His eyes burned and his back ached, and his mind pleaded battle fatigue. He had paid almost no attention to time in the last three days. When he looked at his watch now he found that it was early evening; it occurred to him that he had been living on sandwiches and coffee these three days and that now he was hungry. He would go out for a hamburger and beer and think about nothing more troubling than baseball. Dante could wait till tomorrow.

It was a fine evening, still light, the air just hinting that summer was becoming fall. He drove along the lakeshore to a restaurant in a marina on the lake. From the back room he could look out over the piers where the pleasure boats were moored. It was calm, and the buggy whip aerials on the powerboats and the masts of the sailboats rocked gently in long lines. Beyond them the lake was darkening, and here and there were glints of riding lights from boats still far out. It was a place that had always pleased Moore, and he and Helen had often come here, even in the winters, when the piers were empty and the lake was glassy with hummocks of ice. But tonight, after a few minutes, Moore found his mind going back to Dante, as his mind had always gone back to the next day's class. Williams' book had reminded him of the oddity of Dante's life. No one seemed sure where fact stopped and Dante's imagination took over. In the *Vita Nuova*—which Moore had not read—Dante apparently said he had met Beatrice in Florence when they were children. He had fallen in love with her then, he said, and he had remained in love with her, though always from a distance, because her beauty made her unapproachable. She had married someone else, then died young. But Dante had not given her up. He followed her into the other world in a vision of his own making, journeyed through Hell, climbed the hill of Purgatory, and from there was led by her into Heaven. Williams had made much of the fact that Beatrice in the poem was not only herself but philosophy as well: Dante had been led to paradise by studying the masters of thought. But Moore, musing on the problem of Dante's two lives (real and imagined) was not thinking of the allegory. He was wondering why he had not discovered in Williams' book what seemed so obvious and unsettling to him now. Dante's *Commedia* was his response to a loved one's death; the poem was what he had made out of that loss. Harker had merely written down book titles, but he must have known that Moore would see the parallel between his own life and Dante's. Moore thought now that it might be one of Harker's ironic reminders of coincidence, but if that was what it was, Moore was sure it was also more than that. But whatever it was, it wouldn't be in an outline of Dante's life, it would be in the work itself. Moore took a last look at the lake, now only endless blackness beyond the lights of the piers, and left for home. He was still very tired, but he knew he wouldn't wait for morning to begin his last reading assignment.

Back home, he splashed cold water on his face, heated some leftover coffee, took a cup of it into the den, and stood at the desk looking down at the Dante books. The *Vita Nuova*, the New Life, and the *Divina Commedia*, the Divine Comedy: the steps that led from Dante's ordinary life to his imagined life, from earth to heaven. Moore picked up the battered copy of the *Vita Nuova*. On the first page he read, "Early in the book of my memory is a heading which says: Here the new life begins." Something in those phrases delighted Moore: the promise of a story told from the inside, a promise of fiction, of lived experience examined. He began reading with a kind of relief.

Two hours later, when he had finished, he laid the book on the desk and for a long while simply stared at it as if it were more than a book. He remembered Whitman's boast about his poetry: Whoever reads my book touches a man. It was what Moore felt about the *Vita Nuova*: he hadn't been reading a book; he had been listening to a man telling him an experience. He understood his reaction. It wasn't a reaction to great art, because the English translation was labored and dull. It was that Dante had entered the discussion that had begun with Harker and Moore and gone on with Moore and Lane: What does human love amount to? For a kind of giddy moment Moore imagined a scene in some pub or bar—like the back room of the Eagle & Child—with the four of them sitting around a table, matching their experiences, Harker in his white coat and half glasses, Lane in his red athletic jacket, Dante in a long robe and tight fitting cap, Moore himself looking from face to face, listening.

Yes, Dante had joined the discussion, offered an experience like the rest of them, but he had done more than that: he had said in the clearest possible terms what the experience meant. He had made the experience into an allegory—Moore knew that—but he was very sure that the allegory wasn't simply a poetic convention. The allegory was the meaning of the experience, and the experience was real. Moore knew it was real because he was sure he had had the same experience. In Beatrice's presence Dante felt that he had no enemies; he felt only a charity that allowed him to forgive all injuries. If someone had asked him a question about anything in the world, he would have responded: Love. I believe I felt that, Moore thought, that night in the pub with Gwen when I made the toast to England. I was toasting everyone there and everyone not there, I was toasting the world. Moore lingered over the experience; even in memory it was exhilarating. But Dante had not lingered over it. He had stated it as a fact and had then gone on to explain it. But the explanation was too much for Moore to take in at first reading. He had to go back to the passages he had marked, like a student reading Einstein's equations over again to make sure they really changed the world. Moore would read them again, but for just another moment he wanted to feel the warmth of that recalled experience that Dante had validated.

But that was somehow not allowed. He couldn't keep the experience present without thinking about it—maybe Dante hadn't been able to, either—but when Moore thought about it his mind wouldn't go forward like Dante's, to explanation, only backward to questions he didn't want to ask and didn't want to answer, like an anchorite who could make even a moment of joy an excuse for further flagellation. Broderick or the London reporter might have asked the question he now asked himself. If the experience is a mark of love, did you ever have that experience with Helen? It was a prosecutor's question, sharp and direct, but Moore could find no sharp and direct answer, no distinct yes or no, only a slow realization that either answer sealed his love of Helen as a failure. He became defensive. Maybe the experience was a mark of real love, but surely it was not the only one? Surely twenty-five years of fidelity counted? Surely twenty-five years of good will and companionship and shared moments of happiness counted? He was sure they did, but in a moment he knew where that argument led. It led to Gwen Morgan and the night when the twenty-five years had not counted. He tried a different tack. Suppose I had the experience with Helen, he said, some time far in the past when we first met. Suppose I had that experience but I've forgotten it. But that was even worse; that was a contradiction in terms. If you could forget that experience it was not the real experience. All right, he finally said to himself, maybe what I felt for Helen was only ordinary love, no different from Lane's, not Harker's kind of love, not Dante's, just run of the mill affection sentimentalized. But if that was so, it was not just a personal failure; somehow, in being small and hollow he felt he had made Helen small as well, and she had deserved better than that. And when he turned back to the experience with Gwen he found himself simply afraid, as Lane had been afraid, and he wondered if he shouldn't simply close the book, as Lane had done, and if he couldn't be good at least be honest.

But to be like Lane wasn't good enough; he had said that to Lane, and now he had to say it to himself. He paged forward to the sections he had marked. He read again the poem in which Dante praised Beatrice to the ladies who understood the true nature of love, the poem with all his question marks in the margins. He went through it line by line but in the end could only make more question marks. The poem seemed to say that real love was known only to a few and that those few would find salvation in love: not pleasure or contentment but the salvation of one's soul. The loved one was an occasion of grace. Moore didn't need the footnote to realize that this notion was the foundation of the *Commedia*, where Beatrice would actually lead Dante into the presence of God. Moore's question marks were all concerned with those few who knew the secret meaning of love. How did they come to be these happy few? They weren't chosen, apparently, not predestined to be initiates. It was something that they did. Moore, still haunted by the intense experience he had tried to put aside, was afraid he knew. They were the ones who had had the experience and had acted upon it, set themselves to understand it. The experience was only a fact, not important until it was understood. If you asked how it could be understood, Dante's answer came at the end of the book. There in another vision he saw "things" which made him determined never to speak of Beatrice again until he could speak more worthily. "To attain this end I study as hard as I can," he said, in order "to write of her what has never been said of any woman." What he wrote of her was the *Commedia*, and the *Commedia* was the meaning of the experience. But the *Commedia* was possible only after years of study, after Dante had mastered not a tiny book list like Harker's but the cumulative wisdom of a thousand years—Aristotle and Augustine and Boethius and Albertus Magnus and Aquinas. The experience had been only a dot beginning a long line of thought that eventually led to the poem. That was what

Moore found so incredible: that Dante could not believe the experience to be valuable unless it was also explainable, if not immediately, then after years of study. The happy few were scholars as well as lovers.

Moore went to bed thinking about Dante's invincible belief that the human mind could attain important truth. But when he was half asleep he was thinking, too, of the parts of the *Vita* that weren't rational—Dante's dreams and visions. That thousand years of thought that Dante had examined was what he called Philosophy, but for Dante that had meant Theology as well. Dante's view of the mind echoed Aquinas: the merely rational mind went as far as Aristotle took it; after that there was the revealed knowledge from theology and scriptures. But there was revelation outside of theology and scriptures—visions, epiphanies, mystical discoveries, true dreams. Dante believed this. So did modern thinkers like Otto and Underhill and William James. Dante's dream of Beatrice wearing the red dress of her childhood may have been only a dream, but when Dante said at the end of the book that he had had a vision, Moore was willing to believe him. What was significant, though, was that the vision did not dispute the findings of theology and scripture; it confirmed them. Moore fell asleep and dreamed his own dream: in it Aquinas levitated before the altar of the church at Iffley and sunlight streamed through the window of the Eye of God.

The next morning Moore started on the *Commedia*. He read the *Inferno* in a day and evening and the *Purgatorio* in a second day and evening. He read them as he had read the *Vita Nuova*, as if they were meditative and fantastic fiction, read them as he read *Moby Dick* and James' ghostly tales. Dante's continuing story seemed as persuasive to Moore as the search for the white whale or the presence of doppelgangers in James. A medievalist would have told Moore that he was misreading Dante in this way, but Moore didn't care. He knew he was projecting his own life into Dante's poem in a way that a psychologist would call fantasy, but he didn't care about that either. He was after a kind of truth, and it seemed irrelevant whether he found the truth in books or in himself. He saw something of himself in a good many of the sinners in both Hell and Purgatory: in the apathetic ones, in the hypocrites, in Paolo and Francesca tossed forever in the winds of sexual passion, unable to stop for thought. And he saw something of himself in Virgil, who was able to lead Dante through Hell and Purgatory but was barred from Heaven by his absence of faith. He found himself moved, like Dante, when Beatrice first appeared at the end of the

Purgatorio and Virgil vanished. Dante, overwhelmed by her beauty, at seeing her in the crimson dress of her childhood, had turned to tell Virgil that he trembled even in his blood, but Virgil was gone. He had led Dante as far as he was allowed and now would be replaced by Beatrice. The injustice of this bothered Moore, and it had bothered Dante as well, but it was not the injustice that moved Moore most. It was the conjunction of loss and replacement, Virgil's sacrifice for Dante's happiness, Helen's death in that high-ceilinged room for Moore's happiness in the smoky bar of the Fox and Grape. Dante had cried at the loss of Virgil, but soon he was bathed in the stream of Lethe and then the stream of Eunoe, so that before he entered Paradise he had forgotten evil and pain and remembered only good. But there wouldn't be any mythic streams for Moore. Reading his life into the poem, he knew he would carry memory with him like a genetic inheritance.

His mind brooding on the notion of exchange, Moore noted that Beatrice's first words to Dante after years of separation and a change of worlds were not happy words but words of reproach. He had been given a vision of love in that mortal world, and even after her death she had appeared to him in dreams that continued that first vision, but he had failed her. Moore, full of his notion of Gwen as his Beatrice, was forced to see Helen as his Beatrice as well and to feel again his failure. Harker's puzzling words came back to him—that hint that Helen dead and Gwen alive were somehow not really separate, or that if they were separate in themselves they were not separate for him. Perhaps only a few models, Harker had said, but many replications, many repetitions with endless variations. For just a moment Moore felt a light touch of meaning, like movement not really seen but sensed in peripheral vision. The single human nature that the philosophers argued endlessly about was varied in him and Harker and Lane and Morgan, and in Helen and Gwen and Nancy Morgan. In the eyes of God, Dame Julian had said, all men are one man. Adam, and out of Adam Eve, and out of them all the rest of us, all different yet really all the same. Lane thought the breed proved separateness, but Lady Julian said the breed proved unity. But Lane and Lady Julian lived by their ideas, Moore thought, and all I do is keep them both in mind, like a man who buys books and stores them in the attic.

He turned back to the mythic tableau at the end of the *Purgatorio* that he had found bothersome—that procession of saved souls, biblical figures, and symbolic animals of which Beatrice was a part. His sense of story had demanded a lover's reunion between Dante and Beatrice, some private and personal scene. But Dante had made Beatrice a figure in a public extravaganza, so that the private love affair had become as public as a marriage of royalty. Moore read through the tableau again, and when he had finished it he thought he knew why he disliked it so. It wasn't just that it was allegorical. It was that Dante had refused to make his love story merely linear, the way Moore wanted it. He had made it open out into that dimension that had been hinted at in the *Vita Nuova* and that Moore had found frightening. Beatrice's words to Dante—"We are Beatrice," which must mean "God and I are Beatrice"—were like the conclusion to a syllogism: if you love me you love the God in me. Somehow Moore had hoped for a more evasive statement than that, some softer suggestion that love of a woman was in some way like the love of God, but not the very thing in itself. Moore, transposing again, telling his own story in Dante's terms, saw Helen coming toward him at Gatwick out of the crowd of tourists, saying, "We are Helen," and saw Gwen turning toward him in the crowded bar and saying, "We are Gwen." They hadn't said these words, but if Dante was right they hadn't had to say them; Moore should have heard them anyway. There was no mistaking what Dante meant. A few lines later Beatrice looked at the figure of the griffin, the emblem of Christ, both human and divine, and Dante saw its reflection in her eyes. Nothing could have been clearer. It was like an equation in algebra, Moore thought, but an equation he had never solved. He closed the book and went to bed. He had gone with Dante through Hell and Purgatory, and tomorrow he would read the *Paradiso*, but he didn't think he would be with Dante there. He was not of the elite, not one of those who understood love. He would be like Virgil, always outside the gates, not good enough or lucky enough to enter.

The next day, low in spirit, he began the *Paradiso*. It might have been appropriate, he thought, if his reading had taken place at Easter time, if he had read the *Inferno* on Good Friday, the *Purgatorio* on Holy Saturday, and the *Paradiso* on Easter Sunday. But he was reading in the fall of the year, and with a foreboding that if there was to be joy in the *Paradiso* it would be joy described, not joy experienced. The first several cantos confirmed his expectations. They were, he thought, lectures. They were remarkable lectures, but still they were lectures. Spokesmen for God explained the meaning and justice of God's creation—Dominic and Bonaventure and Aquinas and the blessed souls who formed a symbolic eagle in the sky and spoke with a single voice. And the later things, too, Moore understood and appreciated without being moved: the ascending order of the angels as Dante was lifted into ever higher spheres of Heaven, the appearance of the Virgin, Dante's entrance into the mystical rose. Moore remembered all this from his catechism and from the prayers at Mass and from his theology courses. Dante had made all these things grand, but they were still only the things that Moore had always known, and they were not what he was looking for. He found himself wishing that the poem had ended with the *Purgatorio*. There he had been told of his failure at love: that he hadn't been good enough or bright enough to see that human love ought to lead to love of God. He could be sad about that, but he could accept it. In time he might even come to see it like Lane, as hardly a failure at all, as only a human limitation. He didn't believe now that dramatized theology would take him any further.

He plodded on, but really only to finish his assignment. Then—he couldn't have said at what point in the book—he forgot he was reading theology and forgot his sense of a story being abandoned. He had been aware, as Dante and Beatrice rose through the spheres toward the sun, that the brightness had increased and had become almost blinding for Dante—dark with excess of light, Milton had said—but with the light there was also increase of warmth. From the sun, of course, but what Moore finally understood was that the light and the warmth were the same thing: light was knowledge and warmth was love, but they were not separate things. Part of his mind said, Yes, allegory, but another part of his mind was suddenly satisfied that the story had resumed. It was just what Dante had said at the end of the *Vita*: the love was in the mind as well as in the heart. For those who understood, they were the same thing. The single substance, Harker had said, not hydrogen and oxygen but water: that is the truth about humans. And Dante had completed the equation: that was also the truth about God. It was all in Dante's final vision of God—the end of the story—the mystery of the Incarnation.

Moore read and read again that final vision, read it in the English translation and found his eyes sliding leftward to the facing page of Dante's original, catching here and there the music of the Italian, so that he had the impression of at least half reading the original. Dante, nearly blinded by light, saw all of history as a great book, opened, the turning pages of the story bound together by love—*Legato con amore in un volume*—all substances and all accidents related and intertwined in the book that was the mind of God; all the objects of the will, everything ever desired, all together and understood by the author of the book, all human actions merging in a vast circle in God's mind, and on this circle imprinted the image of man—*nostra effige*—the meaning of the story, the Incarnation. Dante's story had been taken up into God's story. Dante's story was a love story, but so was God's: it was love that moves the sun and all the stars.

Moore sat back in his chair. All his instincts told him that Dante's final vision was great art, that Dante's imagination had shaped something so grand and satisfying that Moore could only think of comparisons, the end of Beethoven's Ninth Symphony, Michelangelo's Sistine ceiling. For several minutes that was enough for Moore, for several minutes it was enough to feel that he and Helen and Gwen and the others were part of that grand vision, that they had a kind of dignity and significance by being characters in that story by a divine author who understood them so well and loved them so much that the notion of forgiveness was almost irrelevant. They had been wrong, but they were understood, and they had the kind of stature that Melville had given to his meanest mariners and renegades and castaways. Dante's vision recalled for Moore Dame Julian's mystical assurance: All things are well, all manner of things are well. Moore lighted his pipe and got up and paced the room, feeling reprieved. That was all anyone could ask for, to be understood.

But the vision was grand only if you accepted Dante's theology. For those few minutes Moore had put that theology aside, as he had put it aside when he had read Dante's description of Beatrice's effect on him in the *Vita Nuova*. But he couldn't put it aside any longer; Dante was too insistent. If the love experience was important it was important because Beatrice was an effect of the Incarnation; she was proof of the Incarnation; seeing her, Dante was seeing Christ in her. Dante in his final vision was seeing more fully what he had seen only in a glimpse on that street in Florence in that other life: he was seeing the human face imprinted on the blended figures of the Trinity. Seeing this union, Moore thought, but not understanding it. Beatrice and St. Bernard and various others in the *Paradiso* had explained fine points of theology, but there was no one to explain that final vision of union. It was simply there, as the overwhelming conclusion to Dante's quest.

Matching his story with Dante's, Moore felt himself confronted now by Dante's ending to his story, and once again felt himself outside the gates with Virgil. When he tried to think of the doctrine of the Incarnation he could think only of images: the nuns in grade school and their pictures of the bleeding heart of Jesus, the bumper stickers that said "Jesus loves you" and "God is love." It was easy to dismiss them: did Jesus love the mumbling and drooling Alzheimer's patients and the children buried alive in earthquakes? Moore could remember a hundred arguments about the illogic of a loving God allowing unspeakable pain. He knew them all. He even knew some of the answers on the other side: God had suffered those same unspeakable pains, in his human nature as Christ; he was mankind's fellow sufferer. But even so, why? What was the point of it all? The arguments went round and round. God was not omnipotent. There was no God, only uncreated natural forces. God was an evil jokester, a brute and blackguard. Pain and death were illusions. All existence was an illusion. Or Job's answer: you cannot read the divine mind. Moore had been over all the arguments, and he wondered now why he had thought that falling in love and reading Dante would bring him an answer. He turned back to Dante's final lines: all things were moved by love. But he found it unimaginable that a human could love anyone other than another human; to love God was a notion without meaning. But then that was the point of Dante's theology: Dante hadn't loved God directly; he had loved Beatrice and without knowing it had thus loved God, or at least the human element in God. You weren't asked to love an abstraction, only asked to love another human; mystical theology would take care of the rest. Moore trudged back over his life, but could find no evidence of sustained and continuous love of another human, nothing like Dante's lifelong devotion to Beatrice. But then it occurred to him that he was giving Dante too much credit, that Beatrice had rebuked Dante for not being faithful to his first vision. He was blamed for his lapses, Moore thought, but they were not fatal lapses, because they were understood. But Moore, looking again at his own life, seemed to see not occasional failure but only occasional success. Scattered images came to him like pulses of pain from a toothache. Ruthie as a baby: he was pushing her in a stroller past a stand of pine trees in the winter; there had been a gust of cold wind and he had stopped and wrapped her blanket more closely around her, thinking at that moment that he would have died to keep her warm. Helen being wheeled into the operating room, holding his hand until the very last moment before the automatic doors swung open: it struck him like a physical blow that she might die and as he turned away it seemed to him that the universe had dropped out of being. Gwen, hardly more than a voice out of the shadow of her little car, saying goodbye, leaving him wordless, marooned. He thought these were moments of love. They were all he had to offer. He could only hope they were enough. The last lines from Goethe's poem on holy longing came to him like an echo of his own thought:

> And so long as you haven't experienced
> This: to die and so to grow,
> You are only a troubled guest
> On the dark earth.

Three weeks after Labor Day, he was mowing the front lawn when the postman came by, still wearing his summer shorts and cork sun helmet. Moore took the mail and sat down on the front step to look through it. The weekly letter from Ruthie, the electric bill, a letter from Wallingford, a letter from Madison. He sat for several minutes with the unopened envelopes in his hand, staring at the half-cut lawn still green and healthy. A little boy went by on a bike and said hello and Moore waved to him. Two of the tenants in his mental house were going to talk to him today, by coincidence. Maybe it *was* only coincidence, he thought; surely there were coincidences that weren't meaningful, little oddities that didn't count.

He opened Gwen's letter first. It was a single page. She'd put the house up for sale but hadn't had any offers yet. The weather had stayed cool and damp. She'd been to London and applied for positions at several firms but hadn't heard anything from them. She hoped his back was mending. Love, Gwen. No more. Just a note. Just a reminder, he thought, like her mother's letters to Lane. A stranger reading it would learn nothing about her.

He opened the Madison letter, wondering what Lane could have to add to that conversation that had seemed so final a few weeks earlier. The letter was two pages long and typed. "Dear Mr. Moore," it began. Moore turned to the second page and looked at the signature: Marion Lane. He looked away from the letter, back to the lawn again, suddenly cold. Not news from A, he thought, news from B. Bad news. The little boy on the bike came by again and Moore waved again. When he turned back to the letter he was sure he knew what he would read.

Dear Mr. Moore,

I wanted to write you sooner, but I didn't have your address then. Bob died a week ago, suddenly, of a heart attack. I thought you would want to know. I tried to find you in the Detroit directory, but I didn't even know your first name. It wasn't until I looked through Bob's desk today that I found your address. He must have looked it up. I suppose he was going to write you.

He died in the den, watching a ballgame on television. I came in to say goodnight to him and at first I thought he'd fallen asleep. I called 911 and they came with the emergency squad, but it was too late. They said he must have died an hour or so before I found him.

He told me you and he had talked that day I saw you, and I know you must have tried to help. Maybe you did. Maybe that's why he looked up your address. I don't suppose we'll ever know that, but Betty and I thank you for at least trying.

He's buried in the family plot. It's in a country cemetery, about halfway between Madison and a little town called Oregon. His parents and grandparents are buried there. His father served in World War One and his grandfather served in the Spanish-American War. The inscription on his tombstone is the same as theirs. Just the name and dates and "Husband, Father, Soldier."

The funeral was quite large. He was very popular here. But I wish you could have been here, because there wasn't anyone else to represent that part of his life that must have been so important to him.

Please stop and see us if you ever come this way again.

Sincerely,
Marion Lane

Moore folded the two letters together with Ruthie's letter and the electric bill, shoved them in his back pocket, went back to the lawn mower and started it up. As always, he felt the need to move when things became heavy in his mind. He pushed the mower back and forth across the wide lawn, neatly overlapping each newly cut lane, while his mind tried to put order to the news in the morning mail. But for a long while only a kind of refrain went through his mind: Wallingford reports life, Madison reports death. That was the coincidence, of course. From the time he had finished the Dante reading he had been sure he must somehow act. He had phrased the question for himself: Knowing what I know, and knowing myself as I do, what shall I do with my life?

But he hadn't answered the question, had only kept repeating it, and now the morning mail had put the question to him again. He bent over to unlatch the grass bag from the mower and felt a sudden tightness and pain across his chest and for a few seconds his mind screamed Heart Attack. But in a moment he knew it was Lane's agony he felt, not his own. And then it occurred to him that Lane was out of it now too. Of all the characters in that story set in Oxford and Wallingford only Gwen and he were left. It had been a long story, spanning more than thirty years, and two countries, and a world war had figured in it, but its center was in the old places along the Thames, north of London—the ancient halls of Corpus Christi, the ordinary little pubs and paths and graveyards of Oxford and Wallingford. And Moore had a quick, cold feeling that the story might be more nearly over than he had thought. Shivers of mortality ran over him as he put the lawn mower away in the garage, and he thought, If I'm to die soon I want it to be in the center of all that's happened.

He went into his study and sat down at his desk and in a shaking hand wrote out two telegrams that he would read over the phone to Western Union. One was to Ruthie: Leaving for England. Unfinished business there. Will write or call soon. Love, Dad. The other was to Gwen: Leaving for Oxford tomorrow. Will wire you from there. Love, Jim.

When he had sent the wires he telephoned the airline and made a reservation for the next day's evening flight to London. After that he went to the bank and got traveler's checks and then came home and packed a suitcase. By then it was dinnertime, so he showered and shaved and went out for a hamburger. As a last step he went down to Windmill Pointe. It was dark by then, the breeze coming off the water was cool and for the first time seemed to have a touch of fall in it. The Windsor lights across the river were clean and white in the night sky, and just before Moore left, the ghost of a freighter passed, downbound, a long flat festoon of lights like a Christmas tree tipped over and floating on its side in the black water.

Driving home, and again before he finally fell asleep, Moore thought of Lane and the letter Lane hadn't written. The shrill, rhythmic noise of beetles or crickets came through his open bedroom window, regular as the tick of a clock, and framed his thought. Just before he fell asleep he was no longer thinking of what Lane had meant to say. He was thinking that Lane had run out of time to say anything at all.

CHAPTER 11

Oxford

The night flight to London seemed very short to Moore, and yet he neither read nor slept to pass the time. He picked at the dinner tray the stewardess gave him at ten o'clock, walked the aisles three or four times to ease the stiffness in his back, and then the eastern sky ahead of them began to brighten and the short night was over. He drank his breakfast coffee while they were passing over southern Ireland, and once or twice he caught glimpses of dark green and slate gray where the land and the sea came together. The landing pattern at Heathrow took them out over the Channel in a long loop and then back toward London, and as the plane banked Moore saw cameos of the river and Tower Bridge and the parliament buildings. He looked at the sights with interest but not with the tourist flutter of excitement he had once felt. And then he wondered whether it would have been better to meet Gwen in London. It would have been safer than Oxford. But though he hadn't thought beyond the mere meeting with her—hadn't thought of any particular words to say or things to do—his mind had somehow shaped the meeting to be in Oxford, and no place else would do. Again he thought: Oxford is my central city; London is only a suburb of it.

He rode a bus from Heathrow into Victoria Station, but when he got there he found that he couldn't bring himself to make the walk from there to the bus depot. There were certain things now he knew in advance he could never repeat. He could never go into Gwen's parlor again, or the Fox and Grape, or the room in Corpus Christi. But there were other things that he only gradually discovered he couldn't do: certain streets in Detroit that were too painful to drive on, certain corners of restaurants that were too empty even when they were crowded. So now he discovered that there was a stretch of a London street that he would never willingly walk again, because he had walked with Helen there, and he could add that to the other places in Oxford that he would never see again—the White Horse, the Turf, the path along the Cherwell behind Corpus Christi.

He waited in line for a taxi to Paddington and the slower train ride to Oxford, and for the first time since he had left Detroit he felt tired. He found himself dozing in the taxi, and at Paddington he had trouble counting change for his ticket. He'd only been in America for a few weeks, but in that little time England had become strange to him again. He was still a tourist here, he thought, and though his life had changed here in ways he couldn't yet fathom, he was still coming into this world from the outside.

He stood at the gate for the Oxford train and stared up at the great dusky glass panels overhead, reminded again of Holmes and Watson, but without any lifting sense of embarking on an adventure like theirs. He felt simply dull and torpid. He sat down astride his suitcase and watched the spectacle of Paddington as passively as he might have watched a television set that happened to be showing a documentary film of London. People formed in line behind him: neat men with rolled umbrellas and newspapers, two or three groups of ladies with wicker picnic hampers and clusters of quiet, well-behaved children, leaving for a day in the country. The aroma of pastry came to him from a lunch booth fifty yards away, and overhead an almost unintelligible voice came over the PA system announcing arrivals and departures.

It was past noon when the Oxford train was opened to passengers, and Moore gratefully struggled aboard with his suitcase and found a compartment in the smoking section. He felt better when he'd settled down beside the dusty half-opened window and felt the train begin to move smoothly away from the platform. He felt as he had felt on the plane: that he was moving purposefully but without the necessity of thought, like a soldier obeying an order. When he got to Oxford it would be time to think again, so he leaned back and dozed, thankful for the interlude of no thought, and was only half aware of the pauses in the rhythm of the train when it stopped at Beaconsfield and High Wycombe and Stokenchurch. But a minute or so before the conductor called Oxford he was suddenly wide awake, as if some inner odometer had been ticking off the miles. He eased his suitcase off the overhead rack, still favoring his back, even though it did not really bother him any more. And when he stood on the platform under the Oxford sign he thought simply, Well, I've come back. As he went down the steps under the tracks and up the other side something of the old feeling for Oxford came back to him for a moment, but only for a moment. That feeling had been before the Fall, when death in Oxford had been decent and historical. He had projected the presence of Shelley at University and of Newman at Oriel and St. Mary's, presences that were benign because they were safely and comfortably in the past.

But the presence in the room in Stairway Twelve that he projected now, and that came to him in his dreams, evaded the laws of time and change, stayed stubbornly what it was and went on happening. In those dreams memory recalled the darkened room and the shadowy figure of a woman sitting on a narrow bed and crying, and he knew it must be Helen, but the sound he heard in the dream was that of a child crying, frightened and alone.

When the taxi driver asked him where he wanted to go, he said "Eastgate Hotel," without hesitation, though he wasn't aware that he had been thinking about it. And as the cab went through the shabby outskirts toward the center of town he thought, Well, why not the Eastgate? After all, Ruthie had stayed there. But then, even though his tired mind was working slowly, he knew there was something more than that to it. The Eastgate was as close as he could come to Corpus without actually being there. What had ended for him had ended at Corpus, whether it was his world or the model of his world, or only Helen's life. Some vague urge for symmetry, some half-formed hope for pattern, said that if anything new was to begin it should start to life where the old thing had died, even if it was only a replacement and not a resurrection.

Besides, he wasn't known at Eastgate. Wasn't known. He caught himself trying to hunch down in the taxi, leaning back from the window, as though people in the street might recognize him at a glance, as they would a movie star or a president. But of course only a few people in Oxford might actually recognize him: the owners of the White Horse, one or two people from the Turf, Harker and a few other people from Radcliffe, Broderick. Broderick. As the cab circled around the shopping mall behind Carfax Moore had a quick image of the car stopping for a traffic light and Broderick suddenly leaning in the window, smooth and urbane in his dark suit, saying, "So you've come back, Professor. We thought you would." But the cab stopped at a light and then moved on, and Broderick wasn't there. He didn't have to be, Moore thought, just the idea of him was enough. But then Moore forced himself to sit upright. Whatever he was, he wasn't a criminal, and for just a moment he nearly wished he *would* meet Broderick. Because at least he was reasonably healthy now, and dressed and shaved and able to stand straight. He would never be able to explain to Broderick why he had come back, of course, but he had a feeling that at least Broderick would not be able to overwhelm him with righteousness again. If Moore had had to put his thought into words he would have said that if he was not right in coming back, at least he was more nearly right than Lane in not coming back, or at the very least he had a chance to be more nearly right than Lane. He knew what Broderick and the lesbian reporter would say about that distinction in terms, but it was what he had to live by now, that and the sense of the shortness of time that had been with him ever since he had read Marion Lane's letter. At one time these two things had been separate, but now, if they were not the same thing, at least they appeared together in his mind like a sound and an echo or a presence and a reflection.

The cab rounded Carfax and headed down the High Street, still crowded but no longer overflowing with summer tourists. Now the people that Moore saw in front of the John Menzies shop and the tobacconist's and the covered market seemed to be mostly young men—boys, really—back for the beginning of the Michaelmas term. They looked scruffy and adolescent to Moore, and it was hard for him to realize that these were the current students at Oriel and Magdalen and Corpus Christi. A few of them wore their academic gowns over their open long-sleeved shirts, and they all seemed to Moore to walk in the same affected way—stoop-shouldered, a little bent forward, taking over-long strides. Two of those he saw, Moore thought, might be the ones who lived in his old rooms in Staircase Twelve. He wondered if the students made jokes about the rooms. Probably. Probably the rooms were notorious by now among the undergraduates, like the rooms in a house where a ghost has been seen.

The scaffolding at St. Mary's Church was still there, Moore noted, as they passed King Edward Street, and the Old Barclays Bank looked as prim as ever, and in front of him were the spires of Magdalen. For the first time it occurred to him that he would hear the bells again, all through the days and nights, as long as he stayed in Oxford. He had forgotten them. He couldn't remember ever hearing them at Radcliffe, as if they had stopped on the night that Helen died.

The cab turned into Merton Street and stopped at the corner, across from the Eastgate. When he had paid the driver Moore stood for a moment looking down the stretch of a hundred yards or so to where Merton Street bent sharply and ran out of sight, past Merton College and then to Corpus Christi. It was almost here where he was standing that he had helped Helen off the bus from London, it was almost here that she had opened her eyes and seen Oxford for the first time. What a brief time, he thought, not even one full circle of the clock. An afternoon and evening; two pubs; a walk down to the river on Dead Man's Walk; some lovemaking; a bitter quarrel. And then the unthinkable, the thing that even now Moore kept in a special part of his conscious mind reserved for things that were true but unacceptable, like his own inevitable death, things whose reality he could not assent to.

At the little counter in the hotel lobby Moore wondered for the first time where he would go if the Eastgate was full. But when he asked for a room the thin man behind the counter nodded and handed him a registration card to fill out. "For how long, sir?"

Moore hesitated; he hadn't thought about that. "Tonight. And tomorrow night." He picked up the pen to fill out the form and had written "Mr. James" when he thought suddenly that his name might be familiar here even if his face was not. He scratched out what he had written and, without thinking, wrote "Mr. Robert Lane," paused for a moment, then added "and wife." He pushed the form back to the clerk. "My wife will be coming in tomorrow," he said.

His room was a small and pleasant one overlooking the High Street. He took off his coat and shoes and lay down on the double bed with his hands locked beneath his head and closed his eyes, content for a few moments that another leg of the journey was over. All over Oxford the bells chimed two o'clock, and he was sure he recognized the bells of Merton and Christ Church. He was thinking that he had to tell Gwen he was here when he quite suddenly fell asleep. Just before the three o'clock bells woke him he was dreaming of Helen, and as he awoke his hand was searching for her on the other side of the bed.

He sat on the edge of the bed for a few minutes, staring numbly at the window, too tired to move but not able to go back to sleep. He knew it was the jet lag, and he knew he had to push himself into some sort of action. Traffic sounds came up to him from the street below and then the bells of the quarter hour. He listened for the final chime from Christ Church, as if for a cue to act, but he knew what the act should be. He had come here to see Gwen, and now it was time to tell her he was here. But he had the feeling that he had been in a speeded-up movie ever since he had read Marion Lane's letter and that his mind had not yet caught up with his body. He wanted to slow the film down. He looked around the room and was relieved to see that there was no telephone. He would wire her instead.

He stood up and went over to the wash basin and doused his face in cold water and forced himself to get his pipe and tobacco and ballpoint pen from his jacket pockets. When he had lighted the pipe he sat down at the little writing table in the corner of the room, found a sheet of paper in the drawer, and began the wire. After several false starts he finally wrote, "Staying at Eastgate Hotel in Oxford. Can you meet me—" Here he stopped, wondering where they could meet. He thought she would come by bus. So he wrote, "Can you meet me at the bus stop in High Street tomorrow? And when? Please reply to R. Lane. Will explain later. Can you stay a few days? Jim." He stared for a moment at what he had written. He imagined her taking the telegram into the parlor and opening it there, standing by the fireplace. He tried to see the words as she would see them. Words on paper had always seemed more real to him than spoken words. Words on paper were words you couldn't take back. His hand trembled a little as he crossed out "Jim" and wrote "Love, Jim."

He didn't want to give the wire to the desk clerk, so he decided to send it from the main post office. He dressed hurriedly, unable to remember the post office hours, and walked fast up the High Street toward St. Aldate's, past the familiar fronts of the camera shop and the ice cream parlor and the shop that displayed the Oxford gowns. But when he had sent the wire his spurt of energy ended. He walked slowly back through Blue Boar Lane, past the walls of Christ Church and into the familiar curve where King Edward Street became Merton. He stopped, with Oriel on his left and Corpus just ahead on his right, then walked even more slowly past Corpus and looked through the archway. He was momentarily surprised to see that it all looked the same. The scaffolding was still there against the far wall. The stone tiles that had been taken down for cleaning were stacked neatly in the quad, and Moore knew that each one of them was numbered and would be put back in precisely the old place, so that Corpus would look just as it had always looked for four-hundred years. The pelican, high on its pedestal, glowed with golden fire in the late afternoon sun. Everything just the same, as if Helen and Morgan had never existed, as if there had never been blood in the room in Stairway Twelve and a corpse at the foot of the pelican. If this were a poem or a story, Moore thought, Corpus would somehow register those horrors, as Milton had made nature weep at the time of the mortal sin original and Poe had made the house of Usher crack and crumble because of insanity and incest. But there was no one to chronicle those horrors,

Moore thought, and only Gwen and himself even to remember them. He went slowly on, past Merton, and back to the Eastgate.

At the lobby desk he waited until the thin clerk got off the phone, then told him, "I'm expecting a wire some time tonight. I'll be somewhere in the hotel."

The clerk nodded and made a note on a memo pad. "You're Mr.—," he said questioningly.

"Lane."

"Yes, of course. Mr. Lane."

"It's important," Moore said.

"We assume all wires are important," the clerk said snappishly.

For a moment Moore wondered if the rudeness was directed at him as an American or if it was merely a generic snub of a foreigner. Bad manners had always annoyed Moore the way bad grammar did, but as he began to frame a retort it occurred to him that he should do nothing to call attention to himself. And then it occurred to him, too, that this prudence would probably be a way of life from now on. He wondered if Gwen had thought about that kind of life, the life of people trying to stay unnoticed in the background, like people in a witness protection program.

Back in his room he bathed and shaved and then pulled an arm chair over to the window and sat looking out over the High Street, half dozing, listening to the bells, and finally fell asleep and dreamed that he was dreaming of Oxford. In the dream within a dream he seemed to be always coming out of King Edward Street and then stopping to look at St. Mary's and thinking again that Newman had preached there. But when he crossed the street and went inside, the man in the high pulpit was Lane. He was wearing his red Badger A. C. jacket, and he was preaching that love is bullshit. And then Moore was somehow up in the pulpit, and in front of him were countless ranks of people in the pews, waiting for him to preach and to refute Lane. He tensed himself for a mighty effort, as if he were going to lift a great weight, but when he finally began to speak all he could say was, "Really, you should talk to Dr. Harker, and you should read Dante and Aquinas," and he could feel the wave of disappointment come up to him from the congregation, and he was grateful when a bell rang to end the class.

The bells were chiming half past six when he woke up. The traffic had thinned on the street below him, and the far side of the street was slipping into shade. He dressed and went down to the dining room and lingered over dinner, waiting for someone to bring him a message, but no one did. Finally he went into the bar and got a lager and took it to a far corner of the room. A jukebox blared American country western music, and the bar began to fill up with young people, and Moore remembered now that it was the jukebox that had kept him away from the Eastgate. He drank his lager slowly, because already he was beginning to feel as if he had taken one of Harker's pills. When he tried to think of what he might do tomorrow or the next day he found that he couldn't. He couldn't think beyond the next immediate event, and that event would be Gwen's return wire. He remembered what Ruthie had said at Radcliffe about Helen's death: I felt as if I was going up a flight of stairs, and I didn't know where they would take me.

At nine-thirty the thin desk clerk came into the bar and looked around. Moore raised his hand, like a pupil in school, and the clerk came over to the table. "Wire for you, Mr. Lane," he said, and handed Moore a sheet from the memo pad.

Moore thanked him and waited until he had turned away before he looked at it. It said: "Will arrive bus stop 10 A.M. Love, Nancy." Moore stared at the name, wondering if she'd thought his giving Lane's name had been a bad joke that she had to play along with. But at least the next event had happened and now he could go to bed. He stopped at the desk and asked the clerk to have him called at eight. "My wife is coming in," he said.

When he got to his room he found that he was so tired he could barely make himself undress. When he got into bed he fell deeply asleep almost at once, and dreamed of arrivals, over and over. Someone was getting off a plane at Gatwick, and someone was getting off a bus at Radcliffe, and he was waiting anxiously to see who it was.

He had tea and toast in the hotel dining room the next morning, and by nine-thirty he was at the bus stop. The sky was overcast and the air hung heavy and damp like the air in a laundry. Chilled in spite of his raincoat and cap, Moore walked tautly like a sentry as far as the polished doors of the Barclay Bank and back again. The next event was about to happen, the next turn of the page, and for whatever it might bring he felt footless and unprepared, and for just a moment he envied Lane the ugly peace he had made for himself when he had burned away everything worth hoping for. But then Moore remembered Marion Lane.

The bus was nearly fifteen minutes late. Gwen was the fifth person to get off. She was wearing the mackintosh that he remembered and carrying a small plaid suitcase. She stepped down into the street and stopped and looked around, and then she saw him. For a moment neither of them moved, only stood looking at each other, and Moore thought, I know what she's thinking, the same thing I am: Are we meeting at Wallingford or at Radcliffe? For just another instant he looked at her, thinking of the picture Marion Lane had showed him, matching the two serious faces and dark eyes, and she simply stood there, waiting for him to make the first move, the beginning of the next event for her. Feeling as if he had somehow left Lane and Harker standing behind him on the sidewalk, he stepped off the curb toward her, and what she saw in his face must have been what she had been waiting to see, and she put out her arms to him.

"Welcome back," she said when they had pulled apart. She said it seriously and a little breathlessly, and then they both became aware that there were people all around them and that they were in the way of passengers getting off the bus. Moore picked up the plaid suitcase and they walked arm in arm away from the little crowd and stopped in front of the bank. He set the suitcase down and they turned to each other again, and once again Moore was surprised at how tall she was.

"You look good," she said. "Are you all healed?"

"Almost as good as new," he said. "You look fine too." She did. Back at Radcliffe she had seemed worn and tired to him, and older than her years, but now she looked like what she really was, a striking young woman in her late twenties.

"Now tell me about the telegram," she said. "Why are you R. Lane?" And when he had told her she nodded and said, "I thought it might be something like that. But then I thought maybe it was a kind of code. That's why I used my mother's name—to show you I understood the code." She smiled and looked at him in that direct way that Lane had seen in her mother. "But then after I thought about it I wasn't sure that's what you meant at all, and if it was a code I didn't really understand it. By the time I left I wasn't quite sure what I'd find when I got here."

"But you came anyway."

"Of course," she said. "I was sure there'd be a reason."

"You're as sure of everything as ever, aren't you?" He took her arm and they began to walk toward the Eastgate. "We have a lot of things to talk about," he said, "a lot of things to decide."

"I brought my suitcase," she said. "I'm in no hurry."

They turned into the Eastgate and went through the lobby. "Remember you're Mrs. Lane if anyone asks," Moore said.

"I'm not likely to forget," she said. "It's what my mother wanted to be. At least I suppose that's what she wanted."

Moore didn't answer her until they were in his room and he had hung their coats in the little wardrobe and put her suitcase on the foot of the bed. She was wearing a gray pantsuit and a high-necked blue blouse, and she looked trim and almost boyish except for the helmet of heavy dark hair.

"You're wrong about your mother," Moore said. "She didn't care about getting married. She just wanted Lane. I know. I saw him."

"That surprises me," she said. "I thought she was more conventional than that. We're more alike than I thought."

"You even look like her," Moore said. She looked at him in surprise. "I saw her picture," he said. "Lane's wife showed it to me."

"I remember you said you'd seen his wife and daughter. That surprised me."

After a moment she said, "Was it all very ugly? For you, I mean, but I suppose I mean for them too."

"No, not ugly," Moore said. "No sordid scenes, no harsh words, not even any raised voices. It was all very civilized." So civilized, he thought, that Marion Lane and her daughter had not even cried until after he left. "I suppose the best word is sad."

She went to the window and looked down at the High Street and they both waited while the bells chimed the quarter hour. Then she said, "Tell me about it. Tell me about Lane."

I have more to tell her than the last time she asked, Moore thought, remembering that night in her parlor when like ignorant conjurers they had said Lane's name and called up his presence for the first time. He went over to her and they stood together looking out the window while he told her, told her everything, hiding nothing, shading nothing, like a boy making his first confession. When he had finished, the Oxford bells were striking eleven.

"That poor woman," Gwen said, but she meant Marion Lane, not her mother. Then after a minute she said, "So he wasn't coming back? He never intended to?"

"No."

"He and my mother were just like us, weren't they?" she said quietly. "It all happened the same way. Only he didn't come back." She turned away from the window and looked at him. "Do you think he loved her?"

"Yes, I do. But he didn't trust love."

"But you came back," she said. "You must trust it then."

"I trust it more than he did," Moore said. "I'm not sure how much more."

She put her hands on either side of his face and made him look directly at her. "*I* trust it," she said. "At least I trust it with you. We're different, you and I."

Moore put his arms around her. "No, we're not," he said, "but maybe we have a chance to be."

"You mean something by that," she said, "something big and donnish that I probably won't ever understand, or ever want to."

"Oh, yes you will," Moore said. "I think you understand it already."

She kissed him, then stopped, then kissed him again, longer. "I'm glad of that," she said, and then she looked at the bed. "If you moved the suitcase we could make love."

"I can move the suitcase," Moore said. "Maybe I can even move mountains."

They lay in bed for a few minutes, touching each other almost tentatively, and Moore knew again that she must be thinking what he was thinking: that this was not a continuation of that night in the parlor in Wallingford; deaths had made what they were doing now something different, something new. He moved his hands slowly down her body and she put her arms around his neck and began to draw his face down to hers. Moore felt his heart begin to pump harder, but part of his mind was full of Lane and Harker, images nearly as real as that of Gwen's face beneath him. Something new, his mind said, but just a new case of an old thing, or something really new? The scent of her hair came up to him like the scent of flowers from a secret garden, and he knew that in a moment it would erase Harker's words, and Lane's words too—the warning not to begin a cruel and transient thing. "I love you," he said, and it seemed to him that her eyes looked though his own eyes and into his mind as if she were looking through a window into a room. "It's easy now," he said hoarsely. "The trick is to make it last. I mean to do that."

"I'm not worried," she said. "I never have been."

And Moore's last thought before she enveloped him completely was what Lane had said about her mother: she had faith. The street noises sifted into the open window and around them like jazz music, the tooting horns and the grinding gears of the buses and lorries, and the Merton bells and all the other bells of Oxford, and then the final heavy chime from Christ Church, and Moore lay contentedly against her, and lifted a long wing of her heavy hair and rubbed it against his cheek like a talisman. After a few minutes she sat up and leaned against the headboard and cradled his head in her lap and looked down at him. "You're thinking again," she said.

"I suppose I am," Moore said. He put his hand up to one of her small breasts and left it there. And then he remembered what Harker had said about himself and his wife: we touch a good deal, we never talk without touching. Bringing together the two aspects of the single substance, the body and the mind. With his fingertips on the nipple of her breast and the spiky hairs of her groin against the back of his neck, without any introduction or preamble he began to tell her about Harker, and Harker's book list, and the world that had seemed to open out for him as he read. The world of Harker and Dante and Aquinas had become very real to him in the past few weeks, but it was a private world, secluded like the meditative world of an anchorite in a desert. Now he had to translate that private world into the public world, into Gwen's world, and he felt fumbling and inarticulate, as he had been in his dream of being in the pulpit in St. Mary's. Coincidence and pattern, the single substance, Dante's love, people sharing existence with other people: he told her of all these things, and as he went on he was not sure whether he was repeating Harker and Dante or whether he was talking for himself but talking in a way that they had not only made possible but necessary.

When some ingrained professorial instinct told him he was repeating himself he finally simply stopped, defeated, ashamed that he had done so little justice to beliefs and ideas that moved him so deeply. "All this," he said, "is what I meant when I said we have a chance to be different. I can't explain it all, and I don't know how much I really believe. What I do know is that I can't be like Lane. But I'm afraid I can't be like Harker or Dante either." He looked up at her. She had been looking down at him while he talked, but now she was looking away, toward the window. Moore had the sinking feeling he had had a few times in class when something personal and inappropriate had somehow crept into his lecture and made his students uncomfortable. He moved his hand from her breast and touched her face and she looked down at him. "Lane said people like Harker are out on the edges," he said. "I suppose he would have said the same thing about Dante and Aquinas. And me. Do you think I'm out on the edges?" The question slipped out, unintended, and surprised him. He hadn't meant to ask her to pass judgment on him. And then, when she didn't answer for what seemed like minutes, it came to him that in his muddled report of his own debate he had forced the same debate on her, and was asking her now to pass judgment on herself as well as on him. He had been wrestling with his problem as if it were a private problem, but it was anything but private, it was in fact the next thing to universal, the problem for all the people who had ever been in love, or thought they had been, or had been and weren't any longer. I've been staring at my own navel, he thought, and haven't realized that I'm asking her to examine herself and her marriage and her divorce—to justify her life. He had treated her as if she were merely a listener. He felt like a moralistic inquisitor, felt in fact like Broderick.

While he had been talking she had been looking down at him, but now she seemed to be looking through him, as people do when they are thinking. Finally she said, "I don't know if you're out on the edges, I suppose because I don't know where the center is, or even if there is a center. If Lane is the center, then I'm out on the edges with you. But I wonder if we're not just playing with words, talking about centers and edges." She lifted his head from her lap so that he was sitting up and then she moved so that they were sitting cross-legged across from each other like two Buddhas. "No offense, my dear," she said, "I know what you mean. You want to be as far away from Lane as you can be. But remember what you said about people not being really as separate as they think they are? That startled me, because I'd been thinking something like that for weeks. I never knew your wife, but I've had dreams about her. I've been in colleges like Corpus Christi; I can imagine the room she was in; I know it would be ugly and shabby and have a high ceiling. In my dream she's in bed, and she wakes up frightened of something, but then she's not the one in bed—I am—I'm the one in bed and I know who's coming toward me, and I know what he's going to do, and I begin to scream for him to stop. The screaming wakes me up."

She stopped, and Moore knew it was because she saw pain in his face. She put her hand on his knee for comfort. "I know it wasn't like that," she said, "I know I make it worse because I know everything she didn't know.

But what I mean is that somehow I feel very close to her. I almost feel as if I know how she felt about you. And lately I've often felt as if I were my mother—as if I'm saying things she said and feeling things she felt. You said something about all men being in some way the same man, and all women the same woman, like Adam and Eve. It made me think of something I read somewhere: that sooner or later all men will play the parts of all other men, and women will be all other women. And I thought as you talked, when you've been all the men in the world and I've been all the women, everything will be over. Between us we'd have been everyone and done everything, and it would be time for God to shut up shop. And you'd have been Lane, you see, and would understand him, and you'd have been my father, and understood him." She stopped, as if something had just occurred to her, and unexpectedly she laughed. "If we're Adam and Eve, we're dressed for the parts," she said. "Or undressed."

Moore laughed with her. "I think you've sketched out a complete philosophical system," he said, "or at least the bare outline."

Suddenly they were laughing as if they had made the funniest jokes in the world, but when they finally stopped they looked at each other guiltily, like children caught giggling in church.

"I wasn't making fun of anything," Gwen said defensively. "Except us, I mean."

"I know," Moore said, and he thought he did know. Someone wholly detached from them could make low comedy out of two naked people philosophizing in bed, but only by ignoring the events that had got the people there, and that was what he and Gwen had done for a moment.

Gwen pushed her hair back from her face, serious again. "What you said about coincidence frightens me. It seems to me you're saying that all these terrible things that have happened have happened in order to bring us together. I can't believe that, it's too horrible. I know what you said about that: that these things weren't planned so that we would be together, that they just happened and we should take advantage of these other people's bad luck. You said that coincidence shows that there's a pattern in the world, that everything is connected to everything else. Well, I suppose I believe that, or something like that. When I was a young girl still going to church, I heard sermons about providence, how God cared about even little things like the fall of a sparrow. I believed that, I suppose, if I thought about it at all. Later on I suppose I questioned it, like most people. I still question it. I mean I don't understand it. I think the only people who can really believe in providence are the ones who have good luck. But I can't believe there isn't some sense to things somewhere. My father had a collection of classical recordings, and I grew up listening to Mozart and Bach and Brahms. I can't believe that music like that, music so marvelous and so orderly, could be made in a world that didn't make some sense. But I don't believe that your coincidences show any pattern except one that terrifies me. I don't want to be singled out as an example or a model of perfect love. I don't want to be Beatrice, or at least if I should become Beatrice for you I don't want to know about it. Isn't there a joke about someone who said he was a reverent agnostic? That's probably what I am, if I'm anything. I think there's a meaning to things because I can't not think that, but I don't think we can know the meaning. Or at least I don't think *I* can."

Moore, watching her, listening to her, felt the teacher's special joy of watching intelligence at work, though he had had no part in training that intelligence. Probably serious, like her mother, Lane had said, but he hadn't meant it as a compliment to Nancy, only as a fatal complication. But Gwen had listened to Moore's disjointed account and had understood it, and she had sifted through it to find what she could accept and what she could not. Moore was surprised to realize that he was not disappointed in her reaction, that in fact he felt as he had sometimes felt in arguments with people he admired: that they were not really disagreeing so much as simply seeing something differently. He looked with admiration at this young woman who said, without pretentiousness, that she was agnostic—could find nothing in the world to explain the world, yet believed there had to be an explanation—and he remembered the lines from another intense and agnostic woman—

This world is not conclusion—
A species stands beyond—

She waited for him to reply, and when he did not she said, "I have to say something else. It's about love, or what you said about love. I'm very much in love with you right now—intensely, as I suppose you would say." The statement was so direct and so surprising to Moore that it was a moment before he could even feel the thrill of pleasure it gave him. "I believe I'll stay in love with you," she went on, "but not just like this. I don't believe I could endure being this intense all the time." She paused. "I was intensely in love with my husband when we married. We were both very young, maybe too young really to love anyone over a long period. I found him very attractive, I thought he was as handsome as a film star. Then after a year he didn't seem so attractive—I don't know why—familiarity, I suppose. And there was nothing beyond the attraction. I mean I could still see he was handsome, and he was still amusing to be with, but that wasn't enough any more. Now with you, dear, it's nearly the reverse." She patted his knee. "I don't mean to be unkind, but you're not nearly as attractive as he was. But that night we had together I thought I saw something in you that was better than attractiveness. I don't quite know how to say it. You were interesting, but it was more than that. You seemed to be decent, in an old-fashioned kind of way. Interesting and decent. I suppose the old term would be 'gentleman.' I thought these things even at the end that night, when you told me you were married. I cried a lot that night, but I still thought your wife was a lucky woman. I still think these things. I'll still think them when my heart doesn't beat faster when I see you, the way it does now. You said love should be more than body love; you called it love of the single substance. Well, I'm trying to say that that's the way I feel about you. When I say I love you I don't mean I just love having sex with you, I mean I love you because you have those things I can't find proper words for—honor and kindness, the gentleman's qualities." She stopped again for a moment and frowned, as if she were searching for just the right words. "Your single substance isn't a new discovery," she said, and again she patted his knee and he knew she thought she might hurt his feeling. "It's what every woman with any sense hopes for when she marries, hopes that she isn't being married simply to be hustled into bed. I love you for what you are beside your body. Well, a woman simply wants to be loved the same way. I'm sure your wife must have felt this way."

"Yes, she did," Moore said, "yes, she did." Yes, Moore thought, it may have been the last thing she thought before she died. She had said, You can't be Peter Pan, we can't stay young forever, if you love me it must be for what I am and always was, not for what I looked like twenty years ago. She had told him that and then she had died. She had died, and then he had found that she was right, and that what Gwen was saying now was right. Harker had known it was right, too, Moore thought; probably even Broderick knew. But as soon as Moore spelled it out for himself like this he knew he had been deluding himself till now. Gwen had said the doctrine of the single substance was not esoteric philosophy but common knowledge, to women especially, yes, but really known as an ideal to men as well. So he had known it, too, he hadn't had to go to Dante and Aquinas to discover it. He had known it that night in the Corpus room, listening to Helen crying. Hearing Gwen speak of love now, of loving him for qualities she valued, he was hearing a reminder of what he knew, not a special revelation. Qualities of a gentleman, Gwen had said, lacking a modern term, but Moore, staring so deeply into himself that Gwen and Oxford and even his sense of his own body vanished, performed an examination of conscience that was like a disemboweling, and concluded that what he knew now with Gwen he had known with Helen, that he had known what Dante and Aquinas said before he ever read them, that it was not ignorance that started the chain of events that began in Wallingford and ended in the Radcliffe mortuary, not a failure of knowledge but a failure of will. Aquinas and Dante would have called it sin, and Moore could think of no softer term for it. Looking at himself, he mourned for himself, as if he were at his own funeral.

He felt Gwen tapping his knee and heard her saying his name. "I was saying something to you," she said, "but you didn't seem to hear me."

"Sorry," he said, and took her hand and held it as if to keep her from going away, because, he thought, if she ever saw in him what he saw in himself that was what she would do. And then it occurred to him that perhaps she already saw that, and forgave it, as she had forgiven Lane.

"Lane said Harker sounded like a spoiled priest," Moore said. "I suppose he'd say the same thing about me."

"I don't know what that means," Gwen said.

"It's an Irish expression. It means someone who's holier than other people, someone who should have been a priest."

"Well, then, you're not that," Gwen said. "You're a don."

"That's a profession," Moore said, "not a category."

"Oh, but it *is* a category," she said. "It's not only what you do but what you are. It's what makes you feel things and do things in a donnish way. You live in your mind—and in other people's minds, in Dante's mind and Harker's mind and Aquinas's mind. I think the world needs dons, but being a don makes you very harsh on yourself. Most people judge themselves by comparing themselves to other people they know. But people like you compare yourselves to saints and heroes. Lots of men cheat on their wives, my dear, and if they're decent men they're sorry for it, but they don't put themselves in the company of the world's great sinners. For most men that would be—what's the word?—grandiose. With your conscience, I wonder that you don't accuse yourself of the sin of pride."

Moore took in her words, as he had taken in the words of Harker and Dante and Aquinas and Lane, and was sure that her words were somehow definitive. He had mourned his failure of will, but now he saw that even that had been an evasion. He was a don. He had condemned himself in other dons' words, as if words from lesser minds than Aquinas and Dante were not good enough for him. Because he was a don. This naked young woman sitting cross-legged in front of him, in two or three almost casual sentences, had snatched away his last rag of self-respect. Even in his penitence he had been a don, calling great minds to witness his sin. For a long moment he looked back over his life and wondered if any part of it had really been untainted.

Gwen's voice came to him as from a distance. "You're not a monster, you know. Two women have known you and they've both loved you."

"Is that true?" Moore said. His voice seemed choked and raspy to him. "Yes, I suppose it is." He had always thought of himself as a rather complex person, but now it seemed to him that there really hadn't been all that much to understand. Gwen had been able to put it in a word. He felt flat and one-dimensional, like a character in an obvious allegory. "There doesn't seem to be much to me," he said, and immediately wondered if there was a taint of pride in that statement too, as if he might secretly be claiming the title of the hollowest man in the world.

"Oh, yes there is," Gwen said. "I wouldn't love you if there wasn't. Trust me."

"All right," Moore said, "I will. I do." As he said these words, Moore was aware for just a moment of something he couldn't identify as either physical or mental, something that seemed part thought and part feeling. It was gone at once, and only when it had left him did he determine that if it wasn't what had occurred so many years ago when the priest had muttered absolution through the confessional slot, it was at least the memory of it. And he had something like the sense he had had then, not so much of being cleansed and purified, as of simply being able to go on. He cleared his throat and said, "That's enough about me. Now let's talk about us. We must make plans."

"I know," Gwen said. "I haven't thought very much about the future. Not at all, really, till I got your telegram. I didn't need to plan much if you weren't coming back. I would have just let the future be whatever came."

"I wasn't able to think beyond today either," Moore said. "I mean I wasn't able to think beyond seeing you. And now that I have to think beyond today I hardly know where to begin." He stopped, remembering. Lane had said it had been when he and Nancy had begun to think of the future that he'd begun to ask himself whether it was all worth it.

Gwen looked at him steadily but said nothing, and Moore thought, She's like her mother, she's wondering if her lover is having second thoughts. The quarter hour bells all over Oxford chimed in chorus, and Moore found himself wondering if the bells of St. Mary's were among them; the notion of doubt had made him think of Newman. Speaking of Christian doctrine, Newman had said that ten-thousand difficulties do not make a doubt. Before the bells stopped Moore took Gwen's hands in his and groped for words to destroy doubt. "I'm on medical leave till the end of the year," he said. "That gives us time for a long honeymoon."

He felt her hands tighten in his. "Only married people take honeymoons," she said quietly.

"I know."

She looked down at their hands. "You don't have to marry me," she said. "You don't have to prove anything."

"But you remember that I'm old-fashioned," Moore said. "Old-fashioned people marry when they're in love."

She was silent for a while. Then she said, "I won't say I haven't thought about our being married. Fantasized about it would be more accurate, I suppose. I never got very far into the fantasy, though. You can guess why not, what stopped me."

"Yes," Moore said. "America. My daughter."

"I know her name," Gwen said. "I even saw her picture in one of the papers." She paused, then went on very slowly, as if carefully choosing her words. "It wasn't America that bothered me, really. We see so much of it here in the films and television that it's hardly even foreign to us. Rather like Scotland or Northern Ireland. It was your colleagues and your friends, all the people who knew you and your wife. I could imagine how terribly awkward it would be for us. But when I thought of your daughter—well, at that point I couldn't even imagine how that would be. And I still can't."

"I know," Moore said. He felt her hand on his knee again, the touch of sympathy. He was grateful for the touch, but he hoped she didn't see him now as he saw himself, because he knew he was picturing himself as the suffering moralist, the gentleman how worried about the measure of pain he was going to inflict, as if he were God in an unimaginable moment of indecision. The room seemed suddenly crowded with minds other than his own: Harker's and Dante's and Aquinas'—all of them saying that pain was not his to distribute, that to believe that he had that power was the same old egotism that Gwen had helped him vanquish. Knowing what these other minds had told him, he should know that his function was to choose between right and wrong, not to play a judging God. No matter what he did, there would be agony enough to go around.

He folded her hands carefully in his and said, "We came here because we knew it was the right thing for us to do."

"Yes." Her voice was hardly more than a whisper.

"Then this is our beginning," Moore said. "Time begins here. The world begins to forget us now, and we can pray that the people we care about will someday understand us and forgive us if that's what's needed."

"And your daughter? You'll write to her? What will you tell her?"

"Everything," Moore said, "but not all at once. An inch at a time."

Gwen was silent for a moment. Then she said, "An inch at a time. Weeks, months, maybe years."

"Yes, I suppose so."

"Maybe, after a long time," Gwen said, "when she had got used to our being together, I could write to her. I don't know now what I would say, but I know I couldn't go on forever as a silent enemy."

Yes, Moore thought, she would feel compelled to write, waiting for the proper time that might never come. And what would she write at that imagined time? Only in her own words what he would begin to write as early as tomorrow. A lawyer might say that all they could do was to state their case, over and over. Somehow they must say, "We never meant to cause you pain. We hope you can forgive us." That brief statement carried their message. If he tried to say more he knew he would stay into the forbidden territory of self-pity. Because what he really felt alongside his message of apology was another blunt statement. "We are not criminals; we are not Bonnie and Clyde fleeing from the law. We are not guilty people, yet a sense of guilt clings to us the way old cigarette smoke clings to clothes. I know you too well and love you too much to think that you can be happy if you know our feelings. Love, Dad" Tomorrow, his secret feeling unsaid, he would write Ruthie, would set down the first inch of the journey out of the present into the veiled future.

He was about to say something donnish to Gwen about time, about present time fusing almost imperceptibly into the future, when a sudden burst of music seemed to explode in their quiet little room. For a moment they gaped at each other in astonishment, before Moore had realized that the music was coming from outside. He snatched his trousers from the bedside table, put them on and went to the window. Their room was on the second story, and directly beneath his window was what at first seemed to be a first story but was really the upper deck of a tour bus painted in gaudy reds and yellows. Thirty or forty people sat eating picnic lunches from cardboard boxes and drinking what Moore could tell from the odor was beer or ale. In the center aisle, two couples were dancing to a pounding rhythm that came up from a stereo of some sort on the lower deck. Moore was so struck by the sudden appearance of this other world beneath his window that he was surprised to feel Gwen's hand on his bare shoulder. She had put on the robe he remembered from Wallingford.

"I don't think I've ever seen a tour bus in Oxford," Moore said. "They must be on their way to somewhere else."

"I suppose so," Gwen said," but maybe it doesn't even matter where they're going. They're having a fine time on the way."

He put his arm around her waist beneath the robe. "Maybe we should get dressed and go down and join the party."

Gwen laughed. "A don dancing to disco music. That might draw a crowd."

"Is that what we're hearing? Disco music?"

"Yes, my dear. It's a song called 'Dance with Me.' It's very popular. Probably all your students know it."

"Not music for a fusty old don, I suppose."

"Why don't we see?" Gwen said. They had been crouching below the windowsill, but now she led him to the little open space between the bed and the wardrobe. "Come on, my fusty don. Come on and dance with me."

"Okay," said Moore, "I'll try. But I'm barefoot."

"No excuses accepted," Gwen said. "Dance with me."

So with the disco beat pounding from below, Moore moved his feet in failed attempts at rhythm. "Never mind your feet," Gwen said, her face against his shoulder, "just hold me."

"I can do that," Moore said, and he did.

Down below there was sudden quiet, then the roar of the engine as the tour bus pulled away from Eastgate. Gwen, her arms still around Moore's neck, said, "I enjoyed that immensely."

"You're joking," Moore said.

"No, I'm not," she said. "I'm very serious. It doesn't matter that you're not Fred Astaire."

"I'm just a clumsy don," Moore said.

"Yes, but not the clumsiest of all dons. Remember that."

"I will," Moore said. "No more superlatives for me."

When they were sitting down on the bed again, Moore said, "I don't know what those other people were celebrating, but we have our own reasons to celebrate today. Maybe we should give it a name."

"We don't have to call it anything," Gwen said. "It's just the day we began our new life."

"Exactly right," Moore said, "the new life, Dante's *Vita Nuova*."

"There's no curing you," Gwen said. "Once a don always a don."

"Well, if we're leaving tomorrow on our wedding trip or honeymoon or whatever we want to call it," Moore said, "we need at least a semblance of a plan. We need to tell each other where we might like to go."

"All right, "said Gwen. "You go first."

"Well, I thought of something while we were dancing," Moore said.

"I hope you weren't thinking of Tahiti," Gwen said. "I've only brought a small bag."

"No, not Tahiti and not America," Moore said. "America can wait for a while. No, I was thinking of England, or at least a part of it."

What he had been thinking about, now that he would finally be leaving Oxford, was the travel video he and Helen had watched in what seemed years ago, before he had come to Oxford. They had talked often of where they might go after the Oxford program ended: to Wales, or Scotland, or the Lake Country, or Cornwall. Cornwall had been his choice then, and it still was. The video had begun with dramatic pictures of the cliffs that rear unexpectedly out of the Atlantic. Then the camera had moved inland to show the little village that claimed to be the "real" Camelot and Plymouth where his own ancestors had set out for America (he loved the peculiar mixture of English and Celtic place names: Mouse Hole, St. Ives, Penzance, Bolventor) and the enormous stone monoliths that had survived from some ancient age, monstrous stones that were not orderly and meaningful, like those of Stonehenge, but stones simply scattered like the debris of some battle of mythic giants. Then, Moore remembered, the narrator had remarked that Cornwall was grounded in English history but was not bound by it. Pirates both real and legendary had called Cornwall their home port, and Gilbert and Sullivan had set their pirate story in Penzance, and modern writers like du Maurier still set their gothic stories in the tiny hamlets along the rocky shore. But, the narrator had pointed out, Cornwall's greatest addition to history was of course its creation, or discovery, of the Arthurian tales. The narrator had closed with a little joke: all the castles were Arthur's, all the pools were the water Arthur's sword had been thrown into.

Moore tried to summarize all this without lecturing, but he was, after all, a lecturer by nature, and he could only hope that Gwen would be patient with him. When he paused, she said, "I've never been to Cornwall, and I don't suppose I know any more about Arthurian tales than the ordinary person in the street. I mean I've seen the films, and somewhere in the dim past I've read some of the stories. I do remember that Lancelot in the film was very handsome. And of course we all saw the Broadway version of *Camelot*, and all the men I knew tried to talk like Richard Burton. It should be fun seeing these things with you."

"Then I vote for the new life to start in Cornwall," Moore said, and began to tell her what he'd learned from the travel videos about the monoliths and the pirate legacy and the fascinating language, but he found himself talking mostly about the real appeal of Cornwall, the body of Arthurian tales that seemed to borrow equally from history and from myth: Camelot and the Round Table and the sword in the stone that only Arthur could remove—all the impossible loves and hates and treacheries and betrayals that for English-speaking people were as real as the recorded sins and joys in the Bible. Merlin and Gawain and Lancelot and Mordred; Guinevere and Isolde—none of them real, yet more than real, Moore thought, epic presences, heroes, and villains larger than life but somehow sharing our life and dramatizing our life, putting our ordinary life in italics. And it suddenly occurred to Moore that what he found thrilling in the Arthurian tales, and in Milton and Shakespeare, and in *The*

King James Bible was simply the language that brought these figures to life. Arthur and Hamlet and Adam and Moses were significant for him because of the language that gave them their existence. He'd looked for the essence of England in places and people and actions, but it wasn't there; it was in the language itself, in Shakespeare's images and Milton's rhythms and the sonorities of the King James version of the Bible. It was his language too, as an American, but the ancient roots and early flowering had been here in England, and that was why Americans like him found themselves homesick for England. The essence of England wasn't any single place or trait or quality; it was the language that named these things and thus brought them into being.

He heard Gwen's voice and realized she was asking him something. "Tintagel sounds marvelous," she said, "but do the trains go there?"

"Let's find out," Moore said. They swung themselves off the bed and reached for their clothes. They had sat naked in bed and talked without embarrassment, but now they dressed awkwardly in each other's presence, and Moore thought that Gwen must feel as he did the brevity of their intimate time together.

They went down The High, past St. Mary's and the covered market-place, to the British Railway office. They looked at railway maps, following the colored lines from London down to Somerset, then Devon, and finally to Cornwall. On impulse they decided to take the train as far as possible into Cornwall and simply start their wandering from there. Penzance, it turned out, was their destination. They would take an early train into London and leave for Penzance from Paddington (like Holmes and Watson, Moore told Gwen; the game was afoot).

They walked back up The High, arm in arm, and at King Edward Street, Moore turned and Gwen looked at him but said nothing. They went down the curving brick street, past the entrance to Oriel, and stopped in front of Corpus Christi. The massive wooden portals, crafted centuries before to keep out the rabble, stood open now to visitors and tourists like them. From where they stood, Moore could see the base of the pelican and the passageway that led past the dining hall and out into the other quad and then to Staircase Twelve. He took Gwen's hand and they walked slowly through the archway and into the ugly, barren quad, all ancient brick paving stones not graced with a single blade of grass. A ragged circle of tourists stood around the pelican, mostly Germans and Japanese, Moore thought, with cameras and guidebooks. One Japanese man knelt by the base of the monument, taking of picture of the crabbed Latin words, but most of the people with cameras were circling slowly around, trying out angles for pictures of the pelican.

Moore and Gwen stood outside the circle and looked at the monument where Gwen's father had died. We don't have to take pictures, Moore thought, and we don't have to read the inscription. We know what the pelican means. It means beginnings and endings, and love and hate, and past and present, and chance and coincidence and pattern. It means all those things running together, like the colors in a painting of the world where the paints weren't given time to dry, so that no one can tell where one starts and the other ends. He stared at the monument for the last time, really seeing it for the first time. He'd given hasty guidebook answers to Helen's tourist questions about the pelican. He hadn't been thinking of murder or betrayal then, but he was thinking of those things now, and he thought it might be their presence that made him see more in the monument than he had ever seen before. It hadn't occurred to him till now that the pelican, tearing at its breast with its beak, sat high above the sundial at the base of the monument, suggesting that the suffering and atoning Christ was above time and history, that his atoning power stretched backward to the start of time and forward to its end. Thus Cain was atoned for, and other murderers yet to come. Corpus Christi, Body of Christ: the college had been named for this atoning substance, and the pelican was its appropriate coat of arms.

But, looking across the quad toward Staircase Twelve, Moore for a moment was nearly overwhelmed by a sense of the pervasiveness and persistence of evil: not just murder, not just Cranmer and Latimer burned at the stake in the Haymarket, not just Helen slaughtered by a man who'd never seen her and who never really saw her in the darkness even when he killed her, not just the Jews huddled in shower rooms waiting for the Zyklon B tablet to drop; not just murder but the more subtle evidences of evil, what theologians called the deadly sins—envy and pride and contempt for the unfortunate. He understood a little better the logic of the doctrine of Christian atonement: it had to be qualitative, not quantitative; human evil was so enormous that only a divinity could atone for it. And he felt the strength of the Calvinists' view of original sin as an aboriginal and universal blight, felt it for a moment, and glanced quickly at Gwen, as if he might catch her in some unexpected immorality. Then the moment of bleakness passed. He touched Gwen's arm and they turned and went back through the archway onto Merton Street without looking back.

That night they lay in bed and talked about Cornwall, about Tintagel and Camelot, and about the signpost at Lands' End that pointed toward America. Land's End, the end of England, and St. Michael's Mount, where Milton had placed England's guardian spirit.

When Gwen had fallen asleep, Moore moved so that his face just touched her hair and lay listening to the Oxford bells for the last time. Then he was abruptly asleep and dreaming. He and Gwen were at Land's End—it looked just as it did in the video—and they were standing on a chalky white cliff in front of the signpost. Moore looked up at it and could see that it pointed precisely west and that it said, "USA 3291 miles," and he said to Gwen, "It's like Ireland, it's the last parish before America." And then he was flying, but not in a plane, because he could look straight down and see the Atlantic, calm, terraced like desert sand. He saw the white fringe of foam on the southern Irish coast, then for hours endless gray water. He knew he was flying west because ahead of him it was still daylight.

Then he was over land, but generic land, not land that he recognized, and then he was on the ground at the foot of a long gently sloping hill. Without effort he started up the hill and saw that it was the cemetery where Lane was buried. Darkness was finally coming on now. The crest of the hill was still trimmed with red, but angels and crucifixes and obelisks threw long shadows down the hill toward him, as if the pattered darkness was coming to meet him. He didn't know where Lane's grave was, but he came on it at once, a plain stone lying in twilight amid the splashes of darkness. He knelt down beside the stone, where he supposed Lane's head would be, because he realized that he had come all the way across the Atlantic to talk to him. I came to talk to you, he said, here where the brooks are "too broad for leaping." Do you know that poem? His mind was bursting with his message, but the darkness was sliding down the hill toward them and he hadn't time to phrase it properly. But he could ask a few hurried questions, and he thought he would be able to hear Lane's answers if he listened carefully. The darkness had seeped over Lane's headstone now and was flowing eastward, toward England. Moore stood up to leave before it was too late and said his truncated message into the darkness at his feet. I wanted to talk to you about love, he said, now that you know all the answers. I want to know why we learned so little when there's so much to know. If we could do it all over, do you think we'd do any better? Do you wish it was 1944 again and we were just waking up in the haystack and everything was fresh and clear in the morning light and we had just seen those little girls sitting on the fence saying how handsome we were? Maybe we were handsome then, you and I, because we *were* young and so were they, and everything was possible then.

The End

About the Author

A native Detroiter, R. J. Reilly graduated from high school in 1943 and, following basic training, was assigned to a U.S. Army Combat Engineering battalion that saw service in France and Germany during World War Two. Discharged in 1946, like millions of other veterans, he went to college on the GI Bill. He received MA and PhD  degrees in English and American literature and began a university teaching career that lasted until his retirement in 1987.

After retirement Reilly's attention turned from scholarly writing to fiction. His four novels and two volumes of short stories include *Over There* and *Weekend in the Country*, novels that draw on his experiences during World War Two. *The Pelican Affair* is set in Oxford, where Reilly taught a summer course at Corpus Christi College. *The Bronte House* and the short story collections deal with people caught up in problems of love and marriage and, occasionally, those of religion and philosophy. Reilly has said that he writes for "literate adults, people for whom fiction is storytelling that portrays the complexities of human existence."

If you enjoy Reilly's fiction, you may want to read his scholarly works: "Henry James and the Morality of Fiction," winner of the Norman Foerster award for the best scholarly essay in *American Literature* in 1967, and *Romantic Religion: A Study of Owen Barfield, C.S. Lewis, Charles Williams, and J.R.R. Tolkien*, published in 1971 and reprinted as an e-book in 2006.

Reilly welcomes your comments at rreilly16@comcast.net.

CPSIA information can be obtained
at www.ICGtesting.com
Printed in the USA
FFOW04n1318200815
16105FF